Conscious

Vic Grout

To Helen, Jack, Danny, James, Heather,
Killian, Lilith & Maizie

No-one really knows the future: just have fun!

Vic Grout
Clear Futures Publishing
Glyndwr University
Plas Coch, Mold Road
Wrexham, LL11 2AW, UK
www.vicgrout.net

Ordering Information:
Quantity sales. Special discounts are available on quantity purchases by corporations, associations, and others. For details, contact the publisher at the address above.

Printed by Amazon.

Publisher's Cataloguing-in-Publication data
Grout, Vic.
Conscious, Clear Futures Publishing.
ISBN 978-1-0819391-3-1
1. Science-Fiction. 2. Hard Science-Fiction. 3. Apocalyptic & Post-Apocalyptic Science-Fiction

First Edition: September 2016
Second Edition: March 2017
Third Edition: August 2019

Foreword (Third Edition)

I first conceived the vague idea for this story about fifteen years ago. I had organised a public debate at Wrexham Glyndŵr University (then the North East Wales Institute of Higher Education) on *'The Future of Computing'*. Four 'experts', drawn from academia and industry, had been assembled into a panel, together with a distinguished chair to oversee proceedings. Each expert spoke on their particular topic for about ten minutes before the panel as a whole answered questions from the audience and allowed the discussion to wander where it would. The event was a partial success – probably no more than that. Other than setting the whole thing up in the first place and priming the chair with a few pertinent questions, should the conversation flag, I took little part in the evening's proceedings beyond the role of interested spectator.

However, at some point in the event, the conversation drifted – somewhat inevitably – towards machine intelligence. Although a well-trodden path indeed, a certain comment made an impression on me. It was simply that – in the opinion of the speaker, 'some years into the future' – the neural size of the Internet would reach that of the human brain. I had two immediate thoughts. The first was fairly obvious: that such a milestone in itself wasn't particularly meaningful because the brain and a collection of logic gates were probably entirely different things. (I recalled watching a TV programme, which had discussed panpsychism, some years earlier but I couldn't remember the term then.) Secondly, it struck me that that point would have already arrived without anyone realising it. If you added (multiplied) the circuitry of the individual devices (network routers, end PCs, etc.) into the basic topology of the Internet, then its overall neural count was many orders of magnitude higher. Whatever the fine detail, if the panpsychists had a point, then the Internet might be showing signs of life sooner than anyone expected! This story – at least the idea behind it – traces its origins back to that moment. I even wrote a few thousand words at the time.

Unfortunately, life then got in the way. I had a growing family and a job that was proving interesting and fulfilling – but demanding. Nothing happened for several years. When I finally returned to the project at the start of 2015, my first impression was that I'd missed the boat: that the idea was already mainstream and the story had been told. People like Christof Koch were discussing panpsychism in relation to the Internet (having made those appropriate adjustments to the calculations, which had occurred to me years before) and Robert J. Sawyer had written the excellent 'WWW' trilogy. It looked like time to move on.

However, having read the available material in a little more detail – both 'fact' and 'fiction', and the essential intersection of 'speculation', it became clear that this still wasn't yet quite what I wanted to say. Firstly, the somewhat one-dimensional focus of the Internet panpsychists on neural complexity seemed a touch simplistic to me. Secondly, as entertaining as Sawyer's *'Webmind'* was, I couldn't swallow the moral reliance on western political axioms or the general level of anthropomorphism throughout. It wasn't that I necessarily thought it *wouldn't* work out like that; I just couldn't see how anyone could be *sure* – there didn't seem to be any reliable foundation to base it upon. But, finally and most importantly, 'emergent sentience' in literature was always just *really clever software*; and I simply didn't see it like that *at all*. To me, it would start with the *hardware* and take it from there. The software, if there even *was any*, would – at most – be an indistinguishable part of it (as it probably is in our own brains). So, although there was always *Skynet* (*Terminator*) of course, like Webmind and many other variations on the theme, this was AI that existed *on* or *in* something. I still felt the need to do something different: I wanted 'it' – the sentient 'whatever it was' – to *be* the *something* – the thing itself, not what lived on it, and I wasn't actually bothered how *intelligent* it was – that seemed like a distraction. It was the idea of 'it' existing *at all* that interested me!

At the same time, debate on the 'technological singularity' was beginning to be played out in public with a comparable array of unfounded assertions – for good and bad – appearing with increasing regularity. Also, the 'Internet of Things' was becoming a reality, which brought its own extra dimension to the story. 'The Internet' was suddenly no longer a separate entity, to be logged on to, as and when: it was *everything* – everything we do on Planet Earth. *Everything* was going to be connected! In one sense, certainly trying to consider all the angles, it all seemed a lot more *complex* to me; in another – any attempt at an underlying philosophy, say – just very *uncertain*; but finally, and paradoxically – in terms of the overall *effect*, somewhat *simpler*. Then, of course, there are some questions that go way beyond just the technology and we really should be talking about the bigger picture anyway. I felt that the whole story needed to be told on a different level, and that I might yet have a job to do. Only readers can confirm or disabuse me of that notion!

I do, however, feel that a word of apology may be needed to hard-core computer scientists, particularly networkers (a group to which I have historical affiliations), and scientists, and technologists in general. In my attempts to make the story accessible for a wider audience, I've knowingly (and possibly unknowingly – I'm not sure which is worse) taken some horrible liberties with both hardware and software concepts in places and freely abused some scientific principles of scale and scope. This is generally true in terms of how, and where, some types of network activity might be *measured*, for example. My protocol discrimination – particularly wireless – has a fair amount of poetic licence too. Also, engineers will argue that some of the technological 'side effects' described couldn't happen because our safety systems (for example) wouldn't allow it. But I'm trying to make a *particular* point here; namely that our understanding of technology is often based on our assumptions and preconceptions and, to a great extent, *custom*. An independent intelligence may not be restricted by any of this and will be constrained only by the laws of physics (not just the ones *we* know). Other than that, I believe (within the normal operational parameters of science fiction) the basic premise of the story to be vaguely sensible but, to describe it in the detail necessary to satisfy everyone, would have taken a book three times as long. Please forgive me: my intentions are good! Similarly, events, places and institutions aren't to be taken too seriously: they're a convenient mixture of the real and made-up with a few geographical and historical – occasionally historic – reference points.

Finally, if I can predict one likely and repeated question that's going to be asked … *No*, this isn't my serious prediction for the future. There are far too many unknowns, which is one of the main points I'd like to get across. The Internet *not* doing what it does in this story will discredit a particular narrow philosophy and this simple empirical analysis will continue. As we build larger, increasingly sophisticated – possibly more human-like – machines, some existing theories of consciousness, for example (panpsychism, powered neural complexity, biological structures, etc.), may be disproved by the relevant technology not becoming self-aware at each stage when it's built. At those points, it will always be interesting to consider the options we're left with and where our revised philosophies may be funnelling us. *This* discussion is also the role of the central characters in the book, having their own various positions on this. Woven into the *actual* storyline in what follows, there are numerous other ideas, theories and opinions as to what consciousness really is, what machine intelligence may look like – or *behave* like, what our technological future may be, concerns we possibly should have and, ultimately, what it will mean for us. Any or none of these may be correct. *Something* will be, of course, but it may be just in the nature of things that we won't know what until we get there. What's definitely true though is that we should be *talking* about this stuff *now* and I don't think we really are. The idea that we might be heading towards one or more technological catastrophes (or *singularities*, if you like) doesn't seem particularly outrageous to me.

Vic Grout, Wrexham, July 2019

Acknowledgements

To my wife, Helen, for loving me, supporting me, being with me, looking after me, and putting up with me for a quarter of a century; this can't have been easy! To my sons, Jack, Danny and James, for being lovable, good kids, and keeping me in the real world. More recently, to Heather, Killian, Lilith and Maizie for being very special additions. Mum, Dad, Vanessa and extended family too. I haven't always shown it but, in all the ups and downs of my life, my family has always meant more to me than anything else – and still does.

On a less soppy note, special thanks to John Cummins for his help with, and contribution to, much of the theoretical discussion of brain function – including a few paragraphs of borrowed (with kind permission) text, which was completely beyond me. Perhaps apologies also for corrupting his ideas in many places to suit my story. If anyone is interested in the finer detail of brain function – particularly aspects relating to the origins of human creativity, they'll find his work much better than mine!

Finally, heartfelt thanks to my colleagues and students in Computing at Wrexham Glyndŵr University and other friends in Chester and North Wales. Not only have their thoughts and ideas, over the years, contributed so much to my own thinking and – ultimately – this book; but their general good humour and camaraderie have often (just) succeeded in keeping me (just) in some degree of sanity. They may not have realised they were doing either! Special thanks to Nigel Houlden for the proof-reading. I'd like to remember a particular colleague, Richard Smith, who died the week the first draft of this book was finished. My thoughts, as I write this, are with his family.

Contents

PHASE ONE: SYMPTOMS

Chapter 1: The Desk

The world had known grander reunions. Two women and two men, in their mid-forties, sat around a small table in a London pub – a London pub on the Strand to be precise. Three pints of London Pride and a diet coke filled the space between them. The pub had all the traditional charm and quirkiness to be expected of its kind: half-floors, stairs, nooks and crannies, and plenty of wood panelling. Charming, intriguing and unique; unique, that is, apart from the hundred or so others that were to be found looking very much like it within a five-mile radius, the nearest being a hundred yards down the same street. It was a mid-December, late Friday afternoon; so already quite dark outside.

So, as class get-togethers went, it was not the biggest or best but that did not seem to matter much. The four of them circled the table, happy and relaxed and, as would be fairly obvious from eavesdropping on the conversation, each of them had done well enough in their own way. They were all clearly content with their lot – just for different reasons. The pleasant result was not much in the way of one-upmanship or competition. Rather, each was happy to listen to what the others had to say; genuinely caring, attentive and interested – interrupting only occasionally and in places where they genuinely did have something useful to contribute.

Aside from the size of the group and the modest location, another reason why this might not have ranked high in the great class reunion lists was that, in fact, this was not even the first time *some* of them had met since university. Although the entire foursome had not sat around a table together as a group for a couple of decades or so, they had met in pairs over the years. In that time they had also, sporadically, maintained some semblance of remote contact through email and, more recently, social media. Once connected through the latter, they had all been saying for some time that this face-to-face get-together was something that they really must do. However, being the busy people they were, it had only just got round to happening now; and, even then, because they had all finally converged to living or working in London. So here they were.

Naturally, given the broken communication that had taken place over the years, each of them knew fragments of *some* of the others' stories, but no-one had the full picture about *everyone* else. So, partly because it seemed the done thing, and partly simply because it was fun, they took turns to give a very brief account of what had happened to them – their careers and wider personal lives – since graduation from university. Where modesty threatened to overshadow fact, the others often supplied the missing information in an entertaining, but distinctly ad-hoc manner. So ...

Aisha Davies had come to England as a teenager, following her mother's remarriage, and studied medicine at university; then had continued her early career with a fairly standard surgeon's training and placement. However, as the years went by, she had begun to specialise more and more in neuroscience and had achieved a considerable degree of prominence in her field. In fact, she was probably the most publicly known of the four, having gained some significant government work and contracts and, more recently, becoming a regular face on television, particularly the BBC. She was recognised as something of an authority on how human and other animal brains worked and, in particular, what made such beings aware of their surroundings, in a creative problem-solving sense – rather than just surviving. Her research largely focused on which parts of the brain were responsible for the 'higher human' activities that appeared to mark them out. Maybe unsurprisingly, she came across as having a hard, clinical approach to both her science and the sometimes unpleasant experimentation behind it. But the other three were able to see without much difficulty that, behind the confident facade, lurked an element of self-doubt and uncertainty; possibly even loneliness. There was no question concerning one aspect of her determination, however: she was entirely career-oriented. She had never married – 'never seen the point'; nor really indulged in any relationship counted in more than weeks. Over the last twenty years, she had worked in various locations around the UK but had just moved, for the last time she felt – or *hoped*, to a London hospital.

Andy Jamieson was born in Edinburgh and had studied politics at university. More precisely, he had started out as a Marxist economist and philosopher. He had always been recognised as the intellectual of the group and, to a great extent, the least money-oriented in outlook. However, as his academic career moved ahead in leaps and bounds, his personal life had begun to fall apart. A notorious bon viveur and party animal at university, drink had quickly become his master after graduation. By his mid-twenties, this had cost him a number of jobs and a brief but painful marriage. Quickly divorced, he had stumbled on 'in darkness' for a few more years before finding salvation in *Alcoholics Anonymous*. This, in addition to saving his physical body and functioning brain, had – somewhat unsurprisingly – changed much of his outlook on life too. Although his fundamental beliefs in equality remained unshaken, they were expanded 'in the spiritual sense'. When he was able to re-embark on a successful academic career, the direction had changed a little. Although he had always been interested in the science – the philosophy really – of the mind, his set texts these days were more along the lines of Carl Jung, C.S. Lewis and Scott Peck. He also was no complete stranger to TV appearances but the programmes tended to be somewhat more 'specialist' (later at night and fewer people saw them). A year previously he had moved from being a university reader in the Midlands, 'after some local unpleasantness', to take up a position of professor of religious and cultural philosophy at a London university. Physically, he stood three or four inches taller than the others and had longer hair. By chance, he and Aisha had met twice over the years at social events and once at an interdisciplinary research conference.

By contrast, *Jenny Smith* was born, and had always worked, in London. Her only prolonged absence from the capital had been her undergraduate years. After graduating at the top of her class in mathematics, she had proceeded to take the rest of her degrees 'back home' in computer science. But, she said, she had 'finished with all that hard, nuts-and-bolts techie stuff' and was now much more interested in the 'bigger issues' of where technology was taking humanity and what each was doing to the other – 'what's going to work and what isn't'. She had achieved a lofty status in her field through well-cited publications and plenty of UK Research Council funding grants and had been a professor of computer science at a London university (not the same one as Andy) for many years. It seemed to the others that, in many ways, she had changed the least: she was still very big on theories and grand questions and described herself loosely as a 'futurologist'. Her current work, as much as she was working on anything in particular, was connected with projects attempting to build computer systems along the lines of the structures used by the human brain. Although passionate about her work, she was also realistic; admitting that she – and researchers like her – were far, far away from any concrete success. She also had no close personal connections. Having 'played the field – the *whole* field, that was' – quite successfully at university, she had 'lost interest in men' within a few years of graduation and, in recent times, had 'pretty much lost interest in the alternative too'. She and Andy had maintained the closest online contact since university and had largely arranged this eventual reunion through 'the somewhat archaic machinery' of Facebook.

That left *Bob Weatherill*. Unlike Jenny, Bob *had* studied computer science at university and had 'stayed true to the faith' for the rest of his career up to this point. He had been recognised, at a young age, in his sphere of the technical world, as an extremely able and intelligent man; and had quickly gained high-profile work with major network companies as a systems trouble-shooter, working for both British Telecom and Cisco on large, successful projects. He had breezed through the supposedly demanding Cisco Certified Internetworking Expert qualification at an early age. He was a gifted problem-solver and seemed to have an ability to 'see solutions' in a way that generally defeated others. 'You have to see inside a network to really get to grips with it' was his formal line, or 'to fix the network, you have to *become* the network' when feeling more flippant. (His rustic Bristol accent often lulled people into underestimating his sharp analytical skills.) In recent years, he had developed 'what everyone thought was' a particularly sophisticated network analysis tool and was beginning to make good money from it. Other than his networking qualifications, he had taken no further education after university but that had certainly not done him any harm. His personal life was comfortably the most complete of the four. He was happily married with a son, daughter-in-law and grandson. He regularly travelled the world and had spent some years living in Europe and the USA but was now pleased to be (at least *based*) on the outskirts of London, returning to his family whenever he could. That he had been one of Jenny's many university conquests before her more permanent lesbian phase was no more than a minor embarrassment. They had crossed paths regularly since and had, that day, been to the same meeting, at the British Computer Society across the way in Southampton Street.

So the ragged group of friends that had been formed – no-one could quite remember how or why – at a grimy bar in the old Westcountry university student union in 1993, now sat reunited around a beaten copper table in a mock-traditional London pub. Frankly, the reason for this was questionable as well. Clearly they had overlapping academic interests and there had been talk of joint research, maybe some funding applications – possibly even a book on the multidisciplinary aspects of the differences and similarities of computers, networks and biological systems. As it turned out, of all the odd things that were about to happen to the group, that was the part that was never discussed ever again. In truth, they were just enjoying the experience of being together once more and soon agreed that the exercise should be repeated on as close to a monthly basis as possible. At one point, Aisha described them as the 'Class of '93'. Jenny laughed. 'Not much of a class; the four of us would only make one desk!' And the name stuck. At first, the group was the *Desk of '93* and, quickly, just *'The Desk'*.

*

As the evening wore on, the conversation drifted all over the place, to the entertainment of all. Although each of them was a specialist in their own field, they were all – to a greater or lesser extent – capable communicators into the bargain. And naturally there were some aspects of everyone's work that interested everybody else. It was fun, with a practical edge, and some more fun. First to get some good-humoured interrogation was Jenny.

"So, this 'building a computer like a human brain' concept," ventured Aisha in a somewhat teasing manner. "Is that just science for science's sake or is there some serious purpose behind it?" She spoke with the forced accuracy of someone for whom English was not (or at least *had* not been) a first language, even if the others always accepted with amusement that it was probably better than theirs.

"Oh, it's entirely serious," insisted Jenny, "and *necessary*." It's something we're probably going to *have* to do if we're going to take the technology we've got today very much further. Certainly, if we want to keep on making the computers smaller and more powerful."

"Why?" asked Andy. "Aren't we doing well enough on that front at the moment? Even I've heard of *Moore's Law!*"

"Well, I suppose we are, *at the moment*," Jenny emphasised. "But really *only at the moment*. Moore's Law might say that computing power doubles every eighteen months or two years or so but it can't last. We can't keep on doing what we're doing any more, or at least not for much longer. We can't just keep cramming more and more logic gates into smaller and smaller spaces on chips with the existing silicon technology. There's a couple of very good reasons for that. One is very simple; the other's a bit more complicated."

"Go on," prompted Bob, a shade more interested than before. He was always the practical one.

8

"Well, the simple problem is this," said Jenny with a wry smile on her face. "The processors are simply getting too *hot*. The denser the circuitry, the harder it is to keep cool. In fact, with some very powerful systems – some of the big high performance computing systems, for example, the cooling systems are costing as much as the processing power. They're certainly taking as much electricity to run! *Power* is becoming very important these days. For personal computers – desktops and laptops and the like, we partially get around it by splitting the processor into multiple cores but this decreases the overall efficiency of the system: you just don't get something from nothing. OK, there may be alternatives: optical computing, biological computing or quantum computing – that sort of thing – but those are still on the research benches."

"And the complicated reason?" Aisha again; this time with the tiniest hint of irony.

Jenny continued, smiling, "The second reason is just how *small* we're making these devices now. We're not that far off the *atomic* scale with some of these logic components and *that's* a problem. You see, normally, when you make logic gates out of, shall we say, *conventional* materials, they behave in a predictable way. In other words, if you put the same inputs in, you always get the same output out. But as you get smaller and smaller, when you're actually counting *atoms* across the logic gate, then the slightest little molecular variation and you're working with a different material, with different properties; and it may not behave the same from one time to the next. So the components aren't *reliable*: they're not *breaking* exactly, but they're not going to behave in a *deterministic* way. And you just can't build computer systems out of unpredictable components with our existing models. We don't *know how* to build systems from randomly unreliable units!"

Aisha's eyes narrowed slightly in recognition but it was Andy who asked the question.

"So how does trying to build them like brains help?"

Jenny continued.

"Well that's exactly what our brains are made of, isn't it: unreliable components? In a sense, the brain is made up of a network of simple processors, a bit like a computer, but each of the individual processing nodes is imperfect. They can fail from time to time in everyday use and eventually the occasional one will fail permanently as we get older. Sometimes, that causes a problem if too many of them go down but, on the whole, we get by perfectly well. Our brain is a fantastic model for a computer built successfully from quite rubbish and unreliable individual components!"

"Ah, OK, yes, but, in turn," interjected Aisha, slowly and deliberately, "there are two problems with *that* too. Firstly, in an obvious sense, the brain is put together in a quite different *way* to a typical computer. Secondly, beyond the superficial, we do not *really understand* the way that it is put together or how it works anything like as well as we do something like a computer, which we have built ourselves. We know vaguely what some parts of the brain seem to *do* but we do not know much about exactly *how* it processes thoughts or stores information or solves problems. Certainly, what we *do* know about the brain makes it look rather different. I may not know very much about computer architecture but I do know that, for example, signals within the brain travel very slowly – just a few metres per second. Also, the brain is *massively connected*. Each neuron in the brain is connected to tens of thousands of other neurons. I am pretty sure a computer is not built like that in either sense; am I right?"

"Dead right," agreed Jenny. "In a computer system, the signals are travelling at a decent fraction of the speed of light. On the other hand, each logic gate is connected to, at most, half a dozen or so others. So, yes, they're very different animals indeed!"

"So, quite a challenge then?" offered Bob, humorously. "Perfect for you!" Everyone chuckled in agreement. Jenny liked to think *big*.

"Of course, looking at it from the other direction," continued Jenny, "thinking about the brain from a computational perspective, it's astonishing that it works *at all!*"

"Why do you say that?" asked Aisha.

"Well, what's the brain got, really," asked Jenny. "It's just a collection of neurons networked together. How's that a processing system? Where's the data actually stored? Where's the central processor? Where's the software? What *programs* is it running? How does it manage to do *anything*?"

"Maybe that is all you need," suggested Aisha. "Perhaps just a collection of neurons is enough. Maybe, these days, we think about it too much from a computing perspective. Perhaps it does not have dedicated memory banks in the way that a computer scientist would understand them. Maybe it does not have dedicated processors. Maybe it is processing *everywhere*, all the time. It might not be running programs at all in the way that you might understand them: software running on hardware. Perhaps the hardware and software is all wrapped up together in some brilliant design that we just have not figured out yet?"

"Well yes, agreed," nodded Jenny. "And that's what we're trying to work out. But, really, that's what we're hoping you people will tell us!"

Aisha clearly had doubts. "It still bothers me that we are assuming that the brain works to *any* sort of computational model," she said, slowly. "We do not know that it does that; we do not know *what* it does. There are some big, unanswered questions. We humans are not just processing and storing data. We are also *aware* that we are doing it to a greater or lesser extent. We are somehow conscious of that. There is something extra. Does that make a difference to the way the system is put together?"

"You're really talking about the *soul*, I suppose?" suggested Andy.

Aisha pulled an almost apologetic face. "I do not think it has to be the *soul* exactly; at least not in the sense of something that is *independent* of the body it resides in. Not something that can live *without* the body or continue *after* the body has stopped working. I suppose you could call it 'soul', if you want to, but I think whatever it is, is *tied to* the body and comes *from* the body. It does not even necessarily come from the brain alone. Many people think it probably does but there are some who believe it does not have to. Other civilisations have felt that this internal self-awareness lived in different places in the body. Some thought it lived in the stomach, others thought it lived in the heart. This idea that our consciousness must live in the brain is actually a reasonably modern thing.

"It is a very interesting experiment to try to clear your mind and 'internalise'. Where exactly in your body is it that *you* live? You can *feel* everywhere, if you are well that is, but where are *you* exactly? Most people nowadays *would* suggest that their consciousness comes from the brain because that is where they have a feeling that their thinking is coming from, but that might just be modern conditioning. Being told that something works a certain way is a very powerful agent and often it can be self-fulfilling.

"Personally, I am inclined to think that our self-awareness *does* have more to do with the brain than any other part of the body but I do sometimes wonder whether it is *entirely* independent of the rest of the body. I mean, clearly the brain needs *power* to work so it needs to be *fed* by the body but it might be that the way the rest of the body is put together contributes to the brain's operation in a manner that we have not quite yet understood. It might be that the model of an energy system and a data-processing system, as two separate entities, is much too simplistic and that it is actually all wrapped up together. In fact, in general, it may be better to talk about a 'nervous system' than just a 'brain'."

"But that still doesn't really answer the question of where exactly this self-awareness comes from in the first place, does it?" insisted Andy, not prepared to give up the argument without a fight.

But nor was Aisha giving in quite so easily.

"True, but just not being sure where it comes from does not necessarily make it an independent soul that we are dealing with, does it? Just because it might be more complex than merely the brain on its own, just because it might need the body as well, does not mean that it cannot still come entirely from within. I admit I do not know but, whether it is just the brain or whether it is brain *and* body, it could be merely a question of complexity. Build something with enough complexity – with enough neurons and connections between them, give it some fuel, and maybe that is all it takes?"

Chapter 2: Changes

More drinks were ordered and the conversation continued to flow enthusiastically. Returning from the bar with the next tray of glasses – three beers and a sparkling water, this time, Aisha shot Andy a quizzical glance.

"Andy, this is not making you feel uncomfortable, is it? The pub, the beer, I mean?"

"Oh God, no!" smiled Andy. "If it bothered me watching people drink booze, I wouldn't have made much of a recovery, would I? No, I'm happy enough – really enjoying it, in fact. I still love a night out and good company. I can go anywhere and do anything these days. I'm not clinging on trying to avoid the sight of alcohol. I'm *recovered*. God's taken the problem away from me."

More than merely the religious angle intrigued Aisha in this, having – sometimes literally – bumped into an alcoholic or two in the course of her work. "I thought you people tended to call yourselves *recovering* alcoholics these days?" she ventured. "And I thought it was all *'Higher Power'* and 'God' had gone out of fashion?"

"Maybe for some," Andy conceded, "but not for me. I tried all that modern stuff. I sat around in meetings for several months when I first came into AA and that's exactly what we did. We had nice cups of tea – biscuits too, quite often – and slapped each other on the back and shook hands and congratulated ourselves on how well *we* were doing. And it was all about staying sober 'one day at a time'. We shared stories about things that had happened and told each other that it was all about *will-power*: 'don't take the first drink'! It was lovely really. The only problem was that it *didn't work*: quite often, every few nights, sometimes most nights, I'd go straight home afterwards and have a drink! Then, after a few days or so – sometimes *weeks* – on the booze, I'd fall back into a meeting and try to pick up the pieces. And I kept on doing that for month after month, just feeling like a failure: that my 'will-power' wasn't strong enough. And people would say to me, every time I came back, that I 'obviously hadn't wanted it enough'! But I was pretty sure that I *had* so I just didn't have a clue what to do."

"So what happened then?" asked Jenny. "*Something* did, obviously!"

"Aye," Andy continued, "Well, eventually, after stumbling from group to group, trying to find a new set of friends that I didn't feel I'd let down again, I fell in with what seemed like a pretty weird bunch at first. They were doing AA the traditional way; the way it's described in the original Alcoholics Anonymous 'Big Book' from the 1930s. They didn't try to make me feel better by telling me it was all going to be all right: quite the opposite, in fact. Instead, they explained to me just how hopeless a case I was. They told me that I was beyond human aid – mine or anyone else's: that I'd sooner or later drink again – however much I tried not to. And that the only hope I had was a massive 'spiritual experience'. So, I started on the proper AA twelve-step programme. It really wasn't fun (at least at first) and I didn't like the look of it, but I did it and it worked. I found *my* God. I *recovered*."

All three of them, under any other circumstances, would have laughed at this point, hearing this explanation from most people. But Andy wasn't 'most people': they all had the greatest of respect for him. Although far from convinced, their minds were open enough not to dismiss the concept out of hand. It was very unfamiliar territory for them but each of them thought in their own way, 'well, who can say?' Aisha was probably the most doubtful but Bob and Jenny had never been 'proper scientists' (as they often put it) and were generally prepared to consider most things viable – even the 'wacky stuff'.

"So, is there some sort of split in AA now?" suggested Jenny, intrigued by the concept.

"Hardly," admitted Andy. "It's all a bit too one-sided to be considered a split, I suppose. There aren't many groups left like the one I found. Most of AA is going along the modern lines now. 'Forget the Big Book'. 'Forget the programme and the steps'. 'Forget God'. 'Just spread the love and pass the biscuits' and everything will be OK. Actually, that *works* if you've just got a bit of a drink problem, or you're going through a 'phase' but it doesn't work for an out-and-out alcoholic." The smile faded from his lips for the first time. "And I guess that's why, on the whole, AA isn't getting *real* alcoholics sober any more."

An observation like that was not going to go unchallenged in such company. Aisha was the first in.

"And is that a fact?"

"Aye," answered Andy sadly. "In the early days, AA's success rate was supposed to be about seventy-five percent in sobering up drunks like me. Even taking a pessimistic view of the numbers – documented figures, it couldn't have been less than fifty percent. Nowadays – and a good few studies have been done on this too, a real alcoholic has less than a *five* percent chance of recovery in AA. And that's not much better than any other approach: signing the pledge, moving house, changing your job or simply going it alone. There was actually a time when AA was seen as the model for a new society: if *everyone* started adopting twelve-step principles and following God's way, it was going to save us all. Now more and more people seem to *need* the real AA these days – the alcoholism problem's getting worse – but *proper* AA is disappearing fast. It's getting harder to find the 'real deal' any more." They could see his thoughts drift momentarily, then he sniggered a little derisively. "Maybe that's just another possible solution to the *Fermi Paradox*!"

Jenny nodded a degree of partial recognition – but still seemed doubtful about the connection. The other two were clearly completely baffled. So Andy continued, smiling apologetically.

"Sorry, I'm kind of paid to come up with daft stuff like that, I suppose! Making weird connections. The Fermi Paradox; it's really a question. Why haven't we seen any signs of life from elsewhere in the universe? If there's an infinite number of galaxies out there, and an infinite number of planets then there must still be something like an infinite number of them that could support life. Where is it? Why haven't we seen it? Many of these solar systems have been around a lot longer than ours. Why has there been no contact? Seriously, it's a valid question. More importantly, it must have a valid *answer*. It's not some abstract hypothetical conundrum. So, what *is* the answer? The problem is, any answer that you can come up with tends to seem a bit unlikely. And there probably aren't *that* many possible answers. But one of them has to be *true*! *Which one?*"

"How about that there just *isn't any*?" offered Bob.

"Aye, that's the obvious one," agreed Andy. "Perhaps we're genuinely alone. Maybe we're unique in the universe. But, from a purely scientific standpoint, wouldn't that seem a bit unlikely? That this wee insignificant planet, in a backwater galaxy, is the one and only place in the whole universe where this incredible thing called *life* happened? Wouldn't that make us rather special? Almost *chosen*? Actually, of course, that's the solution that makes religious nutters like me feel comfortable, but it's hard to sell to serious scientists!"

"OK, what else then?" pressed Jenny. "I guess saying that it just hasn't happened yet or it's just a matter of time before it happens, or we're actually the most advanced civilisation of all the inhabited planets is pretty improbable if there are so many of them. What else?"

"Exactly!" agreed Andy. "There really aren't that many possible solutions, or at least different types of solution, and they're *all* dubious. But it has to be one of them. Another answer would be that the universe isn't really infinite so nor is the potential number of life-bearing planets. But even if it weren't, there'd still be a huge number to choose from, so surely we'd still expect to see *something*? As Arthur C. Clarke said, *'Either we are alone in the Universe or we are not. Both are equally terrifying.'*

"An alternative is that they're out there but they somehow can't reach us. Perhaps there are some universal constraints that we don't understand: some fundamental physical limits beyond Newtonian or Einstein's mechanics, which just make the distances impossible. The problem with that is that there are a huge number of 'Goldilocks planets' – with just the right this, that and the other – that we already know about within striking distance. We've 'reached' them so why can't they reach *us*. OK, there's no guarantee that there's life on any of them but there *might* be!"

"So where do the drunks come in then?" asked Aisha. Andy resumed.

"Well, the final broad group of suggestions is that something *happens* to all these civilisations before they reach the stage where they're capable of long-distance travel or communication. Presumably something disastrous or fatal. Maybe it's a natural part of the evolution of intelligent life, or a global society, that before they get to that stage, they all destroy themselves with their technology. By the time they'd be ready to launch big enough spaceships, they've already blown themselves apart! I was just thinking – not *terribly* seriously, mind you – that it might not actually be something catastrophic but something more like *decline*. Perhaps they all become *decadent*; you know, like the Romans. Or perhaps they all become *addicts*!"

The conversation moved on.

*

When Andy returned with the next tray of drinks, Bob was being grilled on his 'new invention'. With fewer beers inside him, he would probably have been a little more circumspect but he knew he was with people he could trust.

"It's not exactly an *invention*, I suppose," admitted Bob. "It's more a combination of existing techniques for analysing networks – usually for trying to diagnose problems – wrapped up in a single box … well, *nearly* a single box. I've often wondered why it's not been done before. There's a little bit of new hardware in there and a little bit of new software but not that much of either. There are already plenty of tools for tracing data around networks but the problem is they can't always distinguish particularly well between different *types* of problem. For example, if someone or something's trying to break into a network – in other words human or automatic but *deliberate* – then the data will look quite sensible but it will have malicious intent. You need to ignore individual streams of data in isolation but look at the overall patterns it's giving. Patterns are often the clue to cyber-attacks: or just plain *hacking*. On the other hand, if the network isn't set up properly – that's probably human but *accidental* – then the data might be *structured* properly but the *figures* will probably be wrong so you really need to be doing some maths. However, if it's the equipment itself that's faulty – *broken kit*, then the data might not even be put together properly at all. You could have the wrong voltage levels or timings, for example. There might not be properly-formed data frames at all. That's really pretty obvious if you think about it but, if you're trying to analyse IP-packets, say, to see what's up with your network, whereas it's gone wrong in a more primitive way, then you might miss it all together. Basically, if all you know is that you've got a problem somewhere but you don't know what it is, it can be difficult to know where to start looking. Networkers generally know to look 'from the bottom up' when diagnosing problems but there's still a lot to look for. And because the modern technology is so complex, it's very hard to find a network manager anywhere these days who actually understands their network on *all* these levels!

"So what I did was to embed some basic hardware; diagnostic, packet sniffing and intrusion detection software on a reasonably powerful processor. In fact, that's the bit I keep updating to keep it up to speed. In principle, it'll run on anything but I always use the newest hardware I can find and rewrite the algorithms when I come across new cases. It's always a cat-and-mouse game between the hackers and the defenders. Then I added what's effectively a glorified oscilloscope to analyse the network at a much lower level, and with more accuracy and better timings; and set it up so that the system could automatically switch between the different states – either when *I* wanted to or when *it* thought there was something to look at. Then I wrote some software of my own to pull all the different parts of the system together under a common interface. The software is about the only clever bit; the only *new* bit anyway. It runs another load of AI programs that connect the individual routines together. They use a kind of *fuzzy logic* to try to second-guess what's going to happen next on the network and either be ready for it when it does or, at least, respond to it much quicker than existing tools. Also, it *learns*: the more networks it analyses, the better it gets. It's so simple but it amazes me how well it actually works! Sometimes it actually diagnoses network problems entirely on its own. Other times, it might not but it gives incredibly clear pointers as to where I ought to look. Someone asked me what it was called once so I had to give it some sort of name. I pretty much made up *'Holistic Analysis Tool'* on the spot; so initially it was called *'HAT'*. But, after a few beers one night, I started calling it *'Hattie'* and it's been that ever since. It's (She's) not much to look at – in fact she looks like an overflowing box of junk! But she does the business!"

Bob's face took on a reflective expression. "And that's where it got interesting. To be quite honest, when I first starting using Hattie, I couldn't really see that I was going to get much use out of it (or *her*) – at least, not for very long. I honestly thought it was a bit of a novelty product. I tried it out on a few private contracts and, yes, it worked very well. But because I knew how simple the architecture behind it was, I thought that it was just a matter of time before other developers managed to come up with something similar and I'd lose the market edge. But there were a couple of things I just didn't see coming. Firstly, no one yet *does* seem to have worked out exactly how she works, so the package itself is still in great demand. Secondly, on the one or two occasions where I took a risk and gave her to other people to try to use on their networks, they just didn't seem to be able to use her! As simple as I thought the package was, it almost seemed – still does, to be honest – that I was the only person that was in tune enough with her and the networks to be able to diagnose whatever problem it was we were looking for. So between the two of us – Hattie and me, we still seem to have cornered the market!

"After that, I started getting some really big work, from some of the major companies, who were struggling with their own systems. It still seems slightly bizarre, when you consider all the resources that these people have at their disposal, that they should have to call in little old me and my box of tricks! But that's exactly what they do! I've got a pretty busy week coming up before Christmas, for example – practically a European tour. I've got five networks to investigate in four different countries. And in the middle of all that I've been called to a European Commission meeting in Luxembourg. That's actually about something entirely different, I think, and I'm not even sure *what*. But I seem to have built up such a reputation now, being this great network troubleshooter, that I'm being called in for all kinds of things – well, Hattie and me, that is. I really don't know how long it can last but I'm certainly enjoying it while it does! And it's not doing the retirement fund any harm either!"

"So, how big is this thing, then? How do you move Hattie around?" asked Jenny, curiously. "Does she fit in your briefcase?"

"No, not really," admitted Bob. "The main box is a bit bigger than a suitcase; and there are one or two extra bits, which can be connected if I need them. And, of course, it's fairly delicate so conventional 'hold luggage' air transport doesn't work. Hattie has to be looked after: either ground movement or private plane. What generally happens is that she goes on ahead of wherever I go by private courier. I've found a specialist team that understand exactly what's needed and sorts the logistics out for me. Occasionally I travel with her; more often I meet her where I'm going. The couriers charge the earth, of course, for that sort of treatment but it's worth it and I just build it into costing my contract quotes. People still seem happy to pay when there's no alternative!"

The looks Aisha and Jenny gave Bob, on finishing, were warm, good-humoured and friendly – but not entirely without a hint of envy. Andy just smiled. Bob grinned in recognition and went to buy the final 'quick' round of the evening.

*

When he returned, Jenny had reclaimed the floor and was describing something that was vaguely familiar to his ears.

"Yes, I guess the problem with *Kurzweil*," she appeared to be in full flow: he had obviously missed the start of this, "is that it sounds too much like science fiction. The idea of a super-intelligent, super-efficient, super-strong race of robots taking over the planet doesn't sound like the sort of thing that a serious computer scientist ought to be talking about. But, if you look at it one step at a time, what's to stop it? Look at what we're already doing at the moment. We have automated production lines, often with very little human intervention. Most of the precision work is done by machine. So we have, in effect, machines *making* machines. What we also do, quite routinely, is use design packages – and these are often very automated too – to design machines. When I say design machines, I mean either on a large mechanical scale or on a small, precision level, such as circuit design or microchip layout. So again, effectively, we have machines *designing* machines. And, of course, all of this is joined together and automated these days by the *Internet of Everything*.

"So we have, on the one hand, machines *designing* the next generation of machines and, on the other, machines *building* the next generation of machines. All you have to do is put those two things together to produce a class of machines which is capable of designing *and* building the next generation and what have you got then? What you've got, in essence, is a generation of machines that is capable of *replicating* itself automatically. To all intents and purposes, the machines will *reproduce*; they will give birth to the next generation. Now, once that starts happening, they're going to get better and better at it very quickly. Each new generation will be better than the last. So, again to all intents and purposes, the machines will *evolve*. They will evolve to be better and better over time and the pace of the evolution will increase. There's going to come a point beyond which it's very difficult to predict what's going to happen. This tends to get called the *Kurzweil Singularity*, or sometimes just the *technological singularity* – although it's debatable, in the truest mathematical sense, whether it's an actual 'singularity'. But that doesn't really matter. The point is, the acceleration of this machine evolution could get to a point where we simply don't know what's going to happen. A lot of people are even suggesting that this could happen in *this* half of *this* century! What happens if and when it does? We're going to have a new race of intelligent machines that, presumably, are better than us in every conceivable way. What's going to happen to us then? Will these machines still want to serve us? Will they have anything like the same set of morals that we do – for good *or* bad? Will they become the superior race? Will they have any *use* for us whatsoever and, if they don't, what will become of us?"

She looked around. She knew that her friends were game enough to take this seriously but it seemed like they were unsure quite *how* seriously! She realised Andy would have problems with some of these assumptions for a start. It was probably best to bring the subject down to earth a little.

"Now, OK, that might all seem a little far-fetched! Well, it may or may not be; I don't have a strong opinion really. But what I *am* interested in, taking the viewpoint that *some* of this – if not necessarily *all* – *is* likely to happen, is trying to get an idea of what the *wider impact* will be. It's been concerning me a lot recently that, because these are mainly seen as technological issues, we're almost invariably, and exclusively, letting the technologists, like Ray Kurzweil – that came up with the ideas and theories in the first place – tell us what the effect will be in a wider social sense. Now, that worries me. I'm always happy to listen to technologists talking about *technology* but I'm a little bit more reluctant to place too much emphasis on what *they* think the *effect* of that technology will be on our future society, the environment; what the legalities and ethics of it all are, the political implications and all that sort of thing. The trouble with technologists, I think, and of course I say this as *one* of them, is that we can often fail to see this *bigger picture,* so we can be scurrying around trying to solve our individual little technical problems, usually on a pretty small scale, and we can completely miss something way more important. There's always a 'bigger picture'."

She could tell that she had caught Andy's attention with all this. He was nodding enthusiastically as she was concluding. This was as much his field as it was hers, of course; certainly when you put it the way she had. There should indeed be a lot of sympathy between them on that score. However, the particular examples he chose to support what she was saying, took even her by surprise.

"Aye, that's right," he agreed. "And when we get hit by a big enough asteroid or that big bugger of a volcano under Yellowstone Park erupts, it probably won't matter much whether you're a human or one of these super-machines. It will quite probably do for the lot of us; there's the 'bigger picture' for you!"

*

That seemed to round the evening off nicely. They downed their shorts and prepared to leave. Although still fairly early by London Friday standards, *The Desk* had successfully conducted its first meeting and agreed to reconvene – 'same time, same place' – in the New Year. As its members were quietly – and for three-quarters of them, somewhat unsteadily – vacating the premises, Bob's attention was caught by a chain of lights hung around the window of a shop across the road. They were clearly programmed to turn on and off in timed segments, giving the impression of a pulse of light circling the display. However, as he watched, the pulse stopped, and was replaced by a random sequence of on and off for each light, resulting in a chaotic flashing effect. It only lasted a second or two before the normal operation resumed and the pulse restarted its circling pattern. Most people would have barely noticed but Bob was an

24

experienced analyst and had a basic feel for things that should and should not happen. Even he, however, managed to give it merely a tired first look but not a second.

'That sort of thing's happening a lot lately!' he thought; then, within the same second, stopped thinking about it, and thought of home.

Chapter 3: Warning Signs

The Desk collectively hugged on the corner, then turned their separate ways home; Andy and Aisha along the Strand towards Charing Cross, Bob towards the river for Embankment and Jenny for Covent Garden.

As she walked towards the tube station, Jenny glanced at her smart-watch to make sure the tracking was on. It was but then she had second thoughts and pulled out her mobile anyway. She was getting to 'that age', she thought to herself; this was the modern equivalent of going back to check you've locked the front door when you *know* you have. Her older brother was staying with her at her flat for a few days and he would like to know where she was this time of night. Every few seconds, of course, the watch would send him her precise location on the system he was watching movies on at home (and probably to anyone else interested enough to be looking as well, she thought with a wry smile) so there was no real need to send an additional message. But she knew he worried and did not entirely trust all this 'new stuff' so she thought it might be best if she did.

"Home in three quarters of an hour with any luck: Send to Richard," she spoke quietly. There: that was job done. She should probably have that message stored on a voice-key somewhere, she thought; she seemed to say it often enough when Richard was visiting.

Jenny still carried a mobile phone, almost like a security blanket. Most of the functionality she needed from day to day, including its own 5G unit, was now on the smart-watch but she liked the backup of the device in her jeans pocket. Also, as she sometimes pointed out to people when they queried it, she was more likely to lose or have stolen one than the other in different circumstances so this was just another level of security. Just to complete the set, she carried similarly-enabled smart-glasses in her jacket pocket but had not got to the point of wearing them much as yet. In fact, she reminded herself, she still had some basic configuration to do at home some time to properly link them to her online identity. (One day, she thought absentmindedly, all this would be replaced by something implanted directly into her head.)

She turned into the station and headed towards the two new entry gates at the far corner. Jenny was a 'volunteer technical evaluation expert', or *'veetee'*, for the new Oyster Card system; no longer a card at all, in fact. In its alpha testing stage, the smaller, cheaper, more powerful, more robust RFID chip was hung, somewhat primitively, on a plastic strip around her neck. (Future NFC versions were planned to be integrated with people's mobile technology.) On this occasion, it worked; as she approached, about a metre away from the gate, the Perspex panels sprung apart to let her through and closed equally rapidly behind her. That did not always happen, she reflected with a grin. Only last week – at Goodge Street, she had been running late and the gate had refused to acknowledge her. She had spent close to a minute contorting her neck towards where she guessed the sensor to be before an attendant had come to her rescue and let her through with a manual key. 'You've just got to love that new technology,' she chuckled to herself.

Some things were already a bit more reliable though. Once downstairs, she waved her *eCard* at a bottle of apple juice in the vending machine half-way along the platform. The cover opened and she took her purchase. She recalled how there had also been issues with this technology in the first year or so but the system was more robust now. This transaction would be automatically recorded and the amount instantly debited from her bank account. The nutritional information would also be loaded directly into her personal diet plan and the plastic logged with her carbon footprint app, as would the train journey she was about to make. If she disposed of the empty bottle at a recognised IoE recycling station, the penalty points would be automatically credited back to her. She had enough faith in all of this working these days to probably not bother checking any of it later.

In fact, she mused, this whole *Internet of Everything* really had come on leaps and bounds over the last year or so. That it was happening in the first place was no great surprise to anyone with any level of technical awareness but the *pace* of development was impressive nonetheless. The idea of an *Internet of Things* had first been given serious attention around the turn of the millennium, initially as an ambiguous blend of new technology (the tags) and a new concept (get *things* talking directly to each other without involving people any more than necessary). The idea of fridges automatically reordering the milk, watering your plants remotely while you were on holiday and instant transactions such as her bottle of juice were seen as gimmicks at first but had quickly caught on. At some point, some of the big corporations had obviously decided that the *Internet of Everything* was a more impressive-sounding name than merely an *Internet of Things* and the *IoT* had seamlessly become the *IoE*. Probably somewhat premature, she had thought at the time; *you're likely to wish you'd hung on to that one until it was actually justified*!

Nevertheless, over-hyped or not, the IoE was here, and here to stay – and expand, it clearly would. Grand promises were being made to the world at large of intelligent integration on an almost unimaginable scale. Everyone and everything was to become part of initially closed, then local, then open, and finally global networks connecting people to businesses to public services to government to just about everything else you could think of. *Already*, buses and trains were, to a large extent, scheduling themselves, blocked drains were automatically calling up for repair, appliances at home were cooperating to run at the most economical times of day, traffic lights were now changing dynamically in response to shifting traffic patterns and, one day, everyone's car would drive itself automatically anyway. There was even talk of an IoE *toilet*! Life would be easier than ever before. One day, but not yet: the IoE, like any new technology, was having the usual teething troubles. But that was not going to stop the developers. Already, even now, almost everything that functioned was likely to be networked: *hardly anything was separate from the Internet any more.*

But clearly – *surely* clearly – there was a darker side to all this? There were a quite a few things being overlooked here, thought Jenny. Possibly foremost amongst what was *definitely* being overlooked was the fact that it would not be necessary to *tag* things to *watch* them. Unfortunately, there still appeared to be a widespread, implicit assumption that 'joining in' with the IoE would be a *voluntary* choice. The belief was that individuals would *choose* to have their items (or themselves) tagged and identified. This had already been happening in practice, of course, for years, with so many people carrying a mobile device around with them: as a society, we were already sacrificing privacy for the 'pay-off' that technology delivered. But tags were not the only way of identifying *things*. *Things* (including *people*) could be recognised by their *own* characteristics. Once *things* were *known* in the system, they could be *tracked*.

There were numerous ways in which people, and what they owned, could be drawn into the IoE, she reasoned. Cars could be tracked by their registration plates (in addition to the other things people filled them with); serial numbers could be scanned; fingerprints, DNA, even breath – as had been recently proved, could be detected as unique identifiers. Effective face-recognition might still be developing but it was improving all the time and realistic, accurate identification was becoming a reality. Also, any technology you *carried* would obviously identify you. The day would come, she was sure, that stepping outside your door would instantly integrate you into a *global awareness*, from which it was impossible to hide or escape. (Staying at home would probably not help much either.) Such was the vision Jenny was beginning to call the *Real Internet of Things* (which just happened to abbreviate nicely to *RIoT*). She had already written a few papers on the subject but none had received much attention and one had been rejected outright by a top journal as 'speculative and unfounded' but she remained undeterred. This RIoT would be a very different world, and not just in a technical sense, she thought: it was going to affect how everyone *behaved*. All kinds of new social questions would arise. How would we live our lives when we really could not hide? When our faces, for example, could be accurately and automatically recognised everywhere, how could there be any privacy? Would anyone ever be able to protect their personal information or to have any *secrets*?

Also, she mused, what was being done with IoE technologies at that point in time was both limited and reasonably legal, but was that likely to be the way it stayed? The answer was almost certainly *no* on both counts. Without much doubt, we were destined for a form of *global awareness system*, which would be very difficult to control or escape from, and it was unlikely that legislation would offer much protection in either the short or long term. Jenny had seen this before. *Conventional* laws always lagged badly behind the technology, which the lawmakers usually did not understand. They could try, and generally did – often admirably, she thought, but they would always be 'playing catch-up'. More significantly, there would always be loopholes and simple mistakes. She knew there was another essential privacy axiom related to this: once data was 'out there', it was *out there*; once an individual was drawn in, albeit involuntarily, they *stayed in*; there was no going back. That was the way '*big data*' worked in practice. The wrongdoers *might* get prosecuted and punished but that was always too late for the individual; the damage could never be undone, even with the original Internet, even less so with the IoE (or RIoT).

Another point was that it was all so very easy to *mine* data nowadays, often quite accurately, but it was so very easy for it to be wrong too. The business models of the Internet had always been different to their offline counterparts; profits were to be made from dredging through huge quantities of probably useless information in the knowledge that the occasional pay-off from the relevant material would still be worthwhile. Spam/phishing was the clearest illustration of this; even if 99.99% of recipients failed to respond, the exercise was still useful for the wrongdoer for the handful of cases that *did*. However, she returned to the same thought: once the information was in the common domain –

approved, valid, *validated or otherwise*, the damage was done. An individual might consider it private or inaccurate but it was unlikely that any legislation would protect them effectively. They might be able to force it down on one page – even punish the perpetrators – but it would probably appear somewhere else. The reality would be that if anyone was interested enough to find out about us, they would be able to. If you considered the combination of this global *knowledge* of everyone with the RIoT's ability to *track* their every movement, then obviously the connected world of the future would be a very different place indeed. *'Big Connectivity'*, she might call it.

The final, albeit minor misconception, she thought, as the incoming train hooted towards the platform, was that this use and abuse of 'big data' would be limited to governments and major institutions. The past few years had seen a succession of cyber-security spy scares and business hacks, each one more politically or commercially damning or damaging than the last, and it should have been obvious to everyone by now that there was *no* such thing as private data any more. The only surprise really was that people were still *surprised*! But, clearly, it would not stay that way for long; use or abuse of big data and big connectivity would not remain the preserve of the powerful elite. Data had value; anything with value could, and would, be sold on; those doing the selling would sell it wherever there was a market. All this personal information *would* find its way into common distribution – it was naïve to think otherwise; the great new god of data-obsessed technological entrepreneurship and private enterprise, *'Technocapitalism'*, would see to that!

As Jenny stepped aboard the empty train and slumped exhausted into the nearest seat, a discomforting scenario played, almost dreamlike, through her mind. She was at some event, a few years into the future, meeting someone for the first time during a coffee break. He introduced himself as *'John Green'*. As he was speaking, the headset she was wearing (smart-glasses, maybe, or perhaps it was an implant) scanned his face and analysed his voice and breath and other characteristics. It matched it all against an online global database and reported back to her, in seconds … *"No, this isn't John Green. This is Paul White. He's 45 years old and lives in Sheffield; married with three children. He was arrested in 2007 for shoplifting and declared bankrupt in 2011. He works as a landscape gardener but his attendance record isn't very good. He smokes and has a chronic lung condition, which is making it difficult for him to get insurance. He votes Liberal Democrat. His favourite type of porn is …"*

She came around just in time to get off at her station and ambled slowly home, still deep in thought. As she walked towards the shared front entrance of the apartment block, the security camera of the adjacent door whirred into motion. She knew that her neighbours spent much time away from home and used a number of these, controlled remotely over the IoE if they felt like it, to watch over their property from afar. Now, however, this particular device was obviously not interested in her: it never looked her way. It seemed broken somehow. Instead, it performed a curious – and pointless – Z-shaped movement before tilting backwards and coming to a stop, gazing impotently upwards towards the dark, cloudy sky.

'That kind of stuff's been going on a lot lately!' she thought, forgetting it immediately upon turning the key in the door and stepping inside.

*

Aisha and Andy walked briskly towards Trafalgar Square, quiet for the first part of the short route. Andy was the first to break the slightly uncomfortable silence.

"I'm really intrigued by this notion – if I've understood it right – that internal awareness comes from the whole body rather than just the brain," he offered as a conversation strategy. It seemed easier to start with a question that appeared to divide her from her peers than one that possibly divided the two of them. "Are you getting a lot of support for that?"

But Aisha saw through it easily. "I have not really asked," she smiled. "I am not even putting that forward as a particularly serious proposal. What I *am* saying is that I think it is quite likely that we do not need to look *beyond* the body for whatever it is that causes its contents to be capable of high-level reasoning. I do not see the need for an independent mind, or soul. Yes, there is much that we do not understand but it remains possible that self-awareness is merely the result of neural complexity, whether solely in the brain or not. It may be that if you take a system with sufficient complexity and give it fuel, it becomes sentient – whatever that may mean in practice. But maybe it is more complicated than that; perhaps the complexity and power are all part of an integrated system we do not yet understand. These are just different ways of looking at the question." Her smile turned to a grin. "It is even possible that your God has designed it that way, really!"

"True," conceded Andy with a sigh. "It's possible. If I remember rightly, *Alan Turing*'s original 'theological defence of artificial intelligence' was along those lines. He pointed out that we shouldn't say that a machine *couldn't* be intelligent because that would be telling God how the universe worked! God might *like* AI, for all we know! But, at the same time, science itself comes from God. He's laid down the rules. If something can't be done then we can't change that – and that's the same whether or not you think God made the rules in the first place." Aisha grimaced some form of acceptance and they ended the evening as friends. They would never be anything less. In fact, Andy felt comfortable enough to propose something he would not have done five minutes earlier.

"Actually," he suggested, "I need to write a wee piece for one of these 'spiritual science' publications I'm involved with." He used term in a deliberately self-depreciating tone. "I was thinking of doing something combining the 'What is machine intelligence?' question with Jenny's 'technological singularity' thing. But I'd like to take it from the basic definitions rather than pure technology. If I was able to put together something over the next day or so, which I was happy with, would you like to look it over – and perhaps add your thoughts – before I show it to the two 'techies'?

"Of course!" Aisha smiled. She was unsure whether he really meant it or was trying to rebuild bridges that were still intact, but she appreciated it. As it happened, Andy *was* serious and spent much of his later journey home planning an initial draft in his head.

As they neared the crossing to take them over to the entrance to the tube, the pedestrian light conveniently turned green and they stepped directly into the road, unaware that, in fact, the traffic lights pointing in both directions up and down the street had remained unchanged. A taxi screeched to a halt, horn pumping loudly and the driver shouting crude Highway Code advice from his open window. They flinched like sprinters in starting blocks and ran to the other side, coming to an abrupt, breathless halt once safe on the pavement.

"Is it just me," asked Andy, "or are those kinds of thing happening more and more these days?"

"No, not just you," agreed Aisha. "I've noticed it too."

*

Bob's journey home was uneventful, but productive. Once on his train, he viewed and deleted most of the evening's messages on his smart-watch. There was just one that would need attention when he got home. More precisely, it would need a discussion with his wife, which he was not entirely looking forward to. After that, he scanned for news. There were some odd stories about various technology failures around the country: it mostly looked like pranks of some sort. Other than that, the ongoing debate was the rising unemployment rates caused by machine automation: yet more factories in India and China had laid off many tens of thousands of people in favour of robots, causing extensive public unrest. A new, even more virulent and life-threatening, variant of the MRSA bacterium was appearing in hospitals around the world and people were being warned to take extra care. Another terrorist attack had taken place in Rome. Climate-change concerns were still growing with long-term predictions becoming graver.

Jill opened the door as he arrived. She had been tracking his progress for the past hour. It was almost exactly midnight.

"How was it?" she enquired.

He considered briefly. "It was nice," he said. "I'm not really sure we're likely to get much actual work done between us but it was great to see everyone together again. We said we'd try again after Christmas so we'll see. Anyway, I need to talk to you about something."

Jill knew exactly what that meant from long experience. "As long as you're home for Christmas, I'll live with it!" she grunted.

"I've just had a message from a guy in Zaragoza," he explained, apologetically. "I've been working on dates on the way home. I was hoping I could fit it in between Madrid and Cork; that would have been the obvious way to do it, but the flights won't work out for me and Hattie. I'll have to spend a day or two there at the end instead. I'll still be home by the twenty-third."

"It's OK," she smiled. "We'll understand. Anyway, you'll have plenty of time to get some nice Christmas presents!"

He was not entirely sure she really *did* understand and the beer was giving him a sense of mild paranoia. "The thing is, I *do* need to be taking these contracts now," he said. "I can't guarantee I'm going to be getting them much longer. There's going to come a time when other people will be doing what I'm doing and I won't be in such demand. Then there'll be competition all over the place and I'll get undercut – certainly outside the UK. It probably won't be worth doing these trips soon. I'm just making the most of it."

"I said *it's OK!*" she insisted, a firmer edge to her voice. "Now, get yourself off to bed, you old sot. Chris and Heather and Ben are going to be here for breakfast tomorrow." Her severe tone was betrayed by her smile.

Chapter 4: Weird Stuff

Bob was usually an early riser – a family trait, it seemed – and, even with no alarm set for the weekend and a mild hangover, he was downstairs by 7am, not much later than usual. Even so, the rest of the family was already busy feeding themselves and each other in the kitchen-diner. It felt colder that it normally did – there must be a window open, he thought absentmindedly. His grandson, Ben, was strapped into his high-chair, looking out over the back garden and Jill, his son Christopher and daughter-in-law Heather were fussing over him and generally getting in each other's way. Ben, for his part, was altogether more interested in the two dogs playing under the garden spotlights than any amount or variety of food his parents and grandmother could attempt to cajole him with. A broken conversation was taking place about something Bob could not determine. He caught words such as 'strange' and 'no-one seems to know' once or twice but, before he could get any focus, he drew attention away by entering himself.

"Hi Grandad," Heather and Chris chirped in unison. Ben glanced at him briefly but the accompanying gurgle could have been intended for anyone, or anything.

"Hi guys," beamed Bob.

Saturday breakfast, with or without, company was never a grand affair. People grabbed cereal from cupboards; milk and juice from the fridge, and made toast or fried the odd egg or rasher of bacon in a communal pan as and when suited them. The five of them were only eventually seated all together at the table when most had finished eating. A glass jug of coffee was the centrepiece. Ben's chair had been turned round to face inwards at a particularly inconvenient time for him. It was beginning to brighten outside, bringing into view a world infinitely more interesting than the interior had to offer. He exercised himself by straining to peer over alternate shoulders to recapture sight of the glory that had been stolen from him. Bob felt very content with all this. He knew they were lucky that

Chris and Heather lived reasonably close so that family get-togethers such as this happened frequently. He thought of the other members of The Desk; not everyone was so fortunate. His mind wandered back.

He and Jill had met while he was finishing at university. They were both too young back then (he thought now) but they had 'got away with it'. They were already engaged when Jill found she was pregnant with Christopher so that rather set things in concrete. As he had to admit, it was not the best recipe for a lasting relationship but sometimes these things were just meant to be. After Chris was born, there never seemed to be the right time for a second child so there never was. No-one really regretted that. Eighteen years later, Chris had outdone his parents by marrying even younger and here they all were.

"Mum says you're still in big demand, Dad?" said Chris, through the steam of the coffee cup he had just taken from his lips. (Yes, why *was* it so cold today?) "Off again, I hear?"

"Yes, that's right," admitted Bob, probably trying to look a little more downcast than he absolutely needed to. "Off on Tuesday. Paris, Darmstadt, Luxembourg, Madrid, Cork and Zaragoza. Not exactly an *optimal route* but the way it's worked out unfortunately."

"Don't be daft," snorted Jill. "You'll have a whale of a time. Fancy hotels and being taken out to dinner everywhere as usual!" Bob made no attempt to answer this time, merely allowing himself a theatrically reluctant smile of acknowledgement.

"So is it more of the same, Grandad? More misbehaving computers?" suggested Heather, whilst trying to coax Ben into eating the last piece of toast. She always spoke as if through Ben. Both she and Chris were newly qualified teachers; bright, able and enthusiastic but hardly au fait with the subtleties of network analysis.

"Indeed," agreed Bob. "Those naughty computers – well *networks*!"

"So what's it this time, Dad," asked Chris. "Anything challenging? Anything up to a man of your calibre?" The sarcasm was entirely good-humoured. He admired the work his Dad got involved with, albeit without understanding too much of it.

"Well, it's always hard to tell before you turn up somewhere," said Bob, as much in self-reflection as in direct response. "There's a couple I can make a fair guess at before I go but, usually, it's a question of dealing with whatever they throw at you when you get there. The Darmstadt one doesn't seem to make any sense at all from this side of the water but it'll probably be simple enough when Hattie and I get to look at it. Anyway, at least I know what *type* of work it'll be in the companies. I've absolutely no idea what The Commission want me for!"

"Commission?" Heather enquired. Everyone knew what, or *who*, Hattie was!

"*The European Commission*," Bob explained. "Basically the guys in charge of the *European Union*, the *EU*. Most of my contact with them recently has been through their research funding. I've worked on a couple of *Framework 6* and *Framework 7* projects in the past. The current round is called *Horizon 2020* and I've already done some work for them as an expert reviewer for the early proposals and now they've asked me to do some more. Obviously, the UK vote to leave made no real difference to *me* in the long run but it's really hurt people in the universities like Jenny Smith. She and I were thinking about putting a proposal together with some other European partners for a few million Euros – but I won't be able to do both because there'll be a conflict of interests. Getting funding isn't easy but it's *big* if you do. Most of the time the EC works out of the *Berlaymont* in Brussels but they're spread around in bits all over Europe. Luxembourg's not unheard of."

"So this is about a project?" suggested Chris.

"No, it can't be," said Bob. "There's nothing currently in the pipeline." He paused for a moment of reflection. True enough, he *had* been included in proposals in the past without much prior knowledge but, even if that had happened with *H2020*, no-one would ever call *him* in just to talk about *that*. "No, I think they want to talk to me about something specific. It's either going to be a technical issue or I've done something wrong," he joked. "I'm hoping it's the first one!"

"It's not going to be to do with this *Weird Stuff*, is it?" suggested Jill as she picked up Ben's rejected toast from the floor and threw it to one of the dogs.

Judging by their smiles, everyone seemed to know what this meant except Bob so he looked suitably quizzical without difficulty. He guessed this was the basis of the conversation he had walked in on but that did not help. Jill continued.

"You must have noticed over the last few days? Things just behaving oddly? Not working properly? Things going off at the wrong time, displays going funny, automatic systems doing their own thing; that sort of stuff. The newspapers are having great fun with it. There was a piece on Breakfast TV this morning. Apparently *#weirdstuff* is trending on Twitter."

Heather nodded in agreement. "A woman Mummy works with," through Ben again, "has one of those automatic cat-flaps that only lets in the cat with the right chip. The night before last, it wouldn't let the cat in. Then, in the middle of the night, it opened up and stayed open. Yesterday morning, she had a kitchen full of cats, who had eaten all the food she'd left out."

"Yes, and I've just remembered," murmured Chris, "the man at the garage this morning said one of the fuel pumps was giving away diesel for free for twenty minutes until someone spotted the meter wasn't running."

"Yes, that sort of thing," agreed Jill. "Burglar alarms going off for no reason, for example. And old Mrs. Harris, down the road, had her telecare system automatically call the support team twice yesterday; she's only just had it serviced and she was at home both times and the alarm didn't go off in the house itself. Come to think of it, did you notice the heating wasn't on this morning? That's because the timer reset itself last night. That's always been your trouble, Bob," she laughed. "Your head's so full of your technical nonsense, you can't see what's in plain sight; everyone *else* is talking about it!"

Bob sat open-mouthed for a few moments. Conflicting thoughts fought for attention in his mind. It was going to be a close run thing as to which won the race to be articulated into words. *Yes*, of course, now that he was forced to think about it, obviously he *had* noticed a few rather odd things over the past few days; *yes*, probably more than normal; true, he *was* inclined to be rather absent-minded – noticing on the periphery but not taking things in. And there *had* been something in the news the previous night. *But*, on the other hand, this just *had* to be coincidence, surely? These things happened. No-one was suggesting a national phenomenon … *were they?*

"Well, yes, I suppose I have … Yes, I definitely have," he almost stuttered. "But things *do* break and play up from time to time, don't they? Coincidences happen. This isn't supposed to be part of a big pattern, is it? How could it be? All these devices do entirely different things; they work in completely different ways; they're made all over the place by different manufacturers; they're different technologies entirely; they're on different systems, different networks; some are barely on networks at all; *there's no connection.* How can there be any link in any of this nonsense?" He looked around, honestly expecting, for a moment, an instructive response. All he received were pulled faces and shrugged shoulders.

"No-one really seems to know, Grandad," said Heather, from which Bob was almost inclined to infer that no-one cared too much either.

He politely resisted the urge to jump straight onto his tablet to investigate further but this *Weird Stuff* effectively dominated the conversation for the next three quarters of an hour. Apparently, there were anecdotes galore across the length and breadth of the country. There seemed to be very little doubt that, if these events had to be put down to a coincidence, it was a coincidence of truly massive proportions. Something *had* to be going on and he was itching to find out. Eventually, it was time for Heather and Chris to leave. They all finished their second round of coffee and said their fond goodbyes as Ben was being strapped into the car.

"You're going to be checking this out right away, aren't you Dad?" smiled Chris as he climbed into the driver's seat. It was not hard to see just how intrigued and confused his father was.

"Got that right!" admitted Bob with a pained expression. "This has really got me thinking; but, but it just doesn't make any sense."

"Do you think the Government will be calling you in for advice?"

Bob considered for a moment. "No, I doubt it," he said. "Firstly, it just doesn't seem like a *networking* problem. I've no idea what sort of problem it is but it doesn't *feel* like a networking one – certainly not like anything I've come across before. Secondly, I've never really been very high in the UK Government's picking list. I go down well in Europe and America but I've never seemed to be in much demand in Britain. They probably know how I vote!" he joked.

*

Sure enough, the crudest of web searches, as soon as Bob could lay hands on his tablet, revealed the growing extent of the story. Some of the pages were rather slow to download, which he put down to high levels of interest that morning overloading servers. However, it did not take long for the picture to emerge. Whatever the 'weird stuff' was, it could *not* be coincidence. Also, it was immediately apparent that this was not merely a British phenomenon. Stories were flowing in from around the world. Tweets on the #weirdstuff tag poured through in their thousands. Someone had produced an official name; the *weird stuff* was beginning to be known as *Random Failure Syndrome*, or *RFS*. Governments were being pressed for statements. Most seemed reluctant to oblige. No-one was claiming responsibility or even any level of understanding. However, vague suggestions – then actual claims – of cyber-terrorism were beginning to surface. Naturally, those organisations that might well have had any idea about what was going on – the US military were at the top of most people's list – were remaining tight-lipped. Whether this was a sign of culpability or cluelessness was impossible to determine. Worldwide, a few fatalities – accidents supposedly attributed to RFS – were already being reported, although it was often hard to be sure what was (and was not) the cause. As he scanned the BBC website, a story broke about a passenger plane in difficulty – possibly missing – after ground contact had been lost early that morning.

Tracing RFS back to its beginnings looked problematic and the attempts were in their early stages. However, there was a general global impression that the first signs of odd activity – as in something that might reasonably be considered statistically significant – had appeared a week or so previously. Unsurprisingly, the first few days of this had caused merely localised amusement and annoyance in equal measure. It was only in the past forty-eight hours that reports had started to become connected. It was also difficult to tell for certain if the rate of RFS events was changing. Naturally, earlier problems had not been reported as accurately as later ones. However, even taking this into account, it *could* be that the problem was growing.

Bob cupped his mouth and chin in his left hand as he flicked through screens with the right. This made no sense. What was happening? How could this RFS be occurring across the globe on such a range of completely unrelated devices? That single thought pounded in his mind. *This makes no sense!* There was no rational explanation he could muster that would come even close to dealing with it. But happening it clearly was.

'Surely this *has* to be malicious?' he eventually muttered to himself, then repeated it from time to time. Somehow, somewhere, *somebody* had to be responsible for this. Beyond that, he had very little idea. Was it *malware*? If so, was it hundreds of different types or some astonishing cross-platform variant? Even then, how could that work? Of course, it was an accepted fact in technological research that the military were always far in advance of everyone else and it was generally impossible to know what they were up to. Also, over the past few years, a number of radical groups, even nations, had also shown themselves to be extremely adept at exploiting both emerging technologies and weaknesses within them for their own ends. The terrorism/counter-terrorism battle had moved into cyberspace some time ago.

But if these were *attacks*, the question of who might be behind them was of secondary interest to Bob. He was entirely absorbed by the *how?* The more he considered it, the more impossible it seemed. There was *no similarity* between the devices that were malfunctioning – other than the fact that they *were* malfunctioning and nowadays were all part of the global IoE. The more he threw a quarter of a century of networking experience at the question, the more impenetrable it looked.

*

He was hardly surprised to get a call from Jenny Smith the following morning. He was putting together some final reports for the most recent contracts he had worked on. Bob liked to submit a brief concluding note along with his invoice for services rendered. He doubted anyone actually read them. He often admitted that, 'if an expert comes in, explains to you what was wrong with your network, fixes the problem and explains whatever it is that you mustn't do again, why would you bother to read a report a fortnight later that tells you the same thing?' However, it gave him a sense of completing the work properly, so he always wrote them. His smart-watch buzzed and he jabbed at the screen.

"I take it you've seen this RFS thing?" Jenny snapped, clearly short of temper.

"Well, seen it, yes … but absolutely no idea what it *is* or what any of it *means*," asserted Bob quickly, lest there be any misunderstanding.

"Damn!" grunted Jenny. "I was hoping you were going to help me out with this."

"Er, *help you out?*"

"Yes, I got caught by surprise by the University's Marketing Department late last night: that'll teach me to answer the phone half-cut! The BBC wanted someone to talk about RFS on the lunchtime news today. I actually suggested you but they said they wanted an academic. It was late and I was tired so I said 'yes' almost before I'd thought about it. My thinking then was that no-one would know what this was about so I'd be as good at saying that as anyone else." She sighed. "But thinking about it fresh this morning, I'm doubting that's the impression they've been given. They may be expecting some sort of insight from me and I don't think I can deliver that. Have you *any* idea what's going on?"

"Well, it *has* to be some sort of malware," suggested Bob. "I just can't see what else it can be. It's not as if tens of thousands – I don't know, maybe hundreds of thousands; maybe *millions* – of peripheral devices are going to independently develop faults. The networks themselves seem OK and ..." He paused, reflecting on some of the earlier download delays. "Actually, come to think of it, the network – the Internet, I mean, obviously – was a bit of a pain this morning. Maybe the faults aren't just on the edges?"

"Anyway," he continued, "whether they are or not, this can't be coincidence. There has to be someone behind it; nothing else makes sense. But I can't get much further than that. *Who's* behind it and *how* it's happening, I've no idea. This isn't a conventional cyber-attack, for a start. It's bigger than anything that's ever been seen before, it's spread across more platforms, it's just utterly random and I can't see any evidence of how it's coordinated or whatever malware it might be is being spread. And *who's* to benefit? Also, there's just no consistency: it's not as if *everything's* breaking; just the odd thing here and there. That's simply not the way it normally works: even malware tends to be predictable – *deterministic* really."

"You mean *deterministic* as in same-thing-in-same-thing out always?" suggested Jenny. She was aware that there were definitions of the word beyond computer science.

"Yes, that's right," Bob confirmed. "This *isn't* deterministic. Whatever these devices seem to be responding to, it doesn't always have the same effect. It's as if it's not conventional computer logic at work here. It's almost ..." He paused to reflect. "It's almost *fuzzy*."

"OK, well, that's pretty much what I was going to say!" laughed Jenny nervously. "And I might quote you on that!"

*

Bob rarely watched TV, certainly not on Sundays, but he naturally made an exception now. A few hours later, he was nestled in his armchair in the corner of the lounge, with a cup of tea, ready to see Jenny on the lunchtime news. He could have stayed and watched it in his office but this was his weekend compromise. Jill was getting Sunday dinner ready in the kitchen.

If the interview was an unpleasant experience for Bob to witness, it must have been a whole lot worse for Jenny. The piece started well enough but descended rapidly. Naturally, it was the lead news item and began with a short documentary-type summary of the emerging phenomenon, the delivery shared between the anchor-woman in the studio and a couple of reporters out on the streets. A problem the TV channels were having was that it was proving difficult to catch RFS events actually taking place. Generally the best they could do was after-shots of devices that had already malfunctioned, either stopped inappropriately or returned to normal. So, for anyone still unaware of what was unfolding around them, the story had a slightly spoof air to it. However, for the non-sceptic, the sight of the two reporters explaining malfunctioning displays, signals, controls and devices in general would have already been familiar. The focus then returned to the studio, where 'Professor Jenny Smith, now joins us to shed some light on these strange happenings'. Bob winced inwardly.

"Professor Smith," started the interviewer, "so, what do we think is behind all this RFS?" And it went rapidly downhill from there.

If Jenny had started with a frank admission that neither she nor anyone else had the faintest idea, the interview would probably have been short, disappointing but reasonably painless. However, she made the fatal mistake of opening with a somewhat more non-committal answer.

"Well, it's hard to say for sure," she said nervously (inadvertently giving the impression that she might, if pressed, be able to say *something* or at least suggest it without being *sure*), and then proceeded to outline all the things she *did not* know about RFS. She repeated essentially what Bob had said about there having to be some malicious intent behind it all but that it was impossible to say who or indeed exactly what. She managed to list a few things it *could not* be but had little – nothing really – to offer by way of firm suggestions. At one point, she began to hint towards military research gone wrong but realised, in mid-sentence, that she could not justify any such claim. She then shifted towards the possibility of cyber-terrorism.

Neither did she have any real suggestions to offer for what type of technology the attacks (if indeed that was what they were) might be using. 'How are so many different types of device being affected across the world, Professor Smith?' She did not know. Again, there were plenty of things to say about how this could *not* be effected but no insight into how it *might*. The interviewer initially tried to help by turning to new questions but each new question merely turned out to be another Jenny failed to answer. Gradually the tone became more confrontational. *Why* could the academic and scientific community (of which she was apparently being offered as the spokesperson) *not* explain what was going on? What were people like her paid for if they could not step up to the mark when their country, and the world, needed them? Who *should* they be talking to if this was beyond the experience or ability of the scientists? In total, her humiliating descent from respected senior academic to pointless schedule-filler took less than eight embarrassing minutes. The concluding 'Thank you, Professor Smith' had a distinct '*Thanks for nothing!*' undertone.

But Jenny was tough, and not one to stay down long. Within the hour, she was back on the line to Bob and both were laughing at the daft futility of it all.

"And what exactly did they expect?" she giggled almost hysterically. "I told them they'd be better off with you!"

"Oh, yes," snorted Bob derisively. "That would have made all the difference, of course, wouldn't it? Because I've got *all* the answers!"

They were interrupted by a ring at the door. The couriers had come to collect Hattie.

Chapter 5: The Singularity

There were a couple of pieces of better news the next morning. Firstly, the missing plane had landed safely, albeit in something of an emergency fashion and not at the intended destination airport. Failure of ground-based communications systems had been the biggest problem; the plane's own navigation system had, on the whole it appeared, behaved. The authorities were in some doubt as to whether this had been a 'real case of RFS' or 'a conventional equipment fault'. *That's a stupid thing to say*, thought Bob, with mild irritation. If you don't know what's *causing* RFS, how can you make arbitrary judgements whether something's been *caused* by it? That's like saying you don't know whether that *unexplained* thing in the sky was a real *UFO*! He genuinely wondered sometimes whether the average inhabitant of Planet Earth could, left to their own devices, think their way out of an unlocked shed.

The second welcome news was to be found in a message from Andy sent hours before. (Andy appeared to be an even earlier riser than him these days. Bob reflected, with some amusement, that he had not been like that at university. He had nearly failed his first year as a result of only ever attending lectures in the afternoon!) Andy was asking for some more exact details of Bob's European itinerary as he thought they might be able to meet at some point. After a haphazard dialogue throughout the day, it was established that they indeed could, in Luxembourg to be precise, the evening after Bob's appointment with The Commission.

There was an international conference on *The Ethics of Technology* in Luxembourg City the following week, Andy explained, which had unexpectedly lost its keynote speaker and guest of honour at the last moment. Under normal circumstances, such an obligation was one of the most binding commitments an academic could enter into and not to be withdrawn from for all but the most exceptional of reasons. On this occasion, however, the intended speaker had died unexpectedly and was to be forgiven.   However tolerantly the conference organising committee were prepared to look upon such a 'no show', though, it did leave them somewhat in the lurch, so Andy, who knew one of the conference co-chairs, had agreed to save the day through the lure of an all-expenses-paid trip and a welcome break from his normal routine.

Bob was staying in a hotel on the east side of the city, mid-way between the centre and the airport. He had chosen it for its proximity to the *Jean Monnet Building* used by The Commission. Andy was going to be able to stay wherever he liked, being in the position of offering the conference such a favour. Although, his conference was more central, the whole place being so small and taxis reasonable, the conference committee would agree to Andy staying at the same hotel without any question. They arranged to meet there for dinner on Saturday, the evening before Andy's talk.

Andy's final message of the day had the following addition.

"BTW, Aisha and I have knocked out the attached over the weekend. I'd been asked to do something 'futuristic' as an editorial for an ethics newsletter so we worked together on it. I wrote the first draft, then it went through the 'Aisha filter' and we've batted it to-and-fro since. It's probably not quite the piece I would have given them, left to my own devices, but I think it reads quite well. See what you think? (I've sent it to Jenny too.)"

Bob opened the attachment on his reader, settled back with another cup of tea, and read with interest.

'How Singular is the Singularity?' (Andrew Jamieson and Aisha Davies)

> *If recent headlines are anything to go by, opinion on the likelihood – and impact – of the 'Technological Singularity' is diverging rapidly. Is this largely because we don't even agree on what it is?*

'*Artificial Intelligence*' (*AI*) is certainly in the news at lot at the moment. But so are *robots*; and *Kurzweil's Singularity*; and machine *evolution;* and *transhumanism*. Are these the same

49

thing? Are they even related? If so, how? What exactly *should* we be arguing about? Are we worried *precisely because we don't even understand the questions*?

Well, perhaps to make a start, we should point out that *intelligence* isn't the same thing as *evolution* (in *any* sense). That's obvious and accepted for 'conventional' life-on-earth but we seem to be getting a bit confused between the two when it comes to machines. Developments in both may proceed in parallel and one may eventually lead to the other (although which way round is debatable) but they're *not the same thing*.

Biological evolution, as our natural example, works by species continuing to adapt to their environment. If there's any intelligence at all in that process, it's in the ingenuity of how the algorithm itself solves the problem – not the species in question. Depending on what we mean by intelligence (we'll have a go at this further on), an individual within a species may or may not possess intelligence – if the individual doesn't, then a group of them collectively *might* – but either way, it's not *required*. Evolution works through random mutations producing better specimens; neither the species nor an individual can take credit for that – it's all down to the algorithm fitting the problem space. Many species are supremely adapted to their environment but their individuals would fail most common definitions of intelligence.

For a slightly tangential example, we might reasonably expect ongoing engineering advances to lead to continually improving travel (or communications or healthcare or safety or comfort or education or entertainment or *whatever*) but these improvements might arise in other ways too. *Engineering* isn't the *same thing* as *Travel*. *Intelligence* isn't the *same thing* as *Evolution*. So which of these is involved in 'The Singularity'?

Well, the clearest – but somewhat generic and by no means universally accepted – definition of the *'Technological Singularity'* (*TS*) is a point in the future where machines are able to automatically build other machines with better features than themselves. There's then an assumption that this process would soon accelerate so that new generations of machines would appear increasingly quickly and with increasing sophistication. If this improvement in performance becomes widespread and/or general – i.e. it goes beyond being simply better suited for a particular, narrow role – then it becomes a bit hard to see where it might all end. It's debatable, in a pure scientific sense, whether this makes for a genuine 'singularity' (compare with black holes and $y = 1/x$ at $x=0$) but it would clearly be a period of considerable uncertainty.

And it's not a particularly mad idea really. We already use computers to help *design* the next generation of machines, including themselves; in fact, many complex optimisation problems in layout, circuitry, etc. are entirely beyond human solution today. We also have machines *producing* machines – or components of machines, from simple 3D printers to complex production lines; and, once again, the efficiency and/or accuracy of the process is way beyond what a human could manage. In principle, all we have to do is merge together automated design and automated production and we have *replication*. Repeated replication with improvements from generation to generation is *evolution*. No-one's explicitly mentioned *intelligence*.

OK, there are a couple of reality checks needed here before we go much further. Firstly, the technology still has a long way to go to get to this point. The use of software and hardware in design and production is still pretty piecemeal compared to what would be necessary for automatic replication; there's a lot of joining up to do yet. Computers largely *assist* in the process today, rather than *own* it; something altogether more complete is needed for machines 'giving birth' to new ones. On the other hand, common suggestions for the arrival of the TS (although almost entirely for the wrong reasons) centre around 2050. This is quite conceivable: three decades or so is a huge time in technological advancement - almost anything's *possible*.

Secondly, we may not have explicitly *mentioned* intelligence on the road to automatic replication but some of this adaptation might *sound* like it? Autonomously extending optimisation algorithms to solve new problem classes, for example, certainly fits most concepts of 'intelligent software'. This is more difficult and it depends on definitions (still coming) but we come back once more to *cause* not being *effect*. In a strict sense, replication (and therefore evolution) *isn't* dependent on intelligence; after all, it isn't with many conventional life forms. It's possible to imagine, say, an industrial manufacturing robot, which was simply programmed to produce a larger version of itself – mechanically *difficult* today, certainly, but not *intelligent*. Anyway, the thing that might worry us most about a heavily-armed human *or* robot wouldn't necessarily be its *intelligence*; in fact, it might be its *lack* of it. (More on this later too.)

So intelligence isn't directly required for the TS; rather the establishment of an evolutionary process. In particular, when people say things like "The TS will occur when we build machines with the neural complexity of the human brain", they've missed the point spectacularly – both conceptually and, as it happens, even numerically (still to come). However, it can't be entirely denied that some form of machine 'intelligence' will probably have a hand in all this. At the very least, developments in AI are likely to continue *alongside* the filling-in-the-gaps necessary for machine replication so we're going to have get to grips with what it means somehow …

And right here is where it gets very *difficult. Because there's simply* no *standard, accepted, agreed definition of 'intelligence', not even for conventional life; in fact the word is clearly used to mean different things in different contexts.*

We won't even begin to attempt to describe all the *different*, and multi-dimensional, definitions of intelligence here. Even on a single axis, they sit somewhere on a spectrum from the crude *intelligent=clever* extreme to the (in fact, equally crude but with a deceptive air of sophistication) *intelligent=conscious*. It will even upset many to use 'self-aware' and 'conscious' as synonyms, but we will here for simplicity. No *single* definition works. By some, conscious life isn't intelligent if it isn't 'clever enough'; by others, an automaton might be if it solves fixed problems 'fast enough'.

And of course, it gets worse when we try to apply this to computers and machines. By some definitions, a pocket calculator is intelligent because it processes data quickly; by others, a robot, which was superior to a human in every single mental and physical way, wouldn't be if it was conventionally programmed and wasn't aware of its own existence. (Is an AI robot more or less intelligent than a dog, or a worm, or a microbe?) We sometimes try to link AI to some level of *adaptability* – a machine extending its ability *beyond* its initial. design or configuration to new areas – but this proves very difficult to tie down in practice. (At which point is a computer *really* writing its own code, for example.) Furthermore, there are two philosophically different types of machine intelligence to consider: that which is (as it is now) the result of good human design (*artificial* intelligence) and that which arises from the machine somehow 'waking up' and becoming self-aware (*real* intelligence).

This fundamental difference in *types* (not *definitions*) of intelligence is possibly more *interesting* than *problematic*. We won't digress in this piece to consider the social implications of 'real' machine intelligence (such as the ethics of 'robot rights', for example) or the different models of intelligence that might allow 'real' intelligence to be created (neural complexity, panpsychism, the biological dimension, spirituality, etc.) That's an argument in itself. But for now, anything that's exciting or scary about the TS applies broadly the same if we're dealing with something that really *is* intelligent or just *appears* to be. And remember, the TS is primarily a question of *evolution*: *intelligence* is a worthy but related secondary issue.

In fact, this might be a good point to dispel another myth in relation to the TS. It has *nothing whatsoever* to do with the circuit complexity of any given processor or any collection of them. The point at which a computer's neural mass (presumably measured in number of logic gates) reaches that of the human brain is often portrayed as some significant point in AI development – sometimes even as the TS itself – but this is nonsense. The almost endless reasons why this doesn't make sense include these deal-breakers:

• The structure and speed of a computer device (including any network of them) is utterly unlike the brain. Each brain neuron is directly connected to many, many thousands of others. Signals, however, move fairly slowly – just a few metres per second. By comparison, computer/network nodes (gates, switches, etc.) generally connect to just a handful of neighbours but signals travel at electron speed. In graph terms, *the brain is dense but slow while a computer is sparse but fast.*

53

• Whilst it's often admitted that we don't know what algorithms the brain runs so it would be difficult to replicate them, the truth, in fact, is that *we don't really know if it runs algorithms at all* – in any sense that we would recognise. The conventional notion of software running on hardware may have no equivalent in the brain. Its structure and operation may be inextricably linked in a way that we can't (yet) recreate in a machine. (There may be a biological foundation, for example.) Its hardware and software (perhaps even its *power*) may be inseparable. We may eventually understand how this works and seek to design machines on this basis but we're not even close now.

So a computer is very unlike the brain; the TS can't be *measured* or *counted*. It's what *happens* that's important.

His reading was interrupted by Jill poking her head around the door.

"Did you turn the cooker off?" she asked irritably.

"No. Why would I?"

"Well, someone – *something* – did! This is getting stupid," she frowned. "Dinner's going to be late," she grumbled as she withdrew.

Bob resumed his reading …

The real question we have to somehow get to grips with is how we might expect these highly-evolved machines to *behave*. This seems to be the focus of most of the recent scare stories. Again, intelligence may be something we have to consider here but it isn't the driver. A new race of machines (in fact, probably many different species of them), superior to humans in every physical and mental way, could clearly be considered a threat. But it's not obvious, in this respect, that an 'intelligent' machine would be any more worrying than one that wasn't – that 'strong, fast and clever' is more dangerous than 'strong, fast and thick' – because, for example, we know the human (and animal) world often doesn't work that way. And all of this is made more difficult by having never really worked out what these terms mean in the first place.

But an obvious key point here is whether we're going to remain *in control* of what these machines do. The implied concern behind a lot of the AI-related headlines is that we *won't*. If, over the long-term and beyond the TS (and the notion of 'beyond' may be why 'singularity' isn't such a great term), machines only *ever* do what we tell them to, then humans remain responsible for whatever use and abuse may occur. The machines are effectively extensions of ourselves (tools) so, even accepting that legislation often struggles to keep pace with developments in technology, we might hope that 'conventional' human moral, ethical and legal codes can be eventually applied (not to the actual machines, of course – that wouldn't make sense – but to the way we *use* them). Whether these human social codes, *in themselves*, are fit for purpose is way out of the scope of this piece.

A much more serious situation arises if, as is generally expected or feared, machines evolve to the point of (at least *appearing*) to think for themselves, either by the autonomous extension of 'artificial' intelligence to new domains or the acquisition of 'real' intelligence. At this point, we have to genuinely consider the rules or framework by which such a machine might 'think' and therefore 'behave' and, if what's gone before was difficult, this takes us into entirely new, deeper, uncharted and murkier depths ...

Frankly, what axioms do we have for dealing with this? Why do *we* even *think* the way we do? OK, we have many models but they range from hard neuroscience, through different psychological theories, including and leading to concepts of the soul – and they're intersected by various arguments for and against pre-determinism and free-will. C.S. Lewis, for example, describes the *'Moral Law'* binding humanity (and there are more scientific versions available for the spiritually faint-hearted) but can any of this be a foundation for predicting the way *machines* will think and behave?

On the whole, humans try their best to apply logic to an, albeit difficult to define, moral foundation. We're not particularly good at this in practice. First of all, few of us really know what this starting point *is* and we have even less idea where it *comes from*. Second, we're not expert logicians in following an optimal line: we make *mistakes*. Third, real life usually gets in the way of the logic and a form of 'needs must' thinking overrides clinical reasoning. Fourth, we often *knowingly* deviate from what's clearly the right course of action because we're all – to a greater or lesser extent – flawed, which might for some even include not wanting to try in the first place. (Obviously there's a sense of fundamental human 'goodness' in this model, which isn't universally accepted.) However, in principle at least, we have a sense of *direction* through all of this. We either make some attempt to stay on course or we don't.

So the question is can or will this sense of 'moral direction' be instilled in – and remain with – artificially-programmed intelligent machines and/or will it be evident in machines achieving their own sentience? In particular, *what* would be their initial moral code? This seems like a very important question because we might reasonably assume that the machines' logic in putting the (moral) code into practice would be impeccable and not prone to diversion as it tends to be with us. But does the question even *make sense*? (Let's be utterly clear about this - Asimov's Laws of Robotics, in this context, are useless: simple fiction and already frequently violated in the real world.) What *might* highly-evolved, super-powerful (*possibly* intelligent) machines regard as their 'purpose', their *raison d'être*? Would they serve, tolerate, use or replace humanity?

And we just don't know. We can define the question in as many ways as we like and analyse it every which way we can. *But we just can't say.* We can easily pluck unsubstantiated opinions out of the air and defend them with as much energy as we wish but there's really nothing to go on. Just as we can only speculate on what would motivate an alien race from a distant planet, it's anyone's guess as to what might drive a new technological species that either we've created or has evolved by itself. (This is all assuming we've surrendered control of the process by then.) In this respect *at least*, some amount of concern in relation to the TS seems *justified* – even if only because we can't be *certain*. It's taken us a long time to get to this position of doubt but concern relating to uncertainly isn't irrational.

Looking to tie this up somehow, if it's difficult to say whether we can ultimately coexist with intelligent robots then is *transhumanism* our insurance policy? As we put more human features into machines, will we take on more of theirs? Is the future not competition between 'natural' and 'technological' species but their *merging*? *Cyborgs?* Some futurologists see transhumanism as a fairly inevitable destiny but does it really help?

Well, *maybe*. But it's a maybe with the same problems as the uncertainties of the TS itself. Because it still depends on how the 'pure' machines will see the world. If ordinary humans are tolerated then probably so will 'enhanced' humans be. If not, then this level of improvement still might not be enough if machine logic takes a ruthless line. Again, the standard futurologist's view of transhumanism implies we'll still have some control but it remains to be seen if that's the case.

And finally, possibly even optimistically, a word of caution ... If this potential elimination of humanity by a robot master race (repeated across equivalent worlds) might seem like an answer to the *Fermi Paradox*, we might have to think again. (Another version of the 'civilisations naturally create their own destruction before they can travel far enough' theory.) Even if the 'developer race' was lost in each and every case across the universe, why aren't the machines talking to each other? (Or are they?)

And there we are ... already at the end of the piece and *we don't know*. Many people have written a lot more, and a lot less, and they claim to know but *they don't*. There are just too many unknowns and we'll have to wait and see. Should we be scared by the TS or not? Well, in the sense that it's uncertain and unpredictable, *yes*. But lots of things in life are uncertain and unpredictable. For some of us, *death* itself is uncertain and unpredictable.

So, is the TS really a 'singularity'? In a strictly *Gödelian* sense, it *might* be. Probably, we'll know when we get there – but not before!

*

Bob smiled. Although not really one for all this 'arm-waving futurology' business, as Jenny often described it, he never failed to be impressed by Andy's essential grasp of the raw ingredients of a subject some distance from his own. True, he had been applying his philosophy to various aspects of science for some time now but his instinctive ability to get to the core of complex issues – with no relevant educational background – was not to be dismissed lightly. Maybe, in fact, having the subject-independence he had was actually an advantage – allowing him to strip away peripheral material without prejudice or bias, and then to abstract and distil. Anyway, he was always a good read!

Nor was it difficult to see Aisha's influence on the piece. There were sections he was fairly sure would not have been that way in the first draft. He could almost picture the two of them arguing over concepts – even exact wording – in several places, before coming to an uneasy compromise. It was interesting that, despite the two of them coming from almost diametrically opposite fundamental points of view, they had managed to agree to a large extent on the conclusions – even if those conclusions were that there were no conclusions!

Anyway, thought Bob. That was enough of that. It was time to turn his thoughts to the 'nuts and bolts and numbers' of real networks. As he turned to his main desk display, it went blank for a few seconds for no particular reason, then reappeared.

PHASE TWO: DIAGNOSIS

Chapter 6: Many Failures

Tuesday, the day of Bob's departure did not begin so well. Interrupting the array of, generally entertaining, stories of RFS being served up on different breakfast TV, radio and Internet channels, appeared to be the first British fatality that could be directly attributed. A pensioner had been killed at a level crossing late the previous evening. One of the gates had inexplicably raised on his side of the tracks. Ignoring the other – it was thought, probably correct – signals, he had driven part-way over without realising that the exit was still blocked on the other side. He had attempted to reverse but became stuck on the tracks and did not quite clear the area in time. The train had only caught the car a glancing blow but that had been enough.

The media were clearly struggling with how to cover RFS – or even to decide when an event was or was not part of the phenomenon. As serious as such events as this were, there was much potential for amusement as well. The UK tragedy was followed by a short piece from Las Vegas. Over the weekend, a casino's centrepiece slot machine had apparently paid out a million-dollar jackpot twice in quick succession. Despite the American reporter's seemingly reasonable observation that 'Surely, these things will duplicate by chance occasionally?', the owner was furious. He had 'paid good money for this particular model' and these random fall-outs in customers' favour 'totally shouldn't happen!' In New Zealand, an automatic farm security system had reported a remote herd of RFID-tagged cows missing; an entire rural police force had been activated in response. The cows, it emerged, had not gone anywhere.

Bob slipped out of the door quietly to find the taxi waiting at the end of the drive. His wife was still in bed asleep. He was dressed casually as always: people paid for his expertise – not his dress-sense. He lifted, rather than pulled, his case round towards the boot so as not to make a noise on the gravel. A cold, fine rain – almost a mist – made him shiver as he slipped into the passenger seat. The taxi was too warm inside and the driver not much for conversation; Bob nodded drowsily, the soft tunes on the radio seducing him into a conviction that he was awake too early, as they cruised towards the airport. The journey seemed unusually short.

An automatic door at the entrance to the departures area was refusing to open as he rolled his case towards it. A small queue had formed as a maintenance man levered the two parts apart with a steel rod that looked a lot as if it could have been designed for the very purpose. Inside was relative normality although the odd information board reset itself from time to time and the check-ins were having the occasional issue with the network systems. On the whole, the place was functioning without too much difficulty although traces of RFS were evident everywhere in the margins. There were some delays, including to his flight, but everyone was getting by. Normally, these malfunctions would have passed without much more than mild exasperation but, knowing (or at least, *suspecting*) them to be part of a wider phenomenon, cast it all in a different light. Bob turned it all over in his head for the hundredth time, but to no avail. He *still* did not know what it *was* and it *still* did not make *sense*.

*

The next nine days were a routine Bob knew well. Planes, taxis, offices, restaurants, more taxis and hotels. A blur of departure lounges, roads, glass buildings, too much food and over-soft beds. Hattie and he followed a continentally similar, but locally different, path; meeting as and where needed and usually parting immediately afterwards to take their separate routes to the next destination. There was no set pattern for this or how it worked. The couriers knew what was needed, where and when – and worked it all out, and were well rewarded for it, including the careful treatment of their delicate and precious cargo. But, all the time, RFS was getting visibly worse.

*

There were two places to visit in Paris. The problem at the first was trivial: a simple set-up issue. There were probably people in the building at that very moment, Bob thought with some amusement, who could have fixed it. They had not needed him or Hattie. Nevertheless, he had switched everything on and made a token attempt at taking some readings before making the necessary changes to configuration files. Bob felt he had to make it look as if they were getting their money's worth; they were going to pay handsomely for the over-the-top attention so he, at least, was happy.

There was even time for some Christmas shopping in an up-market French shopping centre. In the space of an hour and a half, he was able to eat a light lunch and buy the sort of presents for Jill, Chris, Heather and Ben that would be difficult to find at home: this might keep people happy when he returned, he chuckled to himself. But, even here, RFS was very evident: lights, tills, interactive displays, parking meters, the public address system, even the occasional alarm or security system; all were proving problematic from time to time. Most things were taking longer than they should and public bemusement was mounting.

He was able to make the second technical visit, as planned, the same afternoon. This next network proved to be something more of a challenge – although hardly a difficult one. It eventually transpired that there were *two* separate problems – at different network levels, which were each managing to obscure the exact effect of the other. With a reasonable amount of networking knowhow and experience and a bit more time, they *could* have been diagnosed in a more conventional manner but Hattie's 'holistic' approach made short work of it and the company cheerfully signed off the completion document without question. Over the whole day, Bob mused as his taxi swept him to his overnight hotel, RFS had caused him a fair few more problems than these two French networks had.

But Darmstadt was different.

Bob's appointment was at *HGMS-Ion*, a research facility on the outskirts of the town. He flew into Frankfurt airport, was met by a suited driver and driven by private car – by autobahn save for the last few miles – directly to the front gate, to be met at the security desk by *Ulrich Bär*, the contact with whom he had arranged most of the visit. He had decided, in advance, that this one was going to be slightly 'odd'.

Ulrich was dressed as a typical managerial scientist. The only concession he seemed to be prepared to make to his elevated role was to replace the default scientist's t-shirt with an open collar; the jeans remained the same. He welcomed Bob warmly; and had his enthusiasm returned equally. Once the initial pleasantries were exchanged and security processes complete, Bob moved in on the business in hand.

"So what have you got here?" he opened as they walked together towards one of several large buildings at the centre of the complex. "What's the problem? What's not working?"

Ulrich smiled mysteriously. "To take those questions in reverse order, Mr. Weatherill, *nothing* is *not working*; we are not sure if we *have* a *problem*; but whatever we do *have*, we are hoping you can tell us what it *is!*" It was Bob's turn to grin, his curiosity already raised; he had expected something like this from their remote discussions before he had left London: it appeared he was not to be disappointed.

HGMS-Ion – sometimes just HGMS – was a heavy-ion accelerator plant, which had been open for about thirty years from modest beginnings. It specialised in certain types of controlled atomic collisions, which were difficult to produce in conventional research centres. Scientists from all over Europe – and sometimes the world – came to run specialist experiments in booked sessions with time and availability always at a premium. The centre could support a few dozen such guests at a time and had a growing reputation for results across a range of scientific research fields including biophysics, materials and medicine. Several advances in cancer radiation treatment, for example, had been made there in recent years.

While the experimental research community was generally of the visiting variety, HGMS retained a much larger core of resident support staff. These local engineers and scientists were responsible for maintaining the operational capacity of the centre. In his job as Senior Technical Officer, Ulrich was responsible for coordinating home teams of physicists, chemists, mechanical and electrical engineers, computer scientists and networkers. Instantly, Bob did not envy him in such a role: herding cats sprung to mind.

HGMS was expanding, Ulrich explained with some pride. Over the next eighteen months, the old hundred-metre linear accelerator and twenty-five-metre synchrotron ring were being replaced by a new hundred and sixty-metre accelerator and ninety-metre ring, both of which would increase the centre's experimental scope considerably. Several other aspects of the site were also being upgraded and improved; some sections were entirely new. Much of the physical work was complete. The engineers and physicists had fulfilled their roles; most of the hardware – from concrete to precision equipment to wiring – was installed and the computer scientists and networkers had moved in ... at which point the '*issue*' had come to light.

"Quite simply," said Ulrich quietly, followed by a considerable pause, "there is *noise* on the network. That is it, really; there is *noise*." He continued quickly, "We do not know what it is or where it comes from. It does not seem to be doing any damage at the present time but it is *there* and we do not know *why*." We believe we have eliminated all sources of external interference but it is still there. Bob offered nothing at this point beyond a slight raising of the eyebrows so Ulrich continued.

"We are worried that this may become a much bigger problem in the future. You see, the purpose of the network is essentially to carry timing signals around the system so key events across the accelerator can be synchronised and recorded. It needs to be – and it *is* – incredibly accurate. We are talking *nano-second* precision here to keep the physical parts of the process in time. Most of the essential network processing itself is chip-based; you will be familiar with *Network on a Chip* technology?" Bob nodded. "That part is not causing us much concern," Ulrich said deliberately. "But, of course, the signals themselves still have to be distributed over the physical network to and from where they are needed or produced; and these have to have the same nano-second accuracy – after all, that is the whole *point*!

"So, naturally, when we have been testing the system, we have been looking at the carrier lines in considerable detail – on a very minute scale – and this is where and when we start to see the noise. We would not have noticed it if we did not need to look so closely."

"What sort of noise, exactly?" asked Bob. "And why isn't it affecting the operation of the network?"

"Once again, the second question is easier to answer than the first, Bob," smiled Ulrich with a trace of embarrassment. By this time, they were inside the central unit building and at the door of the main control room. "The timing signals we are currently using for testing the system are sparse – there are few of them – because the atomic events are currently not real. We are simply generating test events to monitor the behaviour of the system and the network. But the noise itself is discrete, rather than continuous, and also sparse and – at present – they generally do not coincide: one is not interfering with the other. However we suspect that we may have a problem when we try to switch the timing network across to the real system."

"I would imagine that's pretty likely," agreed Bob, thoughtfully. "And the first question? What sort of noise have we got?"

"I'm a quantum physicist, not a computer scientist," grinned Ulrich. "I think it may be as well for you to look for yourself!" He opened the door and motioned to vast racks of equipment on two sides of the large room. Bob whistled at state-of-the-art kit he only recognised from catalogues. A large display screen was fixed on a third wall. A woman and two men, in their mid-thirties – also casually dressed, sat around a table in the centre but rose together as Bob and Ulrich entered. "As I said, Bob, we are still in a testing phase – not yet live. Please go where you will and do as you choose; and ask for anything you do not see. I put my team and my facilities at your disposal," he said by way of introduction. An open door in the far corner showed another similar room beyond and a familiar package on a sturdy trolley against the adjacent wall: Hattie was already there.

Quickly, Bob was properly introduced to several others in the HGMS senior network team and given a hurried tour of the facilities, meeting further key personnel along the way, including the Network Manager, *Karla Heintze*. He visited the ion source area, the accelerator line, the storage ring and finally the delivery centre: a huge warehouse, in effect, where massive, somewhat ad-hoc, caves of concrete denoted the end of the line for any given ion beam – and where the results of individual experiments were recorded. They finally returned to the network control centre to discuss the problem. Bob asked Karla and her team as many questions as seemed sensible at the start but, beyond the facility's basic operation, they could offer little insight into the problem itself. He therefore soon started up Hattie and began to take readings; initially at the network centre, then around the facility. As a slightly clearer picture began to emerge, other questions followed and slowly he started to see what was happening. At least, that is, Bob could gradually see the noise itself – the *effect*; the *cause* was another matter entirely.

He had been briefed very well. What he was seeing was both discrete and slight. It came in small bursts rather than being continuous background noise and it was generally – although not always – at a somewhat lower voltage than the signals the network was designed to carry. Although Hattie picked it up fairly easily, the HGMS folk had done well to notice it at all. Occasionally, of course, Hattie picked up a legitimate data frame, which made calibration easier – fortunate because neither of them were familiar with working at this ultra-precision scale.

Despite Ulrich's (and, it appeared, Karla's) assertion that the noise was not currently interfering with real signals, Bob was fairly confident that, if he waited long enough, he *would* see this happening: it seemed a statistical certainty. Sure enough, after a while – and with Hattie's accuracy ramped up close to her limit, they witnessed a frame collision and monitored the subsequent retransmission of the data from source. That certainly *would* present timing problems when the system was operational, Bob reasoned, but, other than that, the system seemed to be behaving normally. The only issue was what the noise was and what was causing it.

And it seemed to be everywhere. Hattie sniffed the network from the central matrix to the extremities of the test system and the spikes were network-wide. Occasionally, they saw something more than simple low-voltage spikes: the odd signal was either slightly higher voltage or longer in duration and, *very* occasionally, even seemed to have something like a square-wave binary data form – although generally no more than the equivalent of a few bits. That was *really* weird; but it might just be coincidence at this stage.

Bob adjusted Hattie again; this time to look for and record the longer periods of noise. He set her to run for half-an-hour while he joined the others for coffee. When he returned and looked at the oscilloscope log, he was able to focus on the 'bigger' noise, which made up less than a hundred-thousandth of the total signals Hattie had processed. On the whole, the results confirmed what he had thought before: among the random electrical spikes, were a very small number of longer, larger noise signals that looked a little like fragmented binary digits. One, in particular, stood out: comprising what *looked* like (even if it was unlikely that it *was*) about thirty bits – several *bytes* – of data. Either way, it was pretty obviously a hardware fault; but where was it coming from and how was it managing to propagate across the entire network? Normally, bogus data from a malfunctioning transceiver would not get past the next device. Were *all* the devices faulty? Unlikely, he thought.

He left Hattie running – scanning links across the whole network – and went to ask some questions. But he did not get many answers; at least not any that helped much. 'When had they first noticed the problem?' No-one was quite sure; it had been mentioned two weeks or so before but only documented the previous week. 'Had it started suddenly or gradually? Had the pattern changed at all?' No-one could say. 'What about background interference? Radiation perhaps?' No, they had measured and tested for all that: there was nothing to be found away from the network itself. 'Could it be a bad batch of equipment? Was all the kit from the same supplier?' No: there were at least three different suppliers for different levels – regulations required that. Moreover, it had been ordered and delivered at different times: a production problem was impossible.

For the first time in a while on a real case, Bob was beaten. He had no idea what the problem might be. The network was properly configured and it was hardly credible that all the equipment was failing simultaneously across the whole network – after all, to all intents and purposes, it was *working*. It was just noisy – *dirty* almost. What else could it be? He did not know. He stayed late, until the end of the afternoon became the early evening, but eventually switched Hattie off and confessed to Karla, then Ulrich, that he could not help. Of course, there would be no bill; even so, he would look at the data he had logged in more detail when he had time later. It was still possible that he might yet get some insight, but he might not. What hurt his pride even more was, in addition to the admission of defeat, he could not help but think that Ulrich seemed less than surprised. There was almost a resigned – perhaps a *knowing* – look from him as they parted. The car took him back to the airport in Frankfurt, where he checked into his hotel. Early the following morning, he flew to Luxembourg.

*

However, Bob barely stopped thinking about the *Darmstadt Dirty Network*, as he started to call it, through most stages of the journey and in the quiet of his hotel room. Hattie had gone off with the overnight couriers; she would not arrive before him this time as the EC had explicitly said that they wanted to talk to him – not run any diagnostics. She would be there the following afternoon if it turned out she was needed after all. However, Bob had copied the complete log from the final four hours at HGMS onto a memory pen and was able to scan through it on his tablet. For want of anything better to do, he started on it in the departure lounge.

On the whole, the afternoon's records were much more of the same: huge numbers of meaningless spikes, what looked like a few bits' worth of broken data (suggested by something like a square-wave form) and, very occasionally, a longer sequence of (what might be) binary code (or it might just be random patterns) – but nothing really that he had not seen from the shorter half-hour session earlier.

One such block, however, caught his eye. Perhaps a lifetime of peering at network traffic had given him some unusual insight but one of the longer blocks had a vaguely familiar shape. The individual bits (if that was really what they were) actually looked to be *organised* into eight-bit bytes; he could see this from their tendency to be packed (filled up) with default ones and zeros. Furthermore, some of the early bytes even had a recognisable shape, something vaguely like a *protocol flag*. Could this be a real network *frame*?

His first thought was that Hattie may have somehow picked up a valid frame amidst the noise she was set to look for. However, he dismissed this idea quickly for two reasons. Firstly, the data was too short – it was an incomplete or aborted frame at best. Secondly, the flag and structure he thought he recognised for the would-be frame was for a protocol he knew would not be running on a network of that kind. It looked like an ATM cell but the HGMS network was running a high-speed extension of a simple EtherCAT protocol. Either way, Hattie would not have detected a legitimate frame like that. He was either wrong or it was pure coincidence or ... perhaps the noise was playing '*Shakespearean monkeys*'?

The plane was landing so he gave it no more thought.

*

Aisha Davies was at home, reading from her tablet.

"A key element of *creativity* in humans involves *abstraction*. I don't know how abstraction occurs, but we know that there is a very low energetic differential between the 'fire' and 'non-fire' states of neurons to save energy, and we also know this leads to massive randomness of firing. A likely implication is that to extract a useful signal from this sea of noise, there could be some sort of 'regularity spotter'. This would be a neural primitive, probably at the level of description immediately above biophysics: perhaps regular firing is an energetically desirable state because it's simpler to maintain?

"Whatever happens at the primitive level, it may have been conserved and perhaps scaled-up with variation, perhaps to high level abstraction in humans. But there are two potential problems before we can generate and manipulate abstractions. First, some emotion or affect associated with abstractions (or potential abstractions) in memory may have to be diminished or we would remain forever trapped in a deterministic world. Second, any proposed activity has to sit within the overall global imperative of all neural systems, that of using an appropriate structural-functional substrate. So I believe that the global imperative of the brain is not minimisation of surprise, error or uncertainty, but minimisation of *assessments* of *lack of control*. As regards a possible structural–functional substrate, it seems to me that an individual neuron could act as a *comparator*, evaluating what it *expects* to see against what it *really* sees and signalling any mismatch. In fact, this role may lie behind predictive coding formulations of hierarchical inference in the brain. This is surely rich with implications?

"I argue that all nervous systems are basically *collections* of comparators at all levels of description, from individual neuron-comparators up to assemblies of neuron-comparators that form ever larger comparators. In this model, comparators at all levels of description can have variable goal states and actual states and, crucially, can *learn*. All neuron comparators, individually or in assemblies, are seeking to minimise assessments of lack of control. Thus, I suggest that all nervous systems only really ever process *control*, not *information*, though for convenience we can treat some abstractions of control as something we call 'information'. This commonality explains how nature can 'bolt on' a wide variety of sensors and actuators across the range of species – indeed, it is difficult to see how these faculties could do anything other than grow incrementally out of a pre-existing (distributed) control–based context – and it resolves, at least conceptually, the related problem of how different processes in an individual brain can talk to each other without an overly burdensome 'translator'.

Aisha was in conversation with an Italian colleague – or possibly 'acquaintance': she was unsure as they had never met physically – on the origins of creative thinking and problem-solving in humans. She had been considering some of the more abstract aspects of intelligence since writing the 'Singularity' piece with Andy. Somewhat unusually for Aisha, she was largely in agreement with Professor Paulo Di Iorio (her current correspondent) on where creativity *came from*; they were merely having a protracted discussion on how it might be *measured* or *simulated* – and it really was not getting anywhere. She typed a terse response.

"OK, that makes sense as a theory; but what advantage do we get from a model like that? How would we *apply* it?"

Chapter 7: Connections

The arrivals area at Luxembourg Airport was fairly quiet. Emerging from the security area, Bob was met by a suited man carrying a tablet displaying his name. He was accompanied by a woman, dressed similarly smartly. The man introduced himself as *Carl*, 'his driver', but looked and behaved as unlike a driver as anyone Bob could imagine. The woman was never introduced, either by 'Carl' or herself, and never said a word throughout the journey. They walked to what seemed to be a private car park. Carl held the doors open for Bob and the woman to step into the back of a large black car, with heavily darkened windows.

As they drove away, signs of RFS were becoming commonplace: every few minutes suggested an example. There was a general air of dysfunctional chaos everywhere. Automatic systems, such as lights, controls and sensors – which had always been taken for granted, were misbehaving from time-to-time. Confusion was rife, leading, in the main, to good-humoured amusement, and occasionally frustration; but accidents were also happening. Dealing with the problems was being made harder by a gradual loss of confidence in the technology being used to do it. But still, the majority of issues were short-lived: often dangerous – but transient.

Bob was unfamiliar with the city so had no idea where he was going and was a little unnerved by the officious nature of his reception. To make conversation, after a minute or so, he turned to the woman and enquired – rhetorically, he thought – "So we're going to the *Jean Monnet Building* I presume?" The woman said nothing but Carl spoke, with a slight turn of his head, over his shoulder.

"No, not Jean Monnet. We're going ... somewhere else."

Although there was no clear change in tone, there was something in the way he heard *somewhere else* that made Bob reluctant to enquire further. So he stayed silent and watched the unfamiliar streets and the occasional manifestations of RFS blur past outside.

After about ten minutes, the car turned off the main carriageway and slowed before an imposing set of security gates, which opened quickly as they approached. They parked immediately inside in what appeared to be a closed courtyard. As lost as he was, Bob knew this wasn't Jean Monnet.

They all climbed out of the car. Carl remained behind as the woman strode to an arched entrance in the courtyard corner.

"Follow me please, Mr. Weatherill." They entered a short corridor with a single door at the far end. The woman opened the door for Bob, ushered him through and closed the door behind him, remaining outside herself. He never saw her or 'Carl' again.

Bob found himself in a small, roughly circular room with a desk on the side away from him, also curved to fit within the wall. On the other side sat two men and two women of a similar age to him – give or take ten years (determining ages was not one of his strengths). They were all smartly dressed but no seniority was apparent. However, the woman on the far left spoke by way of introduction.

"Mr. Weatherill," she began abruptly. "Welcome to Luxembourg. My name is Claudia Oudeyer and I work for the European Commission."

"I'm very pleased to meet you," Bob said, hurriedly – and somewhat untruthfully, given his reception. He made a small movement towards the panel to shake hands but realised that the attempt was not reciprocated so stopped quickly and sat instead on the chair on his side of the desk, within its arc.

"So, Mr. Weatherill; now that we have broken the ice, so to speak, I shall update that information. That is *not* my name and I do *not* – to all intents and purposes – work for the Commission." A slight chill passed between Bob's shoulders. 'Claudia' continued, "On that basis, and using the same model, I will not waste the time of any of us by introducing my colleagues. I'm sure you understand?"

"Er, well, I suppose I understand *that* bit."

"Good, then we can proceed."

The second woman spoke.

"Mr. Weatherill," The light behind her flickered off, then back on, as she spoke. She glanced at it with an air of confirmation. "We have a problem. We may have two problems. We may have a problem that looks like two problems. My colleague here," gesturing to one of the men, "will explain. Then we will find out what you know. Then we will discuss what is to be done."

Bob was so entirely speechless now that even the thought of trying did not occur to him. The woman continued.

"But first, my other colleague will provide us with some setting for what we are about to discuss." The second man leant forwards and began, in a low, slow monotone.

"Mr. Weatherill, do you know where you are?"

"No."

"That is good. It is not our intention to be unnecessarily uncivil but there is some information that it is good to share and there is some that it is not. Who we are and where we currently are is not particularly significant. Suffice to say that we act in the general interests of Europe – as I am sure do you. This is all good."

Bob sat transfixed, hoping very much this was indeed 'good'. The man continued.

"Mr. Weatherill, we believe that, across the world, our electronic systems have come under sustained attack. We do not yet have an explanation. We need expertise that we may not have within our unit. We believe you may have that expertise. We have asked you to come here rather than discuss this remotely for the precise reason that we do not know what we are dealing with or how great is the threat.

"Mr. Weatherill, you are considered an expert in your field. We wish to consult with you. This will be to the benefit of us all, we think. The problem is already known, to an extent, and will become more so soon. Therefore, we do not wish to bind you to secrecy; nor do we wish for you to feel threatened. You are free to discuss these issues with those who you think may be able to help and it is not necessary for you to withhold detail. We ask only that you give us your assurance that you share our interests and purpose. Can I take that as agreed?"

"Well, as far as I understand what we're talking about and who you are, then, I suppose … yes."

"Good." The man remained abrupt to the last. "My colleague will now conduct the technical part of the discussion." He nodded to the first man, who began, in a much lighter tone than the other three.

"Mr. Weatherill; may I call you Bob? I believe that is your more familiar name?" Bob nodded.

"Bob, I will start with the obvious; then we will get into the detail. I assume you will be familiar with *Random Failure Syndrome?*"

"Yes."

"Do you know what is causing it?"

"No."

"Do you have any hypotheses as to what may be causing it?"

"No, although I'm guessing it must be some form of cyber-attack. But, beyond that, no. It's weird. In fact, some colleagues and I tend to refer to it as *weird stuff*: it's a term that seems to be popular in the UK."

"Good; this places us in the same position with regard to RFS – your *weird stuff*. We believe that the first symptoms can be traced back to the first or second week of this month but we are unable to be precise. We know that it attacks all physical electronic systems, not merely those concerning communication, and we find this difficult to explain – as I imagine you do. We know that the problem is getting worse. We do *not* know what the cause is or what to do about it. Naturally, we are concerned."

The held each other's gaze for a few moments before the man continued.

"Bob, what else do you know?"

Bob was completely thrown by the sudden change in line. He nervously muttered, "Nothing. Well, no nothing. Not on this, anyway; *nothing*."

The man smiled. "Bob, where have you just been?"

"Well, I've just come from Germany: Darmstadt, if that's what you mean?"

"Yes, that *is* what I mean. And what did you do in Darmstadt?"

"I was working on a network problem." He was beginning to consider how much client confidentiality he would need to protect and whether it would cut much ice with his current audience.

"And did you solve the problem, Bob?"

"Er, no." That surely was as much as he was going to be able to say.

Another long pause.

"Well," the man continued, "what you saw in Darmstadt, Bob, we are referring to as *Potentially Disruptive Noise*, or *PDN* if you like acronyms. But do you have your own name for that too?"

Bob looked stunned for a few seconds, then smiled ruefully as he slowly understood the depth of the set-up.

"Well, I suppose I was calling it a *dirty network*." He considered for a moment as connections forced their way into his mind. "So, did you *find out* that I'd been to Darmstadt or did you really *send* me to Darmstadt?"

"The latter, really. It seemed like an appropriate place to 'direct you', shall we say? And, as a partially federally-funded institute, we retain some influence there." Another pause.

"To be fair, Bob," he continued. "HGMS *was* one of the first places PDN was found. Only that level of precision and that accuracy of measurement detects it easily. Until very recently – only the past week or so – we have not been aware of its presence on more conventional networks. But we are now. They agreed with us that you should visit them. Bob, we are aware that you possess both diagnostic tools and skills that may shed light on the problem?"

Bob thought carefully. "Well you know I *didn't* solve the problem, I guess? Hattie, er sorry, my *holistic analysis tool*, took a huge amount of data from the network, which I'm still trying to analyse offline. That may yet give some clearer clues as to the *effects* of the problem; I can't say if that'll get me anywhere nearer to understanding the *cause*."

"It goes without saying, Bob," the man struck in, "that we would be extremely interested in any such findings – or any other, for that matter."

"I'll see what I can do," Bob agreed, slowly – further connections making inroads into his head. "But, so, are you suggesting that this PDN is on *other* networks, now? Other LANs? WANs? Analogue *and* digital? Across the *Internet*?"

Another pause. "It's on *all* wired networks, Bob."

And then the penny really did drop. Bob spoke slowly and deliberately, barely believing what he was saying.

"Even on non-data networks? Even *power* networks?"

"Even on non-data networks, Bob. It obviously takes a variety of forms on various networks: power networks are very different from data networks. But, in some form or other, it is on *all* physically-connected electronic systems. *All* the networks are *dirty*."

They looked at each other for a full minute. By the time he eventually spoke, the words that fell out of Bob's mouth seemed obvious to the point of imbecility.

"*So, are you saying that the dirty networks are causing the weird stuff?*"

The man drew a slow breath. "We are certainly saying that RFS and PDN are *linked*. We cannot assume with certainty which is cause and effect but we think we can discount them being unconnected phenomena. Both the timings and nature of their appearance suggest interdependence. Most of us would support your assertion that the network noise is affecting network behaviour: PDN is leading to RFS or, as you put it, the 'dirty networks are causing the weird stuff'.

"So, you see, Bob, I may condense my thoughts thus. We have a universal network problem (PDN), which appears to be having serious consequences (RFS), which in turn are getting worse with no sign of stopping or slowing down. You are one of Europe's top men in complex network analysis and you possess diagnostic tools and capabilities, which we lack. We need your help."

'Claudia' interposed briefly at this point. "There can be no payment for this cooperation – other than your expenses; we trust you will consider it a service to society." The man glanced sideways, appearing slightly annoyed by the interruption and its lack of immediate relevance, and continued.

"So, it may not be unreasonable of me now, Bob, to ask the question again. What else do you know?"

"About PDN?"

"Yes, about your dirty networks."

Bob reflected. "I'm not sure. Yes, I suppose it's possible. I did manage to observe a collision between a noise spike and a sync frame on the HGMS network, which then needed retransmission. That would have had an effect on the timings at that level of accuracy if the network had been live. But, it's hard to see how that would affect most networks … or *systems*," he added as an afterthought.

"So, your measurements suggest the noise to be entirely random?" The man's eyes narrowed slowly.

"Yes, well, no, not exactly."

The man leaned back in his chair again and said, with a slight sigh:

"We need to be open with each other here, Bob. I suspect you may be working close to the limits of your technology? We are certainly at the limits of ours." Yet another pause. "However, we do not observe the noise to be completely random. Our technical specialists say they can detect some limited form of structure. Would you agree?"

"Well, it's not as simple as that," Bob said defensively. "Most of it *is* random: just spikes and stuff. But very occasionally you see something that could be a few bits of binary code. Very, very occasionally there's some longer 'data' – if it *is* data. And once, I thought I saw something that looked like it might be the start of a network *frame*; but it was incomplete. In fact, if I read it right, it shouldn't have been on that network at all

– certainly not on that part because the kit should have cleaned it off before the bit where we measured it. I'll need to have another look at that, I guess," he said softly.

The man's eyes widened at the mention of *frame*. "That would be very useful to us all, I expect," he smiled.

The first man spoke again. "Mr. Weatherill, I think now may be a good time for us to introduce you to some more colleagues and for you to see what we have been doing here." The two men stood; the two women remained seated. The men led Bob towards, and through, a door on the right side of the room. The women he never saw again in his life.

*

Over the next seven hours or so, Bob was shown three or four more rooms and met around a dozen more people. Beyond that level of recall, he could subsequently have no more described any human aspect of his day's work than he could have delivered it in Latin. He shook hands (these people *did* that), answered and asked questions, moved from one room to another, sat down, stood up, ate a sandwich and drank some coffee. If people were a blur, however, the outcomes were in sharp focus. It was clear that these guys were technically more on his level and they had equipment that, although differently conceived and constructed to Hattie, delivered network analysis results to an almost similar level of accuracy.

It was immediately clear that the anomalies Bob had observed in Darmstadt were to found everywhere. There were network traces, logs and scans available from across Europe and beyond. Generally, they appeared to take the same form, once the difference in speeds, transmission media, and suchlike were taken into account. There were also records from electrical power networks, both domestic and supply, and various other control systems that used a huge variety of different carrier technologies.

And the patterns (possibly the *lack* of patterns) was effectively the same. Mostly the noise was random and meaningless but rare occurrences appeared to have more shape. It was not quite so clear, from the readings these people had, that the longer pieces of noise might represent data fragments (the signal forms had not been so accurately captured) but, knowing what he had seen earlier, Bob was reasonably convinced they did. The non-communication systems (mainly the national power grids) showed less variety in their interference but the presence of the random noise (it still seemed utterly random there) was clear for all to see.

"How much data do you have here?" Bob asked.

A woman who appeared to be charge of the team he was currently talking to, or possibly the room he was in, or possibly both, answered.

"We have the equivalent of approximately thirty-thousand hours of observation here, from across the world; although about ninety percent is from Europe. Approximately seventy percent of the material is from data networks, the rest from cabled phone networks, control and power supply networks."

"You captured all this *here*?" Bob asked doubtfully.

"No, from our facility in Brussels."

"Is it possible to just look at the very longest periods of noise from all the data networks?"

"Of course."

One of her team stepped across to the nearest workstation and brought up a file showing a graphical waveform image of twenty-five of the longest traces, then zoomed in on the top three in a rectangular window. Bob's intake of breath was so sharp the air almost whistled between his teeth.

There was absolutely no doubt. These were *frames* – or, at least, *partial* frames. Most were incomplete but the structure was clear. The individual bits were arranged as bytes and these bytes made up network frames. He could see protocol flags, addresses, and padded fields. They were sometimes imperfect in their make-up but the overall pattern being attempted was distinct enough. He pointed this out to his companions to some considerable astonishment but not disbelief. Once Bob, aided by his years in the business and his experience from Hattie's clearer images earlier, pointed the structures out, they could see – and they concurred. Some of the noise was forming bits of data; some of the bits were combined into bytes and some of the bytes were forming (not always entirely successfully) frames. All were in agreement. Then discussions began in earnest.

Firstly, could this be random? Some simple statistical calculations showed that it could not. Although there was a huge amount of noise to be observed, the 'Shakespearean monkeys' model of spikes randomly forming the occasional bit, then sequence of bits, then bytes and frames was not credible, at least not in its purest form. True, there was the occasional flaw in the make-up of what should have been a certain structure but, as few and far between as the larger sequences were, there were still too many for random chance. Among the general noise there *were* fragments of structure and this structure had to mean *something*.

Secondly, could the noise be causing the network (and other) malfunctions? (Was PDN definitely causing RFS?) There was quick agreement that it could be – at least *theoretically*. A hastily formed working hypothesis was reached … If occasionally the noise resembled data bits and, if even more occasionally the bits made bytes and frames, then eventually – following some *currently completely unknown logic* – a very rare frame might have sufficient meaning to be understood by the link device that received it. Then, even more rarely, a combination of properly constructed frames and receptive network device states could (*very* theoretically) be meaningful to a higher layer network protocol, which in turn might then affect the *behaviour* of a network device or end system. The chance would be billions and billions to one but that would be enough in principle. True enough, no-one had yet observed such a *frameset* but it seemed highly likely that they would exist, considering just how much noise there was across all systems in operation. Individual manifestations of RFS were possibly precisely that – the eventual, and ultimately *probable* appearance of just such an individually unlikely event. It was not 'Shakespearean monkeys' as such; rather the logical extension of a process they could observe – even predict – but could not understand.

Thirdly, was the problem growing? Yes, it seemed to be. Earlier traces were, understandably, not as comprehensive or accurately documented as later ones – measurements had slowly been taken more seriously as RFS, and then PDN, had become more noticed – but it was clear that noise levels had increased over the short time they had been observed. There was also an indication that the rate of 'conversion' from spikes to bits to bytes to frames, and so on, was growing. In other words, the ratio of structured data on all levels – though still tiny – to unstructured noise was increasing. However, it was difficult at this stage to prove this with statistical certainty.

Finally, *what was producing the noise?* How? Where was it coming from? *No-one had any idea whatsoever!*

*

By the time he left, Bob had – to all intents and purposes – joined the team. He had no idea, other than conceptually, what the team were trying to do, who they worked for or answered to, what precise roles they played or even any of their names. There was a good chance he would never see them again. But they were working *together* in some ill-defined struggle against a problem, which could now be named (as *PDN* or *RFS* or *dirty networks* or *weird stuff* as made no odds) but could barely be described, and certainly not explained. Bob had also given the team some suggestions as to how their monitoring equipment could be improved along the lines of how Hattie combined high- and low-level traffic tracing.

The friendlier of the two men led Bob out through a small door, which led to a small alley. A small car was parked directly in front of the door. The man drove them to the end of the side road, then out on to a larger road and quickly onto one of the main thoroughfares through the city. Looking back, Bob knew he would be unable to reverse the journey even if he had wanted to: he was as lost as he had been that morning.

There was no point now in Hattie coming to Luxembourg. But Bob had some difficulty in getting through on his smart-watch to the couriers to reschedule her for the next stage of his trip to Madrid. Was this just the result of normal network problems or RFS? It was always going to be difficult to tell with network failures. (The 4G and 5G phone networks were obviously not affected but there would still be 'infected' *cables* involved at some point in between.) However, outside, the evidence was clear. There were numerous signal failures, equipment malfunctions and a few more accidents as a result. As they drove past a car-park exit, a cyclist was lying beside a buckled bike. An automatic bollard appeared to have risen at the wrong time. If the relaxed but grim manner of the paramedics was any guide, the outlook was bad.

Eventually Bob contacted the couriers and rearranged Hattie's movements and – weird stuff aside – the remainder of the journey was uneventful. The two of them talked for most of it about what might be behind PDN (and therefore RFS), largely succeeding only in reinforcing both what they knew and what they clearly did not. Was it a sophisticated cyber-attack? Perhaps. Eventually, the man enquired:

"So, are you going back to the UK tomorrow, Bob?"

"No, I've other work to do around Europe for the rest of the week."

"Where, if you do not mind me asking?"

"Don't you *know*?" Bob asked wryly.

The man laughed. "We do not know *everything*, Bob: we are not spying on you!"

You could have fooled me! Bob thought but answered good-humouredly, "I've got work in Spain, then Ireland, then back to Spain again."

"Network problems?"

"Yes."

"Are they likely to be PDN-related?"

"No, they look fairly standard, but they'll give me plenty of opportunity to *look* for PDN and take a whole load more readings with Hattie. That little bit of extra resolution might shed some light on things."

"Good," nodded the man with a satisfied grin.

After fifty minutes, which apparently would have been about a quarter of an hour without the traffic chaos, Bob's companion pointed out, with some shared irony, the Jean Monnet Building as they passed it. This meant the hotel must be near. Sure enough, a minute later, they turned off the large carriage-way onto a paved car park and the man announced:

"We are here."

As Bob got out of the car at the hotel, the man leaned across the passenger seat, to shake hands, and spoke through the open door.

"It will not be convenient, Bob, for you to contact other people directly. I will contact you tomorrow with my phone number, message IDs and email. You may use any of them to reach me; it *will* be me – no-one else will answer."

Bob nodded agreement; then an idea struck. "Do you have a name?" he enquired hopefully.

The man thought, smiled and nodded. "You can call me Stephen if you like."

"And is that your real name?"

"Of course not."

Chapter 8: Rights and Wrongs

Bob was considerably later arriving at the hotel than he had planned. Andy was waiting in the entrance bar, having just made enquiries for him at the reception desk. They shook hands warmly, Bob – more than usually – relishing the sight of a familiar, friendly, smiling face. He checked in quickly, Andy and he deposited his luggage in his room with minimal ceremony and they went down to the restaurant, both with considerable appetites.

Bob had much to tell, of course; but he was not quite ready. The previous days' events were still so crowded and jumbled in his mind that he wanted time to let them settle. As far as Andy knew, his was a routine set of visits: there was unlikely to be much out of the ordinary. Bob was happy to leave that assumption unchallenged for the time being: his chance would come. Instead, once seated, he started with harmless questions.

"So, how's the conference going?"

"Not really started, yet," Andy shrugged. "Just early registration and pre-conference tutorials this afternoon. My keynote's tomorrow morning."

"Have you written anything yet?" Bob asked mischievously. He still remembered the Andy from university days: the one who barely handed an assignment in on time for the whole of his first two years.

Andy feigned a wounded character by wincing. "Of course I have!" he then grinned. "In fact, I've gone one stage further: I've actually written a discussion paper!"

"That's not usual for a keynote, is it?"

"No, but the proceedings aren't published until after the conference. So, I thought I might as well give them a wee something. Slightly old-fashioned, I know but it was sort of a thank-you for the last-minute invite and paying for everything. Also, having the short paper made it easier to put together the presentation." He reached into his jacket pocket. "Here: would you like to read it?"

Bob glanced at the title, in larger font at the top of the front page, as the paper was waved in his direction. *'Sex with Robots! An Illustrative Discussion of Technological Ethics'.*

"But hardly an old-fashioned title!" he suggested with a laugh, glancing up at Andy as he was about to read. "Remind me what the conference is about, again?"

"*'The Ethics of Technology'*, it's called. I thought I'd give them something to remember!" Andy grinned. "As you can see, Jenny put in a bit of the technical detail."

Bob read quickly:

'Sex with Robots! An Illustrative Discussion of Technological Ethics' (Andrew Jamieson, with thanks to Jenny Smith)

This paper is not for the faint-hearted or easily offended. With the First International Congress on Love and Sex with Robots already having taken place in Portugal four years ago and the second banned by the Malaysian government the year after, once again, many of the key issues relating to emerging technology extend well beyond the purely technological.

Without labouring on detail, there's a certain type of spiritual confession, which takes place all over the world, in which past sexual conduct is a major aspect. Some crude advice often given to those (males, in this case) about to confess is along the lines of, "Don't worry: I've heard it all before. In the end, there are only five things you can really have sex with: a man, a woman, a child, an animal and a milk bottle." So … in the AI simulated world of the future, does that taxonomy still work? Is an android sex-machine still a milk bottle or something more?

The abstract for one of the original conference papers, *"Entertainment vs. Evolution: Cyber Love and Relationships. Should We Draw the Line?"*, asked:

"Just because we can, does it mean we should?" and expands …

"Technology continues to advance at an exponential pace. We are living in an ever-changing environment; one where machine intelligence is constantly evolving and taking a more active role in society.

This paper attempts to examine and raise awareness of the issues and problems in the development and operation of intelligent machines and the current failure to address ethical and social factors. It considers issues concerning the future of human-machine relationships and raises questions for an exploratory discussion of the social implications and concerns they present. In particular, these questions should be asked in preparation for the many scenarios and impacts involved with future cyber-love, sex and relationships. We need to be aware and have consideration of the social involvement and the psychological well-being of people as a result of using them."

So, what are these *'issues'*?

Well, let's start with a couple of socio-technological principles, which we might argue as having been established over the past few decades:

• Technology – existing and emerging – is generally used and abused in about equal measure, and will probably continue to be, although it's often a matter of personal opinion as to what's actually good or bad. Just as one man's terrorist is another's freedom-fighter, one woman's pleasure is another's sin.

• Appropriate legislation always lags some way behind the changes brought about by emerging technology and there's really no credible history of short-term social, moral or ethical objections being effective in restricting long-term technological advance and deployment.

The *additional* premise behind this particular argument is that – at some point in the future – pretty much *anything* by way of entertainment will be possible; at least in simulation and without much difficulty if we're prepared to accept limited quality/realism in the early stages. The Star Trek Holodeck may be a good few years off yet but the individual components are appearing and most of what we're going to discuss here doesn't require anything like that level of sophistication. Moorcock's *Dancers at the End of Time* it isn't but then it doesn't have to be.

These three principles are, in a strictly propositional sense, the axioms for this piece.

2010 saw the release of *Foxxxy, the 'love android*, or 'real companion' to give it its company description. There should be no real surprise in this. The period of time between the invention of plastic and the arrival of the blow-up doll market wasn't huge either. And, in fact – visually at least, Foxxxy doesn't look that much different to an inflatable sex toy. Now we're in the AI age, however, the claims made for Foxxxy are that *"She will know your name and what you like, can talk to you, listen to you, understand you, comfort you and so much more! She is anatomically perfect so you can do whatever you like! She is always there and waiting for you! Talk or 'play' – the choice is yours!"* (although none of this has been verified – empirically or otherwise – in the research for this paper!) Foxxxy is also configurable (by the manufacturers) in the basic features of eye, hair & skin colour and breast size to reflect personal 'taste' [sic].

What's being offered here is fairly crude in both senses of the word so there may or may not be academic AI interest – technological or social – at this stage of Foxxxy's development. However, if there isn't yet, there certainly will be soon, particularly as the robot's configurability improves, both in terms of hardware (appearance) and software (behaviour) but, to continue this discussion, we're probably going to have to stop calling it Foxxxy – that may be too restrictive a concept. And, if that need to generalise sets alarms ringing, it probably should.

It doesn't take much imagination to project the 'love android' into a future where much more convincing configuration is possible. *Now, there's no suggestion here that the current makers of Foxxxy will get involved in any of the shady stuff we're about to consider* but others could easily jump on the bandwagon. Generally, where there's money to be made, a market appears: *'Technocapitalism'*. If there's something (or someone) to be exploited, someone (or something) will do just that. (A fairly self-explanatory product called 'Self-Blow' reached its crowd-funding target in a very short time indeed recently.)

In fact, and in time, what manufacturers are prepared to ship by way of factory configuration may not matter much. Making Foxxxy's skin, hair and eyes in a range of colours and her breasts in different (but presumably matching?) sizes is hardly the future of robotic sex. All that's needed instead is to supply a configurable system to the customer; then they can get on with it themselves. It's not hard to conceive a combination of:

• a body with the necessary mechatronics to change shape; larger and smaller overall and fine-tuned individual detail wherever required (even if there are still a few 'base models' initially to facilitate this), and

• smart-material for skin, which can take on any appearance, or any image (configured through a variety of means), wherever required across the body's surface.

Put these two hardware concepts together, and add the necessary software to convincingly drive it, and you have the complete package. One way or another (very unscrupulous suppliers *or* full customer configuration), we have to consider a future in which the sex robot that you buy can be *absolutely anything you want it to be.*

So, having hopefully covered our legal backsides, exactly what sort of 'configuration' might we be talking about? As if we can't see it coming …

Well, we have to take a deep breath here and recognise that, laying morality and legality aside – at least for now, a sex robot:

1. *Doesn't have to be a woman*

2. *Doesn't have be adult*

3. *Doesn't have to be human*

4. *Doesn't have to have any counterpart in the real world at all*

Now, that's done it, hasn't it? What's interesting to observe is that, whilst this list might be in the natural order of constraint relaxation from the conventional female sex doll, the levels of outrage caused by each in turn won't be. Remember we're not implicitly condoning or condemning any of these but it's likely that the first could be taken as a simple matter of equality (if that's what's wanted) and the last probably seen as just weird. However, the third will make most people feel uncomfortable and the second will have them screaming.

Or will it in fact? Is it actually wrong? Or does it being a robot we're talking about here make it OK? *This is probably the central question.* Right, have you chosen your moral position? Good. Let's see if it's really as simple as that then …

The problem is that this really *isn't* a straightforward ethical decision to be made in moral isolation. It has some hard-edged practicality to it. Consider the following questions and scenarios:

• Is a sex robot fundamentally (legally, morally, ethically, whatever) any different to simple masturbation? Where does the physical stimulation overlap with the mental image and how much is this affected by the other senses being played on? And does it actually matter or is it really just an expensive milk bottle?

• There's often an implicit assumption that this will be a male-oriented market. Should it be? Will it be? The world is a big place and sexual standards and preferences are pretty non-homogeneous. Can we always assume that equality is equivalence and both are to be encouraged?

• Would an appropriate use of a 'real companion' be to, say, recreate a departed partner for emotional continuity? OK, how about an ex-partner … against their wishes? How about someone whose essential data you've just captured – completely without their knowledge – in the street on your smart-glasses? How about your neighbour's twelve-year-old daughter? Could celebrities 'sell' themselves?

• If the idea of a child sex robot *is* utterly abhorrent, how about the alternative proposal that precisely this technology could be used to *treat* paedophiles? Is it just possible that there might be a positive side to such a sickening idea?

• To what extent would it be acceptable to use a sex robot to 'experiment'? Obviously the technology would allow individuals to engage in activity they probably couldn't easily in the real world but would there then be more of a tendency to push boundaries, try things they probably wouldn't 'in the flesh', test personal sexualities, etc.? Is this OK?

• Is it OK to *abuse* a sex robot? (Of course, 'abuse' is a somewhat subjective term in relation to sex: some people pay for 'abuse'.) Is it OK to rape or 'kill' a sex robot? Does its simulated appearance have any bearing on this? In fact, should robots have 'rights'? After all, we seem to be talking about sex slaves here.

• If you still don't like the sound of *any* of this then, apart from grumbling in coffee shops or writing irate letters to newspapers, what do you *really* think you can do to *stop* it?

• And we've not even mentioned animals and extraterrestrials. (Well, we have now.)

Morally, there *may* be a difference here between, say, child pornography and a child sex robot. Child pornography clearly abuses children in its creation; on the surface, a child robot doesn't. But would it encourage it? Or would it actually decrease it? (Perhaps, we really shouldn't be asking the technologists these sorts of questions.) [A comparable issue divides vegetarians: if 'real' meat could be constructed from a molecular process, with no actual animals involved, would that make it OK? Similarly, why do many vegetarians like to eat soya protein shaped like a pork chop? Is that 'dirty' vegetarianism or simply helping them remain vegetarian?] Is convincing sex robot simulation something shameful or to be considered better than its alternative? Are we all ever likely to agree on this? Frankly, no. Are those groups that see themselves as our spiritual or moral guides ever likely to agree on this? An even franker 'no'. This may seem like a localised affair at the moment but it truly has the potential to further split the scientific and religious communities.

Whatever we decide, or *try* to decide, effective legislation may be difficult anyway. Emergent technology as a service often pulls together a number of individual threads, which are innocuous in their own right but devastating in combination. The hardware and software necessary for a realistic sex robot would have numerous benefits elsewhere in society and would be actively encouraged as research. On the other hand, in practice, there would be little to prevent a sex robot being supplied in diminutive appearance to reflect a particular model or ethnicity, say – to *not* do so could be seen as discriminatory. The 'home configuration' required from that to a child would then be minimal. Outrage may have its place but how effective is that likely to be? Many are still outraged by pornography and sex toys; have they been eliminated? No; there is no effective legislation, *even for the pornography industry, which is known to be exploitative.* Ultimately, we simply keep it out of the public view and individually choose whether or not to partake.

So where does all this leave us? Well, probably nowhere, really. Even if there was to be some great legal and ethical consensus on this, which then became enshrined in law or moral code, it could still be ignored – and it would be. The problem is that people just don't all think the same and sexual morality and conduct may divide them more than anything else. Ultimately, this may – yet again – be something that we have to get to grips with ourselves; and this isn't a legal – certainly not a *technological* – process.

Jack DeGioia, of Georgetown University, a few years ago, in a talk in North Wales on the impact of social media, warned, *"I wish to signal my concern that our new technologies, together with the underlying values such as moral relativism and consumerism, are shaping the interior worlds of so many, especially the young people we are educating, limiting the fullness of their flourishing as human persons and limiting their responses to a world in need of healing intellectually, morally, and spiritually."*

However, he then suggested the need for, *"deepening self-understanding, self-awareness, self-knowledge – resources that support the interior work of seeking inner freedom. If we establish as a goal for each of our lives, Herder's idea* "that each of us has an original way of being human" *– that the goal of our lives is to identify what Charles Taylor identifies as* our most "authentic" self, *such a goal can only be attained through demanding interior work. An authentic self is one living in accord with one's most deeply held values."*

He wasn't talking about robot sex, of course, but the *"we each find our own way of being human"* principle may well apply to this and many other areas where we wrestle with the moral implications of emerging technology. It's likely that individually we're the only one on our street that thinks about sex the way we do; it's likely that we're the only one *in the world* that thinks about *everything* the way we do. On that basis, what chance do we have of fitting someone else's morality? Ultimately, the best way of answering to an unknown higher code is probably to (*genuinely and truly*) answer to ourselves. *But how good are we going to be at that?*

*

"Well, they'll remember that all right!" chuckled Bob, not really knowing where to begin with it. Then a thought struck him. "This 'spiritual confession' you've mentioned; is that *AA*?"

"Aye, that's right," nodded Andy. "It's part of the 'spiritual awakening' that comes from the twelve-step recovery programme. Admitting your past comes right after handing yourself over to God and before trying to put it right. Of course, as I said last week, it's an approach that's going out of fashion in the secular world." He bit his teeth together then sighed. "I'm telling you, Bob, we're losing the plot. I'm not just talking about AA here. The whole world; it's lost sight of almost anything that's not science or technology-based. Whether or not we *should* do something hardly seems to get considered these days so long as we *can*. There's a much bigger picture that people aren't seeing."

Bob was hardly in the mood for this: he knew of another 'big picture' that people currently 'weren't seeing', although it would only be a matter of time. "And who's 'Moorcock'?" he asked to change the subject.

"*Michael Moorcock*. Science fiction writer – amongst other things – very prolific. Mostly simple futuristic punch-ups but some much deeper stuff in places if you look for it. '*Dancers'* was more of a social commentary than sci-fi. Set in a far future where technological power made *anything* possible. In fact, the power was essentially hidden: there was no-one left who even knew how it worked – it was just activated when needed. So, once that simple concept was established, the more interesting question was *what would people do*? 'How would they behave?'

"And how *did* they behave?"

"Er, pretty decadently, on the whole," Andy laughed, "but possibly with just a bit of C.S. Lewis's 'Moral Law' in there somewhere! But this is part of the point I'm trying to make. We're looking to a future where we might be able do just about

94

anything through technology. What are we going to do with that power? Can we be trusted with it? Because, at the same time, we're possibly about to create machines that are even better than us. What will a machine do if it's, to all intents and purposes, *intelligent*? Will *it* have any moral code and, if it does, will it be same as ours. We really need to get to grips with this. But we can hardly expect to deal with intelligent machines if we haven't figured *ourselves* out first. But we're not trying to do that. We don't really understand what drives *us* so what hope do we have of predicting the 'thinking' of an all-powerful machine, whether it's modelled on ourselves or *not*"

"*Or not?*"

"Well, I'm just saying that intelligence might not be something we create *in our own image* as it were. It could evolve from much simpler beginnings, which we *did* understand, but that evolution might produce something that we *didn't*. Or, if the panpsychists are right, we might not have any control over it at all."

"Remind me?"

"Well, the theory of mind that says that *everything* is conscious to an extent. How much consciousness something has might vary – based on the size of the brain, for example – but everything has it. On that basis, we could conceivably create a robot one day with a big enough brain for it to just 'wake up'. If that happened, presumably, whether or not it thought like us would be dependent on something much more fundamental than programming?"

"Presumably, not a theory you're that keen on?" Bob suggested.

"Well no, not exactly. I tend still to believe that consciousness is external from the body – or at least separate. 'God-given', I would say, of course. But, someone pointed me at Turing's 1950 paper a while back. 'Computing Intelligence'? Something like that. Anyway, he was posing the question, *Can machines think?* He devised a game in which a machine tried to trick a human into thinking *it* was human."

"The *Turing Test*," Bob agreed.

"Aye, well, that's what it became known as. Turing called it *The Imitation Game*, of course. But anyway, he then went on to discuss a number of possible objections to the concept of machine intelligence. One of which he called 'The Theological Objection'. Now, Turing had no time for any of that sort of thing, of course, but his argument *against* the objection was actually quite good. He basically put, to anyone who said that consciousness is a gift of God – only given to humans (possibly animals), 'why do *you* think you can tell *God* how the universe works?' He's the omnipotent one: not you! Surely, if God's chosen model of intelligence is based on neural complexity, for example, who are you to argue with it? I guess he was sort of saying that maybe God *could* be waiting for us to build something with a big enough brain for him to make it conscious. OK, I can't say I like the idea but it can't be dismissed out of hand."

Andy smiled as he slowed down. "Heh-heh. Sorry for the wee rant. Anyway," he added, as an afterthought, "How was your day?"

"Ah, ...," said Bob.

Chapter 9: Dirty Networks

Bob spoke, almost entirely uninterrupted – apart from a few expressions of surprise from Andy, for over half an hour. He related – with some theatrical intent, he would later have to admit – his experiences of the previous three days in sequence, beginning with the relatively uneventful day in Paris. He then described his (apparently) unsuccessful visit to HGMS in Darmstadt, only subsequently explaining the deeper meaning of what he had seen as he revealed, in even greater detail, his adventures in Luxembourg that very day.

Then, having presented the facts in chronological order, he offered Andy a summary.

"So you see, it seems that the noise is everywhere: *all* networks are dirty and they may well be getting *dirtier* all the time – they're calling it 'Potentially Disruptive Noise': PDN. And that's not just local networks and wide-area networks; not just Internet-based systems. There's noise on electrical networks of all kinds too: every type of *physical* electronic system. *Everything.* And it seems pretty likely that the noise is causing the weird stuff – the RFS. Because the PDN isn't really completely random: buried in it, there's some almost *sensible* stuff. *Somehow*, on comms systems, it sometimes manages to look like real data. Then we think it's, very occasionally, managing to produce something that actually looks real enough to be understood by a network device. Then, very, very occasionally, there a sequence that's good enough to change the network behaviour or the device that's connected to it. Then something silly happens. That's what we end up seeing. Now we have to find out why!"

Andy sat, wide-eyed, in silence when Bob had finished. Now it was his turn to not know where to begin. Eventually, he managed to phrase a question.

"And does that make *sense*? Could this 'random but not really random' noise be causing the weird stuff?"

"Well, yes, on one level," Bob admitted. "It's certainly true that the progression we've seen, rarer and rarer, from low to high noise spikes, to bits and bytes and frame fragments, could eventually form something that did some damage. We haven't actually *observed* one of those complete frames yet but the signs are there that they might well be. Hattie *did* get something close to a decent frame from Darmstadt but that was very odd because it wasn't a frame that should have been on the HGMS network in the first place – it was the *wrong protocol*. Mind you, I may have made a mistake there – I still need to check that out.

"Also, of course, just about *everything* is networked now – the *Internet of Everything*. This would all have been completely daft a few years ago before the IoE kicked in. But there's hardly anything by way of electronic equipment now that's not connected. All the problems we're seeing are from systems that are networked these days but wouldn't have been a few years ago. In principle, yes, a massive, global Internet problem could affect just about *everything* we use and do." A passing thought struck him. "Actually, our *Christmas tree lights* are wifi-enabled for God's sake – so that they can be programed from a mobile. It's madness really but, from *that* point of view, it makes sense."

"*But?*"

"Yes, *but* … that's all fine, *but* we still have no clue what's causing the problem in the first place!"

"Not even the slightest?"

"Not really. We've a general feeling that it must be some sort of sustained cyber-attack, possibly a type of sophisticated malware but no-one's really got any idea what. It just doesn't seem possible. What on earth can you do to each and every end device, system, network, network of networks, *in the world*, the bloody *Internet itself*, plus the power grids, for God's sake, that puts quasi-random noise across everything? Everything! Regardless of type, technology, material, equipment, carrier, protocols and function? How can a single attack do all that? It *can't* be done, surely?"

Andy smiled, regaining some composure. *"When you have eliminated the impossible, whatever remains, however improbable, must be the truth."*

"What?"

"Sherlock Holmes!"

"Hmmm ..."

"The point is, *something* must be causing it, mustn't it? It's like the Fermi Paradox. There *has* to be an answer. It might seem a bit far-fetched but you have to focus on what possible and what's not. And I'm not being flippant here, or saying it for the sake of it: someone *does* need to sort this out. The news this afternoon was suggesting that RFS may have killed several hundred people worldwide: it needs fixing *quick*! So, I'd suggest nothing even vaguely credible, however improbable, should be dismissed. Wouldn't you agree?"

"Go on, then. Try me with some improbable stuff ..."

"OK, *coincidence*?"

Bob snorted. "What, *every* network device in the world has developed the *same* fault, but in its own way – on its own system, but that has the *same* effect? No, the odds against that are barely even finite!"

"Does it have to be *every* device? Could it be just *some* of them?"

Bob gave this a fraction of a second before replying, "No, it couldn't. If just some of the kit was broken, the good stuff wouldn't pass the noise, or the broken data, on. This has to be either generated simultaneously across all networks, via some process we don't understand, or injected centrally, then distributed somehow, allowing it to propagate across networks and devices ... again via some process ... we don't ... understand." He slowed and stopped as the complete hopelessness of it overpowered him. But Andy had not given up.

"OK, *environmental*?"

"What?"

"Environmental. Maybe the change in global temperatures, atmospheric variations, or something, has had a catastrophic effect on all the equipment?"

"Heh, heh; nice idea, but that just wouldn't work. There's so much variety of kit and carrier media: it couldn't *all* go wrong. Anyway, much of it's in climate controlled areas so there wouldn't be any effect."

"*Political?*"

"Well yes, political is one possible motivation if it's a cyber-attack, but that doesn't explain *how*."

"No, I mean *organised* political. Geographically distributed groups of individuals, all working to a common purpose, but each taking care of the networks in their region?"

Bob paused a little longer but shook his head ruefully. "No, that's just not credible, is it? Thousands, maybe tens of thousands, of individual groups working surreptitiously without a single one being caught? It couldn't happen. You know that as well as I do, surely?"

"Maybe they *have* caught some of them but no-one's told the likes of us?"

"No, I think these Euro guys would know that, and I think they're being straight with me."

Still not to be defeated, Andy reeled off several more unlikely suggestions in quick succession but Bob soberly and grimly dismissed each one. They stared at each other for a while longer before Andy resumed:

"Well, it's got to be sorted out somehow, Bob: it's getting worse. We're both saying that, aren't we? You're saying this PDN is growing and it's clear that RFS is becoming a bigger problem. Hundreds of deaths already but, presumably, soon, it'll be a lot worse?"

*

They finished late, after a good meal and several hours in the bar, prolonged by a complete failure of the hotel's online payment connection. They talked of little but dirty networks and weird stuff. Bob tried a variety of local lagers and Andy worked his way through their range of fruit juices. They parted after midnight, having agreed to meet again in London shortly after Christmas. Although tired, and somewhat the worse for wear, Bob made a point of checking the data he had downloaded from Hattie the day before and comparing it against standard frame structures. In fact, he *had* been *right*: if Hattie had recorded the signal properly, then she had captured a protocol frame that had no right to be on the HGMS network. Had *Hattie* made a mistake? She never had before. Once again, Bob found himself half thinking – half muttering, '*it doesn't make sense*'. At home, this had been his initial reaction to RFS; now the same could be said of PDN. Whichever way he looked at it, neither the cause nor the effect had any logic at all. It took some time for tiredness to get the better of his confusion and, when he did sleep, he had strange dreams.

*

On one level, the rest of Bob's week was routine. Three more jobs in three more locations: Madrid, Cork and Zaragoza. It was hardly the ideal schedule (travelling from Spain to Ireland and back to Spain again) but the order in which the visits had been originally agreed dictated it. However, Bob was a seasoned traveller and took such things in his stride. In reality, though, the experience was anything but typical. Failures, mishaps, accidents and other signs of RFS were visible everywhere (and Tuesday's news suggested the worldwide death toll to be over a thousand) and, wherever he went, Bob was looking for the underlying signs of PDN, now generally (at least within the European 'inner circle' of which he now appeared to be a part) believed to be the cause. Fortunately, by Friday, there had been a few small but significant advances in this respect ...

*

First thing Sunday morning, the day after his evening with Andy, Bob messaged Karla Heintze, in Darmstadt, and received an almost immediate reply. 'No, there should be no ATM cells within the HGMS network. There was likely to be ATM over the simply 'domestic' outside lines they used for a variety of purposes but that traffic would be nowhere near the timing system Bob (really Hattie) had been taking readings from. She also attached the full protocol documentation.

Later in the morning, Bob called Jenny to bring her up to date with his experiences of PDN and the connection with RFS. She listened attentively, with just the occasional audible intake of breath, as he outlined the discoveries of the past few days in a broadly similar manner to his explanations for Andy the previous evening. The exception, given Jenny's computer science experience, was the new focus he gave to the 'frame on the wrong network'.

"I just can't explain it, he said. I've double-checked and I don't think Hattie's made a mistake. OK, it's daft enough there being bogus frame fragments on the line in the first place, whatever's causing it, but this particular one was structured like an ATM cell whereas the HGMS network is essentially an ultra-high-speed Ethernet variant. I've checked their protocol diagrams and there's nothing like it. *That frame should not have been on that network!*"

"To be fair," observed Jenny, quietly, "*none* of those frames should have been on *any* of those networks if they weren't legitimate control or data traffic!"

"Well yes, agreed," conceded Bob, "but I just can't help thinking this is significant. Even given that weird things are happening anyway, I'm sure that should tell us *something.*"

Jenny could not suggest anything that Bob had not already considered. She certainly did not manage the imaginative alternatives Andy had proposed the night before. She *was* able, however, to confirm RFS from personal experience. She had been entering the university library through a revolving door on Friday when the mechanism had suddenly locked. Her walking momentum was such that she was unable to stop in time and had slammed her face against the glass panel. Somehow, her nose had survived intact but instead transferred the force of the impact further back, resulting in a matching pair of black eyes.

At lunchtime, Bob received a variety of contacts from 'Stephen' (message IDs, numbers, emails, etc.) together with an unambiguous directive that anything Bob found out was to be relayed to him without delay. Bob complied immediately by contacting him, describing their 'wrong frame' observation. Stephen seemed less than convinced by the suggestion (almost implying he must be mistaken) but, explaining it again, sent the same question flashing across Bob's mind: *Why would there be a frame on the wrong network?*

*

The European tour continued ...

Bob spent a day in Madrid, reunited with Hattie for the first time since Darmstadt. The network problem he had been called in to look at was challenging – certainly compared to Paris – but, even so, only took a couple of hours to deal with. For the remainder of the day (with the network operators under the impression he was still working on *their* problem) he and Hattie were able to study both the local network and the wider connection to the outside world. The pattern was a familiar one.

Even once the local network had been put right (so far as the operators would be interested, anyway), PDN was clearly visible across each and every link (although only with Hattie tuned to a very fine setting). Once again, the noise was mostly low-level and meaningless but with occasional data fragments. Now that he had a clearer idea of what he was looking for, Bob was able to focus on the higher levels and bigger of these streams and find some more partial frames – a few of these being longer than the one Hattie had recorded in Darmstadt. Their redeeming feature, however – if such an idea applied in this mystery – was that they did at least match the network protocol. Bob performed some simple calculations based on the frequency of these structured streams relative to the unstructured ones. The change was small but statistically clear: *more* structured – potentially meaningful –

data was on the Madrid network than the Darmstadt one. This, of course, could be coincidence or a local characteristic. Alternatively, it might be a sign that PDN was gaining in whatever structure it was tending towards: RFS would then probably increase as a result.

And the pattern was repeated in Cork. Bob had to stay until early afternoon on the network problem he had been called in for: some equipment had to be replaced and the new units were not immediately available. However, this meant he was able to spend four hours looking at the network traffic in detail. Once again, what Andy had described as the 'random but not random' pattern of spikes, bits, bytes and partial frames was there. Once again, the ratio of the various levels of structure to unstructured was slightly higher than Darmstadt.

But Cork also provided two further pieces of evidence. Midway through the afternoon, for the first time, Hattie recorded a *complete* frame. It was valid for the network so Bob had to check and recheck that it was not legitimate traffic, picked up by mistake – but it was not: it was a sensible frame for the network, just not generated (at least intentionally) by a network device on that segment. It had to be the 'Shakespearean Monkeys' or 'random but not random' effect of the wider network noise. Even then, such a frame, in isolation, would not have affected network behaviour – but it all pointed further towards the hypothesis of PDN causing RFS.

The second breakthrough occurred just before Bob finished for the day. Again, it took a considerable amount of cross-checking to eliminate possible error, but Hattie clearly recorded another *wrong* frame. This time, the discrepancy was harder to spot (and few other than Bob would have done so) but the protocol *was* wrong. More precisely, it was the wrong *version* of the protocol that was present. Subtle but wrong nonetheless. The frame had no place on the network. *Why would there be a frame on the wrong network?*

He reported both pieces of news to Stephen that evening. The first – the complete frame – pleased him, and appeared to confirm similar results being detected by his team across Europe. He remained sceptical, however, in respect to the second.

That evening, Bob received a somewhat panicky call from Andy.

"Bob, I'm sorry: I may have said something out of place! I was speaking to Aisha this morning – I was telling her about us meeting in Luxembourg – and, without even thinking about it, I realised I was talking about your dirty networks. She was really interested and, before I knew what I was doing, I'd pretty much told her most of what you'd told me! We even had a wee laugh about some of my daft suggestions for what might be behind it. Then, suddenly, I thought, '*bugger*, I probably shouldn't be saying any of this!' I pretty quickly said I thought I might have spoken out of turn but it was all too late then. I'd trust Aisha with my life; you never know, she might even help. But I hope I haven't got you into trouble?"

Bob laughed, immediately realising that he had needed to for some days. "No, it's fine, Andy. I'd always assumed that Aisha would be told; I can't see any reason not to: she is part of '*The Desk*', after all," he chuckled. "The guy I'm in contact with from Luxembourg said it wasn't particularly to be kept secret – that I could talk to anyone that might be able to offer anything. I don't know that Aisha's going to able to help much, with her background, but it won't do any harm. And I think it's generally accepted that most of the detail will be publicly known pretty soon anyway."

"That's a relief!" admitted Andy. "So, how's it going?"

"Slow," Bob said after a brief pause to consider the question. "We're starting to see the same patterns in PDN. It all seems to point in the same direction. We're starting to see the longer frame sequences that might be causing the RFS. I've also found another frame on the wrong network. But that's the bit I'm having trouble convincing the Euro guys about."

"Do you think you *can* convince them?"

"I don't know. I think they may have to see it for themselves."

*

Fortunately, that was exactly what happened …

Bob's plane had barely landed in Zaragoza when he received a call from Stephen. His tone was both excited and deferential at once.

"Bob, I have some news from the lab. And I have to apologise to you. Our technical people have found a number of frames of the form you describe. Frames with protocol structures that are alien to the network on which they are to be found. Until, now our equipment has not been sufficiently accurate to measure this with any certainty but we have modified it according to your suggestions and now we can do this. We have been able to identify at least fifteen 'misplaced' frames across our European measurements and three in the USA. There are likely to many more of course."

"Millions, *billions*, probably," agreed Bob, relieved. "We're only picking up a tiny fraction of all the global traffic, remember. What we're looking at only scratches the surface. We have to scale up the figures from our observations to the real world. The numbers will be huge. They have to be really because, buried in there somewhere, will be the frame sequences that actually cause the changes in behaviour: that's our speculation, anyway."

"*Not speculation.*" Stephen's tone reverted to his normal calm and measured one.

"Pardon?"

"It is no longer speculation, Bob. We have found such a sequence."

Bob swallowed hard. "You've found a frame sequence in the noise that *affects* the network?"

"Yes, at least, it *could* have had that effect. Whether it actually did or not, would depend on the device state; but, in this case, *if* there had been a *Telnet* session open, the sequence would have closed down the interface. It is a small, specific example but the point is made, we think?"

"Yes, that's right!"

"So we think that we have established the principle of PDN causing RFS?"

"Agreed!"

*

After those colossal pieces of news, the remainder of the Zaragoza visit was something of an anti-climax. The original job proved to be trivial and Bob's additional analysis of the network, whilst providing ample confirmation of much that was already known, did not advance their cause. However, on the way to his hotel that evening, Stephen called again.

"Bob, I just thought I would update you on two other points, in case you have not figured these out for yourself yet – you probably have, of course: but in case it helps your thinking at all."

"OK." Bob suspected there was still some element of amends in Stephen's tone: making up for not believing him about the 'wrong' frames.

"You see, our guys in the labs have been widening their tests; experimenting with some of their ideas; trying some rather unusual configurations out."

"Go on ..."

"Well, we have identified a couple of places where we do *not* see PDN."

"Ah!"

"Yes, we do not see it on *completely isolated* networks. If we build a completely separate network and power it independently (with its own power source), so there is no physical connection at all, we *do not see PDN*."

Bob was uncertain of the significance of this. "What do you mean by an 'isolated network'?"

"Well, we connect a few routers and suchlike together and run it off a stand-alone generator, so there is no network to the outside world and nothing is plugged into the mains; if we do this, there is no PDN."

Bob whistled, thinking quickly. "I guess, on one level, that makes sense," he muttered. "If the noise isn't being generated simultaneously *everywhere*, it has to *come* from somewhere. If you make a completely disconnected system then I guess whatever it is can't get through." Another thought struck him immediately. "So, how about *two* independent networks that are only connected by wifi, but no cables?"

"No," confirmed Stephen. "In fact, that is the second point: we do not see it on wifi *at all*!"

With something of a bolt, Bob realised suddenly that this was something he had not considered. All of his work over the previous few days had been on wired networks. He simply had not given any thought whatsoever to *wifi*, or *wireless* in general.

"What, *never, nowhere?*"

"No, Bob. *There is no PDN on wireless.* It appears to only be present on *physical* networks, where there is an actual, cabled connection."

Bob continued to speak at about the speed of his thoughts (and that varied). "So, there has to be a physical electrical connection, then? No, wait; what about *optical*? Is it on optical networks?"

"Yes, Bob; it is on optical networks. It is on *all physically connected wired networks*; but not *wireless*. Does this help us?"

"No, not really."

*

In the morning, Bob headed for the airport, looking forward to going home for Christmas. But still the questions rang in his head: *Who, where or what was PDN coming from?* And, in particular, *why would there be frames on the wrong networks?*

Chapter 10: Awakenings

It was Boxing Day. Aisha Davies was reading from her tablet again. She had received a response from her Italian co-researcher, Professor Paulo Di Iorio. They were still discussing the cause of human creativity and how it might be measured or simulated.

> "As to what advantage a comparator-based system might have over standard connectionist models in understanding intelligent processes: well, existing (artificial) connectionist models have difficulty with hierarchical processes, which are essential for control systems and for some types of creativity that are not just combinatorial. Here, perhaps, the goal state may represent the top-down element of a hierarchy and the actual state the lower level, and clearly one could have a cascade of such processes. Neuron–comparators at all levels of description will be situated within (mostly negative) feedback control loops, and the exercising of control is commonly hierarchical in nature. As to *how* comparisons are made within a comparator, nature is economical and it is possible that the neuronal primitive of regularity-spotting is involved, with the comparator seeking to identify regularities shared by goal and actual states. This sits well with regularity of firing as a desirable energetic state: that is, when goal and actual states share some regularity in common, the assessment of lack of control has been minimised, and there is therefore no output signal to indicate that there has been a prediction error. I don't really understand why researchers seeking to simulate neuronal activity, and researchers in AI and robotics, are apparently not using, or at least exploring the use of, a framework based entirely on neuron-comparators, and assemblies thereof to build larger comparators. I call it a 'comparators-all-the-way-down' approach."

Once again, Aisha found nothing particularly to disagree with in Professor Di Iorio's thoughts. She was simply struggling to find the relevance to her own work – *anyone's* work, in fact. She responded again in her typically brief style.

"Fine, I would not argue with that, but what *use* is it? Apart from anything else, how would we *prove* it?"

She scanned her BBC app for a time while she waited. There was little good news out there: several thousand deaths worldwide were now being attributed to RFS. Travel and communication were disrupted. People were beginning to find themselves stranded on holiday or business trips. A train had derailed at speed in Kenya – survivors unknown but probably few; a chemical plant had exploded in Canada with many casualties assumed.

Eventually, the message app alerted her to Paulo's reply.

"Well, let's start by thinking about what an architecture might *look* like then ... A cartoon-like simplification might be this: At the bottom is the metabolic level of description, in which the brain burns glucose and oxygen to make energy available to do work. Above this, the 'neuronal energetics' level concerns the ways in which the flow of energy made available to do work drives and influences basic 'control-processing' by neuron-comparators and assemblies thereof, subject to the global imperative to minimise assessments of lack of control. This is where much hierarchical processing occurs. The level of description above this concerns the way in which memory is organised to handle different types of control-related information. Above this, presumably, is the level dealing with the more familiar divisions of memory, such as semantic, episodic, and declarative, and the integrated sensor-motor-affect simulations. At the top is domain-general intelligence that may interact with memory.

"So perhaps we could prove the theory by actually *building* such a system? Maybe building an intelligent and creative device modelled at least loosely on living nervous systems? (*I'm serious! Why not?*) I suggest following the general trajectory that nature may have taken. Build from the ground up, and begin with general principles, especially neuronal energetics, and use comparators as the basic building blocks. As a *cheap* (relatively – compared to Jenny Smith's 'Big Brain Project') project, one could consider having a 'core' or 'hub' of one or two research institutions, who begin by designing, say, half-a dozen different basic types of (virtual) comparators that can be fitted together like building bricks. These comparators are then made available, over a shared network, for the wider research community (including computer and brain scientists), as tools to experiment with as they wish. Nature's scheme is conceptually mostly fairly simple, but there have been numerous fine-tunings in different species, and this is where the sophistication lies, I suggest: hence the proposed 'open-source' & 'crowd-source' empirical approach of 'understanding by building'. Functionality can be improved as the project progresses, as in nature. Specific goals can be loaded onto specific comparators. It seems to me that comparators will fall into two main types; those where neuronal energetic protocols manifest fully minimised assessments of lack of control by not outputting any signal, as in the case of (usually) comparators regulating higher–level goals, and those manifesting fully minimised assessments of lack of control by outputting a regular signal, as is often the case with lower-level comparators such as those neurons in specific visual areas that only fire when a specific incoming signal is detected. The core group of researchers designs and retains control over the main architecture, but this is very simple and flexible, like a living nervous system. Comparators can be situated within negative feedback control loops, incorporating virtual sensors or actuators, in a virtual environment. If there is a 'general explore and reinforcement-learning' protocol, this should lead eventually to some form of virtual functionality. The key point here is that if one substitutes interfaces having 'real world' sensors and actuators for the virtual ones, one is on the way to a robot with primitive functionality. As a major safeguard, of course, an ethics committee/core group has to ensure that the system remains isolated: such a system needs to be 'hermetically contained', both to stop it getting out *and* so that it's not influenced by the outside world!

(Alternatively, we just find something that we think might be doing all of this already and see if we can measure any of this!!)"

*

Oh, good grief! That was quite enough of that! That last sentence was probably no more than a throw-away comment to end with but it was too much for Boxing Day! Aisha sighed quietly and put down the tablet she had been reading from. Anyway, to an extent, she realised, all this was just trying, for a while, to keep her mind off what everyone else was talking about and that was not really working either. She reached for her glass of wine but saw, as she did so, that it was empty.

She now sat thinking quietly on the sofa, toying with the empty wineglass, with what little attention she had for the external world divided about equally between the TV in the corner of the room and the small child playing with trains on a rug in front of it. The wine, sofa, TV and room, indeed the house she was in, belonged to Jill and Bob Weatherill. The child was their grandson, Ben. Jenny Smith sat beside her, her two black eyes not yet entirely faded, apparently similarly engaged in thought. *Her* empty glass sat on a small table beside her. The only noise came from Ben, his trains and the TV. Aisha and Jenny, as Ben's delegated babysitters, sat in a mildly wine-subdued silence. Aisha reflected sombrely on what she knew of the past few days. The Desk had not planned to meet this soon but events had moved on – domestically and on the wider stage.

It had not been a normal Christmas for any of them, or for anyone else for that matter. Bob, and to a lesser extent Andy, had returned from their European trips with little on their minds, and not much else to talk about, other than 'dirty networks' and 'weird stuff'. In one sense this hardly singled them out from the crowd. RFS was now the main topic of every news programme across the globe and, on Christmas Eve, the various reports of *Potentially Disruptive Noise* – or *PDN* – broke. Almost in an instant, it was being recorded and reported worldwide. Suddenly everyone knew about dirty networks (so far as the media could describe it and the public could understand it) and how it seemed to be causing RFS – the *weird stuff* – and that it appeared to be *getting worse*. Experts were routinely consulted but contributed little. No-one knew what was causing it but the effect was plain to all. The TV now agreed five thousand known deaths globally – almost certainly many more in reality, once news had fed in from all regions – and huge numbers of injuries and widespread disruption. For the first time in weeks, the well-worn world stories of terror attacks, galloping unemployment caused by the robot workforce and the new, very unpleasant, MRSA strain – '*MRSA-ZS*' – had been forced into the background.

But, even allowing for its obvious seriousness and the global obsession with PDN and RFS, Bob, in particular, had been especially 'difficult' over the past few days, certainly 'not very Christmassy', as Jill had put it – sarcastically and with deliberate understatement. He had exploited almost every chance to take himself off from everyone else and run tests with Hattie. (She had arrived back home the day after him.) Now that he knew the scale of the problem, he was able to experiment on their home networks as easily as any external ones – and he lost no opportunity to do so. He had spent a lot of time talking remotely with Stephen and Jenny and, to a much lesser extent, Andy and Aisha. Even when he had been with the family, he was clearly distracted. Not that it appeared to have got him anywhere: he still had no idea what PDN *was* and this slowly made things even worse. His attention, never great at the best of times, was now practically non-existent and, when not spoken to for even a few minutes, his thoughts would clearly drift away, often relapsing into his muttered mantras, such as *Where's this coming from?* and *Why would there be frames on the wrong networks?* His wife, son and daughter-in-law, in an attempt to lighten the atmosphere, had even taken to mimicking him, singing these in chorus whenever he appeared.

Eventually, by the end of Christmas Day, Jill had had enough. Not knowing exactly what it was going to achieve, she demanded contact details from Bob for Jenny, Andy and Aisha and invited then round for Boxing Day. Andy had other commitments for the day but Jenny and Aisha had so far spent Christmas largely on their own and been only too glad of the company. Once there, Jill had played a clever card. In return for a warm fire and a large lunch, she (and Chris and Heather) were going to get Bob out of the house for a few hours, to take his mind off dirty networks, and they could babysit Ben, *couldn't they?* Of course they could

– and in fact they were glad to. So the three of them had the house to themselves while his family dragged Bob reluctantly around the sales. Jenny and Aisha now sat peacefully: as peacefully as RFS would allow, of course. Ben played with his trains and train-track on the floor. He had been given two different sets for Christmas. One, a small plastic affair – just an engine and eight curved pieces of track forming a circle and, the second, a larger wooden set with two engines, some carriages and a more complex layout of lines and junctions. The sets were no longer separate now but jumbled together on the rug and he was getting a little mixed up between the two. Aisha gazed, absent-mindedly as he played. A wall light randomly snapped off and on. *What on earth was causing this?*

Although, of course, Bob, on his return, had immediately consulted *The Desk*, and told them all he knew, Aisha had felt somewhat left out of the process. She had not been in Luxembourg like Andy, nor was she a computer scientist like Jenny. She had sometimes been part of the group phone conversations and suchlike but felt she had little to offer – even though she had probably given the matter just as much thought. Worse, she could not shake off the impression that the others secretly, possibly even subconsciously, shared this view. She only happened to be there now, she thought, at Jill's request, and then nothing more than a baby-sitter. Not that she particularly minded that bit: that, at least, made her feel useful – that she was contributing something to the group. In truth, she was as interested in the 'PDN/RFS thing', as anyone but what was a neuroscientist going to contribute to a technical problem with the Internet? *Not much*, she thought. She smiled wistfully as she watched Ben try to make one of the large wooden engines run on the smaller plastic track. It would not, of course, but that was not going to stop him trying. Ha! *Only a child would do that*, she thought. Then, *All part of the learning process*, she supposed. She laughed quietly to herself, as thoughts of trains, dirty networks, weird stuff, children, brains, more networks and more wine stole over her. There was obviously enough in that mix for what then happened but she would never really be able, at any future time, to explain it fully: it just did.

Because the light suddenly came on in her head and almost blinded her …

*

Jenny sat alongside Aisha, also with mixed thoughts and in a similar frame of mind. She was trying to distract herself with a court case for which she was to be called as an expert witness. A couple alleged to have had an extra-marital affair (not the central subject of the case but a 'feature') had both posted data from their fitness sensor watches on an open online repository. An aggrieved partner had located the data, run a series of analysis programs and shown a strong (almost certainly statistically improbable) correlation of intense physical activity, at intervals over time, between the two devices, even though their respective owners claimed to have been nowhere near each other. This 'accidental' or 'de-anonymising' use of big data analytics was becoming increasingly common and this one had all the hallmarks of a significant test case, not to mention the fun the media were having with it: 'FitBit on the side!' and other variations were rife. At another time, Jenny might have been amused or interested but, right now, she was just fed up.

Aisha could not have known it but Jenny felt every bit as low as her. Aside from her eyes still hurting, although she might understand different aspects of the PDN problem, she had no more idea now of what was causing it than when she had been embarrassed by her interview on RFS on the TV before Christmas. (She had not been asked again: the media seemed to be focusing on cyber security experts now for their speculation.) She and Bob had discussed it at length, of course, but with no resolution. She had heard each and every one of Andy's inventive explanations from Luxembourg and had dismissed them in the same manner as Bob. She even recalled Andy's Sherlock Holmes logic: *"When you have eliminated the impossible, whatever remains, however improbable, must be the*

115

truth." That was all very well, she thought, but nothing even seemed to reach the level of *improbable*: everything appeared *impossible*. There appeared to *be* no explanation – but there *had* to be one. In fact, all Bob had really succeeded in doing was to transfer some of his fixation, including his mantras, to her. She shared his belief in the significance of the misplaced frames but could not explain them. She now sat quietly, notionally looking towards the TV, which temporarily lost and then regained the signal as she watched. She reached for the control to turn it off, with the same questions in her head. *Where's this coming from? Is it random or isn't it? Why would there be frames on the wrong networks?*

And then Aisha seemed convulse next to her …

*

The movement was violent, then gone. Aisha appeared to twitch from her head downwards through her shoulders and body. The empty glass slipped from her hand and fell softly onto the carpet. But now she sat motionless, her arm half-raised – in an attempt to point at Ben, it seemed. Her mouth formed primitive, but as yet silent, words. Jenny eyed her with alarm, picked up the dropped glass with one hand and grasped her forearm with the other, in an attempt to reassure her.

"*What's the matter?*"

Aisha said nothing – she seemed unable. But she managed to extend a finger slightly; still with a weak, curved arm, but clearly trying to point at Ben, as he vainly forced the large engine onto the smaller track.

"Aisha, what's the *matter?*"

Eventually, some words came. Slow and disjointed at first, but gathering in speed and coherence as she gradually composed herself.

"Train on the wrong track."

Jenny glanced at Ben. "Er, yes; so?"

"*Why would you put a train on the wrong track?*"

"What?"

"Why would you put a train on the wrong track? *Why would there be frames on the wrong networks?*" She dropped her hand and looked at Jenny for the first time.

"What are you talking about, Aisha?"

"*It is learning!*"

"What is?"

"All the dirty networks. *The Internet*, I suppose. The disruption. *It is learning.*"

"*What?*"

"*The Internet is learning.* It is putting trains on the wrong track, putting frames on the wrong network because it is learning. It is experimenting; trying things out. Lots of things do not make sense when you randomly try things out but that is how you learn." Jenny's eyes widened in utter disbelief and it was her turn to freeze, speechless; so, after a pause, and slightly more firmly, Aisha continued.

"It is learning. The noise and the rubbish and the broken data and the occasional part that makes sense: it is finding out how to *do* things. I suppose I do not really mean quite like a child: it is nothing like that advanced. But it is learning in the same way as our brains may do when they first become active, when they first attain some essential critical level of complexity. The signals are experimental but, slowly, both the signals themselves become more refined and the brain acquires an in-built central control sense of what it is and what it can do ... and how."

Jenny continued to stare at Aisha incredulously.

"But where are the signals coming from? How are they being put on the network?"

"They are not being *put* on the network. They are coming *from* the network."

"Where? Which part?"

"*All of it.*"

"How?"

"From some sort of primitive neural instinct to assess control: *lower* than anything that might be *put* on it. From its own in-built central awareness of its structure."

"In-built central awareness?"

"Yes, something like that."

Another pause.

"Are you saying the Internet has become *sentient*?"

It was Aisha's turn to reflect on what was being said.

"Well, I suppose that depends on exactly what you mean by *sentient*. But, exhibiting a form of independent behaviour? Yes, I suppose so. Looking to make sense of itself: or, at least, to minimise its internal assessment of lack of control, as a colleague of mine would put it? Probably."

This was too much to take in. The only way Jenny could approach the concept was, bizarrely, to raise the stakes.

"And *exerting* control?"

Aisha considered again. "Well, perhaps. Maybe at some point. But I do not think that is what it is doing yet. It is *experimenting* at best. We know that most of the noise is useless and only very occasionally – in terms of the overall count – does it manage to produce anything that has an effect. At the moment, that seems effectively random. But it appears that it is getting better at this. The levels of valid signals are increasing. It will slowly – maybe quickly – find itself doing more things properly. It will come to associate cause and effect and it will assimilate this into what it is currently probably building: a *framework* for its global imperative of minimisation of assessment of lack of control."

Still too much. Jenny floundered for something constructive to say, or ask.

"So, you're saying ... ?"

"I am saying that the Internet has reached some critical mass in terms of its neural size or complexity. From its hardware has emerged a framework for independent internal control assessment, and possibly action."

"You're saying the Internet has become *conscious*!"

"Yes, perhaps I am."

PHASE THREE: PROGNOSIS

Chapter 11: Scepticism and Belief

"It's basic *panpsychism*."

"Oh, good grief! No!"

"Why not? Panpsychism: the theory that *everything* has consciousness to some extent or other; if you create something with enough neural complexity, it eventually reaches some critical mass and becomes aware of itself." Andy shrugged his shoulders and opened his palms as almost to suggest, 'What did you expect?' Aisha's eyes gleamed. Jenny and Bob were clearly less convinced.

The Desk was complete once more. Following Aisha's revelation earlier in the afternoon, she and Jenny had spent two hours hammering the concept to-and-fro between them like tennis players: Aisha trying desperately to force the idea on Jenny who, in turn, was determined not to accept it. Having the strangest of notions that he might actually support her on this, Aisha had eventually called Andy, who had, only slightly but immediately, cut short his visit elsewhere and made arrangements to meet the rest. By the time, the extended Weatherill family had finished their afternoon shopping, he was waiting at Euston to be picked up on the way back. Now they were all together again. Jill's defence against any discussion of dirty networks and weird stuff had dissolved and there was only one topic of conversation. Now, however, they were a doubles match, rather than singles; a strange alliance of the spiritual and scientific against the practically technical.

"So, are you saying you think Aisha's *right*?" There was an incredulous tone to Bob's voice he could not disguise.

"You think the Internet's *woken up*?" pursued Jenny, no less sceptically. "It's *come alive*?"

"Well, something like that, perhaps," said Andy. "*Why not*?"

"Well, let's start with *you*!" Bob suggested after a general pause. "Surely, you of all people don't buy the idea of consciousness just being the result of neural complexity? Don't you live in the world of the spirit these days?" His tone was more mocking than he intended. "You'd want God to be involved, wouldn't you?"

"Perhaps He is! As Turing pointed out, who are we to tell God how His universe works? Maybe that's precisely the way He's designed it. Maybe He's just been waiting all this time for us to build something big enough for Him to put a soul into?"

Jenny snorted. "A *soul*?"

"Well, maybe; maybe not. *Something*. Whether it's God-given or hard science: something capable of independent thought and response, anyway. Why not?"

"OK then," Jenny continued the attack. "Because it's not *big enough*! Because the Internet is only just approaching the neural size of the human brain and we know it's a very different thing. Presumably, the brain does what it does in the most efficient way it can. The Internet's not wired up anything like the brain. Each device is only connected to a handful of other devices. Each neuron in the brain is connected to tens or hundreds of thousands of others. The Internet's not densely connected enough. For it to become a functioning brain, it would have to be many orders of magnitude larger to make up for that, surely?"

Bob almost winced as he spoke, hesitantly. "Actually, it already ... sort of ... *is*." All three shot him quizzical glances. He continued.

"The Internet itself, just taken as a collection of network devices, is one thing. But think about all the other stuff – the end systems – that are connected to it. Think about the internal circuitry of *those* things *and* the routers and switches themselves. Taken as just a collection of connected logic gates – at a much lower level, with no preconceived interpretation of structure – it's already *massive*: way, way bigger than a human brain. And *everything's* connected to the Internet now – there are more 'things' on it than people nowadays: it's the *Internet of Everything* – the *IoE*." He waved a hand carelessly around the room, taking in the lights, TV, the entertainment console, the Christmas tree. "*All* of this stuff is connected. And then there's the *power* ..."

"*Yes!*" Aisha could not restrain herself; Bob continued.

"The Internet is a logically organised *data* network, as are all the devices attached to it really. But it's tied to another system to keep it going: the *power* networks. If you add those in, you've got a fair bit of extra complexity too. Not only that, but a power network often provides a *physical* connection between the main Internet and any other networks that wouldn't otherwise be connected to it – many *wireless* segments, for example."

Jenny spoke slowly, and with an air of resignation, as if she hardly believed what she might be conceding.

"And ... we know ... that there's noise on the ... power networks ... too!" She put her head in her hands in despair. But Bob had not yet switched sides so easily.

"That aside, I think my main objection to the idea is that it's just *daft*! It's science fiction stuff. I mean, a conscious Internet; *really?*" Jenny raised her head and nodded but there was no other response as all four retreated, for a few moments, into their own thoughts.

Aisha quickly scanned the faces of the other three, and took a deep breath before taking her opportunity. She had now had time both to collect herself fully and refine her theory a little.

"Think about it. I know it sounds mad but *think* about it! In animals, the brain and body, working together, are essentially a powered nervous system. There comes a point where it is difficult to separate the two parts of the bodily process: *everywhere* are signals and *everywhere* is power. It is likely that our own consciousness comes from just this combination of signals and energy: there is no need for anything else." A sideways glance at Andy, who merely shrugged. "The brain, our nervous system, is made up of a biological substrate on which neurons can fire data around. OK, we do not exactly know what this data is or how it does it: we can argue about whether it is *information* or *control* that is being passed. But it probably comes down to the same thing. *Somehow* it manages to do it, and we cannot deny that it *does*: we could not be having this discussion otherwise. No-one tells *us* we are not conscious just

123

because we do not know how or why. Well OK, some philosophers might," another glance at Andy, "but generally we accept the idea. Somehow, the right foundation allows for this sufficiently complex powered network to assess its own *existence*, then its ability to *predict*, then to *control*. It tries, it learns, and it gets better. Any notion of higher levels of intelligence *must* be built on this foundation somehow. In fact, if an Italian friend of mine is correct, the brain learns to *abstract*: the whole thing is to do with the nervous system working to a fundamental, low-level imperative to minimise its assessment of lack of control. Everything that happens after that builds from there." No interruption so she continued.

"Now, consider the Internet, and the power networks it is connected to across the world. What have we built? We have built a massive – *really* massive – *powered neural network*. And its very *function* is to communicate. Every link is a carrier *designed* to communicate – we *made* it that way. Its end points are specifically *designed to transmit and receive information*, or *control*. The nodes and the links are *made* to work together: there is nothing left to chance, in fact." She looked at Jenny. "OK, it is not connected in the same way as the brain but it is actually much, *much* bigger – if you consider *all* of it, which may compensate. That may also mean that it does not do things in *exactly* the same manner as the brain but it might do something very *similar*. The point is, it has all the necessary ingredients for self-awareness that the brain has. It makes little sense to worry about how *exactly* that might actually come about because we do not know how it happens in our brains either.

"So, in a pure sense, it is not exactly a panpsychic model, I suppose, if I understand that properly: this does not suggest that a rock or a mountain could achieve consciousness but a *sufficiently complex, custom-built, powered* system *might. We* have provided the structure and the power and the fundamental, low-level mechanisms for communication – we have *built* that. There is no need for an evolutionary process such as humans have emerged from: the Internet is *made-to-measure* as a *global nervous system.*" She paused and raised a finger slightly to focus attention on what she was about to say. "But in fact, we have done much more than that: we have *shown it how to work*!"

The others continued to listen, speechless. Aisha continued.

"Rather than just provide the Internet with the *physical means* to communicate, we have shown it *how*. It is already awash with *our* control and data, properly organised and packaged. There are numerous different protocols in its different parts and there is much more basic material, which we introduce too – whether we mean to or not: aborted data, corrupted fragments … and *noise*. It has a complete demonstration package for how to work (and how not to). Not only does it have its *materials*, it has its *instruction manual* too!

"And this is where I think it is in this process now: at a very early stage in what we might consider to be its *development*. Its very complexity has reached some essential tipping point in which it has acquired a fundamental internal, but global, imperative to assess control, possibly to seek to minimise *lack* of control. Perhaps it is *that*, which we might call *consciousness*. I do not know that I am entirely comfortable with that word but it matters little. I suspect that it does not really know *what* it is doing right now but it is *aware* that it is doing *something*: doing all it *knows* how to do – and that may be what it has been *shown* to do.

"So, it starts with just noise; probably quite low-level noise because – in the brain at least – we think that randomly switching between very close 'on' and 'off' states seems to be an efficient thing to do. It has transmitters and receivers that attempt to send and answer this noise internally but, on the whole that does nothing because there is no response from anywhere: it does not notice any *difference*, whatever it might do. But slowly, with a continued element of randomness and trial-and-error – *localised genetic mutation*, if you like – on a truly massive scale, it occasionally increases the difference between the two states in response to recognising some correlation between cause and effect and it gains in sophistication. This might have something to do with its equivalent of the brain's 'regularity spotter' or whatever it has." She tailed off, uncertainly. "I am not quite sure how it might do that though," she acknowledged thoughtfully.

Bob broke in, shaking his head, also seemingly unable to believe what he was saying.

"Well, I guess the low voltage noise doesn't have any effect at all: it doesn't even *interfere* with anything. But, eventually as the level increases, it's going to coincide with some 'real data' – *some of ours* – and the combined signal will be high enough to register a collision and force a retransmit. I suppose, over time and with enough data, it might get to recognise that and start to favour the higher voltage noise in cleaner spikes over the low-level, continuous white noise type. Perhaps that's the stage we're at now. It's learnt that decent level noise spikes sometimes do something but it's not sure what yet? I guess the same may be true at all levels: individual logic gates, device connections, network links and major data trunks?

"But then maybe, occasionally, the noise takes on a shape that resembles a data bit? After all, it's doing that all the time with the legitimate data we're asking it to carry so it's a reasonable thing for it to gradually learn. A single bit also does nothing but it takes a tiny fraction of time longer for it to be rejected by a receiver, and in a logically *different* way, which it will *notice*. And, of course, it 'sees' all of this because it's happening internally as far as it's concerned. Slowly, it produces a few bit sequences amongst the noise, then some bytes, then some frames. Still none of this actually *does* anything proper but it still sees a difference so it's learning all the time and it has billions and billions, trillions, whatever, of data samples to work with." His eyes suddenly grew wide in realisation. "And *that's* why we see the occasional frame fragment with the *wrong protocol on a different network*! It's just playing silly buggers, experimenting: learning what *doesn't* work just as much as what *does*. It doesn't particularly care about *our* arbitrary divisions: how *we* use the kit determines that; but it may not be limited by that eventually?"

Was this tacit agreement from Bob? Perhaps. All three now turned to Jenny. She rolled her eyes, opened her mouth wide and stupidly, offering her palms in supplication, and, so, *so* reluctantly, attempted to complete the narrative.

"Then, eventually," she said slowly, "partly by sheer volume of material, partly by chance, and partly from learning what it's been shown and seen, it manages to produce something – a compete frame, a meaningful signal, a recognisable command – that actually *does* something. So something comes *on*, or *off*, or *resets*, or *switches*, or *breaks*?" She sighed hopelessly in resignation. "OK, *it's a theory*."

Andy smiled, and said softly: "*When you have eliminated the impossible, whatever remains, however improbable, must be the truth.*"

But, if anything, Jenny glared at him even harder.

*

"Right: just, supposing for a moment that there's *any* sense at all in *any* of this," Jenny narrowed her eyes at each of the other three in turn: almost daring them to agree, "we're talking about a *single entity*; yes?"

It was the following morning and they were having breakfast. They had all stayed the night with Jill and Bob. Aisha and Jenny had used the two single beds in the spare room, Chris, Heather and Ben having left the previous evening, and Andy had slept downstairs on the sofa in the living room. All, apart from Andy, appeared the worse for a bad night with little sleep.

"Yes," agreed Aisha. "It has to be a single thing. It is connected; it is one. It would be too much of a coincidence for there to be more than one at present."

"At *present*?" Jenny's eyes opened a little.

"Well, I suppose there is no reason why whatever has happened could not be replicated. But I would imagine this is not the situation here."

"And," Bob suggested, "we're assuming there's an element of *size*, *complexity* at work here, aren't we? We're saying that some essential mass has been reached that's made this happen. That's almost certainly the whole thing, the Internet, the bigger, powered IoE; not some coincidence across more than one section. Also …"

The others looked expectantly. He continued.

"Also, Stephen says that there's no noise on wifi – or any other wireless systems; nor on the satellite links or anything like that. I've checked with him again this morning. There's no noise on the cellular 4 and 5G phone networks either. It's everything connected as the Internet *or* by the power networks (or both) but there needs to be a *physical* connection for a network to be included, by the look of it. Separately-powered, physically disconnected networks don't seem to be a part of it; nor does wireless *itself*. Yes, it seems to be a single, connected thing."

"*It?*" queried Andy. "Is that the best we can do? *It?*"

And, it appeared that it was. Among themselves, it would never be anything other than '*It*'.

The conversation continued.

*

"OK, let me make something *absolutely clear*," announced Bob, as the morning drifted towards lunchtime. "I am *not* calling Stephen to tell him *we think the Internet's woken up!* I'm pretty sure that would be me straight off the case!"

"Is that because you do not believe it?" Aisha asked, smiling. "Or because you do not want to appear silly; or because you do not think you can convince him?"

"A bit of all three really," admitted Bob.

"Same here, I suppose," said Jenny thoughtfully. "Same thing really, of course."

"Good; so let's think about how we can address the whole thing then," suggested Andy.

"How?" the others asked, largely together.

"Well, what can we do to convince *ourselves*?" asked Andy. "We have a model, of sorts. We're not entirely in agreement on some fundamentals," smiling at Aisha, "and we're a bit vague on

128

detail," a nod to Jenny and Bob, "but we have a rough hypothesis. How can we test it? If we can convince *ourselves* well enough, we should have the armoury to take the argument to someone else, surely? So ... what exactly *is* our model and what does it *tell* us?"

Aisha considered the question. "I suppose, in those terms, we are saying that the Internet – taken as the complete union of *all* devices physically connected together globally, *either* as data *or* power – generally *both*: what we now seem to be calling '*It*' – has, in addition to carrying the data *we* have put onto it, *achieved a control imperative of its own*."

"And what does that mean in practical terms?"

"Well, it means that, at the lowest level, individual logic components, possibly pairs or small clusters, have started acting as neuron comparators; assessing observation against expectation as a primitive mechanism for minimising assessment of lack of control. These are probably working within negative feedback loops, formed logically within and around these comparator units."

"Right, *then* what?"

"Then, presumably, if our brain models are correct themselves, these low-level comparators cluster together to form higher-level comparators – again with feedback logic, which are capable of higher-level control assessment and more functionality, and so on, up through a hierarchy that eventually leads to coordinated sense/response, understanding; then possibly reason, problem-solving and creativity. There will be a lot of repetition, even *recursion*, in this layer building. But we do not know how far along that path we are with *It*, yet. I suspect, not far."

"Good, so how could we measure that?" asked Andy. Aisha's thoughts flashed back to her question to Paulo Di Iorio."

"I suppose we would need to determine what was unique about that structure and behaviour, in a way that we could test; in a way that we could tell apart systems that were like that from those that were not. What makes our brains, and possibly It, *special?*"

"So, some sort of attempt at sensor-based random firing energy-minimisation, with feedback loops, but extended repeatedly and recursively across multiple hierarchical levels and units might be a feature then?" suggested Bob, smiling at his ironic attempt to imply simplicity. "That sounds like '*self-similarity*' and '*scale-free networks*' to me."

"I'm not so sure about the scale-free aspect," said Jenny. "True, both the brain and the Internet are known to have scale-free features but that's usually talked about in terms of structure: the *hardware*. We already have that in place. We built that. We're more interested in the signals themselves. You might have a point with the general self-similarity thing though, if we're thinking about it in terms of data traffic."

"Self-similarity?" enquired Andy.

"Self-similarity is the tendency of a system to have repeated patterns over both the long and short term," explained Jenny, "or over large and small scales. I think it was first noticed measuring Nile river levels or something, but it's recognised that many systems have self-similarity. Internet traffic itself is self-similar because its data tends to be in connected streams rather than independent units like old-fashioned phone calls."

"So, that won't help then, will it?" suggested Andy. "If the Internet's doing it already, how can we measure if the new stuff's any different?"

"Because it is going to be more than self-similarity in neuron pairs," argued Aisha. "We may also see it across hierarchical levels and geographic regions, irrespective of the underlying technology: that might be a *big* clue? Also, we think everything will be embedded within negative feedback control loops as well. I would imagine this would provide particular patterns *within* comparator units as well as *between* them?"

"And," Bob suggested, "we have what we could call the '*signal to noise ratio*'. The fraction of the data that's meaningful, rather than random or useless. That seems to be changing but I guess we could measure it easily enough if we could just compare current activity with data retained from last week or yesterday, say?"

"Yes, that might also give an idea of how much control was being registered and recognised," agreed Aisha.

"So, can we put all this together into something measurably *unique*?" asked Andy.

"Well, we measure basic self-similarity with the '*Hurst Parameter*'," Jenny explained. "Named after the guy who first looked at the Nile levels: usually written as just '*H*'. The H parameter is measured as the average difference between data points over points that are both close together and far apart: it's calculated to be in the range *0* to *1* and any measurement much over *0.5* can be considered significant in terms of possible self-similarity. But what we need here is to extend this to look for the other features we think might be present in the brain such as the self-similarity possibly applying over both distance *and* logical level. There's a kind of '*two-dimensional*' relative similarity here possibly?"

"Also," prompted Aisha, "we need to somehow factor in what effect the feedback logic will have."

"And the signal to noise ratio," Bob reminded them.

"And, once we know what we are looking for," Aisha suggested, "we may be able to take measurements from *actual* brain activity so we know what kind of values we should be getting if It is behaving in a similar way. It is possible that Professor Di Iorio may be able to help with that: it is more his line of work than mine."

"So," Jenny breathed deeply, "if we can somehow combine the 2D self-similarity scores with the feedback control and the signal to noise ratios, then normalise this against known brain figures, we might be able to formulate an '*extended Hurst Parameter*', which we could then use to test for similar activity in It?" She laughed. "Not much then!"

"We'll call it the '*S Parameter*'," joked Andy.

"Why?" asked Jenny doubtfully.

"The '*Smith Parameter*'," explained Andy.

"Don't you dare," Jenny threatened.

But, of course, they did.

Chapter 12: Nodes, Edges and Faces

They worked frantically. Bob immediately connected Hattie to the network adaptor on his office laptop to record some noise readings to compare with later in the day. Jenny spent the rest of the afternoon trying to wrestle through the mathematics of combining self-similarity across both logical layers and physical regions with the patterns normally to be found in negative feedback control loops and the anticipated increase in the signal-to-noise ratio of the meaningful to nonsense data. Aisha made repeated calls to Professor Paulo Di Iorio to establish what aspects of these measurements were known from human brain studies. After a considerable amount of difficult clarification, he was eventually able to send through some relevant results from an H2020 project he was working on. Later, Bob carefully added extra code to Hattie to enable her to take the necessary readings from a network and crudely calculate the new '*S Parameter*'. In the evening, with Aisha's input from the human brain data, Jenny was able to refine the maths and Bob gradually tweaked Hattie further until they had something that all three of them felt was a good as it was likely to be. During this time, Andy made several pots of tea.

None of this (apart from the tea) was easy. As soon as she looked up the details of the H Parameter (hampered, as was usual now, by a very slow Internet response), Jenny was reminded that it was essentially a theoretical figure: difficult to calculate exactly with real, finite data. The *S value* would almost certainly have to be approximated as best they could, with a complexity (and run time) that could be tolerated. (Jenny at first resisted use of the term 'Smith Parameter' but gave up when Bob shortened it to 'S Parameter' and finally 'S value'.) She spent a couple of hours working out an appropriate neural network-based heuristic algorithm to estimate the S value for Bob to implement in Hattie, who was fairly powerful for a stand-alone system but no super-computer so some simplification was needed.

Also, the data Aisha received from Paulo Di Iorio on feedback loops in the brain, whilst useful and relevant, was not exactly in the form that was going to give her the calibration that Hattie would need to find the S value in real networks. Professor Di Iorio had never intended it for this purpose and was very curious as to what Aisha might want it for. Having given both her thanks and an unconvincing sequence of non-specific reasons why she needed it, she then spent three hours turning the information over in a spreadsheet to get the figures they required. Then finally, Hattie had to be set up in a mode that would allow her to automatically ignore the 'proper' user data and only register PDN noise so that this could be used to measure the increase in the signal-to-noise ratio, which also fed into the S value calculation.

*

At about eight o'clock they were ready to test the new-look Hattie. From a memory pen, they loaded in the complete, aggregated set of Professor Di Iorio's brain sample figures. Bob set Hattie to run manually on the data; she had been configured to run Jenny's heuristic AI approximation algorithm for about a minute. Longer would give a more accurate result; shorter, a less accurate one. No-one was entirely sure how much difference that would make.

Bob had made no attempt to refine Hattie's user interface. The *'Processing'* message scrolled across her screen as the 60 seconds passed. Then, entirely without ceremony, the result appeared.

$S = 0.751$

"Is that good?" Andy asked innocently.

"Yes," said Bob, beaming a little. "That's what we were trying to normalise the figures to."

"Anything in the range *0.5* to *1* might represent some level of self-similarity, feedback and signal increase, which could be associated with what is being measured having achieved some control imperative," Aisha explained. "The higher the better: *0.75* is what we get from a typical adult human brain."

"So, it looks like we've got the calibration about right," suggested Jenny, "and a minute seems to be enough for the heuristic to get a decent approximation."

"So, anything above *0.5* means *conscious*?" suggested Andy.

"It might not be as simple as that," Aisha said, wincing slightly, "but it may give an indication of that type of neural activity."

"So, shall we try it for real?" asked Bob.

"Yes, let's do it. Let's get her onto a real network!" agreed Jenny.

But this proved to be less conclusive than they hoped. They first reconnected Hattie to Bob's laptop. They then set her to run and waited for the minute to pass with even greater expectation than before. After what seemed like an eternity, the '*Processing*' message was replaced by the result.

$S = 0.523$

"Ah," said Andy.

"*Hmm,*" mumbled Aisha.

"*Damn!*" said Jenny.

"*Bollocks!*" spat Bob.

"So, where does that leave us?" asked Andy. "At least it's above *0.5*?"

"Not enough," said Aisha, dejectedly. "Not conclusive."

"I can't go to Stephen with this," complained Bob.

They sat in silence for a while. Suddenly, Jenny started forwards.

"Hang on a minute; you're *wifi* here aren't you?"

"Well yes, of course," agreed Bob. "and yes, I know that PDN itself isn't on wireless networks. But this machine's still plugged into the mains so it's still a part of It, isn't it? The noise is still visible: *look*." He pointed to one of Hattie's oscilloscope displays in justification.

"Yes, but it's only on the *edge* of It, as it were," Jenny suggested. "It's connected through the power network but nothing else. Perhaps we're going to get lower figures on the periphery?"

"If I've understood Paulo's figures properly, that is not the way it would work in a human brain," Aisha interjected.

"But we know It's not *exactly* like the brain," pursued Jenny. "It's just based on the same rough model." (The others smiled at her sudden, enthusiastic conversion to the cause. She noticed but continued undeterred.) "I don't think we're looking far enough into It here. We might be getting some local self-similarity and feedback but probably not anything from a wider area. In fact, if you think about it, we're not part of any *hierarchy* here. We would be if the wifi was a part of It but it isn't. There's not going to be any self-similarity or feedback across regions or through levels. Perhaps we'll get a better result – a higher figure – if we measure something a bit closer to the business end?"

So, they quickly tried another experiment. Bob took the cover off the broadband box and connected Hattie to the incoming ATM line. Those earlier weeks of programming her auto-configuration features might be worthwhile after all, he thought to himself. Hattie set off on her measurements and calculations and, after her allocated minute had elapsed, reported:

$S = 0.551$

"Strewth!" groaned Bob. "Does that tell us anything?"

"It's higher," noted Andy, somewhat obviously.

"Not high enough," said Aisha.

"The problem is, I guess," suggested Jenny, "that we're *still* pretty much on the edge. Whatever It's up to, we're getting a sight of some of Its control data," glancing again at Hattie's oscilloscope, "but still not enough. We're not seeing far up the ATM link and there's effectively nothing below us because the wifi's cutting off the rest of the house. We need to get further in to It to really test the concept."

"So, in many ways, it would make our life easier if It *had* learnt to use wireless, then?" suggested Andy, as the most casual of throwaway remarks.

But both Aisha and Bob gaped at him in amazement: he had clearly said something utterly profound. Aisha was the first to speak.

"Yes, I had never thought of it like that. Learning to use different parts of Its structure is probably part of Its development. Although I suspect Its control imperative came into existence all at once, when Its combined structure reached some critical size, it is likely that It is currently having different degrees of success across different media ..."

"Electrical, optical, etc.?" suggested Jenny.

"... Yes, different degrees of success across electrical, optical, and suchlike, media," Aisha continued, "and with different protocol mechanisms: that does not seem unlikely. The improvement we think we are seeing in Its ability to produce meaningful signals, over time, is probably not homogeneous over Its entire structure. I expect we could trace that process if we had access to enough historical data?" She glanced questioningly at Bob, who appeared distracted by other thoughts. "Even now, It is probably still having varying degrees of success, in different places, as It learns. We could conceivably get different S measurements in different locations, even if the connectivity and hierarchical structures were the same." She paused. "I suppose It will never learn to use wireless links, though, because there is no physical connection?"

Bob had been waiting his turn with considerable difficulty. *"I'm really not so sure about that!"* he said with some force. They all stared at him. He continued.

"Why *shouldn't* it be able to use wireless links? Just think about it for a moment. They might seem to us like something completely different but they're *not*. What's a *physical* link? It's just a transmitter and receiver with a carrier medium in between. OK, it's pretty simple with a cable because, from Its perspective, there's an obvious 'in' and 'out' but it's essentially a 'transmit-carry-receive' system.

"Now, if you think about it, *wireless isn't any different*. There's still a transmitter and receiver. The only difference is that the medium's the *air*. You still have the transmit-carry-receive system: just with a different carrier. OK, there are some issues with signals being multi-directional in a typical wifi environment but there are many wireless signals that are quite precisely focused." As the thoughts in his head outpaced the words coming from his mouth, he suddenly banged the arm of his chair hard with his fist.

"*I bet you It's just not figured out how to use wireless YET!*"

"You're saying It *will*?" Aisha asked incredulously.

"I can't see any reason why It *wouldn't*," Bob answered, slightly calmer. "There's no essential difference. I can understand that it might take longer but I can't see anything to stop it. It's true that *we* find it easier to write network discovery algorithms for wired networks but we can manage for wireless too. Remember It has our data as a guide as to what can go where, and how. It can 'see' both ends of a wireless link because they're both plugged into the mains: It just needs to realise what can happen in between. My guess would be that It first figures out how to use the uni-directional links because that's not hugely different – not conceptually different, as far as the transmit-carry-receive model is concerned – from physical connections. From there, it would a simple step to getting to grips with the whole range of wireless communications. I can sort of understand why it hasn't happened yet; but I'm *sure* it will!"

"And what would that give us?" asked Andy. "What would It become then?"

Jenny was first to reply. "I don't think it would make It a lot bigger, would it? True, a lot of the current structure is over wireless but almost all of those networks and end hosts are connected to the main body through the power networks anyway. I doubt it would increase the overall neural count that much: not by a significant factor."

"But it *would* increase the neural *connectivity*," insisted Aisha. "As it stands, It is quite sparsely connected, as is the way of computer systems designed by humans. And this is dictated by the physical connections we have given It. Even if It was to develop Its own rules for internal communication, as it may be doing, It cannot use physical connections that are *not there*.

"But if It becomes able to control, or at least *use*, wireless connections, then It will be able to communicate internally through the *air* – probably through almost *any* medium. Rather than each network neuron being limited in its connection to those we have given it physical data links to, It will be able to establish a neuronal connection with *anything in range*."

"That might put *scale-free network models* back on the table," said Jenny with some alarm. "So, it would begin to look a lot more like a human brain?"

"Yes; although Its neural size will increase only slightly, Its neural complexity will increase massively," said Aisha. "I do not even know how much."

"Several orders of magnitude, I'd think," agreed Bob. "It would be a different beast entirely."

"Not sure I like the '*beast*' concept too much!" said Jenny.

"Let's hope it doesn't happen for a while yet then," suggested Andy

*

"The fact remains, we're still not getting far enough into It to get a convincing reading," Jenny pointed out half an hour later, after a short tea-break. "For now, let's ignore what happens if It manages to master the wireless capabilities It doesn't realise It's got yet and focus on what we *have*. Is it going to help if we set Hattie off to run for longer? Will that give us a better reading?"

"I doubt it," said Bob, "but, while we're not doing anything else, I guess there's no harm in trying." He leaned over, typed in a couple of parameter variations and set Hattie off again. This time, '*Processing*' appeared on her screen and stayed there. "There: that should finish around midnight. But I don't suppose it'll give us much."

"OK then," said Aisha, "while that is running, how can we get further into It to measure Its control assessment capabilities?"

"You mean Its *consciousness*?" suggested Andy once more.

Aisha smiled. "I am still not quite comfortable with calling it that; but, if you like, yes, Its *consciousness*. But I am only saying that because it is shorter, you understand?"

Andy smiled in return. "So what *is* the best way to get deeper into the beast?" he asked. Jenny gritted her teeth but Bob had clearly been considering this already.

"I wish now I'd had a closer look at the 'Network on Chip' core they had at HGMS," Bob said apologetically. "There would have been obvious network levels above and below that so there would have been more to see, I guess."

"You mean the Darmstadt network?" Jenny suggested. "But even that was isolated, wasn't it? And can Hattie get readings from an NoC? She'd have to somehow *look inside* it, wouldn't she?"

"Well, not without some additional kit, I suppose," admitted Bob. "Yes, I suppose you're right. So, what else *can* we do? There are plenty of places where we *would* see big hierarchies and wide coverage but we can't go and break into a BT box without getting locked up! And we can't just walk into the ISPs and demand to set Hattie up, can we? They'll want to know why. And what would we tell them? That we think the Internet's *come alive*?"

"I've got a few useful contacts," Jenny smiled. "In particular, there's a research team at my university, who are looking at energy minimisation on NoC systems: they might have the means of taking measurements from the circuitry. Would Hattie be able to work on data supplied from an external source?"

Bob nodded. "No different to what we just did to test her with Aisha's human brain figures."

"Also, there's a guy I've worked with at Imperial College," Jenny said, "who may be able to get us into the Rutherford Labs at Didcot. That would give us access to the *Janet Network*."

Bob nodded. Aisha and Andy both raised their eyebrows in query so Jenny continued.

"The '*Joint Academic Network*'," she explained. "*JANET* for short. It's the network used by all the UK universities and most of the further education colleges. It's a pretty serious piece of work, which is what we want and, if my Imperial colleague can get us into the right bit at the Rutherford Appleton Labs, near Oxford, then we could be looking at one of the highest hierarchy nodes in the network. So we'd really be able to put our theory to the test. I can think of one or two other places as well," she added.

The other three nodded agreement. The rest of the evening was spent planning an itinerary for the next day. Jenny made a number of phone calls and sent several messages. By the end of the evening, she had enough useful responses to put together a rough schedule for Bob and her to visit four places of possible value in London, Oxford and Cambridge. Hattie's couriers were contacted to arrange for her to follow safely close behind. (Bob grumbled, under his breath, as to 'someone paying for this at some point'.) Some of the visits would involve taxis and lifts from willing (but largely unapprised) collaborators so it was impractical, and generally considered unnecessary, for all four of them to make the tour. It being the period between Christmas and New Year, Andy and Jenny were on an enforced 'operational efficiency break' from their universities; Aisha had taken leave from the hospital; Bob, of course, was his own boss; so all were free. The plan then was for Jenny and Bob (and Hattie) to make the visits while Aisha and Andy took it easy for a day. They would meet back at Jill and Bob's in the evening. All seemed fairly contented with the arrangements.

Before they went to bed, just after midnight, Hattie finished her extended run connected to the broadband box. A single light on the manual part of her dashboard alerted them. They moved over to look. Her simple text output showed:

$S = 0.553$

"So is that Hattie's increased accuracy?" asked Andy. "Or just random variation? *Or is It getting cleverer?*"

"Who can say?" Jenny mumbled.

*

Jenny and Bob started early in the morning and were at the first London stop – her home university – by 8:30am. Dr. Jakob Sovel, leader of the NoC team, met them at the entrance, not in the best of humour.

"I trust this is important, Professor Smith? I have had to delay a family trip to the country for this. I appreciate you hold a senior position here but I hope you can explain why we are doing this?"

To avoid too many difficult questions, Jenny took a direct, and formal, line.

"Mr. Weatherill and I," she introduced Bob with a wave, "are taking some readings of PDN for the government." She omitted to mention any particular government, which Bob considered to be wise as he hardly felt they knew. "Mr. Weatherill is one of the country's top network specialists and he has equipment that may provide us with some insight." Hattie – looking very much like some old kit to be disposed of on a trolley – was being wheeled by at that moment, to the evident astonishment of Dr. Sovel. "Beyond that, we can't say, I'm afraid." They all followed him to his team's base room.

Inside, a discussion ensued on what data they were trying to capture from the NoC although with considerably less emphasis on why. It was difficult. Dr. Sovel's team were able to take basic electrical readings from the chip but the data was otherwise unstructured from a networking point of view. Bob doubted whether it would provide meaningful results but there was little point in not trying.

Within an hour, Dr. Sovel had followed Jenny and Bob's suggestions as best he could. The result was a huge *MATLAB* table of signals taken from a single central point in the chip's logic layout. With minimal difficulty, this was converted and fed into Hattie, now reset to her original sixty-second run time. She was duly set off on her task and, after the regulation minute, reported:

$S = 0.562$

"Better," suggested Jenny.

"Better," agreed Bob. "But probably still not enough. The problem is, we're still isolated in a logical sense. Yes, the NoC has a fair bit of complexity itself but it's still disconnected from the outside world – apart from being plugged into the mains. Also, I doubt the raw electrical data has captured all the essential message complexity that might be in there. It's hard to spot self-similarity, for example, when the data's pretty one-dimensional anyway – and there's possibly no feedback showing. Maybe we'll get some better figures somewhere else?"

This was hardly the valediction Dr. Sovel was looking for in appreciation of his morning's sacrifice. Despite Jenny's profuse thanks and assurances of playing a small but vital role in their quest, he looked fairly cross as he locked the lab door behind them and hurried away.

*

Their next stop was at another London university. Jenny greeted an old colleague, Dr. Alice Colledge, at the entrance, introduced Bob with the same credentials as before and the three of them went to the nearest available I.T. lab. This was much closer to the kind of configuration the two of them were looking for. The hub for the lab would have logical complexity below it, from the host PCs and their internal circuitry, but was also connected, through the university's routers and firewalls, to the outside world. Although that would still place them on the edge of It in global terms, everything was cabled: unlike most of the newer installations, there was no wifi to break the chain. They both diplomatically abstained from mentioning to Alice this lack of up-to-date kit as having such appeal for them.

They switched everything on and Bob connected Hattie to one of the open ports from the hub and set her off on her minute's run. When finished, she reported.

$S = 0.578$

Bob allowed a small grin to pass across his face. "Better still," he observed. "Still not enough to go to Stephen with, I'd say, but it's progress!" He was not finished though: there was another essential question. "I don't suppose it's possible to isolate this lab from the Internet, is it?"

Alice looked around, particularly at the ducting leading from the hub through the wall.

"Doesn't look like it: not at this end, apart from breaking into that bit there." She pointed. "Or finding the other end: that would involve getting someone from I.T. Services out of bed and, either way, they wouldn't be happy!"

"Rutherford next," said Jenny.

*

Their journey to Didcot took longer but they were still there in time to take a hasty, late lunch with yet another of Jenny's old colleagues, Professor Wilhelm Stengel, 'Willie' for short, now a senior member of the Rutherford Labs network team. They told him as much as they felt they could and he appeared sensible of not asking more. After lunch, he led them to the main switching room.

"So, exactly what part would you like to test?" he asked helpfully.

Jenny hesitated for once but Bob had already chosen his words.

"We'd like to 'look down' on as much of the JANET network as possible, in a data sense, please. But from a position where there's a direct line to the rest of the Internet. We'd like to see the maximum amount of data in and out: so some sort of major switching node would be ideal, if you can manage that?"

"Of course," Willie smiled. He led to one of the newer racks of equipment and unlocked the front panel. "I assume it will be convenient for you if I stay while you complete your tests?" he asked softly. "Naturally I am very responsible – and concerned – for this equipment and the role it performs." They both nodded assent.

"Do you need to know exactly what this node is?" asked Willie.

"Not really," Bob admitted after a brief tussle with his curiosity.

"Good. Then I shall not tell you!" he replied with a curious smile.

With Willie watching closely, Bob carefully plugged Hattie into one of the spare fibre optic ports on the main router's front panel. A worrying thought occurred to him as he did so.

"Will this interface auto-recognise the new connection? We won't have to reconfigure the IOS will we?"

"No, and no, Bob," Willie replied quietly. "Although an alternative answer to the second question is that we would not let you, of course!"

"That's a relief," admitted Bob. He stepped back and started Hattie. She sat processing, then displayed:

$S = 0.603$

"Is that enough for Stephen?" asked Jenny.

"I don't know," admitted Bob, "but it's beginning to convince *me*!"

*

Their final stop was in Cambridge. There was nothing particularly unusual about the network they were about to see other than a couple of features Jenny had determined the night before. The university had recently invested heavily in network infrastructure and all labs in the building they were visiting had fibre connections directly to the university's main control room routers. Moreover, they had identified (without much difficulty) a lab that was unused over the vacation period. Dr. Clare Wheeler met them at the entrance and let them into the lab.

They switched all of the equipment on and Bob connected Hattie to the fibre hub. After her minute, she reported:

$S = 0.590$

Jenny looked at Bob for a reaction.

"No great surprise there," he suggested calmly. "Not as high as JANET. Now, Clare, I understand you can disconnect this lab from the rest of the network? From the outside world? From the Internet?"

"Of course," she confirmed. "Nothing easier!" She reached under the main box and pulled out two fibre optic cables. Still holding them in her hands, she grinned, "I can't say I know what you're doing but I suppose you want to do it again now!"

"Yes please," agreed Bob, with a laugh and a trace of eagerness. He set Hattie off once more and they eventually read:

$S = 0.581$

"Now *that*," stated Jenny with some force, "is *significant*!"

Chapter 13: Degrees of Heresy

While Jenny and Bob took Hattie on her regional tour, Aisha and Andy had had a quiet day in the city. After a brief walk around the sights, they had eaten lunch together and then seen a film – interrupted twice by RFS issues with the cinema equipment. They had then taken the tube most of the way back and stopped at a coffee shop a few hundred yards away from Jill and Bob's house. Its staff were trying to combine serving customers with coping with a minor flood apparently caused by the water supply to one of the espresso machines refusing to shut off. It had been a pleasant day: the company had been good. But the conversation had been slightly limited: they were more than happy to leave the 'techie stuff' to the computer scientists for now and neither of them had attempted anything much beyond the superficial – although both had wanted to. Andy had never passed up an opportunity to congratulate Aisha on her Boxing Day 'It revelation' but such praise was always quickly and modestly rebuffed. Now, however, as the two sat quietly sipping cappuccino, Aisha took a longer look at Andy as he stared, possibly somewhat vacantly, across the street, but with his lips hinting at a slight smile.

"Penny for your thoughts?" she suggested.

He turned back to her; his grin deepened immediately but he took time to reply, as if looking for the right words.

"Not much, really. I was just thinking about what we're trying to do with this 'measuring It' thing."

"And are you comfortable with it ... or *It*?"

"Oh, aye; certainly! The thing I like about it is that we're not really trying to determine what It *is*; we're just measuring if It's *there*, based on how we think It might *behave*. No assumptions: it's sort of *philosophy-independent*!"

"What?"

"Well, I mean we can calculate *how* It might behave, what sort of numbers we might see when we measure It; then we can measure It and we'll either be right or wrong but that won't actually take us any closer to knowing what It *is*. Is It just an innate scientific product of complexity? Or does It have a soul? We can be either right or wrong without knowing that. I sort of like that."

Aisha shook her head slightly. "No, as a scientist, I like to know what I am working with; I am not comfortable with uncertainty."

"But you have to be! We're surrounded by it. Our world, and what we know about it is framed by uncertainty. Even science."

"You think so?"

"Aye, we can't avoid it. There's lots we don't know and lot's we'll never know. We have no choice in that. The only power we have is in deciding how to deal with it." He reached into his conference bag: he was still using the one from Luxembourg. He took out his tablet and jabbed at the screen a few times.

"Here, take a look at this. This is from the blog of a friend of mine, Ruth Jones. She describes herself as a 'technological philosopher'. Bit over-the-top but she sometimes comes out with some good stuff. This is her post from last month."

He passed the tablet to Aisha, who read quickly:

"Known Unknowns"

This month's post may make a valid point. Or it may not. Or it may be impossible to tell, the concept of which itself may or may not make sense by the end of the piece!

How do we handle things we *don't know*? More precisely, how do we cope with things we *know we don't know*? All right then: how do we handle things we *know we can't know*?

The examples we're going to discuss are (at first, at least) taken from mathematics; but there are plenty of analogies in the other sciences. This certainly isn't a purely theoretical discussion.

On the whole, we like things (*statements* or *propositions*) in mathematics (say) to be right or wrong: *true* or *false*. Some simple examples are:

The statement "*2 > 3*" is *false*

The statement "There is a value of *x* such that *x < 4*" is *true*

The proposition "There are integer values of x, y and z satisfying the equation $x^3 + y^3 = z^3$" is *false*. *(*Part of *'Fermat's Last Theorem')*

OK, that's pretty straightforward but how about this one?

"Every even number (greater than 2) is the sum of two prime numbers"

Now, we can start off by trying this out easily enough. Working up: $4 = 2 + 2$; $6 = 3 + 3$; $8 = 3 + 5$. Jumping in at random, $100 = 11 + 89$ (and a number of other ways) so it looks promising.

In fact, this *Goldbach's Conjecture (GC)* has been shown by calculation (computation) to be true for a huge range of even numbers, and no-one's ever found an example where it's not.

However, that's not quite the same thing as *proving* it's always true. We'd need a cleverer logical argument for that (because we can't try out an infinite number of numbers individually) and no-one's managed that yet.

So, at the moment, we don't actually *know* if GC is true or false. If someone can supply the general proof, it will be *true*; if anyone finds an exception (an even number, which *isn't* the sum of two primes) then it's *false*.

Or something else might happen ...

Let's take another example ...

Without going into fine mathematical detail, there are obviously an *infinite number* of whole numbers (*integers*), positive or negative. We can think of the *set* of these numbers as having a certain (infinite) size.

Somewhat counter-intuitively, if we then extend the integers to include the *fractions* (*1/3*, *11/4*, etc.), then, although we might argue that there are *more* of them, in a strictly mathematical sense, the set of fractions has the *same* (infinite) size as the set of integers because we can set up a direct one-to-one mapping from the integers to the fractions. (You might need to look that bit up: it's too much for this post.)

Now, we might attempt to regain some sanity here by suggesting this is so because there's only *really* one infinity. However, this line of reasoning falls apart when we look at the set of *all* numbers (the *reals*), now including all the things that *can't* be expressed as fractions ($\sqrt{2}$, π, etc.).

Because it turns out we *can't* set up a one-to-one mapping from the integers to the reals so we have to conclude that we're dealing with a *different infinity*. If the set of integers is of a *certain* infinite size, then the set of reals is a *different* infinite size. And, once we've managed this, it emerges that it doesn't stop there. In fact, there's an endless sequence of infinite set sizes, getting larger and larger without end. (Again, too much to cover here.)

Now, we don't need to worry about where that sequence *goes* but, now that we know there *is* such a sequence, it's interesting to return to the set of integers and the set of reals and consider their *places* in the sequence. In particular, *are they consecutive in this sequence*? In other words, are they next to each other in terms of infinite set sizes or is there something that produces a set between the two? Is there an infinity *between* the integer infinity and the real infinity? This (proposing that there *isn't*) is the *Continuum Hypothesis* (*CH*).

Well, no-one's *found* an infinity between the integers and the reals. On the other hand, no-one's proved there *isn't* one. So, on the surface, we seem to be in the same position as with the GC. However, for the CH, mathematicians have gone one stage further. The question has been shown to be *undecidable*.

So, what does this mean? Well, it sort of depends on how you look at it ... In terms of the previous paragraph, no-one's *ever* going to find an infinity between the two but no-one's *ever* going to prove there isn't one either. In terms of pure logic, this means both of the following:

- Starting from everything we know of numbers and sets, there's *no* logical argument, no sequence of steps that will show that the CH is *true* ... or *false*. It's logically *'distant'*.
- The CH can be either *true* or *false*, arbitrarily, it doesn't matter which; and it doesn't interfere with the rest of what we know of numbers or sets. It's logically *'independent'*.

And, really, we can paraphrase these (equally valid) viewpoints as:

1. *'It's impossible to tell'*, or
2. *'It doesn't matter'*

Now here's the thing … This is actually what most of us *do* subconsciously when we think about things that we don't know. Even with the day-to-day stuff we *could* know, individually we often make an intuitive distinction between what we can be bothered to find out what we can't. But, when we enter the realm of the truly *unknown*, it takes on a whole new significance.

How do we deal with being told (possibly proved) that something is beyond all human knowledge? Very often, we find ourselves adopting a position of either (1) or (2) above and, which it may be can be as much a social or philosophical stance as a scientific one. In fact, we might even rewrite them again as sort of:

1. *'Wow, that's big'*, or
2. *'I don't care!'*

Take *Heisenberg's Uncertainty Principle*, for example, which, in simple terms, says there's a limit to what we can measure at the quantum level: if we look too closely, we change what we're looking at. Here it's pretty easy to see a likely difference between a scientific amazement (possibly frustration) that we can't get any closer and a wider public lack of interest.

Similarly, Turing's algorithmic *Halting Problem* and Gödel's mathematical *Algebraic Incompleteness* are scientifically limiting principles that may have the same effect.

But, to finish with, let's consider a *really* big question, one that's often considered unknowable. *What happened before the Big Bang?* Or perhaps, what *was* there before the *Big Bang* (*BB*)? On one level or another, this seems to be out of our grasp.

We have various tools to try to help … or hinder our attempt. We can search for subatomic particles capable of appearing from nowhere and catastrophic singularities in space. We can tie together notions of space and time into a single concept so we're not even sure what 'before' means any more. ("Don't ask what was before the BB: there was no *'before'* the BB".) But, at the end of the day, we're left not knowing. It's not that our science has *failed*, as such, but our ability to *apply* it from where we are in the universe is *limited*. We don't have the necessary 'vision'. Perhaps we can't 'see' far enough (in space and/or time). Perhaps we don't live in enough dimensions. If there *was* a 'before', then we can't really comprehend it; if there wasn't, then we don't really know what that *means*. And, again, how we cope with this uncertainty (and many other similar scientific unknowns) reflects our philosophy, maybe our religion – or lack thereof, more than our science.

Because, extending (1) and (2) a final time, we can either say:

1. *"That's interesting. Perhaps we're part of a bigger something that we can't see by scientific means, from where we are"*, or
2. *"Don't ask stupid questions!"*

And that may definitely say more about us than the science!

Aisha read most of the piece with light interest but a frown developed as she approached the end.

"So, is she – *are you* – suggesting that, because there might be limits to our knowledge, that proves there must be a God?" She grimaced.

"No, not necessarily," Andy shook his head, "but the possibility of something much bigger that we can't comprehend."

"OK, but that could be *anything*: a new scientific model, a better set of equations, *the spaghetti monster*: anything! It does not have to be God."

"True. But, be careful. We're not saying there *may* be things we *might not* understand; we're saying there *are* things we *can't* understand. That's significant because it limits what a new scientific theory or set of equations can achieve. But no-one's knocking science anyway. Ruth and I both recognise the value – the *beauty* – of science but we recognise its limitations too."

"But science *adapts*," insisted Aisha. "When better information comes to light, we change the models and get on with it. Eventually, we find the truth. We do not rely on unproven mythology." She spoke the last few words in a strange combination of a confrontational and apologetic tone.

But Andy just laughed, good-humouredly. "Agreed. But, as I said, I'm not having a go at science. I'm just saying, as Ruth says in her piece, that there are proven limits to where it can take us and there may be as yet unproven limits. We're limited, by where we are, as to what we can see. We're having a decent wee go at getting to grips with our universe but what's beyond it? What happened before? What comes after? We may not have the vision to *ever* answer those questions. And that's a concept that certainly isn't done any harm by knowing that there are things *within* the universe that we know we can't do. Bearing in mind that we know there's a limit to what we can see *within* the universe, I think we're being a wee bit arrogant thinking that there's nothing *beyond* it. That's not the fault of *science* – it's the science that *says* that: it's a problem with *us*! For all we know, if we're not living in enough dimensions, or something, 'beyond' and 'within' may even be the same thing! And we'll never know!"

"And you think that all of this is sorted out by believing in an old man, with a white beard, sitting on a cloud?"

There was no lessening of the grin on Andy's face but the tone became just a touch more serious.

"No, not at all. That might be what I try to talk to sometimes but I doubt that's what He looks like. That might be way beyond my understanding, or reason. It might even be too much for me to take. That's one of *my* 'Known Unknowns'. I can live with that."

"But, why does it have to be God, at all?" maintained Aisha.

"Perhaps it doesn't," admitted Andy quietly. "And perhaps there you've a working definition of '*faith*'. What do I *know*? What do I *believe*, because it's *likely*? And what do I *choose to believe* because it's *possible*? Well, I *know* that there are limits to where human knowledge can take me. It's *likely* that there's something massive out there: some great 'truth' that's beyond my comprehension. My *faith* is that I then *choose to believe* that that something massive, that great truth beyond my comprehension, *cares about me and whether I do right or wrong*. That's my *choice*."

Aisha was quiet for a few moments; then said thoughtfully.

"OK, I can see your reasoning behind that – I am not saying I *agree* with it but I *follow* it. But my problem is that your 'choice' cannot be justified: you just have no *evidence* for it."

It was Andy's turn to consider for a time. Eventually, he replied.

"Evidence isn't everything. It might sound like it should be, but it isn't. I'm not sure how to say that properly." He paused again, then clearly a thought came; he continued. "A lot more mathematicians believe in God than what we might call 'hard' scientists: physicists, chemists, biologist, etc. Ever thought why that might be the case?"

"No."

"Well, I guess it's because mathematicians tend to work with the theory of what *can* and *can't* be done rather than scientists, who are more interested in the *how*. Mathematicians are concerned with the *possible* in the abstract, whereas scientists work with the *probable* in the real world."

Aisha laughed. "You are not making a great case so far!"

"Mathematical theory," Andy continued smiling, "starts with '*axioms*', the 'rules' on which a particular system is based. Mathematicians are quite happy to *change* the axioms, the rules, to see what happens because that gives them a new system to play with – and they like that. So long as the system doesn't have obvious contradictions within it, it's probably worth looking at. To a mathematician, any well-structured system is as valid as any other. If there's nothing to say a system is downright *wrong*, then it's potentially *right*. Mathematicians don't look for particular validation of one system over another. Scientists, on the other hand, are generally only interested in one set of axioms: those they think define the universe we live in; and, of course, they have bags of evidence to support the system they've developed and not much in the way of material to argue against it – just a few unanswered questions. So, for them, that's job done. Why look any further? Why consider a different theory that's sitting quietly in the background? It's not needed, is it? But perhaps there's a wee touch of the 'rabbits and carrots' about that."

"Rabbits and carrots?"

"Aye," laughed Andy, "How do we know that carrots are good for the eyesight?"

Aisha was on the verge of trying to reply seriously before she realised Andy was attempting a joke.

"I do not know. How do we know that carrots are good for the eyesight?"

"Have you ever seen a rabbit wearing glasses?"

"I do not understand."

"Well, rabbits ..."

"No, I understand the joke. I do not get the connection."

"Alright, it's not the greatest analogy. But 'Why do we know that there's no God?' 'Because a system that's been devised without Him, doesn't need Him!'"

"Hmmm. I am still not convinced!"

"OK, let's do hard science then instead. Tell me where the universe came from, and how it relates to time?"

Aisha grinned. "A little outside of my area, but I believe there are two general theories. The first is that the universe has *always* been here, from the beginning to the end of time. The second is that everything, *including* time itself, started with the universe."

"Right," said Andy, raising a finger, "Now replace 'the universe' with 'God' in what you've just said and tell me why it suddenly makes *less sense!*"

*

"So, do you follow a particular religion, Andy?"

They were now walking back towards Jill and Bob's house, expecting to meet their friends later in the evening.

"Aye, I'm a *heretic!*"

"*Pardon?*"

"I'm a heretic," he chuckled. "Not by choice or design, you understand, but I've realised over the years that my views are potentially offensive to *everyone*: atheists and theists of all flavours. I've never met anyone who really agreed with me on everything."

"Welcome to the club!" Aisha laughed. "Some of my research is a bit like that!"

Andy thrust his hands into his coat pockets. They turned into Jill and Bob's street. Aisha pulled on her gloves. It was still cold so she put her arm through his.

As they approached the door, they could hear several security alarms sounding in the neighbourhood. A few streetlights were flashing randomly. One or two households were clearly having more serious RFS issues: raised voices of concern could be heard. There were police cars sprinkled around the area, and the occasional fire engine and ambulance. These were outnumbered by swarms of utilities vans containing engineers trying to fight the technology. RFS seemed to have worsened over the past few days. This was all becoming commonplace.

They let themselves in with the key Jill had given them before leaving for her day's volunteer work in the local charity shop. Aisha poured a small glass of wine and Andy made a cup of tea. They both fell somewhat exhausted onto the sofa. Aisha picked up the conversation as if there had been no break.

"But you wear a cross."

"Sorry?"

"You said you do not follow a particular religion but you have a cross on a chain around your neck."

"Aye." Andy gently touched his finger to his throat. "Well, it's true, I suppose, but I like to go to church from time to time so I guess I've sort of 'joined a club' to fit in with the ritual!"

"An arbitrary decision?" She smiled mischievously, thinking of the Ruth Jones post. "*Logically independent?*"

"Well almost, but not entirely. I've always found the closest identification with the things Jesus said: more than any other prophet, or whatever you want to call them. I'm not utterly convinced by the 'Son of God' thing but I like Jesus from a political perspective. I'm not quite sure if that qualifies me to call myself a Christian but I sometimes do. As, I said, I can generally upset anyone eventually!"

"So, what is wrong with the mainstream versions?"

Andy thought. "I suppose all major religions look like failed attempts to interpret God's will to me. I reckon that's better done on an individual basis. Someone once said, 'We all find our own way of being human'. I think that's right. Provided we're true to our own beliefs, our own morality, that's what's important. I'm a vegetarian, for example, but I don't try to convert other people: I just do what I think's right. But better that than blindly following something that's of dubious origin in the first place, then passed down and corrupted over the years, then misinterpreted – sometimes *deliberately*!"

"Such as?"

"Well, take Christianity then. Jesus said, quite clearly, that rich people can't go to Heaven. If they want to achieve the Kingdom of God, they have to give all their wealth away. There's not much wiggle room there. But one of Christianity's two great weaknesses is that we've spent the past two thousand years trying to pretend that he meant something else, because a lot of Christians like their wealth so they need to find another interpretation for their own peace of mind. There's no honesty in that."

"What's the second?"

"That's similar in a way: the 'Lamb of God' thing."

"Which is?"

"The argument that, provided I *say* I'm following Christ, provided I'm 'bringing the Lamb of God to the altar', I can be as big a prick as I like. I can be a hate-filled, right-wing, gun-toting red-neck bigot – just an example, you understand," he smiled, "but provided I'm doing it in Jesus's name, it's OK. I really can't buy that either."

"Does The Bible *say* that?

"Well, it allows that *interpretation*. Just as, with Islam, The Quran allows the interpretation of 'kill non-Muslims' – and that appeals to an unpleasant minority, The Bible allows the interpretation that all I have to do is run the Jesus flag up the pole and I'll go to Heaven. That seems very unlikely to me: and, of course, most Muslims and many Christians, don't take those views. But we're seeing all kinds of problems across the world right now because people choose different interpretations of scripture. I suspect the *root* cause is really *economic*; but that's another story: religion is still a willing vehicle."

"So what is the point of the sacred texts in the first place?"

"Ah, you might have something there. 'In the first place!' My guess would be that, if these writings have any validity at all, they need to be considered in terms of when they appeared. A lot of the explanations given in The Bible and Quran and Vinaya Pitaka and suchlike probably made more sense then than they do now. If we're God's children, then – like all children – we *grow*. You don't have the same rules for a teenager as you do for a wee three-year-old, do you? God's children have grown: we know more now than we did then. I can live with the idea that God sent instructions down through a sequence of prophets: Moses, Jesus, Mohammed, say; but each and every one of those would have been delivered in terms that made sense at the time. The old explanations don't stack up now because we have better science; probably most of the rules don't either: I genuinely find it hard to believe that God made gay people just to be hated, for example. Things change; science changes; *we* change. I reckon that, if God passed down a new set of directions today, it would say 'just climb out of your own arses, people' and then probably describe Heaven in terms of multi-dimensional hyperspace and string theory!"

Aisha laughed her clearest laugh of the day, her teeth gleaming in the fading light of the afternoon.

"Your heresy is very profound!" she giggled.

Andy smiled. "I can probably do better! If I was trying to hack off the largest number of people at once: non-believers, different types of believers, etc.; I'd probably say that *I think good humanists go to heaven, whether they like it or not*!"

"You mean that, ultimately, God judges actions, not words?"

"Aye, I think that's exactly what I'm saying, although I think it's been said before!"

They both laughed and rose to get more drinks. When they returned, they sat slightly closer on the sofa.

Chapter 14: Objections

Jenny and Bob were much later back than they had planned, arriving at the same time as Jill, who had been delayed by RFS problems with broken traffic signals and several accidents in central London, only narrowly escaping one herself. As they kicked off shoes and hung coats in the hall, Aisha came down from her temporary bedroom upstairs. A few minutes after, Andy also came downstairs, apparently from the bathroom. Jenny and Bob's trip report was delivered and received with some relish.

"Well, we're getting pretty much what we expected," said Bob brightly. "We're not measuring the *highest* of figures for the S Parameter but what we're getting is consistent with the model." Aisha and Andy smiled at each other with something akin to satisfaction.

"Yes," continued Jenny, with a curious glance sideways in their direction, "we get higher values where there's more network complexity of one form or another: either more network levels or connected to more parts – or both. Naturally, there's going to be some variance and inaccuracy but it's relatively consistent with what we'd expect."

"And the big piece of evidence," Bob added with clear enthusiasm, "is that we get two *different* S's at the *same* place, depending on whether the network segment we're looking at is directly connected to the rest of the Internet – the rest of It – or not. We get a higher value if it's slightly closer to the centre of It, as it were."

"But that's obvious, isn't it?" suggested Andy. "There won't be much happening if it's not connected to the outside world, will there?"

"But we're not measuring user data, remember," Jenny pointed out. "We're looking at characteristics of the *noise* – the PDN, which doesn't go away, even if we do shut off the data. Whether or not a network segment is connected, in a data sense, to the Internet, it's still connected to It via the power grid and the noise is still there in the same *quantity*. To most measurements, it doesn't change but we're interested in very particular characteristics. Looking at just the noise itself, we should see more self-similarity and feedback characteristics – a higher S Parameter, if you like," she grinned sheepishly, "when it's connected that when it's not. And we *do*." Aisha grinned broadly on hearing this.

There was a brief pause from all four. Eventually, Andy asked, "So what do we do now?"

Bob groaned inwardly: just a sigh escaped. "I suppose I'll have to take this to Stephen in the morning: it's late and they're an hour ahead of us, and I can't face it tonight, and I need to think. Not quite sure exactly what I'm going to tell him, though!"

Aisha considered for a moment.

"That we have taken measurements, based on multiple self-similarity indices, feedback structures and signal to noise ratios, from the combined entity that is the Internet, the national power grids and those networks, which, were it *not* for the power grids, would be disconnected. That these measurements are consistent with this combined physical entity having acquired a fundamental control imperative, broadly in line with similar figures known to apply to the human brain."

"Just tell him the Internet's woken up," suggested Andy, "and we're calling it '*It*'!"

"*Bloody hell!*" groaned Bob, audibly this time.

*

The next morning, the headline across all news channels was that the UK government – in accordance with most of Europe and much of the world, it seemed – had declared something amounting to a state of emergency in response to RFS. People were being advised to stay at home if possible and only make essential journeys. (At present the general definition of 'essential' included going to work.) There was limited additional advice. Private transport was extremely dangerous, largely due to signal failures and problems with utilities and the increasingly random behaviour of motorists themselves in response to RFS incidents. Public transport was better but far from ideal. Cycling avoided some of these issues but remained dangerous. Travelling, with care, by foot was suggested, if possible, for those with no choice other than to venture outside. Hospitals were cancelling some routine operations and many other administrative plans were under review in both the public and private sector. Emergency services were very stretched indeed. Domestic security and environmental control systems were becoming dangerous. A reality TV star had apparently been badly injured but his name meant nothing to The Desk. Some figures suggested that over a hundred people had now died in the UK as a result of RFS. Worldwide, estimates were as high as twenty thousand. Still no-one, it appeared, had any idea of the cause of the underlying PDN. The sustained cyber-attack theory was still by far the favoured one but was becoming somewhat stale, not least because there had been no credible claim of responsibility from any organisation. The press had begun to speculate further: 'Aliens' had been mentioned!

Bob's first call to Stephen went about as well as he expected, which was *not well*. He had chosen to approach him alone, with a personal call, as a first attempt, and to simply lay everything they felt they had before him. So, in as logical an order as he could manage, he outlined the diverse contributions of The Desk in relation to understanding PDN and RFS, the theory they had evolved to explain Its apparent sentience, the measurement they had developed to test for this and the results of their several experiments the day before. After speaking for approximately quarter of an hour, he found himself summing up.

"... So, that's what we think's happened. We're not quite sure *how* but we think that, somehow, the combination of the Internet and the power grids has reached some critical point in Its size and complexity and has started behaving primitively something like a natural nervous system; like a brain. We think the PDN is Its own internal signals; and we think that RFS is when It very occasionally, well … sort of … *gets it right*! We've modified Hatt… sorry, my holistic analysis tool … to recognise the features we'd expect to see in a human brain and we've tested it – as best we can, which isn't brilliantly, we know – in a few different places. And the results tend to support the theory. In terms of the noise, the Internet, *It*, does seem to be exhibiting those characteristics.

A long pause at the other end, terminated by a sigh.

"Bob, please be clear. What are you trying to tell me?"

"Well, that's *it* really. If you want it in simpler terms – although one of my colleagues doesn't really like it put like this, we're saying the powered Internet has achieved some level of *sentience*. It may be *conscious*. The noise isn't coming from anywhere external: it's coming from *It*."

An even longer pause; eventually a louder sigh. Stephen spoke quietly but coldly.

"Bob, we are trying to conduct an important study here. For all we know, the security of the world may be at stake. We have to work together … *sensibly*." He almost spat the last word. "If you and your team are going to engage in flights of fancy, then you are no use to me." The call was abruptly terminated.

"OK, now what?" asked Bob, turning to the rest of The Desk, observing behind him. The nature of the conversation, and its conclusion was clear to all of them. No-one replied. A gloomy air descended. Eventually, Andy suggested.

"Shall we *all* try to talk to him?"

So they tried.

*

It was over an hour before Stephen agreed to connect with them again; when he did, it was with clear reluctance. In the meantime, Bob and Jenny had rearranged Bob's office as best they could to allow all four of The Desk to take part in the video-conference. Eventually Stephen came back online, looking impatient.

"Yes, Bob?"

Bob introduced the rest of the team, unnecessarily it appeared.

"Yes, I am aware of your colleagues and their work, Bob," came the curt reply. Andy, Aisha and Jenny raised their eyebrows in surprise, causing Stephen to continue in a slightly softened tone. "Please do not be alarmed, ladies and gentlemen; it is only a routine precaution we have taken here in the office. We all have to remember we do not know who we are dealing with here." He added, after a pause, "Your work is very much appreciated, let me assure you."

"But you don't believe us?" suggested Andy.

"I find this a difficult explanation to accept," agreed Stephen quietly, after a pause. "The concept of the Internet becoming sentient sounds more like science fiction to me than science." However, this time he waited, as if expecting a response. So Andy continued.

"Aye, I agree. It's daft; it's mad! If there was *any* other credible explanation, we'd be looking at it – *but there isn't*." He paused to see the effect on Stephen, who seemed lost for words so he pressed on.

"We *have* to consider this as an explanation: there's *nothing* else! It might be *improbable* but it's all we're left with now that we've eliminated the *impossible*!"

They could see that this had some effect. The four of them continued to try to drive the argument home over the next twenty minutes. They quickly became quite skilful at this as a team. Eventually, Stephen raised a hand as if to demand a halt.

He put his fingertips together and closed his eyes in thought; finally he opened them again and spoke slowly. "I have two problems," he said thoughtfully. "Firstly I have to convince *myself* that this is credible. Secondly, if I were able to do *that*, I would have to convince the team here – including my superiors – without placing my credibility, and therefore my career, at risk. At the moment, both of those objectives look difficult ... possibly for different reasons." He spoke the last few words almost to himself.

"But will you at least consider it?" suggested Aisha.

"I will consider it," agreed Stephen, in a less than encouraging tone.

*

They waited. Hours passed. They ate a small lunch and continued to wait into the afternoon. Sitting around the kitchen table, they sipped coffee and tea in silence. Eventually, Jenny voiced what they were all thinking.

"He's not going to buy it, is he?"

They all shook their heads in agreement.

"Shall we try to contact him again?"

"I don't think he's going to talk to us any more," Bob said sadly. "From what I know of the guy, he's quite hard to persuade if he doesn't like something." He stood up to clear the lunch plates. Suddenly, Andy leaned back in his chair and said thoughtfully.

"*Possibly for different reasons.*"

"What?" asked Aisha.

"He – Stephen – said 'possibly for different reasons'. What did he mean by that?"

"Does it matter?"

"It might. I guess we're assuming that Stephen's too *practical*, too fundamentally *scientific*, to accept the idea of a sentient Internet. But suppose, that's not it. Suppose he – maybe even someone else he knows on the team there – might have some *principled* objection as to why it couldn't happen?"

"You mean a *religious* objection?" suggested Bob.

"Possibly," agreed Andy. "Perhaps the concept's alien to some assumed belief he has, or thinks one of his bosses has?"

"Maybe. But that doesn't really help us, does it?" asked Aisha.

"Perhaps it could," Andy muttered, pulling his tablet from his bag. "Here, have a look at this. This is Ruth Jones's most recent post. It's a very interesting way of looking at the whole AI thing, although it's based on Turing's original work. Maybe, if we were to put this argument to him, it might at least disturb a few preconceptions?"

Bob brought the post up on the large display screen and they all read:

"The 'Theological Objection'"

This month's post considers a little-remembered part of Turing's otherwise famous 1950 paper on AI.

Just for once, this month, let's not skirt around the generally problematic issue of 'real intelligence' compared with 'artificial intelligence' and ask what it means for a machine (a robot, if you like, for simplicity) to have the *whole package*: not just some abstract ability to calculate, process, adapt, etc. but 'human intelligence', 'self-awareness', 'sentience'; the 'Full Monty', as it were. Star Trek's 'Data' if you like, assuming we've understood what the writers had in mind correctly.

Of course, we're not really going to build such a robot, nor even come anything close to designing one. We're just going to ask whether it's *possible* to create a machine with *consciousness*. Even that's fraught with difficulty, however, because we may not be able to define 'consciousness' to everyone's satisfaction but let's try the simple, optimistic version of 'consciousness' broadly meaning 'a state of self-awareness like a human'. Is that possible?

Well, there's no place to start other than by considering what consciousness *is*. Where does consciousness come from? What are the rules? What *can* have consciousness and what *can't*? What are the requirements?

OK, this if difficult. We're never going to all agree – that's not the point. But, just like the Fermi Paradox, the question *must* have an answer. However unsatisfactory any given answer might be, one of them must be *right*. So what are the possibilities?

Well, here are those generally regarded as the more credible contenders; not each and every one individually, but roughly combined into 'types' of explanation:

1.Consciousness is just the result of *neural complexity*. Build something with a big enough 'brain' and it will acquire consciousness. There's possibly some sort of critical neural mass and/or degree of connectivity for this to happen.

166

2.Similar to 1 but the brain needs *energy*. It needs power (food, fuel, electricity, etc.) to make it work.

3.Similar to 2 but with some *symbiosis*. A physical substrate is needed to carry signals of a particular type. The relationship between the substrate and signals (hardware and software) takes a particular critical form (maybe the two are indistinguishable) and we don't know what it is yet.

4.Similar to 3 but there's a *biological* requirement in there somewhere. Consciousness is the preserve of carbon life forms, perhaps. How and/or why we don't understand yet.

5.Similar to 4 but whatever it is that's special about carbon-based life will remain one of the great *unknowns of the universe* (see last month's post). There might not be anything particularly remarkable about it from a philosophical perspective: it's just beyond *us*.

6.Similar to 5 but there's actually something *very* 'special' about the whole thing. Way beyond us.

7.A particular form of 6. Consciousness is somehow *separate* from the underlying hardware but still can't exist *without* it.

8.Extending 7. Consciousness is completely separate from the body and could exist *independently*. We might call it a *'soul'*.

9.Taking 8 to the limit? Consciousness, the soul, comes from *God*.

Now, there's a sort of progression suggested here. Of course, the human brain could satisfy any of these explanations, which is why they're credible. ('Credible' here means logically non-contradictory: it's got nothing to do with any of our particular preconceptions.) It's generally argued, however, that a robot could only get so far down the list. In other words, with technology improving all the time, we've already done 1 and 2 and, with further advances, 3, possibly even 4, might be manageable. So, if the first four aren't the right definitions, we'll eventually prove it by building a robot satisfying all the requirements, which doesn't achieve sentience. (We'll not consider here the somewhat thorny question of how we'd necessarily *know*!)

The other way this ordering is often informally portrayed is as some progression from the 'ultra-scientific' to the 'ultra-spiritual'. Many people's version of 'common sense' comes somewhere in the middle, often without them being able to precisely articulate it.

However, this is where Alan Turing throws a massive spanner into the works! But, to understand it, we need to recap a little ...

In his seminal 1950 paper, "Computing Machinery and Intelligence", published in the journal, "Mind", Turing starts:

"I propose to consider the question, 'Can machines think?' This should begin with definitions of the meaning of the terms 'machine' and 'think'. The definitions might be framed so as to reflect so far as possible the normal use of the words, but this attitude is dangerous, If the meaning of the words 'machine' and 'think' are to be found by examining how they are commonly used it is difficult to escape the conclusion that the meaning and the answer to the question, 'Can machines think?' is to be sought in a statistical survey such as a Gallup poll. But this is absurd. Instead of attempting such a definition I shall replace the question by another, which is closely related to it and is expressed in relatively unambiguous words. The new form of the problem can be described in terms of a game which we call the 'imitation game'."

That should be familiar enough by now. We've all seen the film! Can a human tell another human and a machine apart? What he had in mind was:

"It was suggested tentatively that the question, 'Can machines think?' should be replaced by 'Are there imaginable digital computers which would do well in the imitation game?' If we wish we can make this superficially more general and ask 'Are there discrete-state machines which would do well?' But in view of the universality property we see that either of these questions is equivalent to this, 'Let us fix our attention on one particular digital computer. Is it true that by modifying this computer to have an adequate storage, suitably increasing its speed of action, and providing it with an appropriate programme, it can be made to play satisfactorily ... in the imitation game, [and convince] a man?'"

And then there's a famous prediction, now almost universally misunderstood as 'The Turing Test'.

"It will simplify matters for the reader if I explain first my own beliefs in the matter. Consider first the more accurate form of the question. I believe that in about fifty years' time it will be possible, to programme computers, with a storage capacity of about 10^9, to make them play the imitation game so well that an average interrogator will not have more than 70 per cent chance of making the right identification after five minutes of questioning. The original question, 'Can machines think?' I believe to be too meaningless to deserve discussion. Nevertheless I believe that at the end of the century the use of words and general educated opinion will have altered so much that one will be able to speak of machines thinking without expecting to be contradicted."

That's water under the bridge as far as this post is concerned. Perhaps few people will ever read this part of the paper properly!

However, the interesting section, as far as our earlier discussion of consciousness is concerned, comes later in the paper. Turing was only too aware of the impact, probably negative, his predictions were going to have in the scientific and spiritual communities and on a wider plane so he tried to head several of them off at the pass. A large part of the paper is devoted to his consideration of several 'objections' presented in the form of an initial anticipated criticism followed by a counter-argument. Top of the list, as predicted by Turing is the *"The Theological Objection"*, which he suggests as:

"Thinking is a function of man's immortal soul. God has given an immortal soul to every man and woman, but not to any other animal or to machines. Hence no animal or machine can think."

He then systematically dismantles the objection as follows:

"I am unable to accept any part of this, but will attempt to reply in theological terms. I should find the argument more convincing if animals were classed with men, for there is a greater difference, to my mind, between the typical animate and the inanimate than there is between man and the other animals. The arbitrary character of the orthodox view becomes clearer if we consider how it might appear to a member of some other religious community. How do Christians regard the Moslem

169

view that women have no souls? But let us leave this point aside and return to the main argument. It appears to me that the argument quoted above implies a serious restriction of the omnipotence of the Almighty. It is admitted that there are certain things that He cannot do such as making one equal to two, but should we not believe that He has freedom to confer a soul on an elephant if He sees fit? We might expect that He would only exercise this power in conjunction with a mutation which provided the elephant with an appropriately improved brain to minister to the needs of this sort. An argument of exactly similar form may be made for the case of machines. It may seem different because it is more difficult to 'swallow'. But this really only means that we think it would be less likely that He would consider the circumstances suitable for conferring a soul. The circumstances in question are discussed in the rest of this paper. In attempting to construct such machines we should not be irreverently usurping His power of creating souls, any more than we are in the procreation of children: rather we are, in either case, instruments of His will providing mansions for the souls that He creates.

Now, we need to be a little careful with this. Firstly, Turing's reading of some sacred texts may be questionable (possibly even offensive; although he would hardly be the first to have managed a dubious interpretation of scripture: we're still doing that). And we can see that he had no time for any God or religion whatsoever: that's unambiguous. However, the interesting bit is his '*OK, just supposing ...*' position.

What Turing points out in his defence to the 'theological objection' is that saying intelligence (*consciousness*, adapted for the purposes of this post) isn't just the result of machine complexity is effectively *telling God what He can and can't do. We* might *prefer* the later options in the list above but it's not *we* that decide. For all we know, God may be just waiting for us to build a robot with a big enough brain for Him to put sentience (even a soul, if you like) into! It's *His* universe, *His* rules, *His* science: *He'll* decide surely, not us!

So the perceived 'ultra-scientific' to the 'ultra-spiritual' progression in our 1-9 list above may not make sense at all, viewed in those terms; not if God can decide *any* of them are right.

In fact, we can actually take God temporarily out of the discussion and muddy the waters ourselves now, by rewriting the list but adding a new 'option zero':

0. *Everything* has consciousness to some extent, even an apparently inanimate object like a rock. The *universe* is conscious. We're just not very good at seeing this. (This is *'panpsychism'*.)

1. Consciousness is just the result of neural *complexity*. Build something with a big enough 'brain' and it will acquire consciousness. So 0 is broadly right but there's some sort of critical neural mass and/or degree of connectivity for consciousness to happen.

2. Similar to 1 but ...

:   :   :   :

8. ... could exist independently. We might call it a *'soul'*.

9. Taking 8 to the limit? Consciousness, the soul, comes from *God*.

Now, 0 leads nicely into 1. Panpsychism (0) suggests that *everything* has consciousness. The next option (1) says its neural complexity just has to reach some *critical point*. But, to most general philosophies, 0 is pretty close to 9 as well. The *'spirit of the universe'* in universal consciousness is some people's way of saying 'God' and our taxonomy has gone out of the window. In fact, it suddenly looks cyclic.

So, where do you nail your colours now?

*

"OK, it's an interesting argument," agreed Jenny. "But will it convince Stephen?"

"Who knows?" Bob sighed. "But what else have we got?" He sent the link to Stephen as a message.

"Please find a few minutes to read this!" was all he could think to say.

Chapter 15: Persuasion

"This does not mean I *believe* you; it means I am prepared to *talk* to you. You are unlikely to convince me but you may *try*."

It was mid-afternoon; The Desk was in video-conference with Stephen once more. The others waited for him to continue, but they waited in vain: he said nothing else, merely sat in silence. However, they already had something of a strategy – an approach – planned in the hours without contact, in the hope that it might eventually be restored.

So, as agreed, Jenny tried to expand the discussion.

"So what's the current situation, Stephen? Are there any developments? Any patterns emerging with PDN and RFS?"

"Clearly getting worse," was his sharp reply. "We are detecting gradually increasing levels of noise on all physical networks. We also think the ratio of meaningful signals on the communications networks is increasing too. And, of course, this is consistent with our observations – *everyone's* observations – that RFS is getting steadily more serious as well. Many countries are now advising their citizens not to leave their homes if this can be avoided or to take extreme care if it cannot.

"Although we do not know the root cause of the problem, we accept that today's '*Internet of Everything*' is playing a role. The fact that huge numbers of operable electrical devices are able to be controlled over the Internet is naturally increasing their vulnerability to attack – *whatever* that attack may be. Most of the damage, accidents, injuries and fatalities are being caused by malfunctioning devices. Our specialist engineers are working hard to address this problem in an effective way. We are currently advising national governments and major supply organisations – those in Europe, of course – of techniques that may make equipment potentially less dangerous. Our experts are helping them to make end systems as safe as possible, putting in extra hardware or software – *circuitry or code* – to try to ensure that they fail in a controlled manner if they are going to fail at all. Much of this should have already been in place by default but it is disappointing how many of these systems are currently failing … *not safe*." He tailed off as his, usually excellent, English deserted him for a moment.

"It's really not *that* surprising," suggested Jenny, taking advantage of the pause. "Just imagine the billions of devices that are connected to the IoE nowadays. A few years ago, very few failed anyway because there weren't so many around. When one in ten thousand did, it was barely noticed. But now that they're *all* under stress … from *whatever it is*," she glanced uncertainly at the others, "there will be a lot going wrong at the same time – you just can't beat those odds. There are *bound* to be accidents – *lots* of them."

"Yes, agreed," Stephen nodded, "which is why we have another approach. Where it is not possible to isolate wired systems or make them safe with confidence, we are now enabling *wireless* connections wherever possible. Since we know that PDN is absent from these networks, they should be safe."

Bob nearly choked on his coffee.

"*I really don't think that's a good idea!*" he spluttered.

"Can I ask why?" Stephen asked calmly but with an undertone of impatience.

"Because, well … look, you just have to play along with our theory for a moment …"

"As Alan Turing did when he dealt with the 'theological objection'?" asked Stephen. They all smiled. So, he *had* read Ruth Jones's post!

"Yes, something like that," Bob continued. "If we're right that we're dealing with some sort of primitive sentience here, It will get *worse* (or, from Its perspective, *better*) if It figures out how to use wireless!"

"Explain?"

Aisha struck in. "It is to do with Its neural size and connection complexity," she explained. "At the moment, if you take into account the Internet itself and all the devices and *things* – as you call them in IoE terms – that are connected to It, *and* all the bits and pieces that are physically connected through the

173

power grids, then you have something that is much, much larger than a human brain in Its basic neural count. However, It is not anything like as densely connected as the human brain: each neuron at the lowest logical level is only connected to a few others.

"On that basis, It appears to be exhibiting *some* essential control imperative, but Its behaviour is restricted and primitive. In relation to a human brain, Its greater size is being limited by Its reduced connectivity. Our measurements suggest that, although Its own signals – what we see as PDN – have *some* of the characteristic patterns of the human brain, these are currently at a much lower level.

"However, were It to begin using the wireless links, this would have a dramatic effect. Although Its neural size would not increase considerably – because much of the wireless infrastructure is already connected through the power grids, Its connectivity density would increase *massively*. Certain nodes would potentially be able to communicate with *any others in range*. Its overall neural complexity would suddenly be huge. It might even be something close to human brain levels when we take both size and connectivity into account."

"It would have many of the self-similar, and *scale-free* characteristics of a human brain too," added Jenny.

Stephen nodded his understanding of these terms. "But why *should* we expect … the wireless links … *to become active*?" He clearly chose his words in a careful, non-committal manner.

"Because there's no *real difference* between wired and wireless links as far as It's concerned," Bob argued. "Both ends are plugged into the mains so It can *see* both ends: it's all *internal* as far as It's concerned. Between the transmit and receive, there's just air instead of cable but that's still a communications medium. And, of course, we're *showing* it *how* to use it all the time with our own data."

"It *has* to be only a matter of time before It figures out how to use wireless," Jenny agreed forcefully. "Then you'll have something altogether worse on your hands!"

Half an hour later and they were in conference again. There was a more desperate edge to Stephen's voice now.

"So, ladies and gentlemen, apart from your *theory*, what do you have by way of evidence to *support* it?"

Bob had already attempted to explain the derivation and testing of the 'S Parameter' earlier in the day but Stephen had been far from receptive then. Realising that he was giving their explanation a little more consideration now, Aisha quickly reiterated the essential details.

"OK, we believe that the combined entity – 'It' – has acquired a fundamental control imperative. That means that Its individual components, at *all* levels, have begun acting as neuron comparators in an attempt to assess control of Its environment and to minimise Its assessment of lack of control. This means that the noise we see, what we are calling PDN, will have certain observable characteristics. We have some data as to how these characteristics may appear in the human brain."

"The signals in the brain," continued Jenny with similar urgency, "have recognisable levels of self-similarity, scale-free networks, feedback loops and increased levels of signal to noise ratios. We've put all of that together into a single ... 'S' parameter that we can measure." She still winced saying it out loud: she certainly was not going to give it its agreed name, but then she had a sudden thought. "That just stands for *'Sentience Parameter'*," she said quickly, poking her tongue out at the others. "We've normalised it to *0.75* for the human brain but anything between *0.5* and *1 could* indicate activity of that form: the higher the more brain-like."

"And we've tested it," said Bob, maintaining the pace, "as best we can. We're getting figures of between *0.5* – never *less* – and *0.6* depending on *where* exactly we are in It."

"That's low," admitted Jenny, "but there are probably two reasons for that. Firstly, we're still close to the 'edge' of It in all of our tests so far – the best result was from the *Janet* network – so we're not seeing what you might call an *integrated* brain because It's not as massively connected as the human version. Secondly, for the same reason, we're not getting the full scale-free effect."

"But we get a higher figure for connected networks than disconnected ones – even though the actual level of noise remains the same. That has to imply some order, some *control*, we think." Bob took his turn. "And, if It *does* start using the wireless capabilities It doesn't yet know It's got, then those figures will go *up* because It will be much – *hugely* – more densely connected and there won't be so much of an *edge* to worry about!"

They all paused for breath. Stephen considered for what seemed like an age. Eventually, he spoke slowly, and clearly reluctantly.

"Here, we have access to parts of the Internet that I think you would consider further from the *edge* of *It* as you refer to it. We could arrange for your tests to be carried out at significant central European node centres. If we were to do that, would you predict *higher* values for your 'Sentience Parameter'?"

"*Yes!*" cried Jenny and Bob in unison. Aisha and Andy nodded.

"And would you consider your theory vindicated if we were to read such values?"

"Yes, certainly." Jenny, Bob *and* Aisha now. Andy, however, had a suspicious look. Stephen continued.

"And would you accept your theory disproven by the absence of such an increase?"

"Mmm, OK," they replied quietly, with distinctly less enthusiasm.

*

"I have discussed this with a single, very trusted colleague," said Stephen, when they spoke again a short while later. "She now shares my somewhat loose opinion that this is an unlikely theory," a pause, "… but one that may be worthy of further investigation." The Desk beamed at one another in satisfaction.

"So, how quickly can we perform your tests here?" asked Stephen bluntly.

Jenny and Bob stared at each other in alarm, realising this was not something they had given much consideration.

"Um, I suppose Hattie and I could be with you in a couple of days," suggested Bob. "Maybe tomorrow night at a push?" He avoided Jill's glare as she came in to collect empty cups and glasses.

"Or, maybe we could send you the code?" asked Jenny, more as an enquiry of Bob than Stephen. Bob looked uncomfortable.

"That's going to be difficult," he admitted. "Hattie's a thing unto herself now." He decided to give up with her formal title once and for all. "She's been adapted and rewritten so many times, the closest thing she has to an operating system isn't much like *anything* else. Getting something together in the way of code that might run on whatever you have there could be very hard indeed. I'd have to pull together quite a few threads from different parts. Then I wouldn't really be able to test it before I sent it … and I'm not sure how we'd validate it … and I'd be surprised if it worked over there, if I'm honest." He ground to something of a halt.

"Nevertheless, I think that is our only option at this point, Bob," said Stephen. "I cannot authorise a visit from you without some justification. My superiors would not allow it: in fact, I suspect they would take me off the case if they knew what we were proposing."

*

So Bob, assisted as best she could by Jenny, tried, over the remainder of the afternoon and evening, to package Hattie's analysis code together in a form that could be sent electronically to Stephen's colleague – a young woman, with a harsh tone, who would remain forever officially nameless. This aspect of their collaboration no longer surprised Bob. They held frequent, short conferences – with and without Stephen – in order to establish what the target platform was and what physical testing equipment

'*George*' (as they began to call her offline) had access to. Stephen's European team now had very sophisticated monitoring equipment that might even surpass Hattie's accuracy and reach; but it was only *modelled* on Bob's description of her operation, not her actual hardware and software. Consequently, the transition was always going to be a difficult one.

It took Bob and Jenny over an hour to pull the necessary code together, with Bob far from optimistic. They then iterated many attempts with 'George'. Sure enough, at first, the code would not load for her at all on her platform. When it eventually did, it produced syntax errors when it compiled. George proved herself quickly to be a developer of no small skill as she gradually adapted Bob's code to her environment. Then she had to debug several run-time errors. Even when running without crashing, the software then would not talk to the monitoring hardware. When it finally did so, it produced meaningless – and obviously wrong – results. Bob and Jenny adjusted and revised and advised. They kept going …

*

In the early evening, while Jenny, Bob (and George) continued to work on the analysis code, Aisha and Andy announced they were going out for a coffee. This was met with a slight nod from Bob and a smile from Jenny. Jill, who was passing through the room to check on the house's climate control (which appeared to be playing up again: RFS undoubtedly), asked with some concern.

"Do you think it's OK to go out?"

"We can't sit inside for ever," Andy grumbled. "Whatever's going on, we have to get on with our lives somehow."

"The government advice is that walking is about as safe as anything," agreed Bob.

"We are only going to the place we stopped off at yesterday, on our way home," explained Aisha. "We will be back in less than an hour."

"Have fun," laughed Jenny, as they let themselves out of the front door.

Jenny and Bob were so engrossed with their work that they failed to notice the hour come and go. Nearly two had passed when Jill came to ask.

"Are they not back yet?"

Jenny cast an alarmed look at the clock. "No, they're not. It's been a while hasn't it?"

"I hope they haven't hit problems," Bob said. "That place is only a few hundred yards away, isn't it?"

"Just round the corner from the end of the street," agreed Jill, drawing the curtain to one side to look. "You can see two-thirds of the way from here. But there's no sign of them."

Another half an hour passed. Jenny and Bob continued to work but with frequent anxious glances at the clock. Jill looked out of the window every few minutes. Eventually, she announced.

"I can see them. That's them. They're coming." Bob blew a silent whistle of relief; Jenny released a deep breath. But Jill continued.

"*Although something looks wrong.*"

The other two rushed to the window.

"What's happened?" asked Jenny.

About two hundred yards away, two figures – one slight and average height, the other a few inches taller and much stockier – were visible in the gloom. Streetlights lit them from random angles as they flashed on and off. The larger figure was being supported by the smaller. Jill and Jenny rushed out to help. Bob made preparations to call for assistance, if required.

As the three of them re-entered a few minutes later, each trying somewhat ineffectually to support Andy, Bob was relieved to see the familiar wry grin on his face. Perhaps more grimace than grin, it might be said, but Andy was clearly in at least a degree of control of the situation. A hastily tied bandage around his knee, his trouser leg torn away above it, threatened to tell a different story, however.

"What the hell happened to you?" cried Bob.

Jill and Jenny relieved Aisha of her share of the burden and helped Andy to the sofa. Aisha regained her breath after her exertions and related the story.

"An accident. It is really mad out there! On the way to the coffee shop, we saw so many things going wrong. There are police cars and ambulances and fire engines everywhere. Also, there are engineers and people like that working all over the place. I suppose they are trying to fix things like Stephen said.

"Anyway, the coffee shop was mostly open but things were not running smoothly. The barista said that all the businesses and shops and outlets had been told to try to stay open. People are trying not to let RFS affect them more than it has to. Everyone still thinks it is a terrorist cyber-attack and they are determined not to let them win!

"So it took a long time for them to make coffee: there was a large queue. Many people it seems are still trying to carry on as normal. *Like us!*" She looked with concern at Andy. "Eventually, we left to come home.

"But we had only walked about fifty yards when there was some sort of crash … in the road, I mean. I am not exactly sure what happened but the signals seemed to go wrong and a car and a cyclist collided. The cyclist hit a sign at the side of the road and came off his bike. The bike carried on and hit Andy. It hit him very hard on the leg," she said with some emotion.

"It's really not that bad," Andy grumbled roughly from the sofa. "The cyclist is in a much worse way. There was an ambulance passing. As Aisha says they're all over the place. It stopped to check us out; but it was already taking one guy to hospital so they couldn't fit both of us in. They took the cyclist because he couldn't stand but they just patched me up and said that was probably the best they could do under the circumstances. They all seem really stretched. *It's really not good out there.*"

*

Finally, the code ran on George's platform. She messaged Bob to tell him and The Desk converged around their monitors. George came online; Stephen joined her.

"I have tested this and I know it produces a result," George informed them uncertainly. "But I have some doubts. Firstly, the code I have managed to get to work here takes longer to converge to an answer than yours. I believe yours takes one minute; here it takes several: five or six maybe. That does not seem right since we have much faster processors here. Secondly, I cannot claim complete confidence in the manner in which the software is polling the sensors for the noise readings. We get a *sensible* result but I have limited confidence in its absolute *accuracy*."

"We can but see," said Stephen quietly. "Shall we run it and see what happens?"

"Yes, let's go," agreed Bob. Then a thought occurred. "So, what have you got access to there in Luxembourg to look at?" As he spoke, George leaned over her console and pressed a key, which presumably started the analysis.

"We are not in Luxembourg," said Stephen in a slightly surprised tone. "Why would you think we are in Luxembourg?"

"Because that's where we met. I just assumed you were still there!"

"No Bob, I have not been in Luxembourg since the afternoon we parted. Since then, I have been in Barcelona, Berlin and Milan. I have spoken to you from all those places. Our systems automatically mask out locations reasonably well. Someone like you would know how to bypass this if required but I suppose you have not felt the need to do this?"

"No," agreed Bob. "I'd just assumed you were still in Luxembourg so I didn't look! So where are you now?"

"We are in Paris," George informed them. "We are currently running your code at one of the largest European switching centres, which we have access to here."

"There will not be any need to divulge further detail at this stage," interrupted Stephen, with a disapproving glance at her.

"Wow! That should give us something," said Jenny, clearly impressed.

The analysis took another few minutes to run. It seemed like an hour. Eventually, George moved forwards just slightly in her chair and announced, "It has finished." She twisted her smartwatch to point at her screen. After a split second of auto-focus, they all read:

$S = 6.14$

They all simultaneously emitted a noise – a sigh, a groan, which was part relief – part disappointment. Jenny was the first to speak.

"It's not *much*; but it *is* higher than anything we've seen in the UK." Bob and Andy nodded. Aisha looked anxious. Stephen slowly cupped his eyes and forehead in his hand. When he removed his hand and faced them again, he looked – for the first time since Bob had known him – like man who was not in control of the situation. His voice, when he spoke, was almost imploring.

"Can I *really* take *this* to my superiors?"

"I think you have to," said Aisha, quietly but firmly.

*

Their final video-conference took place at midnight: a short affair. Stephen appeared on screen looking pale and haggard.

"Well, ladies and gentlemen, I have fulfilled my promise. I have taken your concept of a sentient Internet to the remainder of my team and my superiors. I think it is reasonable to say that they appear unimpressed with the possibility, or the *credibility*, of such an explanation. However, they have agreed to discuss it with me again early tomorrow morning. I suspect they will either embrace the concept in a limited form, along with the various other theories under consideration; so you may be invited to join us here. Or ..."

"Or?" prompted Andy.

"Or," Stephen continued reluctantly, "I imagine I will no longer be a part of this investigation. I would say that would mean that there would be someone else for you to speak to by tomorrow; but it is probably more likely that no-one here will then wish to talk to you at all. Goodnight everyone. I hope this is not Goodbye although I believe it may be." The connection was closed abruptly.

There was nothing more to do or say; The Desk prepared for bed for the night. Jenny glanced at Andy and Aisha, putting away the dishes together, and smiled.

"I'll just collect my things from upstairs," she announced. "I'll sleep downstairs on the couch tonight."

"Why?" asked Bob, astonished.

"Bob," laughed Jill, re-entering his office from the living room, "you may be good at detecting network traffic but you're pretty hopeless with real life!"

*

But, in fact, none of them had quite the night they were expecting.

It happened around three o'clock in the morning, not entirely instantaneously but quickly. The, by now commonplace, occasionally noisy, RFS confusion inside and outside suddenly escalated. Lights flashed and alarms sounded everywhere in the house and multiplied many times, it seemed, in the neighbourhood. As the five of them converged in panic to the kitchen, their first task was to unplug several appliances, which had been hitherto behaving themselves. One of the remote TV screens switched on and screamed broken data. Outside, something sounded like an explosion in the distance. Then sirens.

"*What on earth is happening?*" Jill screamed. Bob held her close and glanced at the wifi router, flashing error lights in the corner of the adjacent room.

"*I'd say It's figured out how to use wireless!*"

PHASE FOUR: TREATMENT

Chapter 16: Extended Horizons

There was an extent to which normality could be restored and an extent to which it could not; and this was slowly unveiled through the morning as both a local and global principle. In the Weatherill household, misbehaving appliances were unplugged as necessary. Some were optimistically or experimentally plugged back in again. If this temporary disconnection solved a particular device's issue, it was left; otherwise it was taken out once more, and so on. Some things could be left on with wireless disabled; for others, this reconfiguration was not so easy – and did not always help anyway: the increased RFS was almost everywhere and now had more than one attack vector in many cases. Also, unfortunately, the situation was not consistent – or stable – or predictable – and many devices then 'reoffended' at a later time or showed their first signs of misbehaviour suddenly and without warning. If the sound from the surrounding neighbourhood was anything to go by, this scene was being re-enacted far-and-wide. '*How* far?' they all wondered as they battled their own local chaos.

It took nearly an hour to exert what was clearly the limit of their control. One thing that could not be fixed quickly was the heating: the house was very cold. Devices were still prone to erratic behaviour from time to time but they had reduced the overall disruption to a level by which these individual RFS outbreaks could be dealt with as and when they occurred. In fact, they had to remind themselves repeatedly that this was 'still *just* RFS': the abrupt escalation made the old problem appear new somehow. The world, which had already become a hazardous place over the past week or two, suddenly seemed even more dangerous.

There was unspoken agreement from The Desk that there was to be no further attempt at sleep that night; it would have been difficult anyway: there were almost no periods of sustained quiet now. Shortly after four o'clock, with as much made right in the house as could be, Bob reconnected Hattie to his laptop interface and set her to take another reading. They all gathered round and read:

$S = 0.710$

"Bloody Hell!" grunted Andy.

"I said this would happen," said Bob with the closest he could manage to a nonchalant shrug.

"And we knew what would happen when it did," agreed Aisha.

Bob also pointed at Hattie's various oscilloscope displays. "Look, there's noise on the actual wifi signals being received as well. We're right: It's figured out how to use Its wireless links too."

"Could that be background?" suggested Jenny. "Crossover?"

"Possible," conceded Bob. "But I don't think so at those levels. *And*, it wasn't there before. *Something's* happened!"

They then connected Hattie back to the broadband box for the outside line and measured there.

$S = 0.719$

"That's interesting," noted Jenny. "It's higher; we'd expect that. But it's not *that* much higher."

"That is because there is not so much of an *edge* to It any more," said Aisha. "It is more massively connected now; more like a human brain in terms of self-similarity and scale-free structure."

"*Just* how much like a human brain?" asked Andy.

"We may have to wait and see," said Aisha gloomily.

*

No-one was particularly surprised by Stephen's coming back online at an early hour. They were, however, taken aback by his appearance. He looked pale and drawn in a way that his presumed sudden awakening might only partially explain. His familiar control now seemed to have completely deserted him. When he spoke, it almost seemed as he was unaware what he was going to say until he heard it himself. Only his civility and his general crispness of language remained.

"I assume we have entered a new phase, ladies and gentlemen." They could not tell whether this was supposed to be a question or a statement. Eventually, Jenny offered something by way of return.

"Yes, we think so. We think that It has learned how to ..." She paused, then continued in a different vein. "We suspect that the PDN problem has spread to *wireless* links."

"It has," Stephen agreed with a fatalistic air. "We have reports and readings from across Europe and the rest of the world. There is now noise on most types of wireless links, both long and short range."

"We *did* say that this could happen," Aisha said softly. She added nothing more but waited for the reply.

"Yes, you did, indeed," agreed Stephen eventually. "But there is something more."

"Yes?" asked Bob, expectantly.

"We think ... our data suggests that ..., since PDN has appeared on *wireless* links, there has been an effect on *wired* links as well."

They all nodded. Jenny's eyes narrowed. "Go on ...?"

"We believe that the appearance of PDN on the wireless networks, has coincided with an increase in RFS in devices on wired networks too, even those with *no* wireless components." He may have been about to continue but was interrupted by Jenny slamming her hand down hard on the table in front of the screen.

"*Yes!*"

Stephen nodded his understanding.

"I would assume you find this information consistent with your model of a large, powered *sentient* Internet? You would argue that the increased ... shall we say 'activity' ... on the wired components is the result of its increased overall complexity due to the extra connectivity provided by the newly activated wireless links?"

They all nodded.

"Yes, It's not hugely *bigger*, but It's more densely *connected*," agreed Jenny.

"More like the human brain," confirmed Aisha.

"So, the increased *complexity* in *some* places has given It increased *activity everywhere*," offered Bob by way of further explanation. "There's no *conventional* network model that I can think of that can explain that. Normal signals – even malicious ones – wouldn't propagate like that. We *have* to be looking at some sort of *integrated* brain activity here!"

"Aye, and we've taken new S Parameter measurements this morning," continued Andy, "and they're quite a wee bit higher. Its sentience measure," a wry look at Jenny, "is close to what we'd expect from …, well, *us*."

"I have also taken that reading here," agreed Stephen. The Desk exchanged puzzled looks. Why would Stephen be taking the reading? Perhaps George was not in work yet: it *was* still very early even if Europe was an hour ahead. They allowed him to continue.

"We have a new figure here for your 'Sentience Parameter' of *0.727*," Stephen informed them. "This is taken from the same network position, with the same parameters, as last night. How does this compare with *your* revised figures?"

"*0.710* on a wireless host and *0.719* on domestic ATM," said Bob.

Stephen nodded once more.

"And we think that this is also consistent with your …," he hesitated, sighed, and continued, "with *our* theory?" he suggested with an air of resignation.

"Yes," said Jenny with something of a triumphant look at the others. "Firstly the figure's *higher* everywhere. Secondly, it's more *uniform* everywhere. There seems to be less of an edge to It."

"Which gives It more of the overall scale-free self-similarity of the human brain," agreed Aisha.

Although no-one made any comment, they all understood the significance of Stephen's choice of words: he may have been won over. But there was something more in his tone that made Andy ask:

"So, Stephen, have you spoken to *other* people about this, this morning? *Since* last night?"

Stephen nodded but said nothing. Andy continued.

"And what did they say?"

"As I already told you," Stephen said slowly, "they were considerably less than receptive last night. Of course, I was less than entirely convinced myself. However, my final words to them, before we left for our homes, were fortuitous. I informed them of your prediction that the wireless links would become active at some point. I also explained what you believed would then happen, based on your theory of a sentient Internet. (I am aware that is something of a simplification of your actual model but I was not prepared to elaborate then.) They dismissed my suggestion somewhat ruggedly, shall we say? They came close to dismissing me too, I believe."

"But this morning?" Andy pressed.

"This morning we have held an emergency meeting to consider these new developments. There was much to discuss, of course, and provision has to be made for dealing with the escalated situation. I would naturally have reminded them of your comments regarding the wireless links but this was not necessary: they remembered well enough."

"So …?"

"So, there is, I suppose, good and bad news."

They waited expectantly. Stephen continued.

"The good news is that there is a balance of opinion here in the central team that there may be some validity to your argument." The Desk said nothing, only waited expectantly, so he continued. "There is a majority view now *that we may be dealing with a sentient Internet*."

"And the bad news?" Andy asked quietly.

"*That we may be dealing with a sentient Internet!*"

*

They were speaking again in less than an hour. Stephen began with a very focused question.

"I have been instructed to ask you, ladies and gentlemen," he began, "taking your theory as a working hypothesis, whether you believe our actions have hastened the events of early this morning?"

They felt they probably understood the question but no-one was quite confident enough to reply. Eventually, Jenny took up the case.

"Do you mean, did the policy of switching wired networks to wireless help It learn how to use Its wireless links quicker?"

Stephen nodded. They all glanced uncertainly at each other. Bob volunteered an opinion.

"I don't think we can really say," he conceded. "It's possible, of course, but not certain."

"It would have happened anyway eventually," suggested Aisha. "It is a natural part of the brain's function to find out how best to use its own structure. That may be the most basic part of its control imperative. This is how it deals with internal damage and copes with new external inputs from artificial implants, for example. It naturally discovers how to make use of its full range of hardware. Often, in the human brain, certain paths do not work so it automatically finds out how to use others. In *Its* – the sentient Internet's – case, the wireless links were there to be used all along. It was *aware* of both ends of each link so it was probably natural that It should learn how to use the channel in between. Of course, once it had discovered how to use just one, or a few, It would have had a global solution very quickly." She paused for breath, but added, "We may never know if we actually precipitated that discovery by giving It more wireless links to observe."

"And does it really matter?" asked Andy.

"It does in a tangential sense," Stephen said carefully. "Three things about you all have impressed me, my team and my superiors. Firstly, we have appreciated your analytical skills for some time; we also recognise how you each bring individual experience to your group and how strong the collective result is. Secondly, if you are correct in your explanation of PDN and RFS, then you are probably ahead of anyone else in the world in this at the present time; this ability to find explanations is valuable beyond measure because we might reasonably expect solutions to come from similar creative sources. Thirdly, if we can place a reasonable interpretation on the events of last night, then you may have considerable insight into how this, this ... *entity* ... may behave in future. At the present point in time, this predictive power may make you close to *unique.*"

They smiled uncertainly at each other. Andy asked the somewhat practical question they were all thinking.

"Aye, well, that's very nice indeed, laddie, and much appreciated! But where are going with this?"

Stephen smiled weakly in turn. "'Going' may 'be a good choice of word, my friend, at least from your perspective. 'Coming' is more appropriate from mine. My superiors believe – and I agree – that you all will be more valuable if you now have access to the facilities we do here. With your permission then, we will make immediate arrangements for you join us in Brussels?"

"Brussels?" queried Bob. "Not Paris?"

"I will meet you all in Brussels," confirmed Stephen. "That will be more convenient for us and still a relatively short journey for you. We will make the necessary arrangements without delay. These will include transportation of all your essential equipment," they all glanced involuntarily at Hattie, "and all the safety and security measures we consider necessary." He paused. "I am sure I do not have to tell you, ladies and gentlemen, that no journey is without risk at present and, with the escalation we now see, today may present even more challenges than yesterday. We will do everything within our power to keep you safe but I cannot force you to do this. The final decision is yours."

No-one spoke. No-one seemed prepared to make themselves group spokesperson this time. No-one even knew if what they were thinking was the same as the others. Almost to buy some time, Bob suggested:

"Well, I suppose we *would* be able to take a whole load more measurements over there, at least. We might be able to build up a better picture of Its development so far. Particularly if we need to start thinking about what happens next ... or even what to *do*."

"On the other hand," said Jenny, no more than playing Devil's Advocate to expand the conversation, "I suppose Geor..., er, your assistant – your colleague – can now take those measurements in some form?"

"I am afraid that is no longer possible," said Stephen darkly. "She is no longer with us. I was able to have her password reset this morning to access her most recent configuration. Consequently, I was able to re-run the analysis she performed last night. That was the revised S figure I gave you. To re-apply the process elsewhere, with different parameters, is beyond me and would take anyone else in my team at least as long as it did yesterday. We will try, of course, but, in the meantime, it would be better if you and your equipment were to come directly to Brussels."

A cold chill settled on every spine. Andy broke the silence.

"What you mean, 'no longer with us'?"

"My colleague was killed by an RFS incident last night on her way home. There was an isolated explosion at a food stall at which she had stopped. We are unsure of the exact cause – although we know gas was involved – but, once again, an end system had not 'failed safe' for some reason. My colleague died instantly; the stall owner a few hours later in hospital."

"We're coming," Jenny said firmly.

*

It was ten o'clock the same morning. The Desk sat waiting for a car, which had apparently been dispatched to take them to Heathrow. Hattie had already been collected. Stephen had arranged these things remotely and quickly, as he had many others. Aisha had contacted her hospital to discuss her possible continued absence. Not knowing how to start the conversation with her senior director, she was astonished to discover that she already knew and had been given to understand that it was 'in the national interest'. She had enquired no more. Aisha, Jenny and Andy had borrowed small bags and cases, a few clothes and travel-sized toiletries from Jill and Bob. Bob retrieved his passport; Andy still had his in his conference bag; Aisha and Jenny found other documentation that would suffice for the EU. The whole panic had a surreal, insulated feel to it. RFS continued all around – inside and out. They knew not what to expect next. They sat with their own thoughts for a while.

"So, what exactly is *It*?" asked Bob, breaking their silence so suddenly that Jenny jumped.

"Surely, we've been through that," she answered.

"No, I mean what *is* It? Not what's It *doing*, or *how*, or even *why*? But what *is* It? Assuming *It* is actually self-aware, to some extent, what sort of *self* are we talking about here?"

Jenny shrugged her shoulders. Aisha and Andy exchanged glances.

"To me," suggested Aisha, first in, "It is an artificial entity that has acquired an essential control imperative from reaching a critical level of powered neural complexity, in accordance with some simple scientific rule, which we do not yet fully understand: much could be said of our own brains, of course. But I imagine Andy would say something very different!" She stopped, smiling at him, by way of invitation.

"OK then, two suggestions from me," said Andy. "It's either a manifestation of the panpsychic universal consciousness principle, but aye ... possibly having reached some essential point." He nodded to Aisha in concession of this last observation. "Or, It's God giving life, a *soul* if you like, to a system that fulfils the requirements for consciousness He's laid down for His universe." He paused grinning. "Or, of course, It may be both of those – or Aisha's model – *all at the same time*! Who's to say?"

"It's bloody science-fiction; that's what it is," grumbled Jenny. "I mean, I don't *doubt* our theory any more: it seems to be vindicated by everything that happens but it's still *mad*. I'm surprised no-one's come up with this in a story before!"

"I guess they have, really," suggested Bob. "If you think about *Skynet* in *Terminator*, that's really a huge network-based intelligence, isn't it?"

"Big difference, though, between that and this," insisted Andy.

"Yes, I suppose, if you think about it, there are a few sci-fi stories out there about conscious intelligence – AI, if you like – running *on* systems, often *networks*," agreed Jenny. "But that's not we've got here, is it? We're not talking about It running *on* the Internet; we're saying It *is* the Internet."

"And a bit more," added Aisha. "The power as well. It is not just a brain: more like a nervous system."

"Aye, big network-based AI has been written about in sci-fi a fair bit," agreed Andy, "but always from the point of view of it being software running on hardware. *Sawyer's WWW Trilogy* is probably the best example."

But they all shook their heads: it was not familiar.

"Robert J. Sawyer," continued Andy. "Canadian sci-fi author. Wrote the '*WWW Trilogy*'. Clever title because the three books were '*Wake*', '*Watch*' and '*Wonder*'. His version of a big AI was a thing called '*Webmind*', which lived on the Internet. Somehow made up from cellular automata, if I remember rightly. But still very much software-based. The hardware was just the *platform* – as it always seems to be in these stories. We're in completely new territory here in the real world. With It, the hardware's critical: *It is* the hardware every bit as much as the software: there's an almost symbiotic dependence." The others nodded mute agreement; however Andy had not finished.

"But, in many ways," he continued thoughtfully, "there's a much bigger problem with fictional AI. *Form* is one thing but *behaviour* is something else again. Generally these sci-fi stories are always so ridiculously *anthropomorphic*!"

"What do you mean?" asked Jenny.

"Well, these AI consciousnesses always seem to have such conveniently *human* characteristics," Andy explained. "They always see the world very much the way we would. Maybe a bit more good or evil in there somewhere and usually a lot cleverer but always essentially thinking like *us*."

"It might make it easier to *tell* the stories like that?" suggested Aisha.

"Aye, that's a fair point," Andy agreed, "but it doesn't help us get to grips with how an AI might *really* behave if it's come to life independent of our programming – with no input from *us*. (Remember that piece that you and I wrote before Christmas?) 'Webmind' was particularly daft in that respect, as it happens. Rob Sawyer is a pretty typical middle-class Western author: well-enough-off, with a standard modern neo-liberalist outlook on life – and he's probably never really had those views effectively challenged by anyone. So, of course, Webmind *had to share that outlook*! It was going to do 'right' and Sawyer assumed he *knew* what 'right' was. If you're *sure* you're *right* about everything then you're going to think that something more intelligent than you will just think the *same* things but be *better* at going about making it happen. It may never actually occur to you that you might be *wrong* and the super-intelligence might think something completely *different*! Sawyer's creation was just an extension of himself so it did what he would do. It started off by getting rid of spam, then it found a cure for cancer; finally, it overthrew the Chinese government. Every 'good' thing it did was something that Sawyer thinks is 'good'. OK, it had to sometimes *learn* the difference between good and bad – from a *child*, interestingly enough: presumably *she* knew better than everyone else in the world! But, in the end, it just fell in line with its author."

"But you could argue that, if Webmind had been conceived by someone in China, or Africa, or from any different social group, its moral code would have been very different. Not to recognise that is pretty arrogant. Even the best of philosophers are products of their time and place (Bertrand Russell said something like that): sci-fi writers aren't going to be any different. It's funny how people who *aren't* starving to death place 'personal freedom' above a fairer distribution of resources, for example! It's highly unlikely that a super-intelligent, ultra-logical AI would see the world anything *like* the same way as a comfortably protected Westerner but we all make those assumptions if we're not careful. Some people do the same with God, of course: they have their own narrow views – often their own bigoted opinions – and they actually assume that an all-knowing, all-powerful God *shares* them. When you see God as an extension of yourself, you're spiritually screwed!"

"*Mediocrity knows nothing higher than itself; but talent instantly recognizes genius*," said Bob, suddenly remembering a piece of Sherlock Holmes of his own.

"*Touché!*" smiled Andy.

"Anyway, it's a fair thought," agreed Bob, trying to get back to the point. "So you're saying we don't know what Its *moral code* is going to be?"

"I don't think we can even *ask* questions like that at this stage. It's ..." Andy cast a questioning look at Aisha, who nodded.

"It has nothing *like* a moral code at present," she interrupted, quite forcefully. "It is just not even close to that stage yet. You could even say It is not actually particularly *clever*. After all, It has just 'woken up' and Its neural complexity is within a few orders of magnitude – more or less, it is hard to say – of our own. It is more like a very, very young child – possibly even embryonic. It is consciousness – yes, *OK*, I said *consciousness* – at a very low level. It is a nervous system looking to implement a control imperative. If it were not for all the things that we have connected to It, we would probably not even *notice* It! It makes absolutely *no* sense to discuss how It might *behave* and it may never do: It is not functioning on that level at all. It will just *do* whatever It can *discover* how to do. It will make whatever things *work* that It can find out *how*."

"And just consider what some of those '*things*' are!" said Jenny.

They all took long breaths.

Chapter 17: Flight

The car's arrival was announced by Jill, from her station at the window. She and Bob kissed a longer-than-usual goodbye and she watched them all out of the front door. Her look of annoyed but resigned acceptance was deliberate; the deep concern she clearly felt was not meant for external expression – but was badly hidden nonetheless.

The official UK government advice was now that no-one should leave home – or wherever they happened to be – unless to do so was absolutely essential. Speculation as to the cause of PDN and RFS had reached levels of complex hysteria but the effect was only too simple and clear. Energy supply networks and end systems were unreliable, sometimes to the point of being dangerous. All leave had been cancelled for power workers, network engineers and emergency services staff. Hospitals were already operating far beyond capacity. (Aisha naturally felt some guilt at this.) Local public transport had been suspended indefinitely. Fuel shortages had already begun to bite. National train networks were running skeleton services and all reservations had been cancelled, although the usual ticket restrictions had been lifted. Most airports were still open but about two thirds of UK flights had been cancelled. Affected passengers had been told *not* to travel to airports as there was no immediate intention to reschedule them onto alternative planes. Stephen, however, appeared to have sufficient oversight to make appropriate arrangements. *Their* flight, he assured them, *would* depart. This only partially addressed their general sense of danger.

Bob was no auto-enthusiast but the car sent to collect them had a similar appearance, he thought, to the one he had travelled in from the airport in Luxembourg, just a little longer to accommodate an extra line of seats facing the normal rear passenger row. Other than size and this being right-hand drive, it seemed identical to his limited observation. The driver was similarly uncommunicative. The Desk slid in and sat down to look out at a chaotic world from behind dark tinted windows.

And chaotic it had truly become. Everywhere were signs of increased RFS and its impact. A considerable level of damage was to be seen; its exact cause not always evident after the event itself. Police cars and emergency repair vans were as numerous as private vehicles since many people were keeping to their homes – *if* they were safe there. Ambulances were also everywhere, and yet there appeared not to be enough of them. Just beyond the turn in Jill and Bob's street, a fire engine was dousing a detached house. One of the walls appeared to have been blown out. Normally, in this quiet area of suburban Greater London, such a rare event would have brought two or three such appliances but there were probably too few to cope now. Also, under normal circumstances, of course, they would have stopped to help people; but the sheer scale of this was beyond them. Bob reflected quietly that these were his neighbours but he hardly even recognised any of them.

They had travelled just fifty yards further, however, when he did see a familiar face. A man of about forty or fifty ran screaming down the path from a bungalow set back from the road. "That's old Mrs. Harris's son," Bob pointed. "Driver, *stop*," he shouted. "… please," he added as an afterthought. Their first impression, despite the man's agility was that he was himself injured in some way. However, as the car lurched to a sudden halt, and he veered to meet it, the real situation became immediately, and alarmingly, clear.

"My mother!" he screamed. Tears and sweat mixed across his face. "I think she's been *electrocuted*. She was ironing clothes. I don't know what happened. She just fell down; she's not moving."

Aisha threw herself from the car and rushed past him into the bungalow. The others followed at an only slightly reduced speed. Only the driver remained in the car. "Have you phoned for an ambulance?" asked Jenny as they ran.

"Yes," the man cried, "well no, not exactly; I didn't have to." He tried to overcome his confusion. "I just hit the button on her telecare system. It sent off the alarm call – I heard it do that – but there wasn't a response; not that I could hear anyway. I was trying to do that resuscitation stuff ... but I don't know what I'm *doing*," he whined apologetically. By this time they were at the door.

As they entered, they saw Aisha performing CPR on Mrs Harris, lying in the square angle of two sets of kitchen units, with an iron and a buckled ironing board by her side. Jenny carefully disconnected the iron by pulling on the insulated power cable forcefully until the plug came reluctantly away from the socket. Andy tried to call the emergency line but there was no response. Bob did likewise.

But Aisha's skills had already worked. They could tell by the change in her, before they could see for themselves in the patient, that some life had been restored. Aisha stopped her frantic chest pounding and mouth-to-mouth and, after a few calming breaths of her own, slowly and carefully straightened Mrs. Harris out further and began to make her as comfortable as possible, checking her pulse and breathing all the time. Her son's tears flowed without restraint now – but from a different emotion.

"OK, do we believe there is an ambulance on the way?" Aisha asked as calmly as she could manage.

"We're not sure," answered Bob. "We thought we'd got through but the line went part way through my giving the address. If the GPS tracking kicked in, or her telecare system is working, we should be OK; otherwise, I don't know. I'll keep trying."

"I'll have to stay with her until it comes," Aisha said.

"Can we afford to do that?" asked Jenny. "We might miss the plane." She knew it was not the most tactful of observations under the circumstances. Sure enough, Aisha cast her a sour look.

"This woman has just recovered from a cardiac arrest," she snapped. "At a bare minimum, she requires medical observation until some other qualified assistance comes. *You* may go but *I* will remain until an ambulance arrives."

"We don't know how long that might be," Andy said softly. "Her son could look after her until then?" The man nodded. Andy continued. "We may have some important things to do ourselves in Brussels. If we all miss the plane, then we might conceivably be letting down hundreds, thousands, *millions*, not just one person."

"I know," Aisha smiled, grimly but gently, "and I *do* understand. That is why I think you all should go – you may have some *purpose* there. But I may not and I *cannot*. We do not even know if the ambulance is coming. I am a doctor: I have *my* duty *here*. It may only be *one* person but this is what I *do*!"

"*I won't leave you*," insisted Andy after a pause. "I'm staying here too." Aisha initially protested but there was something in his tone that was beyond contest.

"I will remember this," she growled.

*

The minutes ticked by. The driver had come to the door to rudely insist they left; otherwise they would miss their flight. They came to a reluctant acceptance that they were to be divided. Andy would remain with Aisha; Bob and Jenny would continue to Brussels: no-one was particularly happy with any of it. Jill had been called (with some difficultly) and was on her way on foot to provide whatever support she could for the Harrises: whichever of them needed it most. There was no time for Bob to even wait to see her again. The Desk hugged their disconsolate goodbyes. Bob and Jenny were on their way back to the car.

And then, at the very last moment, an ambulance arrived. Two paramedics rushed in and took control. Within a minute, Mrs. Harris was on a trolley being wheeled out to the road. Aisha barked a few instructions and pieces of essential information and they were gone. Dazed and emotional, The Desk regrouped, threw themselves back into the car and the driver raced, at an alarming speed, to Heathrow.

*

Making contact with anyone remotely was now proving difficult. Bob was sure that the 4 & 5G phone networks were still PDN-free but the underlying infrastructure used by everyone – originally just wired but now wireless too, of course – was not. Across the global Internet, although 'ordinary' communication was still possible alongside the PDN, there were frequent delays and often complete failures. From the car, he eventually – but far from easily – made contact with both Stephen and Jill. Stephen was able to confirm that check-in arrangements had been made for The Desk at Heathrow and Jill was tidying up in old Mrs. Harris's bungalow as her son accompanied her to hospital in the ambulance. "Don't worry;" she said, "I've understood enough of this to take precautions. I'm not touching anything I don't have to and checking everything that I do!" Still Bob worried.

The news coming over the car radio, in broken form, was horrific. There were no realistic estimates of injuries or deaths nationally or globally: for the time being, major RFS incidents and their resultant carnage were being reported in isolation. 'An explosion in Derby has killed at least twelve people'. 'twenty-three dead from traffic pile-up on the M9'. Elsewhere in the world, there were disasters with fatalities orders of magnitude higher. 'Celebrity' deaths were so numerous now that they were being largely ignored but the loss of an African king was mentioned. Reports were coming in of auto-programmed defence weaponry being fired unintentionally somewhere in South America. No-one was prepared to estimate what all this destruction might add up to globally. 'I wonder how soon before someone tries to put a monetary cost to this,' Andy mused to himself.

Jenny also appeared thoughtful. Eventually, she had to speak.

"Right, there are two things I'm not getting here," she announced with some irritation. "Firstly, if It's managed to work the wireless networks now, why are the phone networks still clear? Surely that's just another type of wireless? So, why isn't It using those? Secondly, why is *so* much damage being done? I know I said before that it was just bound to happen probabilistically when you're dealing with such a massive number of things, but I'm not sure I quite accept that myself now. Why is *so* much going wrong? These things should be so well tied-down physically that dangerous malfunctions are impossible, shouldn't they? Why are systems not failing safe? Why are people getting electrocuted when devices should be insulated?" She winced as more news came through on the radio. "Why are weapons going off, for God's sake?"

"I think I can explain the first," Bob started. "It now seems to have control over everything that's essentially *'plugged in'* somewhere. Whether it's wired or wireless, the transceivers at each end are a permanent part of Itself. So, irrespective of the transmission medium in between, It's figured out how to pretty much use it all. But phones and smartwatches and 5G tablets and suchlike are *physically separate* for much of the time: people carry them around unplugged. OK yes, they have to be connected to recharge from time to time but they spend a lot of their operation as separate entities. Of course, the comms protocols are different too – but I really don't know how much difference that makes to It." He slowed, looking uncertain. "And I wouldn't like to say if it's always going to stay that way. I was pretty confident It would get to use wireless. The phone networks, Bluetooth, that sort of thing? I just don't know."

"There are plenty of 5G devices that *are* always connected," Jenny pointed out. "Some tablets stay *permanently* plugged in: and a lot of IoE technology is Bluetooth."

"Yes, I know," agreed Bob. "I guess there are just some mobile parts It hasn't figured out. I wouldn't like to say what's going to happen from here on in." He smiled grimly. "Best not to tell Stephen that!"

"So are there still other systems that It hasn't mastered yet?" asked Andy.

"Well, anything that It can't, sort of *'see the other end of'*, I guess," suggested Bob. So anything completely physically separated. Mobiles, obviously. But also drones, cars, planes, ships at sea ... satellites, I suppose." He glanced at the sky as a shiver ran through him. "Something to be thankful for, at least?"

"OK, but why so much *damage* then?" Jenny pressed her second question. Bob shook his head slowly.

"I really don't have an explanation for that either," he admitted. "I agree with you. These systems should be 'failing safe' – apart from a few that are physically damaged or those with unknown design flaws. *Why aren't they?*"

Aisha now stepped in.

"I think you may be considering this from the wrong point of view," she said quietly. "You are still thinking about a system, built by *us* and responding to *our* concept of how it should behave. But we have to think more widely now. This is no longer the case. Remember what Andy said about the dangers of *anthropomorphism* when trying to figure out AI?

"The powered Internet – *It* – has now something close to complete control awareness of our global communication network and our collective global electricity supply. (Perhaps now everything except *mobile* technology?) We are fortunate that It has, as yet, actually demonstrated very *limited* ability to exercise this control. But It continues to learn. The failsafe mechanisms we have put in place make sense to *us* but may not restrict *It* as much as we would like to think. In particular, I imagine they largely separate power and data in their operation?" She looked at Jenny and Bob, who both nodded, and continued. "But It is not restricted in this way. To It, It is a single entity with all options at Its disposal. Its hardware and signals are indistinguishable. It can send Its own noise, of all types, everywhere at once – and now It can do this *wirelessly*. Signals can overlap and interfere. Just as a human brain learns to find ways around damaged areas, or to link with new artificial inputs, It may be able to bypass many of the safeguards we have probably considered adequate based on our assumptions that nothing like this could happen. It still does not know what It is *doing*, of course, but It can *experiment*. It can *learn*. Its success rate is still very low but I imagine It continues to improve all the time. I do not think we can take anything for granted any more."

They were at the airport departures entrance.

*

Heathrow airport was chaotic but not overcrowded. Passenger numbers appeared roughly balanced between those waiting for cancelled flights (and refusing to accept that there would be no replacement) and those who had heeded advice and stayed at home. Long queues formed everywhere as system failures multiplied. Medical staff treated a number of people in the check-in area and police tried to keep order.

It seemed initially that there was little chance of catching their flight. On the whole, the planes themselves were not being delayed – with or without passengers aboard – and theirs was due to leave in twenty-five minutes. They rushed towards the back of a dispiritingly long queue for the relevant desk. As they did so, however, two members of the airport security staff, accompanied by two police officers, intercepted them.

"Dr. Davies?" They had perhaps decided Aisha was the easiest to identify.

"Yes."

"And Professor Smith?" to Jenny. "Professor Jamieson and Mr. Weatherill?" glancing uncertainly between Bob and Andy.

"Aye. Yes."

"Come with us, please."

They were taken to a small door in the corner of the foyer. On the other side, was a makeshift security screening station. Their bags and documents were checked quickly and they proceeded through another exit to a waiting buggy. It took them a few hundred yards around the outside of the terminal building to their plane, where they rushed up a set of external steps to join a small group of other passengers filing through the standard exit gate.

Ten minutes later, the plane was in the air. Many seats remained empty.

*

The seat allocation on the plane put Jenny and Andy next to each other. They could have changed, of course, but the journey was to be a short one and this suited Jenny well: she felt in desperate need of some small-talk and this was the first time she and Andy would have had time for a conversation of their own since the Strand pub before Christmas – when the world seemed *normal*. Jumping straight to anything concerning Aisha seemed indelicate so she found something equally obvious but trivial.

"So, how are you settling into your London post, Professor Jamieson?" she enquired lightly.

Despite the contrived nature of the conversation, Andy gave this his usual careful consideration. "Not bad, Professor Smith," he said eventually, but in equal humour. "Not bad at all. The usual issues of getting to grips with new processes and procedures; finding out how to do things and finding the right person to talk to when you can't find out how to do things; but, on the whole, pretty good. I've no real admin responsibilities so, apart from a few hours a week with final-year undergrads and masters students, I'm pretty much free to do my own research. That was the appeal of the job really – apart from the 'chair', of course. I'm slowly putting together a wee team of PhD students but I've got my own personal research too. Pretty happy: I'd sort of had enough of Rummidge."

"So, why exactly did you leave? You've never really been the ambitious sort: mind on higher things, and all that."

"Ah well," he took a slow breath. "That just got a bit silly really. I had a bit of a falling out. With hindsight, I was as much at fault as the other guy – probably more so – but the situation just became too difficult, and I decided it was the right time to go. Even accepting my share of the blame, and I *did* apologise – that's the AA way, it didn't really make anything any better."

"What happened?"

"Well, they appointed a new head of the Business School a couple of years ago. Of course, with my blend of political and spiritual beliefs, that was never my favourite part of the university even before he arrived: I quite often referred to it as the 'Faculty of Evil'. (They were practically *selling* PhDs and they gave a visiting research fellowship to the bloke who sold hot-dogs at the football ground.) But this guy, when he turned up, was a *particular* type of prick. I'm not sure what he was before he came to us: used-car salesman or something, but they made him a professor to get him to take the job and he then spent most of the day strutting up and down the corridors in a shiny suit and silk tie. Everything he did was superficial – no depth to anything, including him; and the school got even worse – which few of us thought possible. Everything was marketing bullshit: there was no academic honesty, depth or integrity to anything they did at all.

"Then one day, they decided to stick up a load of 'motivational' posters on the wall. I sometimes had to walk through that corridor to get to the Theology Faculty. The first time I saw them, I was so disgusted I was very nearly physically sick!"

"What on earth was wrong with them?"

"Well, by-and-large, they were all essentially *spiritual* quotations, by *nice* people, but taken completely out of context. There were quotes supposedly from the Dalai Lama, Buddha, Mother Teresa, Gandhi: people like that, about how to lead a *good life*. Half of them were wrong or made up, of course, but anyway they were all superimposed over a load of people in business suits with the implication that they were instructions for how to grind away until you got rich! I think the one that really upset me was supposed to be from Francis of Assisi: '*Start by doing what's necessary; then do what's possible, and suddenly you are doing the impossible*'. It's a good model of spiritual development; in fact, it's used in many addition recovery programmes (although it's *not* really by Francis); but the Business School corrupted it to promote the concept of selfishness in making your pile. It was horrible! In fact, it put me in mind of that time Thatcher desecrated '*Where there is discord, may we bring harmony*' when she got elected. (Although that wasn't really him either!)"

209

"So, what happened?" Jenny asked initially; then, thinking it through a little, smiled: "So, what did *you do*?"

"Ah," Andy chuckled, "you know me well. Aye, I probably should have just taken a deep breath and walked past."

"But you didn't!"

"No, I didn't. Well, in fact I walked past, right enough! But when I got back to my office, I posted a sarcastic wee comment on Facebook. Suggesting that maybe it wasn't appropriate to use a guy who swore himself to a life of *poverty* to promote *greed*. Lots of people saw it immediately."

"Not the worst thing, I've heard: *academic freedom*, surely?"

"Maybe; except that wasn't quite the end of it. Someone replied arguing that these things were 'open to interpretation' and maybe it *was* an appropriate use of the quote. So I answered, aye maybe, *'perhaps the Business School is trying to suggest that their courses prepare you for a life of poverty'*! That may have been the worst bit."

Jenny laughed hard: she realised she needed to. "Then what?"

"Well, Professor Shiny Suit saw his arse; then there was this almighty row at the next Senate meeting and I was asked to apologise. By that time, I'd calmed down and I was happy to. Aye, I could have claimed 'academic freedom' but I decided to take my share of the blame. But that made me look completely in the wrong so I got hauled up to a misconduct panel and given a slapped wrist. Nothing written or permanent but it all got to me in the end. It just seemed like time to move on."

"Really doesn't sound like you! You always seem so laid back!"

"No-one's perfect! *'Spiritual progress, not spiritual perfection'*, and all that. That was a year or so ago: maybe I've got better since then. Anyway, it made Aisha laugh too when I told her!"

That was the introduction Jenny needed. "Yes, the two of you seem to be, er … getting along nicely?" She had started the sentence before knowing how to finish it and almost shuddered at the end product.

But Andy was comfortable. He had expected the inquisition eventually.

"Aye, I don't think any of us saw *that* coming! I thought I was too old for that nonsense!"

"I don't see why. We're all entitled to a little happiness. Nothing wrong with it. I just never really saw the two of *you* paired up. *Chalk and cheese* comes to mind!"

"Well, maybe; maybe not. We're not that far apart really. We're both in the game of trying to find answers – as we *all* are, of course." He looked at Jenny and past her at Bob and Aisha. "I think we're both honest and capable of being logical so, in that respect, we *think* the same. We just come from *completely* different philosophical starting points. We have almost diametrically opposite axioms as to what life is all about. But that doesn't do any harm: it just makes it … *interesting*! We'll probably never run out of things to talk about – or maybe even *argue* about!" He smiled. "Anyway, it just seems right: just *nice*."

"Yes, it is," agreed Jenny. "It's very nice indeed."

"And, ultimately, I think 'nice' is a whole lot better than arbitrary allegiances!"

Jenny smiled agreement.

*

Aisha and Bob were across the aisle, out of earshot amidst the plane's background noise, having a not dissimilar conversation. Bob, however, lacked Jenny's subtlety.

"Never really saw you and Andy as an item!" he opened with no attempt at finesse.

Aisha smiled. "Neither did I! I suppose, like most of us, I found him very attractive at university but he was always too busy with one girl after another in those days to notice me, other than as a friend. He was a little shallow and selfish then, I think. That was before his 'transformation', of course. He is very different now."

"But different in a *good* way? I mean, he was always a commie but *now*: a *religious* commie? Is that really what you're looking for?" It was said entirely without malice.

"No, that is not what I am looking for *in particular* but that is not what this is about. After all, I did not think I was looking for *anything*; it just *happened*. But he is kind; he is considerate. He is also brave: he tells the truth, as he sees it, and does not worry what others may think of him. I have a great deal of respect for that. He is actually quite remarkable. He is also still very good-looking!" she giggled slightly, as an afterthought.

Chapter 18: Numbers

Although the flight itself was uneventful, no-one was particularly surprised by some difficulties approaching Brussels. Problems with radar equipment in the control tower put them in a holding orbit after their first attempt at landing and something not quite so clearly described (and possibly less well understood) did so again on the second. There were raised tensions on board: even the aircrew had difficulty hiding their anxiety. But eventually, at the third time of asking, the plane was committed to the approach and touched down.

It was different on the ground, however. Having landed, and taxied to a stop, they were met at the gate and speeded through some private arrival procedures with a similar haste to their departure from Heathrow. They waved their documents at people as they passed but no-one looked. Within ten minutes, they were in a now-becoming-all-too-familiar black car, being driven away from the airport.

"Strewth; someone's in a hurry to see us!" Andy joked.

"I imagine they're also trying to keep us out of harm's way as much as possible," suggested Jenny more darkly. Bob nodded. As in the UK, the world outside the tinted windows was a grim one: RFS destruction was all around and emergency services – people in general – were coping as best they could. It was not enough. There was misery, desperation, and – becoming slowly more apparent – *anger*.

The route from the airport to the Berlaymont, where he assumed they were going, was a familiar one to Bob. Jenny and Andy had also each been there separately once before. However, approaching the building across the Schuman roundabout, the car took a different turn and came to a gate facing partly away from the main block. It opened swiftly as they passed and closed behind them. No-one was to be seen. They drove down a curved ramp and quickly lost their orientation in relation to the world above. They stopped in front of a set of thick glass doors with only circles of artificial light all around them. Even here, some temporary back-up lighting appeared to have been installed in a hurry.

Stephen himself emerged from the darkness and opened the car door for them. He and Bob shook hands warmly and Bob introduced the rest of The Desk – completely unnecessarily, of course. Stephen had regained a good part of his composure but was still clearly drawn by recent events. He introduced four others in his team, one of whom Bob recognised from his previous visit to Luxembourg.

"Ladies and gentlemen, we have a job to do." He ushered them through the glass doors and towards a free-standing central column with only an elevator entrance. Looking up through the gloom, it was several storeys before it appeared to regain contact with any of the building around it.

"Do we know what that job is?" enquired Andy, dryly.

Stephen either did not hear or chose not to answer. He pressed a single button marked with a small white circle. The doors closed and the lift moved but they were uncertain whether it was up or down.

*

If Bob or Jenny thought that anything they had previously seen in their technical careers would prepare them for the sight that greeted them on emerging from the lift, they were mistaken. The Desk and Stephen's team stepped directly out into a huge amphitheatre-like room; a rough semi-circle about seventy-five yards across and the equivalent of three or four floors from top to bottom. On the outside of the circle, three rows of seats looked down onto an arrangement of concentric desks, workstations and control panels – over two hundred in total – each apparently with its own design and purpose. These, in turn, half enclosed a smaller, lower semi-circle, in which a dozen or so racks of networking equipment stood with bundles of fibre-optic cables both interconnecting them and leading away through channels in the floor. On the flat wall beyond – the focus of everything in the room, shone a massive display, divided into sections: a large central network map and several smaller analysis windows. Everything in the room, from the seating to the stations to the racks, gazed across the empty space at this screen, and almost seemed to answer to it. A few dozen technicians swarmed around trying to cope with RFS, with limited success.

"Jesus!" gasped Jenny.

"Indeed!" breathed Bob.

"Beats our Cisco Lab; it's like something out of James Bond," she joked.

"Beats anything I've ever seen," agreed Bob. "The desks and the screen are a bit like the 'BT Wholesale' monitoring place in Oswestry but this is something else entirely. It's three or four times bigger for a start and I've no idea what half of this stuff *does*!"

There was time to address only some of this ignorance. Stephen, with his team illustrating and demonstrating as required, pointed out the main features of the facility. Essentially, this *was* a massive monitoring station but with a number of extra features. The map on the wall could be configured to highlight any aspect or region of what might be loosely described as 'The European Internet': different types of traffic, protocols, even small sub-regions, could be highlighted or zoomed into as required and various traffic characteristics – traffic throughput, load, route delay, interference, reliability, etc. – could be shown together or individually. At the moment, it surprised no-one that most of the display was coloured red: both the links and the nodes they connected.

But, they were quickly informed, this was much more than just a remote monitoring system.

"From this room," Stephen explained, with a trace of pride, "we can observe and exert some control over most regions of the *EuroNet.*" ('EuroNet', they quickly realised, was the loose term used to describe that part of the Internet within the rough geography of Europe – complicated somewhat as this was by links to various 'dependencies' connected in from other parts of the world.) "Here we can *see* anything we want to within it and *influence* many aspects of it."

"*Exert some control over? Influence?*" asked Bob quizzically. "What do you mean? How exactly?"

Stephen smiled. "The existence of this facility is not widely known. There might be problems if it was, of course. From here was can observe the EuroNet, but also *control* most of its major switching centres. This control is either duplicated from the physical location of these centres or we can override it locally if necessary. We can also reroute traffic from a number of core carriers through this centre if we need to, ... well, *analyse* any content: for security purposes and suchlike."

"*Reroute traffic?*" Bob gasped. "How on earth are you doing that? You can't overrule BGP priorities from here, can you?"

"If necessary," Stephen confirmed, "we have that capability. Naturally, there has been little cause for us to implement much of this power – at least the control or diversion function – in the past, (on the whole we *watch* but we do not *touch*) but these are rapidly changing times, are they not?"

"Well yes," agreed Jenny incredulously. "But who knows about this *really*? Do the guys at JANET know, for example? What about the *ISPs*? Surely they'd be up in arms if they thought their data routes might be manipulated remotely? Their data even *stolen*?"

Stephen smiled. "I will probably not explain all of this: it is not necessary. But suffice to say that we have very good people in many key places. I believe you know Professor Stengel at Rutherford, for example?" He grinned more broadly at the dawning expression on Jenny's face. "Our 'coverage' – if we can call it that – is far from complete but it is enough; at least, it always *has* been."

"Doesn't doing things with people's data, which they don't know about, violate the European 'General Data Protection Regulation' a wee bit?" asked Andy, eyes narrowed. "Even if it's OK with GDPR, it's pretty dodgy ethically, surely?"

Once again, Stephen did not answer, although the slightest of shrugs of his shoulders showed that he had at least heard this time.

*

It was late afternoon. The introduction to the facility had continued, and gradually changed into a discussion of the problem in hand. Hattie had arrived but remained unused at present. Stephen and Bob, assisted by the others to a greater or lesser extent, put different network representations onto the screen and discussed the significance of each in turn. Naturally, the room itself – the whole complex – was no more immune to PDN and its resultant RFS than the rest of the world. One of the units fused as they tried to use it: they all took additional safety precautions. There were longer delays than usual and many failures. To some extent, the facility was measuring *itself*! *And*, Bob realised with some alarm, during a rare daydreaming moment staring at Hattie, *she* became part of It every time they powered her up, of course!

But they could not work indefinitely: they were all tired from their early mornings. In a short break for them to take some food and drink, Aisha found herself gazing at one of the 'smaller' side screens – still nearly ten yards across. It presented the EuroNet as part of the larger global Internet. A map of the world showed faintly in outline behind a network graph of the main backbone. Most parts were as red as most others.

"*So, is this what the Internet looks like?*" she asked with an intentional air of innocence.

"Who knows what the Internet looks like?" Stephen laughed gently. "I do not think any of us really know that! We can choose to look at the biggest links – those that carry the highest traffic levels – or pick out the biggest nodes – such as the AT&T switches in The States – but we can never see *all* of it. There is simply too much complexity over too many levels. And our American partners keep significant detail to themselves; they say for security reasons but they are economic too, of course.

However, for all these reasons, and more besides, there will never be a *single picture* of the Internet."

'Just like our brains, perhaps?' thought Aisha, but said nothing.

"Too complicated," agreed Bob. "The last time anyone tried that was about ten years ago and, even then, it was largely made up!"

Still Aisha stared at the screen. The core network structure remained constant but a few smaller links and nodes dropped out or appeared – or changed colour or form – as Stephen's team made minor adjustments to the monitoring and control parameters. The impression was one of small undulations: local, quivering changes over an immense scale. There was almost a sense of a living form. Eventually, she asked:

"So is this … *It*?"

The others gazed solemnly in the same direction.

"As close as we'll ever get to knowing *It*, I suppose," muttered Andy. "Like our own brains, I might suggest?" He met Aisha's stare with his own and they both smiled.

*

They continued to work into the evening. Eventually Bob introduced Hattie and powered her up to a mixture of bemusement and distrust from Stephen's team.

"Will we be able to replicate the reading you took in Paris?" he asked.

"Not accurately, I think," Stephen replied after some consideration. "We can certainly *reach* that point from here but we will not be able to recreate the conditions under which my colleague," his face clouded, "undertook your S Parameter calculations. Also, we remain unsure as to how well we implemented the operation of …" he hesitated as he looked at Hattie, "… your *equipment* there. It may be well to make a new start?"

"Agreed," said Bob as he began to set Hattie's controls and prepare her connections. Other than quickly connecting a new fibre optic tap, given to him by Stephen's team, no other modification was needed.

There was a general acceptance among all of them now that, in this facility – possibly across the larger Internet, a reading *somewhere* would be much like a reading *anywhere* since the morning's developments. So Bob connected Hattie to the nearest adaptor and set her running. After a minute:

$S = 0.735$

They shared knowing looks. Andy voiced what they were all thinking. "And *0.75* is what we'd expect for the human brain?" Jenny nodded. Bob repeated the experiment twice more: once on the master console for the room and again on one of the main fibre connections between the racks.

$S = 0.736$

$S = 0.738$

They repeated the last experiment several times under different conditions. Stephen instructed his team to change what non-obtrusive network settings they could across the EuroNet in a variety of combinations. It made no difference.

$S = 0.738$

Eventually, they rerouted a considerable quantity of traffic from two of the core carriers and maintained the settings for two minutes, observing all the time. Still:

$S = 0.738$

They all nodded quietly: nothing needed to be said. However, a few hours later – towards the end of the evening, using the same network settings as before, the value changed of its own accord.

$S = 0.739$

They repeated all the recent experiments to see if this was consistent. It was.

$S = 0.739$

The final value did not remain on the screen for long, however, because Hattie blew a fuse.

*

Just before midnight, they gathered around one of the larger, clearer work-tables and considered what they knew.

"So, practically no edge at all but the S value changes as we look?" Jenny opened. "It's slowly increasing."

"And," Bob observed, "we have to assume that a lot of end-user stuff on the periphery around the world has been switched off or disconnected now – like *we* did this morning – but that doesn't seem to have made much difference."

"It's almost as it we're starting to lose the last of our control of It," mused Jenny. "What we do with *our* traffic doesn't seem to bother It much any more: It gets by on Its own connectivity."

"Aye, It has more of a *complete* feel to it?" suggested Andy.

"Yes, I think It is close to a conventional brain structure now, if that is what you mean," suggested Aisha. "And It is *learning*."

"I am still somewhat unclear what you mean by both these terms," announced Stephen, somewhat formally. The others noticed he was now wearing an earpiece: he also placed a micro-tablet in the space in front of him. He made no attempt to conceal either. "Please explain."

Aisha took a slow breath to help her collect her thoughts: she realised that ears other than those in the room were probably listening now. "So, our theory is that It has acquired a control function from Its complexity," she began, in deliberately minimalist form. "Until this morning, Its internal connectivity was only across physical links and this limited Its structure to something very sparse and hierarchical: very *unlike* the human brain. On that basis, although It may have been obeying a natural imperative to *look* to exert higher levels of control, It would have been restricted in Its ability to do this.

"Now, however, It appears to have, shall we say, 'mastered' *some* of Its wireless capabilities." She looked at Bob for approval; he simply nodded. "This has had several effects. Firstly, It has increased in Its essential level of interconnectivity: Its neural complexity is probably much closer to that of our brains now. Secondly, It now has more consistent scale-free properties across all of Its levels: again, much more like a brain."

Jenny nodded to confirm this time. "Thirdly, and finally, It appears to have," she paused for the right word, "*escaped* from some of our engineering preconceptions as to how It should operate." Her eyes appealed to Bob once more. Stephen's eyes narrowed quizzically.

"Yes," Bob took up the case, also glancing nervously at the micro-tablet, "now that It's got wired *and* wireless capabilities *and* power, I think It might be finding combinations of those that allow it to make internal connections we didn't design It for. Particularly when it comes to bypassing safety circuits, bridging gaps, that sort of thing."

"Are you suggesting that … *It* is discovering *new physics*?" asked one of Stephen's team incredulously.

"No, not new physics, as such," Bob answered hastily. "But applying *known* physics in ways that we didn't design the individual parts for. Maybe It's reversing the concepts of wireless data and physical power. Perhaps It's applying electromagnetic induction over short distances; I don't know."

"Our brains are similarly 'inventive' when they have to adapt to different situations and new inputs," added Aisha.

"In a sense," Bob suggested, "It's been doing this all along. Trying to put frames onto the wrong networks in Its early days was really *It* working out how to use *our* technology. It quickly got better at that and now perhaps Its outgrown us altogether and It's finding Its own way of doing things?"

"But *we* built the equipment – the transceivers for example – to perform certain tasks in certain ways," the woman insisted.

"Yes, but a transmitter can operate across a much wider frequency range than we ask it to," Bob pointed out. "It just depends on what's fed into it. And then an aerial – or any sort of receiver – can capture across a wide band too. Yes, *we're* very restricted in the way we use individual components but, if It's simultaneously running hundreds of billions of these, doing lots of different things, then perhaps It's learning to 'transfer technology', if you like. We do seem to have *power jumping gaps*, for example!" He paused. "OK, we're not really *sure*, are we? But we can't deny It's doing *something* and it's looking very much like something *we didn't build It to do!*"

"Aye, and It seems to be getting *better* at it," added Andy, followed by silence from everyone. Stephen appeared to be listening to his earpiece.

"*We need to prove this,*" he announced, suddenly and firmly.

They all nodded agreement but still no-one spoke. Eventually Stephen continued.

"At some point, we have do three things," he announced, as if relaying third-party information. He spoke with a certainty diluted by reluctance. "We have to pass this information to those in authority in European government: people further up the administrative structures – ultimately our elected representatives; they will *not* be easily convinced by our theory. We also have to consider telling our American counterparts what we believe the situation to be since they control more of the Internet – more of *It* – so they may need to be involved in our discussions. Their reaction is harder to predict – The NSA has a history of sympathy towards," he hesitated, "'odd' explanations for natural phenomena … but they prefer to invent them for themselves," he added wryly, as if he was deviating from a script. "Then, at some point, we will have to make an appropriate announcement to the general public. This worries me – *us* – most of all. Although people at large may *accept* the notion all too easily, there is likely to be widespread panic and alarm." He fell silent once more in consideration – or awaiting further instructions.

"The latter questions are thankfully outside of my remit," he restarted suddenly once more. "However, it would appear that the decision regarding the former is mine." His tone changed to something close to belligerence. "My immediate superiors have taken a, shall we say, less-than-resolute position on this now." He glared at the micro-tablet as he spoke. "If this explanation – our model – is to be taken to a senior level in the European security framework, then it appears *I* have the authority," he checked his smartwatch, pursing his lips as he did so, "and *now* also the necessary *contact details*, to do this. I expect my reputation will keep it company on its journey," he added bitterly. "I repeat, *we need to prove this*."

"So, what can we do?" asked Jenny.

"I can have senior officers in this room tomorrow morning," Stephen said slowly. He was clearly following two conversations simultaneously. "We will need to convince them that our model of a sentient Internet is the only credible explanation. How can we do this?"

"Depends on who we're trying to convince! Will they be technical guys?" asked Bob. "Networkers?"

"How about mathematicians?" suggested Jenny. Another pause from Stephen. Eventually, he announced:

"Yes, at least one of them will – *can* – be."

"Right, leave it with us," said Jenny with purpose, trying to smile reassurance at Bob, who looked less than convinced. An electrical socket burst into flames behind them and was quickly smothered by a technician: they barely noticed.

*

They – The Desk and Stephen's team minus Stephen – reconvened at 7:30am. They had been escorted directly to their hotel almost entirely by subterranean means the previous night and taken back to the EuroNet facility in a similar fashion that morning. They had little idea still where exactly they might be and natural daylight was becoming something of a memory. They did, however, have a plan!

Hattie had been mended: two of her smaller individual fuses had blown and protected the underlying circuit as designed; these were replaced. Her programming was also modified to display the S Parameter on a continuous basis as Its signal-to-noise ratio was now steadier and easier to measure as part of ongoing feedback. This gave an altogether more accurate, stable reading. She was, once again, connected to one of the main rack's fibre ports. It was now easy to recognise, even by eye, that the PDN shown on her 'scopes had better structure: fewer spikes, more clearly defined signals and longer bit sequences.

"So, is this going to work?" Bob asked, his eyes scanning them all but quickly resting on Jenny.

"I'm hoping so," she said softly. "I was working on the maths late last night and again early this morning. It's not easy to apply graph theory when you don't know what the graph looks like:" she joked, looking up at the world display, "trying to find a cut-set when you don't know what you're cutting – but I reckon three big nodes will be enough for us to measure a difference. The big question is whether they'll let us do it!"

"We'll see," agreed Bob, smiling.

On the stroke of eight o'clock, Stephen emerged from the lift, accompanied by two men dressed in almost identical dark suits and matching ties. "Bloody Hell, it's *Thomson and Thompson*," chortled Andy until Aisha's well-directed nudge to his ribs stopped him. Unlike Tintin's adversaries, however, only one of them (Thomson in Andy's mind) ever spoke. Stephen made some general introductions but their real names were never mentioned; Bob knew this drill well.

"So what are we planning to do, ladies and gentlemen?" asked Stephen with the uncomfortable air of an intermediary. "What are you going to show us?"

"And how will it convince us that your crazy hypothesis may be true?" added Thomson.

Jenny, already uncomfortable with this opening, tried as well as she could to explain logically.

"We want to conduct an experiment," she answered nervously. "We want to close down these nodes for an hour or so." She pointed at the monitor in front of them, showing the same topology as the huge room display. She indicated three of the brightest points on the EuroNet map: major switching centres in Berlin, Madrid and Paris. "I think I can predict, with reasonable accuracy, what the effect will be – and I think I can explain why."

Thomson looked unimpressed; Thompson may not have understood for all the acknowledgement he showed. Stephen's eyes bulged slightly; his head shook in quiet warning.

"That will not be possible," said Thomson flatly.

"Why not?" asked Bob. He turned to Stephen. "You have the capability to do that, don't you?" But Thomson did not allow him to answer.

"Capability is not the issue," he said, without intonation. "The issue is *expense*."

"*What* expense? Aisha asked, incredulously, looking around at the equipment surrounding them. "What difference will it make? *How hard can it be*?"

"We are not considering the expense *of* shutting down these nodes; we are considering the expense *from* shutting them down." Other than stressing the essential difference, Thomson's voice remained emotionless.

"*What*?"

Stephen mediated once more, glancing nervously in both directions. "My superior means we have to consider the cost of the lost *data*. European industry, particularly business and commerce, loses millions of Euros in transactions when a large link goes down even for a few seconds. The cost of closing three core nodes at major European cities for an hour would be counted in billions."

"It cannot be tolerated," confirmed Thomson.

"But, the data – well *most of it*, at least – wouldn't really be lost," argued Bob. "It would quickly be retransmitted and rerouted via other nodes. And the essential services will be mirrored anyway. We're talking slight *delay* rather than *loss*."

"Yes, I'm not completely *partitioning* the EuroNet," agreed Jenny. "I just want to decrease its *connectivity density* for a little while: to measure the effect it has on … *It*." She paused, aware how odd that sounded.

But Thomson remained unmoved. "Not all traffic could be rerouted," he droned, "Some BGP priorities do not permit alternatives; not everything is mirrored; encrypted channels and private connections could be broken. Data *would* be lost. There would still be considerable expense to European business."

Aisha had been watching Andy as this conversation had proceeded. The humour had dropped from his expression and she could see an unfamiliar emotion in him: *anger*. Eventually, he could stay silent no longer.

"*Look laddie*," he interrupted, gruffly and with deliberate condescension, "I don't know exactly who you work for but it'll be Euro-government of one sort of another, won't it? Not far from *The Commission*, I imagine?" Thomson stared at him coldly but did not reply. Andy continued.

"You've got a problem laddie. People are dying. Not businesses – *people*. So, where's the EC's priority? People or profit? You see, ever since the Greek fiasco, there's a lot of folk thinking that the EU cares more about protecting European *banks* than European *people*. Now's the time to prove them *wrong*! Will you do it?"

Chapter 19: Patterns

Thompson, with the minutest of head movements, gestured to Thomson. They detached themselves from the group and began a hushed discussion. Body language suggested Thompson might be the senior of the two. After a few minutes, he moved towards the lift and departed. Thomson remained but provided little by way of explanation.

"We wait," was all he would say.

After about quarter of an hour, punctuated by ongoing RFS incidents around the control room, Thomson's smart-watch signalled a call. He wore a Bluetooth earpiece so only one side of the conversation could be heard; that was in French: only Andy understood properly. Towards the discussion's end, Thomson nodded several times and grunted acknowledgement. Eventually he concluded, in English:

"I will ask them." He turned to The Desk, Jenny in particular. "Can you reduce the scale of your 'experiment' to *ten minutes* and *two nodes* chosen by us?"

Jenny considered for a moment. "The ten minutes might work," she conceded eventually. "I've no idea really how long it might take, but it depends *which* two nodes. Unless they're big ones, we might not notice the difference."

This was fed back to (they assumed) Thompson by Thomson. Another brief French dialogue ended with Thomson turning back to Jenny and announcing, "They will be two of your original three."

Jenny nodded agreement.

*

Thompson reappeared ten minutes later accompanied by a suited woman, who appeared to now have seniority over proceedings (and became '*not-Thompson*' in Andy's evolving internal model of European bureaucratic hierarchies). Both were breathless. They had used the stairs as, in the past ten minutes, a decision had apparently been taken that lifts and other 'enclosed systems' were too dangerous to use. As if in confirmation, a large section of the room's main display board hissed, flickered and went out for several minutes; technicians fought to restore it. In the interim, Jenny had reworked some S Parameter predictions for a shorter time, eventually concluding that it might not make much difference. This did nothing for her confidence as to their reliability, however. There were no introductions at all this time.

"Tell me what you are going to do," asked not-Thompson abruptly.

"OK," Jenny answered. "But I need to know which two nodes we're going to shut; then I need about five minutes to work a few more things out. I also need," glancing across to Bob, "the current figure."

Hattie was still connected as the previous evening. Bob ran the familiar sequence and she reported:

$S = 0.740$

"Getting cleverer," observed Andy, smiling apologetically at Aisha, who both winced and shuddered slightly at the terminology.

"So that's our base figure," said Jenny. "Now which two nodes?"

Not-Thompson pointed out two of the original three – the switches in Berlin and Madrid – on the small duplicate screen.

"Clearly not *that one*," she smirked, indicating Paris, as if there was some obvious humour in this. But any significance was lost on the others.

Jenny worked, with a combination of spreadsheet calculations and network maps drawn with pencil and paper, for a few minutes more.

"Right!" she said as confidently as she could. "Here's the plan ..."

She started at the beginning. She first explained their essential theory; then the background to the model they had used. She described the essential features of the human brain they were trying to measure; Aisha supported her with specialist biological detail from time to time, along with the relevant parts of

Professor Di Iorio's work. Together, they spoke of the brain's control function, its use of feedback loops, the self-similarity of its signals and the scale-free properties of its hierarchical structure, as well as how the signal-to-noise ratio on 'It' was increasing in line with it all. The others were all taken aback, to some extent, as to just how much of this they had come to accept without question over the past few days. Hearing it all afresh – in its entirety – it really did sound a bit odd!

But Jenny continued. She described how each of these metrics, together with the Internet and power grid's (*Its*) connectivity density, were combined in a series of complex calculations that eventually produced the S Parameter. Bob explained Hattie's role in measuring and calculating S and that her revised method gave a much more accurate – and *stable* - value. Aisha reminded them all, once more, that a figure of *0.750* would be typical for a human brain. "Although such a precise value may not be entirely reliable here," she murmured to cover herself.

"But whatever, It's already bloody close," stressed Andy.

Using her spreadsheet as best she could (it was not designed as a teaching tool so was somewhat opaque to anyone other than her), Jenny tried to show the effect that removing the Berlin and Madrid nodes would have on the S Parameter. Just *two nodes* – even large ones – would not be a huge loss to It in global terms but she predicted there would be a small, hopefully just noticeable, effect. The calculations suggested a reduced figure of $S = 0.736$. Bob took up the case.

"But you've got to understand the significance of that," he pressed. "We're measuring the brain-like activity of the *noise* – the *PDN* – *not* the user data. After a few seconds, *our* traffic will have been rerouted and settle down, but the noise will depend on the connection density so the S value should stay lower … until we bring the two nodes back on line, that is. None of that would happen unless we were measuring something *like* brain activity." Aisha nodded enthusiastically.

Not-Thompson considered this all for several seconds, glanced at the time, and announced crisply:

"Understood. We carry out this experiment at 10am. I need to make others aware." She left without another word.

*

They were reassembled before ten o'clock. Three more suits had joined the group: Andy's Tintin-based classification system was struggling now. Everyone was prepared. They rechecked Hattie, who still read $S = 0.740$. On the stroke of 10:00, not-Thompson nodded towards Stephen and one of his team standing alongside him pressed the return key to enter the prepared configuration script. They watched and waited.

Hattie showed $S = 0.740$. They all gazed at the giant display. After a few seconds, the two core nodes in Berlin and Madrid flashed twice and faded into the background, taking with them the links that connected them to other nodes. They looked back at Hattie.

$S = 0.740$. Aisha and Andy looked uncertain; Jenny, uncomfortable. Bob was downright worried – and showed it.

They waited; fifteen seconds passed.

$S = 0.740$

Thirty seconds.

$S = 0.740$

One of Stephen's team, stooping over a separate display, announced:

"All the routing tables have been updated. Every traffic stream that can be diverted, has been. We are stable."

$S = 0.740$

A minute.

$S = 0.740$

Not-Thompson wore a petulant expression. She spoke in whispers to one of her newer team.

$S = 0.740$

The Desk looked crestfallen. They peered nervously at not-Thompson.

$S = 0.740$

Not-Thompson took a deep breath and barked:

"*Take down Paris.*"

Stephen was taken aback. "Are you sure?" he asked.

"Yes. Do it."

This had not been prepared so it took a minute to write and send the reconfiguration details. Still Hattie's reading was unchanged. Stephen's team member finished and looked up for final confirmation. Not-Thompson nodded. The return key was pressed.

The Paris node and its links flashed and faded.

$S = 0.740$

Another half-minute passed. The network was confirmed as stable.

$S = 0.740$

Not-Thompson looked conspicuously at the time. It was 10:05. "So, is anything going to happen?" she snapped.

$S = 0.740$

"No, I don't think so," Jenny said quietly, not far from tears.

"Switch everything back on," barked not-Thompson.

The reset commands were sent – from prepared scripts for Berlin and Madrid, by hand for Paris. The massive display showed the nodes flashing and becoming steady again.

$S = 0.740$

"We're stable."

$S = 0.740$

Silence.

*

The extended Tintin team, particularly Thomson, Thompson and not-Thompson, glared at The Desk and were on the verge of an unceremonious departure. The Desk looked hopelessly around at each other. Stephen's team clearly shared their misery. They had failed. Was this experiment too small? Were the calculations inaccurate? Was the model flawed? Or were they just plain wrong about *everything*? *Was this whole sentient Internet thing just complete nonsense?* It was over.

But what Stephen said next, they would remember always. He spoke, quietly and with the hint of a firm smile.

"Ladies and gentlemen, what did you *think* was going to happen?"

"We expected the S value to drop, of course," said Bob, with undisguised irritation.

Stephen's smile grew clearer. *"Why* would you think that?" he asked.

"Because we've disconnected those nodes, obviously," growled Jenny. "So we've made It a tiny bit smaller."

"But you have not!" He shook his head slowly to emphasise the point; the smile became a grin. Jenny raised her bowed head and squinted quizzically at him. Not-Thompson raised her hand to stay her evacuating team.

"What?"

"Forgive me, ladies and gentlemen. I had no wish to be theatrical; but I wanted to make sure I *really* understood your model and the best way to do that was to see what happened if you ran an experiment I considered *flawed.* If such a test failed and, God willing," to their surprise, he glanced upwards at this point, "a better one worked, then every last doubt I might have about your theory would be removed. We are half-way to that point, I believe."

Jenny's voice and expression were a mixture of exasperation and rekindled hope. *"Flawed?* How?"

"You did not remove those nodes."

"Yes, we did. We shut them down."

"But you did not *remove* them. You *turned everything off* as a networker would." He grinned at Bob. "You stopped them operating: running anything, disabled all switching processes and closed down their interfaces so that they processed no traffic. In an operational sense, they are lifeless – yes. *But they are still there.*"

Jenny's mouth fell open. Stephen continued.

"You have explained this to me but now I have to explain it to you. *It* operates how *It* chooses, not necessarily in the manner for which *we* have designed Its individual components. Those nodes are still there. They are still plugged in and powered. All their connecting data cables are still in place. To us, they have stopped operating but to It, they are there nonetheless. They are still part of It: It sees no change."

Everyone was silent for a moment. Aisha was the first to speak.

"So what *do* we have to do?"

"We have to *physically* remove those devices from the network," answered Stephen firmly. "The kit must be disconnected from all power grids and cables removed from all interfaces. It is unlikely that such major switches will have any wireless interfaces but, even if they do, these will be rendered inoperative, from Its perspective, by the node becoming physically remote. We know that – even with Its wireless links now active – It remains a *single, physically connected entity*. Physically removing all wired connections will remove these nodes from It."

"And, how the hell are we going to do that," snarled Bob, the irritation returning. "Shall I hop on a plane to Madrid?" he asked derisively. "Andy, do you fancy going to Paris? Aisha? Berlin? Oh, for God's sake!"

"I have others in place," Stephen said softly. "In Berlin and Madrid, I have people ready to perform the necessary *complete* physical disconnection. Not in Paris, though," he conceded. "I was not expecting that. But our *original* experiment can be repeated properly, I think?" He smiled at everyone, a trace of triumph in his eyes.

"Good; we reschedule for 11am," announced not-Thompson with her usual minimal ceremony. A particularly large RFS spark cracked and flashed from the other side of the room.

*

Most people stayed in the control room. A few left and returned shortly before eleven o'clock. When they were all as one, not-Thompson gave her approval, as before, exactly at 11:00. Hattie still read $S = 0.740$. This time, Stephen had two members of his team, each in direct contact with Berlin and Madrid.

"Disconnect Berlin." "Disconnect Madrid," they ordered in unison.

After a few seconds, the first announced, "Madrid disconnected." A fraction of a second later, the second confirmed, "Berlin disconnected."

On the main display screen, both nodes disappeared abruptly.

They quickly turned to Hattie, who for an alarming second, still read $S = 0.740$, but then:

$S = 0.739$

A few more seconds:

$S = 0.738$

Soon:

$S = 0.737$

"We're stable."

The Desk beamed huge smiles at each other. Hattie refused to offer any lower S reading but this was close enough: the point was made. Jenny grinned from ear to ear; her joy was matched by Stephen's. Not-Thompson nodded – just the faintest of movements, shrugged slightly and raised a defensive hand; but there was clear concession in the gesture. They waited another minute but there was no change. The smiles remained.

Not-Thompson looked again at the time. It was 11:02. "So, is anything else going to happen?" she asked. It was the same question as before but her tone was entirely altered.

$S = 0.737$

"No, I don't think so," laughed Jenny. So was hers.

"Switch them back on," ordered not-Thompson.

"Reconnect Berlin." "Reconnect Madrid." The remote instructions were given. They saw Hattie's value change even before confirmation came back.

$S = 0.738$

"Berlin reconnected."

$S = 0.739$

"Madrid reconnected … Both powered up"

$S = 0.740$

"Rerouting complete. We're stable."

"*Bloody fantastic!*" shouted Andy.

Not-Thompson nodded again and quickly ushered her team from the room. "We will return shortly," she assured them. The Desk watched them leave in triumph, smiled at each other once more and looked back, almost with affection, at Hattie.

$S = 0.741$

"*Eh?*" spluttered Bob.

*

The head-scratching was metaphorical, rather than physical, but the confusion was real enough. Aisha pulled an uncomfortable face.

"Maybe this was just due?" she suggested in a whisper. "It changed from *738* to *739* last night and to *740* by this morning. Perhaps It is just continuing to improve? We know the value has been increasing steadily. Perhaps it is just coincidence that it happened now and this is normal progression?"

$S = 0.740$

"*Ah!*"

*

They waited quietly for the door to the stairs to close behind not-Thompson's team.

"Just a blip, surely?" insisted Andy. Jenny nodded.

"I don't know," said Bob. "Hattie's much more stable now: if she's getting a different reading – even by a tiny amount, I'd have thought there was *something* going on." He thought a moment longer, then shook his head. "No, you're probably right: just a 'blip', I suppose."

"Yes, probably," agreed Aisha hesitantly. "Or …"

"Or what?"

"Well, I know Paulo Di Iorio has done some work on this. I do not think his results are very complete but I believe he has some evidence that the brain exhibits both a localised *and* general increase in activity immediately following a damage-repair cycle, or if new inputs are added: artificial implants for example. It is unproven but it would make sense if the brain showed temporarily higher levels of signals whilst trying to *learn* its way around new connectivity."

"Suppose so."

"The question is whether that model would make sense in an Internet scenario?"

"It might," admitted Bob. "After all, when any network topology changes, or something else comes on board, there's some increase in traffic to cope with it – whether it's new devices handshaking or traffic being rerouted. I guess that's something It could pick up on? Maybe when It sees something 'new', the PDN increases temporarily while It figures out how to use it properly? That might even be part of Its *learning*?"

"Makes sense, I suppose."

"Shall we worry about it then?"

"Let's not."

*

The group that reassembled at noon was smaller: The Desk, not-Thompson, Thomson and Stephen. To minimise RFS distraction (and danger), they used a small meeting room off the main chamber. It contained some videoconferencing and audio-visual facilities but these were powered off and disconnected. There was interference to lighting from time to time and – they discovered – the climate control system had been dual-connected to a back-up source should it be needed. Everyone, from senior management to technicians now wore protective clothing to some extent. That aside, they managed a reasonable attempt at normality.

Not-Thompson began without ceremony.

"I doubt I need to tell you all how grave the situation is," she opened. "The world is now a very dangerous place indeed. We have a problem on a scale, the like of which we have never known. We cannot accurately estimate RFS casualties – the figures rise continually – but there have undoubtedly been close to a million deaths globally and many millions of injuries." An icy chill descended every spine and they all shuddered involuntarily. "Everyone is at risk," she said, "at every moment of the day." She glanced around the room and out into the main control centre. "*We* are at risk; the *whole world* is at risk. Those currently some distance from technology or technology centres – rural areas and developing countries, for example – may be safer than others but they are not entirely protected. Planes and trains have crashed, weapons have been unintentionally fired (non-nuclear, thankfully), essential supplies have been disrupted – often severed entirely. You may have already heard that your own British Royal Family has suffered a significant loss? In the short or long term, *no-one* is safe.

"And a new problem begins to present itself. As people suffer these losses, they become scared; they become angry. They blame governments and they blame each other. There has already been considerable unrest in many parts of the world. People are being killed, and they are beginning to kill each other. A world-wide humanitarian catastrophe looms. This cannot be allowed to continue. It has to *stop*.

"So, let us now suppose we are correct in our explanation of the cause of Potentially Disruptive Noise and Random Failure Syndrome," she continued. It appeared The Desk's explanation had very quickly become *her* explanation, although credit and acknowledgement appeared not to be forthcoming as such. "We then have two questions to answer. Firstly, what do we tell the public – and when? Secondly, *what do we do to stop it*?"

"Surely the public have a right to be told the ...," Andy began but was interrupted by not-Thompson.

"The first question will not be considered by the present group," she added quickly, giving him a cold stare. "*Your* expertise," she scanned the others, "is needed in relation to the second."

There was no response: no-one wanted to take the lead.

"I ask again: what can be done to *stop* – or even *reduce* – RFS?"

Aisha looked around nervously, reluctant to be spokesperson. "I do not think there is any option," she said slowly. "You will have to reduce the level of complexity – *connectivity* – that has given It Its control imperative, Its *sentience*, if you like. You will have to massively *disconnect It; break It*."

"*Kill it*, you mean?" said Andy, thoughtfully, as much to himself as to the rest of the group.

*

The Thompson-Stephen-Desk federation reformed shortly afterwards and discussions recommenced, along with more experimentation and monitoring. For the time being, Hattie maintained a constant reading of $S = 0.740$. They worked into the afternoon; in small groups for small periods, coming together regularly to share thoughts and new information. There was a fundamental impasse, however, which no amount of technical measurement could overcome.

"*The only way to stop It is to disconnect It,*" Aisha found herself saying time and time again in different forms, supported by Jenny and Bob. Andy remained quiet for the most part.

"*We cannot allow that,*" and variations upon it, was the standard reply from not-Thompson and her entourage. Stephen and his team appeared neutral.

"*Think about all the things that are connected to It! EVERYTHING's connected to It! It's only going to get worse! It HAS to be disconnected!*"

"*We cannot allow that!*"

*

"OK, suggest another way then?" Jenny offered during the latest of these exchanges.

"We need to find a solution other than breaking It. Surely, there must be some way to *remove* the noise from the network?" implored one of not-Thompson's team.

"Yes, that would be nice, wouldn't it?" snarled Jenny, in an exasperated tone. "But *how*?"

"You have to understand, we have no *control* over PDN," explained Bob, trying to remain calm. "We probably never *did*, but now that It's doing things Its own way, we *really* don't. You could say It's quite *literally* got a mind of Its own!" He glanced at both Andy and Aisha as he said this but there was no visible objection to either the semantics or science of the statement.

"Can we not drown it out with signals – *noise* – of our own?"

Bob, shook his head. "Anything we could do to block the noise would have the same effect on our data. If you make the channels unusable by *It*, you make them unusable for *us*."

"In which case, you may as well disconnect It," observed Jenny.

"Surely we can find an intelligent way to close down interfaces or block traffic?"

"But, again, that would only disrupt *us*. *It's* found *Its* own way of doing things. We don't have any effect on *It* unless we physically disconnect and unplug kit. We *know* that: Stephen's little trick has *proved* that."

"Perhaps we can run systems at certain times only?"

"You still don't really get this, do you?" Bob's patience was wearing thin now. "We're not talking about clever network settings here. We'd never be able to do that *physically* – which is what we'd need to do – and, even if we did, we'd be back to where we started as soon as things came back on line. We've seen how quickly It reconfigures Itself."

"Can we switch off the power networks then?"

"And let people freeze, and starve? *Nothing* would work then!"

"Some aspects of RFS will be damaging Its own network infrastructure, surely? Perhaps, in time, It will destroy *Itself*?"

"In time, yes, It probably *will*. Obviously, It must be hurting Itself, to some extent, with what It's doing. But the wireless gives It so much more connectivity now. At the moment, It seems to be finding Its way around Its structure faster than It's losing parts of it. It's killing *people* quicker than It's killing Itself. I reckon It'll outlast *us*!"

"So what *do* we do?"

Aisha turned to Jenny, who took a deep breath.

"We have to do some more calculations," she began, hesitantly, "but it shouldn't be too difficult. We have to identify a key set of major comms nodes across the world, which would bring Its essential complexity – Its connectivity – below a certain critical threshold."

"We have to eliminate Its natural control imperative," agreed Aisha.

"Then we have to physically disconnect and unplug those nodes," said Bob.

"And *leave* them that way," Jenny concluded.

"That simply cannot happen," said not-Thompson, shaking her head slowly. "The cost would be beyond calculation."

"More than a million people *dead*?" screamed Jenny, nearing hysteria.

"In economic terms, *yes*."

"Well, if that's really our priority here," muttered Andy, sitting largely uninvolved and unobserved towards the back of the group, "then we really *are* screwed!"

*

A middle-aged man in uniform sat listening on headphones. A woman in a smart grey business suit watched him closely; but his features betrayed no emotion. His eyes wandered, from time to time, between the display screens in front of him and the grass lawns outside the window but his head remained motionless and his breathing steady. Eventually, he allowed just a slightly extended sigh to escape his lips. The woman's gaze increased its intensity. He pressed a button, removed the headphones and turned to face her.

"Well?"

"Well, Ma'am," he said calmly, "the Europeans may know what the problem is."

"Yes?"

"And they may know what to do about it."

"Go on …"

"But you're not going to like either part."

Chapter 20: People

"There has to be another way. *Find another way!*" not-Thompson roared. The passing of a further discursive hour without progress had not changed her position but it *had* made her angrier. "Europe calls on its scientists in its hour of need and you let us down!" Her calm exterior was crumbling and some of her rationality seemed to have escaped her. Her words were a painful reminder to Jenny of her disastrous BBC interview before Christmas. Frequent calls, in a side room, to and from unseen powers suggested not-Thompson to be under pressure from even higher in the European order. The current episode was becoming a rant. "What good was all that research funding for academics and public bodies?" she continued with the onslaught. "You waste our money! If we had given it all to the private labs and businesses, I am sure *they* would deliver a solution for us!"

"We *have* given you a solution," Aisha said quietly. "We have told you what to do."

"And, if you don't like hearing it from us, then open it out to the wider scientific community," suggested Jenny.

"Aye, tell *everyone*; and ask for ideas," suggested Andy, sardonically. "Or, if you can't trust the *people*, just ask the *banks!*"

"Or just wait for It to destroy *Itself* – after It has accounted for *all of us*, of course," Aisha added.

Not-Thompson bared her teeth in anger. The situation aside, she was clearly unaccustomed to being spoken to like this.

"Problem is," Bob interjected, a piercing look in his eyes, "that you're already *doing* this to some extent, aren't you?" The others turned to him in surprise; he continued. "I guessed back in Luxembourg that I wasn't the only guy you were consulting about this! You just wouldn't work like that, would you? You've been speaking with other experts, besides us, all along; yes?"

Stephen smiled: a trace of acknowledgement.

"But the point is," Bob continued, "*they* haven't produced the goods, have they? *We're* the ones who have worked out what's going on – and I'm guessing no-one else has yet. But you've told them *now*, haven't you?"

Stephen nodded slightly.

"So, presumably, now that you've shared our ideas with some other scientists and suchlike," added Jenny, quick to pick up the plot, "they're telling you the *same* things?"

"Ah, right, I see! And no-one is giving you any alternative solutions because *there are none!*" said Aisha conclusively.

Not-Thompson strode back to the side room abruptly, slamming the door behind her. After a brief call, she left the control room entirely.

Thomson spoke for the first time in a long while.

"With regard to your suggestion to inform the public of these 'developments'," he said slowly, "now is not the time; but we *are* discussing the matter with our American colleagues. I will keep you informed."

*

As the afternoon wore on, they continued to monitor the Internet – *It* – as best they could. Stephen's team gradually extended their reach, establishing remote connections to other regions inside and outside of Europe. This (when everything *worked* – and it often did not) allowed them to take measurements from across wider areas and in greater volume. Ultimately, it confirmed everything they knew but told them nothing new. Hattie still read $S = 0.740$. Not-Thompson had not returned and, if anyone *had* mentioned any of this to the Americans, they knew nothing of any response. A news channel, intermittently displayed on one of the side monitors, between bursts of interference, showed destruction on a global scale they could hardly believe. Three million might be dead across the world – perhaps more – initially directly from RFS. But now, a new, possibly even darker, danger arose. Supply networks had failed; vast areas were without food; there were early reports of outbreaks of disease. Law and order was breaking down in large parts of the world: there were riots and looting in several countries. *Nature* and *people* were now as much of a threat to each other as the *technology*. The last available credible public explanation of a massive cyber-attack seemed to matter little now; it *could* have been aliens for all anyone cared: the cause was immaterial – the effect catastrophic. Global society was approaching meltdown.

Personal tragedy slowly mixed with the on-screen horror. News gradually filtered through to the control room of friends and loved ones. No-one was unaffected: only levels of closeness varied. One of Stephen's team ran out in tears without warning; they later discovered he had lost a daughter. A technician left suddenly to find his injured wife. An old school-friend of Andy's had been killed; so had a distant uncle of Aisha's. Jill messaged Bob to say that Chris, Heather and Ben had had a lucky escape in their car: they had promised not to drive again and were all home together as safe as they could manage. Old Mrs. Harris's son had been badly injured returning from visiting his mother in hospital: his chances were evenly balanced. The list grew longer and longer.

Just as they were beginning to think there was little more to do or see in their work, Hattie gave them some further food for thought. The slight, and temporary, increase in the S Parameter reappeared a few times through the afternoon and early evening. As before, Hattie's $S = 0.740$ changed to $S = 0.741$ for a few moments before reverting to $S = 0.740$. This happened three times before, shortly after six o'clock, her value changed to $S = 0.741$ and remained steady. She was not done, however: twice more over the next couple of hours, she moved from $S = 0.741$ to $S = 0.742$ for a short period before settling once more back to $S = 0.741$. Jenny and Bob discussed it at length but could find no sensible explanation. Aisha felt keenly that there was 'some learning somewhere in it' but could not be precise.

*

The smart woman stood on the grass lawn, facing away from a curved white wall. Her business suit had changed from grey to cream but was otherwise identical to before. She was joined by the uniformed man, emerging from the building behind her. As he approached, she turned and opened her eyes in question. He half closed his own in anticipation of what he did not want to say or she to hear.

"Ma'am, we *are* going to have to talk to the Europeans."

*

Almost no-one seemed to have remembered – or even cared – that it was New Year's Eve. Certainly The Desk had given it little thought until Aisha overheard a couple of the technicians discussing plans for the rest of the evening. Originally, the traditional fireworks display had been intended for the *Place de Brouckère* but there was little doubt that this would be cancelled. It was dangerous enough outside anyway without any attempt to use timed explosives in the name of entertainment!

The Belgians, however, were a resilient people. Brussels had seen its share of horror over the years. The terrorist attacks at the airport and elsewhere in the city were still fresh in the minds of its occupants and the New Year's Eve celebrations themselves – including the light-show and fireworks – had even been cancelled in 2015 as a security measure. Rather than cower in fear, a spirit of determined resistance had sprung up in Brussels, as in other European cities. They would be sensible, yes. They would take precautions, indeed, but they would not be driven into hiding. Whatever the threat was, whoever was behind it, they would present a brave face to it and the world.

So instead, a plan emerged on social media, and on the mainstream news when they became aware of it, for something like an urban party as an act of defiance. Place de Brouckère was simply too enclosed and too small for this and there was too much technology – and its associated danger – all around. It was quickly agreed that the *Parc de Bruxelles* would be an altogether better location. The authorities were distinctly less than enthusiastic and, at first, threatened to arrest those congregating in groups anywhere in the vicinity of the palace, parliament or theatre. However, recognising in short time that they lacked any organised strength to prevent it (public services were way beyond breaking point) and realising that there was to be no stopping it, they eventually gave it their limited support and even made some practical arrangements to minimise danger: the power grids were switched off in the area and a rudimentary temporary lighting system was hastily sent in, powered by stand-alone generators. All public wireless networks were disabled.

Aisha announced suddenly that she was going to the party. She needed fresh air and a change of scenery; she also sensed the city's defiance and wanted to share in it. Jenny, after a short debate within herself, agreed to join her. Bob had not yet given up on something useful coming from the network analysis so, despite some rugged attempts at persuasion, he elected to remain.

Andy surprised them somewhat by also deciding to stay. At first, he was slightly elusive as to why and Aisha was both disappointed and upset. Eventually he had to concede the real reason. His leg, injured in the accident in London, was causing him more problems that he had disclosed to anyone: walking any distance was difficult and painful. Aisha took him aside and hastily inspected the wound, which had clearly deteriorated through the day, since she had last seen it that morning. She was annoyed and concerned in quick order and her initial reaction was to stay with him. Andy's promise to have it properly treated and dressed while she was gone, together with his threat to go out himself if she did not, eventually persuaded her.

"You are an extremely pig-headed man," she snarled at him in a mixture of annoyance and affection.

*

Aisha and Jenny left the control room – with two uniformed guards, summoned for that purpose – shortly before 10:30pm. It took quarter of an hour to reach the open air. They were guided along passages, up flights of stairs and through a series of doors of gradually decreasing security until they finally emerged onto the street through what appeared to be the entrance to a residential block near to Maelbeek Metro station. Their escorts would have preferred to accompany them to the park itself but their offer was refused. Instead, they were to return to the same spot at 1am to be guided back to the control room, or to their hotel, depending on where the others might be by that time.

Parc de Bruxelles was about half a mile away and, already, a steady stream of people was moving in that direction. Faces were mixed. Some looked sad, others grimly determined; many at least feigned a lighter expression; a few were even boisterous. Everyone was doing their best to avoid immediate sources of danger but accidents were happening nonetheless. As they stepped from the doorway, they found themselves in the company of a group of about a dozen men in their twenties and thirties, most carrying cans or bottles and already clearly somewhat the worse for wear.

"Sorry, pet," slurred the lead man, as he swerved to avoid Jenny.

"No problem."

"Ah, English!"

"Yes."

"Us too. Stag trip from Leeds. Not sure when we're going home though now all this crap's happened! Where you girls from?"

"London."

"Never mind, not your fault!" quipped another, with a self-congratulatory laugh like a braying donkey.

You can join us if you like, girls," suggested a third, wearing sunglasses against the merciless glare of the Belgian night sky.

"Oh, joy!" whispered Aisha to Jenny, who returned the faintest of smiles.

Most of the group, although fairly lubricated, were sociable enough but there were perhaps two of three of their number who seemed distinctly less friendly. One, in particular, shaven-headed and tattooed and noticeably drunker, glared at Aisha as he barged quickly past. Despite the cold, he wore little more than a white t-shirt – with a thick red cross of St. George – above the waist. It was quickly clear, as they walked on, that his displeasure was not reserved solely for her: about half the population of Brussels appeared to fall short of whatever his personal expectations of a human being might be.

Parc de Bruxelles had been re-landscaped somewhat in late 2016. Some of the parallel paths had been lost and the tree cover increased: new techniques had been used to plant mature trees, which were now flourishing. The result was a reduction in horizontal visibility across many areas, which now suited Aisha and Jenny well. Entering the park, they detached themselves from the group as quickly as they could, reducing their pace and falling behind as they approached the central fountain. The stags continued to display their rutting prowess, by attempting to push each other into the water, swearing loudly as they did so, and generally maximising the annoyance they could cause to the greatest number of people. As they staggered around the pond on its right, Aisha and Jenny took the left path and lost themselves in the crowd.

*

Andy was away in the facility's medical centre. Bob remained in the control room, staring at the central display screen. Stephen's team and numerous technicians fluttered in his peripheral vision. He gazed at the sea of red, which covered the world map, then at Hattie's various displays. Her 'scopes showed no change in the PDN now almost saturating the network and she still read $S = 0.741$. Bob glanced at the clock display, which flicked from 22:59 to 23:00 as he watched, then back to Hattie. As he did so, her digits changed to:

$S = 0.742$

Bob watched both Hattie and his smart-watch. Her display remained at the new value for nearly a minute this time before reverting to $S = 0.741$. This was the longest 'blip' yet but he was no closer to understanding what it meant. He sighed a resigned sigh. At that moment, Andy reappeared – his leg now visibly bandaged and padded under his jeans – and hobbled a few steps down into the control room. Seeing Bob several units away, he stopped and shouted.

"Coffee? I've just found a nice little canteen, on the way back from the medical room, no-one mentioned to us: seems to be free!"

Bob nodded slowly in defeat.

"Have they got any beer?"

"I didn't look; they *might*."

"Coming," he grunted.

*

In Parc de Bruxelles, people were trying their hardest to party. Some makeshift stalls had appeared selling food and drink, powered by local generators supplied by the authorities. There was little light but just enough for safe navigation of the open areas and there were small groups dancing to different pockets of music. A few drones were in the air: some taking aerial photographs; others, it seemed, just for the entertainment of being flown. Between the vast areas covered by trees, however, things were distinctly gloomy and these regions were serving as a retreat for those with more secretive or romantic ambitions. Some, hidden beneath the heaviest cover, seemed particularly determined to take advantage of what might – they obviously felt, for many of them – be their last night on Earth. As always, the drug-sellers and other casual hawkers of just about anything the flesh might desire were plying their trades. There was a crude, dark, almost beautiful elegance to it all: something like the simplicity of an earlier, less-technological time.

And yet these were the hardy minority. Most citizens had chosen to stay at home, where they felt the danger to be minimised. That this was no absolute guarantee of safety was evidenced by the occasional flash, explosion or collective cry in the distance. Perhaps 100,000 people – certainly no more – were in the park itself or milling around its edges. Away from the immediate area, the streets of Brussels were close to deserted. Other than the partiers, only those with a call such as outweighed the peril had ventured out.

At around quarter to midnight, greater numbers of people started to gravitate from the periphery towards the park's central walkway. A temporary digital clock display had been erected at the mid-point for the countdown to the New Year. As pockets of people ebbed and flowed, to their disappointment, Aisha and Jenny found themselves accidentally reunited with their rowdy compatriots. The crowds around them now were too dense for a subtle withdrawal.

"Yo! London girls!" Either Donkey or Sunglasses shouted: they could not tell.

They smiled.

Drunk St. George scowled.

*

In the main control room, Andy and Bob returned from their coffee. Bob looked at the clock; it was 23:50. Too soon for a New Year call to Jill really but it was likely to be difficult tonight so an early start might be advisable. He had managed briefly earlier in the day but not without trouble. Although the 4 & 5G in the air was PDN free, the core switches were pretty screwed. He made four attempts this time without success before hearing the call tone at the other end. Jill answered quickly.

"Hello?"

"Happy New Year, Sweetheart!" He tried to sound as cheerful as possible.

"Bit early, aren't you?"

"Only by a few minutes."

"More like an hour and a few minutes. We've just had a late dinner. Chris and Heather have just got Ben off to bed. He's not sleeping well at the moment: all the noise is keeping him awake."

Bob slapped his hand theatrically to his forehead. Idiot! Of course, Europe was an hour ahead of the UK. It was not yet eleven there. In the general confusion and madness, he had overlooked the obvious point that his family back in London would be in the old year for another hour. Further west, of course, it would take them even longer and, to the east, other countries had already been seeing in the New Year at different times through the afternoon.

Oh. My. God!

"Aaaah, sorry, Sweetheart. I'll call you back later," he stuttered apologetically and closed the call abruptly. Andy eyed him with concern across the table.

Bob spun back to one of the smaller displays and opened the spreadsheet into which Hattie had been dumping her readings throughout the afternoon. It was a huge file but he quickly queried it to strip out the constant values. The few lines that remained showed the several points during the afternoon and evening when the S Parameter had varied. His eyes widened in disbelief – then something approaching horror. He turned to Andy.

"*Look!*"

Andy shuffled over. "At what?"

"These *times*; the times when the S value changed today. When it went up then down again: the 'blips'."

"What about them?"

But there was no time for explanation. The clock showed 23:58.

"*Stephen!*" Bob bawled across the chamber. Stephen came running.

"*Call Aisha!*" Bob barked at Andy. "Tell her to come back. *Tell them to get out of there!* I'll try to call Jenny."

But neither of them could get through on mobiles. They tried both of their tracking apps instead but these were not working either.

*

Engulfed as it might be in its own share of a worldwide catastrophe, Brussels was still a very international and multicultural city and, even under normal circumstances, this was never more evident than at New Year. This year, many people of nationalities with different calendars had even chosen to join in. Neither Aisha nor Jenny had heard a multilingual countdown before. As the temporary digital clock flashed past 23:59, shouted numbers in various tongues could be heard competing to call in in the New Year. The good-humoured contest swayed in many directions as different groups struggled for supremacy.

"*Fünfzig.*"

The crowd pressed ever more closely together. Some joined hands or curved arms around others' backs.

"*Forty.*"

People began bouncing at the knees. The whole park took on the appearance of a sea, formed of thousands of tiny waves and swells.

"*Tredive.*"

Smiles formed on even the grimmest of countenances.

"*Twintig.*"

Still everyone strove to shout louder than their neighbours.

"*Nineteen. Dix-huit. Dix-sept. Sedici. Penkiolika.*"

The excitement approached a level of euphoria.

"*Catorce. Trece. Twelve. Elva. Ten.*"

The stags were determined and began to win the volume battle in their immediate area: not much else could be heard.

"*Nine. Eight. Siedem. Six. Five.*"

People raised their phones, tablets and watches to take photos.

"*Four. Three. Two.*"

People prepared to call distant friends and family.

"*One.*"

A few individual fireworks and flares were set off.

"*Zero!*"

A huge cheer erupted across the whole park in a tingling show of defiance. Brussels would not be beaten! Belgium would not be beaten! Europe would not be beaten! The *world* would not be beaten!

"*Happy New Year!*" "*Felice Anno Nuovo!*" "*Happy New Year!*"

People embraced and called loved ones.

"*Onnellista Uutta Vuotta!*" "*Happy New Year!*" "*Happy New Year!*"

Sunglasses hugged Aisha. Donkey embraced Jenny.

"*Happy New Year!*" "*Happy New Year!*" "*Happy New Year!*"

And then everyone's mobiles stopped working.

PHASE FIVE: COMPLICATIONS

Chapter 21: God for Harry!

Near silence fell within seconds. Only the very few without mobile technology in view (theirs or a near neighbour's) were unaware of what had happened; but even these realised quickly that something was amiss. Isolated cheers and snatches of song could still be heard in small pockets for a short while; then these also faded away and were replaced by the low, dense murmur of confusion, which spread across the entire park.

Exactly *what* happened varied from place to place, from device to device and from person to person. Just as when It had found Its wireless capabilities two days before, the visible effects of Its new powers were inconsistent and unpredictable. Some phones, tablets and watches flashed or vibrated; some randomly opened and closed apps, took photos or played or displayed unknown material; some locked or switched off and some did all, some, or none of these things. Most people still managed to send or receive calls or messages; but many were unable. A few had small shocks or other unpleasant side-effects. Some tried to turn their devices off and found that they could not. A few panicked and ran, fearing worse to come – but fled, unwittingly, into greater danger away from the park; most remained, rooted to their places, wondering what could have happened.

It was the same story for Jenny and Aisha: *their* mobile devices, in fact, were both completely useless. Jenny gazed in wonder at her smart-watch, Aisha with similar disbelief at her phone. Neither of them could send or receive anything – anything they *wanted* to, that was: as Aisha looked at her screen, an image appeared of a man something beyond middle-age.

"That's my brother!" cried Jenny in astonishment, looking across her. "How have you got that?"

"I have not," answered Aisha. "I have never seen it before."

Several drones dropped from the sky; some fell harmlessly into open spaces, but others found groups of people and caused injury. The stags nearby stood in dumb confusion. Around them, the general murmur increased.

Jenny leaned in to speak quietly to Aisha but found she had to raise her voice more than she would have liked, to be heard above the escalating chatter.

"So, are you thinking what I'm thinking?"

Aisha nodded. "It would appear that It has taken control of the mobile networks, the 4 & 5G." A drone crashed into the pond with a loud bang and splash, and was quickly swallowed by the water. "And who knows what else?" she added, nervously eyeing both sky and water.

"Bob did say this might happen; and I thought he might have a point," suggested Jenny.

"So did I, to some extent," said Aisha, also more loudly than she intended, and with an element of wounded pride. "*I could tell* somehow that It was in a new learning phase. I was not sure what but I suspected something was about to happen; it seems like a natural progression of Its development: *almost part of the plan*, if you like. *This doesn't surprise me*," she concluded firmly.

One of drunk St. George's unfriendly friends was closer than either of them realised. It was unclear exactly what he had heard – or thought he heard – but it was enough to catch his ear and interest. He thrust his head between the two of them in an unwelcome lunge.

"What was that you said, girls?"

"Wasn't important," muttered Jenny hastily. Aisha froze and said nothing.

"No, *you*," he maintained, raising an insolent finger to point at Aisha. "I heard *you* say something about knowing what was happening."

"No, I ...," Aisha began in alarm, but was shouted down.

"*I heard* you! *You said it was part of the plan!*"

"I did not; I ...," she tried again but, by now, the exchange had alerted drunk St. George himself, who was even drunker – and less rational – than earlier.

"What's the shit?" he drawled aggressively, taking a step in their direction.

"The fookin' rag-'ed *knows what's going on*," his fellow patriot shouted, placing a restraining hand on Aisha's shoulder. "She knows what's happening!"

"Get off!" bawled Aisha, slapping at the unwelcome touch. Jenny attempted to force her way between the two but was pushed away roughly and fell.

"Knows what happening? *Behind it then, more like!*" snarled drunk St. George. He stumbled into her and grabbed her other shoulder. Aisha screamed.

"We should have fookin' known you Mussie scum would be responsible," the first patriot shouted as they both tightened their grips. "You need teachin' a fookin' lesson!" He raised his other hand to strike.

But they were both drunk and Aisha was sober; they were stupid and she was clever. She turned and bent her knees, and twisted and dropped out of their hold. As the two thugs fell together into the space she had left like a vacuum, she straightened and kicked out at their combined form. At the moment drunk St. George rebounded away from his fellow bigot, her heel struck him a powerful blow high up between his legs. He grunted with pain.

"*Rag-'ed Bitch!*" he roared. His other hand swung backwards and they heard the smashing of glass as the bottle he carried broke against the temporary light-pole behind him. Forwards came the arm once more, his hand clutching the soaked and jagged remnants of the bottle by its neck. It continued on, in the same movement, towards Aisha's face. Jenny staggered to her feet.

The broken bottle's trajectory was more a thrust than a slash but Aisha contributed her own relative movement by trying to duck out of the way. The result was a sweeping contact across her face. A red, seething heat seemed to spread from ear to ear as she saw the glass glint different angles in the light. As Jenny

259

watched in horror, blood splashed from a dark line drawn across both her eyes.

"*That's for my brother!*" drunk St. George spat.

Most of the crowd recoiled in shock; a space opened around the English battle. A few, after their initial surprise, moved in to help; others seemed less certain of who deserved the support. Cries and questions were heard in many tongues but the stags could only understand English. Eventually, someone shouted.

"What's happened?"

Jenny ripped off her coat and used it to try to stem the flow of blood from Aisha's face. Neither were able to reply. Instead, drunk St. George, violently compromised between the pride of his deed and fear of retribution, turned to the nearest of the encircling mass and screeched,

"*This is the terrorist scum behind all this! This is their fault! All of it!*" His arm described a semi-circle, indicating the scale of Aisha's culpability across the park – possibly the world; he still brandished the bottle neck as a symbol of his heroic conquest.

The mood of the crowd changed – not universally or to the last individual – but overall. A lot doubted drunk St. George's claim but, in the passion and confusion of the moment, some clearly considered it credible. A few still appeared concerned for Aisha's injury; others seemed more uncertain. But many had suddenly found an unexpected outlet for their pent-up frustration, fear, and *anger* of the past week or so. After ten days of fending off a growing enemy they could neither understand nor undermine, they at last had a visible target directly in front of them. Rationality might have to wait on revenge. The threat was clear.

Jenny had to make an immediate decision, which she did. The crowd looked thinner in one direction than the others. Still holding the screwed-up coat to Aisha's eyes, she grabbed her arm with her free hand, pulled her with all her strength and ran towards the weakest point in the circle. Most people gave way before them but a few stood firm and several rounded in pursuit. They burst through the first line without much difficulty and into clearer space with fewer people in their way. Beyond the immediate audience of the attack, there was less awareness of the situation and, in principle, less resistance. They dodged and ran about fifty yards, chased by a growing group of several dozen or so intent on further retribution. They threw themselves into the darkness of the trees, avoiding – often only at the very last moment – both human and wooden obstructions. They exploded from the cover into the light on the other side, Jenny's arms and face cut in every direction by the slashing of a hundred branches. The pursuing crowd grew.

But soon they could go no further. The crowd along the far side of the pathway, opposite the trees, was so dense that they were funnelled, without choice, along its length. The vigilantes gained on them. At the far end, they came to a temporary fence behind which most of the portable generators were placed, out of everyone's way. It was too high to climb and crowds blocked any way around on either side. Aisha could not see and Jenny dared not relinquish her hold on the, now drenched, makeshift tourniquet: blood still seeped from behind it. They stopped, turned and faced their fate with their backs pressed hard against the icy wire mesh. Their pursuers slowed, realising that their prey had no means of escape, and moved coldly in for the final act, some brandishing sticks and knives. The stags, by this time, were nowhere to be seen. Aisha understood the impending violence quite as well as if she could see and grasped Jenny's free hand as a last, desperate gesture of friendship.

*

Suddenly there was gunfire: two distinct shots were heard close by. For Aisha, seeing nothing, her immediate thought was that their attackers were even more fully-armed than they had feared: she waited for an impact. Jenny, however, could perceive the rear of the group hesitate, slow and begin to fragment. As they did so, through the gaps, uniformed soldiers came into view, sprinting towards the impending confrontation. More warning shots were fired to alert the leading ranks of the pursuit group. In total, between one and two hundred men and women in uniform appeared to have entered the park.

But the mob's front line was lost in its blood-lust. Some never heard; some heard but could not bring their madness under control. They continued to advance; others turned to face the troops, who became an extension of the enemy. Further shots rang out and people fell. On each flank, the soldiers spread out and pushed forward, level with the leading vigilantes; then began to encircle them. There were cries to stop; some did but many pressed on. Away through the blurred crowds of troops and public, Jenny thought – just for a moment – that she saw Stephen standing between two officers.

Five men, the very vanguard of the avenging group, closed in on Aisha and Jenny. They waved knives and cudgels. The soldiers raised their guns. Further warnings were shouted. The five continued to advance, murder in their eyes: they were within striking distance now. A sharp command was followed by the near-simultaneous crack of twenty or thirty rifles and the five men fell dead before them. Small trails of blood formed quickly, flowing away from the bodies and combining in growing pools between them. Jenny vomited in a mixture of relief and revulsion, then felt Aisha grow heavier against her side as she gradually lost consciousness and collapsed at her feet.

*

S = 0.832
"Jesus, bloody Christ!"

Bob turned round in surprise. He had not realised Jenny was behind him until she spoke. In fact, she had only just arrived; he had been so engrossed in his thoughts – none of them good, that he had not heard her creep uncomfortably down the steps of the control room. He darted her a questioning, but compassionate, look.

"The hospital room's let me go," she volunteered by way of explanation, struggling to hold back tears. Her arms were bandaged and scratches showed vividly on her nose and cheeks;

the last remnants of her black eyes completed a sorry picture. "I think they've got more important things to worry about."

"How is she?"

Jenny swallowed hard. "*Alive*. Apart from that, I'm not sure. I caught a glimpse of her face as they rushed her off to theatre – before you and Andy got there. *She's a real mess, Bob*." She could say no more. Her throat contracted into sobs as she tried to speak.

Bob's head drooped and his eyes stared, without focusing, at the floor. "I just wish I'd figured it out sooner," he moaned softly.

"Wouldn't … have … made … any … difference," Jenny drove the words out in staccato form between sobs. "You didn't … really know … what was … going … to happen. Clever … to have … figured … it out … at all." She sat down beside him; they held each other close, united in their grief.

It was 9:30am on New Year's Day and, already, the hours since midnight lay behind them like a lifetime.

From Bob's perspective, the essential narrative had begun a few minutes before the New Year celebrations. Having, been reminded by Jill that Europe was an hour ahead of London, he had realised suddenly that other parts of the world had, of course, been celebrating the New Year at different points through the afternoon. These celebrations would involve sudden, short increases in mobile data traffic, as people called distant loved ones. Some lines of higher population would produce greater surges than others but there would always be an effect of some sort. Checking Hattie's data for the temporary rise in the S value, over the previous several hours, it was alarmingly clear that the 'blip' always started a second or so after the hour, and continued for a number of seconds after that. 'It' appeared to be observing the new mobile data and its regularity was probably helping It distinguish it from the rest of Its traffic internally. It was 'learning', as Aisha put it. At some point, he had been fairly sure, It would be able to make the transition from observer to exploiter and the change would be permanent. The hour before

Europe's midnight (New Year for some Eastern European countries and much of Africa) had shown a particularly long blip and there was every indication that the next one might be for real.

Of course, Bob's real concern was what *It* might *do* with Its new technological abilities, and whatever other threats might emerge from Its increase in complexity. A riot was far from his mind. He was immediately concerned for Aisha and Jenny, however, and had acted fast nonetheless. He and Andy failed to contact them but Stephen had sprung into action. As soon as Bob had explained his fears to him, as tersely as he could, Stephen dispatched three of his team at once, made two twenty-second calls and left the room himself immediately after. Bob's instinct had been to follow but Andy had managed to persuade him that he would be more use having the technical information to hand 'back at base'. (Apart from a brief visit to the hospital centre to see Jenny – Aisha had already been taken to surgery by the time he arrived, he had been there in the control room ever since. There had been no sleep.) Sure enough, a second or so after midnight, Hattie's reading had risen to $S = 0.742$. This time, however, there had been no retreat: after another few seconds, it had suddenly jumped to $S = 0.830$. On the room's main display screen, any node or link that was any colour other than red became red and they were instantly surrounded by the sight and sound of RFS on a scale they could barely comprehend. There were large sparks, flashes, explosions and several immediate injuries. Mobile devices behaved erratically. Much of their essential equipment had to be disconnected to contain the problem even in limited form. Once again, Hattie's fuses saved her and repair and replacement of sections of the main display screen had become an ongoing project. As the night wore on, a new wave of news of personal tragedies infiltrated the control room. Bob managed to get a short message to Jill but, by then, she already knew, to all intents and purposes, everything he needed to warn her.

*

On Stephen's relaying the news to not-Thompson, a minute before midnight, a number of well-planned and rehearsed processes had launched into action. The remaining few Brussels police (a few dozen) and troops (nearly a hundred) still held on final emergency standby had been activated in seconds, from different bases, and sent to join forces at Parc de Bruxelles. Stephen and his closest deputy had followed behind as the Berlaymont unit had deployed onto Schuman and sprinted towards the park.

According to official police reports, when the closest contingents of the armed squad had arrived at Parc de Bruxelles, they found, for the most part, an air of confusion but something short of outright panic. The removal of the area from the power grids had served to limit some of the large-scale destruction that was immediately apparent elsewhere in the city. There were several injuries, and a few deaths, from drone crashes and other incidents but, compared to the continuing RFS escalation of the past few days, and the new levels of horror beyond its boundaries, inside the park the situation's sudden deterioration was less apparent. 'Its' newly-acquired mobile capabilities were a universal nuisance but not quite so deadly in the park itself. One police unit would later report that, as they entered Parc de Bruxelles past the theatre, a group of drunken louts, ten or more, possibly British, were fleeing in the opposite direction. As they ran along *Rue Ducale*, an explosion blew a wall out; none were seen to rise from the rubble in which they fell.

In the relative calm of the park, reports continued, a particular source of disturbance was easy to locate. Four different armed units quickly converged on the western edge inside *Rue Royale*. The situation clearly required immediate action and, within a few minutes, 'after appropriate warnings were issued', thirteen people had been shot, eleven fatally. Two women in their forties were rescued 'from a threatening situation', both injured – one of them seriously.

Stephen had accompanied Aisha and Jenny in the ambulance that took them to the hospital section of the network facility.

There would be far less pressure on available staff and facilities there, he said. He gave directions for Andy and Bob to be escorted to meet them. Fires raged unchecked and bodies now lay unattended by the side of the road as the ambulance drove the short distance from the park to the facility. Mobs were rioting; shops, open or closed, were being looted. Death was all around. Aisha was taken into surgery immediately on arrival at the hospital. Bob had arrived shortly afterwards and remained nearly an hour. Andy was still there.

*

'Beep' $S = 0.833$

Many of Hattie's outputs were now fed directly into the room's main display and programmed to give notification of any variation. Much of the left-hand side of the huge screen (when it worked) showed her 'scope graphs and there were several lines of breakdown analysis of the S Parameter, along with copious unwanted nonsense It had provided elsewhere – and was proving impossible to eliminate. The S value itself, the most important figure of all, produced an audible signal – a simple, sharp beep – to alert them when it changed. The new value was still flashing as Jenny and Bob both turned to the screen. Jenny regained her composure enough to consider the work in front of them. Stephen and his deputy returned from a meeting with persons unknown.

"So, is it everything we think?" asked Bob. Stephen nodded gravely.

"Indeed it is," he answered sombrely. "Our sentient Internet, 'It', now appears to have complete mastery of *all* communication channels."

"Everything?" asked Jenny.

"Everything."

"The mobile networks? 4 & 5G?" suggested Bob.

"Everything. 4 & 5G, experimental 6G, the newer extended LTE & LPWA, Bluetooth and BluetoothX, Zigbee and OpenZigbee, mobile control protocols, land-based, airborne and marine navigation channels, satellite links … *everything*. It is reasonable to say that It can now potentially interfere with *any* device we might choose to connect to It, *the very moment we do*. The implications of this are, of course huge."

"Not only this," added his deputy, "but the, ah, … 'It' now appears to have a level of control *above* the physical layer."

"What do you mean?"

"We mean," Stephen explained, "that some of the problems we begin to see arise this morning are not restricted to malfunctioning *devices*. 'It' is producing more than successful *signals*. There is clear evidence of movement of *data*."

"Surely that's been happening for a while? We know a lot of data's been lost as systems fail."

"This is not merely *lost* data. 'It' appears to have begun to *manipulate* data of Its own accord. It may still be a *random* process – it almost certainly *is* – but we see information being sent and received *outside of our control*. Often – nearly always, in fact – this is incomplete, as the original control frames generally were when It was in Its early stages of development, but we are beginning to witness a crude level of *manipulation* of *our* information, rather than mere *interference* with it."

Bob considered this for a moment, nodding, watching the fragmented and meaningless text appearing and disappearing from the main display screen. He then, not without difficulty, opened Facebook on the machine in front of him and looked at his own timeline. It was a mixture of legitimate older posts and utter garbage. And in there somewhere was a few lines of something that looked a lot like his most recent credit card statement. Was this just his local view or could others see this? "Bloody Hell", he gasped. "It's playing silly buggers with our stuff!"

"But, how can that happen?" asked Jenny incredulously. "That's *application layer*! How can a load of data flying around where it shouldn't, find its way so far up the protocol stack?" However, she suddenly remembered her brother's photo on Aisha's phone earlier.

"Facebook may be a high-level application," said Bob, his eyes compressed in thought, "but rendering the screen output is almost as low as it gets: I guess *that's* the level on which the data's being moved. Remember It's not playing by our network model rules, any more. It's just doing what It likes, by the look of it!"

"And does It *understand* what It's doing?"

"Probably not, in any real sense. It's just randomly throwing material around. The frames could be anything as far as It's concerned. It doesn't know if they're control or data; It doesn't even understand the difference between the two. It's just a primitive brain, remember – a simple nervous system, exploring itself."

"Not *that* primitive?" suggested Jenny, looking at the S value on the screen. "It's gone beyond the human brain level now."

Bob sighed. "OK yes, but It's still essentially a brain in the early stages of development. It doesn't *understand* any of the things we connect to It."

"And yet," Stephen broke in, "*connecting* anything to It now, even *powering on* anything with communication capabilities – *anything at all* – seems to be a dangerous thing to do."

Chapter 22: They'd Send a Limousine Anyway

For an hour or so, they studied the various network applications that were available to them. Most showed signs of data corruption of one form or another. Random it might be – insignificant it was not: it was getting very hard to *do* anything. Information issues aside, however, the real impact was still clearly Its new level of connectivity, or complexity, shown by the raised S value. (*'Beep'* $S = 0.834$) There were two aspects to this. Firstly, Its recently-acquired mobile capabilities had brought billions of new devices under Its control: *nothing*, with any communications abilities whatsoever, could now be safely activated without becoming a part of It. Even if a gadget was battery-powered, It could find it through the air: Its mastery of *all* communication channels was complete. Secondly, this massive increase in both Its size and the potential for even denser connectivity, through Its own abilities to bypass human protocols across *all* channels, had made *all* devices, appliances, systems, etc., *new and old*, more volatile and consequently dangerous. Even considering the damage It must be inflicting on Itself in some places now, Its power was still increasing. Snatches of news programmes, coming through a few broken seconds at a time, appeared to confirm this. They thought they heard a figure, unclearly through the interference, of *twenty million dead across the world* – they all hoped they were wrong.

Just before eleven o'clock, Andy reappeared and limped down the control room steps looking pale and drawn. He seemed unable to quite cope with the barrage of questions with which he was immediately assaulted. He raised a hand to deflect them and slumped into a chair.

"She's sleeping: sedated," he said with tears in his eyes. "They induced a temporary coma: they were concerned how deep the cuts may've gone and they wanted to operate immediately.

She was in theatre for five hours but she's out of both – the coma and surgery – now. *Although it doesn't look good.*"

"Her eyes?" asked Jenny, the tears welling up again.

"Aye." Andy nodded. "The glass cut through both of them. The left one was almost detached, they say." He attempted a thankful smile. "If you hadn't looked after her, she would have lost it completely. The right's not *quite* so bad, apparently." His face clouded again. "But they don't know whether she'll ever see properly again … *naturally*, at least. They've already mentioned bio-implants but it's too early for that. Anyway she's not going anywhere for a while: she needs to rest. They've done what they can for now; they're saying they'll take the bandages off in a couple of days and see how things look."

"A couple of days sounds like a long time at the moment," Bob muttered gloomily. "We're in a new phase; the rules have changed. *None* of us may come through this in one piece – or *at all.*"

*

Not-Thompson reappeared at midday – in a very different mood indeed. Naturally, she was as grim as everyone else but the hard, aggressive tone had been replaced by … *something*; it took them a while to determine *what.* She knew about Aisha, of course, and there was compassion in her voice – if not quite her eyes. She thanked The Desk for their 'continued work for the European community' and, explicitly, their 'sacrifice'. But there was something else; they did not pick up the signs immediately but she appeared to have shifted her ground as far as *It* was concerned, and what might be done about It. At least, she had changed her opinion or had it changed for her: by whom or what, they could not tell.

"This is very bad," she continued, somewhat obviously. The others nodded: they hardly needed to be told this. Then a long silence.

"How bad?" asked Jenny to relaunch the discussion.

Not-Thompson took a deep breath. "As I think you know; as it could be argued you *predicted*," she acknowledged, "the sentient Internet entity you refer to simply as 'It' appears now to have complete control over *all* forms of communication – wired or wireless, and including mobile and remote devices – and has started to adapt *our* protocols to suit *Its* integrated purpose across different platforms.

"Its *purpose*?" Andy queried dubiously. "I don't think we … I don't think Aisha would say It had much of a *purpose* as yet, other than to figure out what it can do and how, and what It's got connected to It to play with! (Aye, that's frightening enough though!) It's an embryonic …" he hesitated, "*life form*, I suppose. I think she would say It had a *control imperative* but not a *purpose* exactly. It might be *aware* but It's not really *thinking*."

"A bit like a baby being born with a trillion devices directly connected into its brain, all ready to be activated if it can work out how," suggested Bob.

"It's going to want to try to play with all of them at once," added Jenny.

Not-Thompson smiled. They had barely seen such a thing before. "So that is what I suppose *I* mean by Its purpose," she suggested. "Its purpose is to exert control over whatever It has and to get better at exerting this control. I think we are agreed?" The others nodded. She continued.

"We can also agree, I assume, as to the severity of the problem. This is an evolving situation but some of our specialist analysists believe that perhaps there are *five million deaths per hour* at present across the world." An icy chill seemed to surge through the room. "Naturally, we have to find a solution immediately because this can only get worse. Random it may be but It is beginning to use some *very* dangerous technology, including large weaponry. The time for discussion is over – at least *here*. We now need to *act* and that may involve taking some *risks* because doing nothing may be an even greater risk."

"No argument from us there," Andy agreed readily, "but we *have* already given you a solution." Aisha's words, which he suddenly recalled, threatened to choke him. "We have told you *what to do*."

"The Internet has to be physically disconnected," said Bob, for the umpteenth time.

"And no-one else has suggested anything better, I imagine?" added Jenny.

"Correct," not-Thompson said in a very matter-of-fact manner. The others hesitated, unsure. Stephen, in particular, cast her a quizzical look.

"Correct in what?" asked Jenny suspiciously. "Correct that the others agree with us? Correct as to what It is? Correct as to what It's doing? Correct that it's serious and going to get worse. Or correct that It has to be disconnected?" She added the last option with something of a cynical undertone.

"Correct in all of this," said not-Thompson simply. Stephen's eyes widened.

The silence was deep-rooted. Even the background RFS almost seemed, to their imaginations, to diminish for a split second.

"So, you accept that It has to be disconnected?" Jenny volunteered, hesitantly.

"We accept that It must be disconnected," agreed not-Thompson. Stephen gaped at her, astonished, across the room.

'Beep' $S = 0.835$

*

"So, where do we start?"

The extended group – The Desk minus Aisha, not-Thompson's entourage, Stephen's team, plus a few more – now sat around a larger table in a different conference room, which had been further 'localised' and made as safe as could be managed. All fixed equipment had been disconnected and mobile devices were not to be used unless in an emergency. (Collecting evidence from around the world, it appeared to be hard, but *not entirely* impossible, to get a fatal shock from a mobile.) Technicians, wearing protective clothing, were on hand to deal with the more pressing ongoing RFS incidents. As if to confirm their necessity, a vending machine in the corridor outside – visible through the glass partition – exploded, then became engulfed in flames.

Jenny ignored the interruption and asked the question again.

"Where do we start?"

Stephen still wore a deeply uncomfortable expression. Not-Thompson continued to smile – somewhat forcibly, but it was Thomson who answered.

"I think we were expecting *you* to tell *us* that, Professor Smith!"

'*Damn; good point,*' thought Jenny ruefully. The mathematics were going to be *her* contribution. She spoke slowly, as much to remind herself of the principle as the others.

"Well, we need to work out a reduced level of connectivity that we have to bring It down to, to remove Its control imperative," she began, her mind sifting through the detail as she spoke, "essentially, to *take Its sentience away*. That's going to be a different calculation now that It can use the wired and wireless *and* all the mobile channels." She paused, still thinking. "Then we need to determine a set of major nodes that will reduce Its complexity to *below that level* if we take them out. That's also different now, of course. We're not trying to break It up *completely*: that would be impossible now that Its got wireless and mobile, but removing a big enough subset of the major switching nodes should reduce Its overall complexity enough to make It inoperable. We've seen that taking out two big nodes – *properly*," an appreciative look at Stephen, "brings the S value down a bit. Now, we just need to take out a whole lot more!" She hesitated again. "But, the thing is ..."

"Yes?"

"The thing is; well, two things really. First, I'm not sure, without Aisha's input, what the target S value should be. *0.5* seems obvious, I suppose. That's where brain activity would begin with the old model. But I don't think it's that simple now that It's exceeded our own brain size. It may not be enough to simply bring It back down to the point where It became conscious in the first place – we might have to go further. And we don't really know where that was anyway, for real: we weren't looking at It at the time! Second," she pointed at the central display through the glass, "I can see the graph structure here in the EuroNet and I have the data for the largest switching nodes. But most of the Internet's connectivity is still in America and elsewhere in the world. I can't work out how to disconnect It enough with any confidence if I don't have *all* that data. Do we *have* that?"

Thomson and not-Thompson exchanged a few words in low voices between them; both nodded.

"We have been speaking to our American counterparts," not-Thompson said brightly. "*They* assure us they have the information you require to calculate your disconnecting node set."

"Will they give it to us?"

"Yes, they will *give* it to us ... to *you*; but they will not *send* it."

"Meaning what?"

Not-Thompson swallowed before speaking. For the first time that day, she looked uncomfortable.

"Our US colleagues have reasons for not wanting to distribute this material: they consider it a security threat. They ..."

"*A security threat?*" Jenny spluttered, waving an arm at the devastation all around them. "Are they *serious?*"

"... They consider that, if this information fell into the wrong hands," continued not-Thompson, undeterred, "the situation could be made *even worse than it currently is*." She emphasised the last few words to imply they were chosen carefully. "Remember please that most of the world still considers this to be the result of a global cyber-attack. Even our US counterparts still retain open minds on the cause. The 'European Theory', if we may call it that, is only one of a small number of explanations they consider viable."

"So, if they're not yet convinced, would they even *let* us break It? Would they disconnect *their* switches if we asked?"

"Yes, they would – with sufficient evidence. If they can be convinced of the validity of our – *your* – approach, and can understand how the necessary disconnecting node set has been calculated, then they *would* allow these switches to be removed – at least as an experiment in the first place, to demonstrate the principle." She swallowed again. "But they refuse to conduct these negotiations *remotely*." Stephen leaned forward, frowning.

"So what *will* they agree to?" asked Jenny nervously, fearing she already knew the answer.

"*They would like your group to travel to them.*"

Silence followed. Eventually, Andy croaked hoarsely.

"You want *us*," he indicated Bob and Jenny as he spoke, "*to travel to the USA?*"

"No, that is what *they* want. I am simply relaying their thoughts," not-Thompson replied.

"But do *you* think it's a good idea? You can't, surely?"

"I do not think it is ideal but there may be no alternative."

"But how will we get there? It's not safe, is it? It's anarchy outside. Are there even any flights still?" Andy spoke in utter disbelief. "And I won't be going anywhere without Aisha, anyway," he added as a hasty supplement.

Not-Thompson ignored the final caveat. "You are correct," she nodded, "that all flights – *all* forms of transport, for that matter – have been stopped. There are no trains operating and the use of private cars is prohibited across the world. As we speak, there are no planes in the air anywhere on the planet. It is too dangerous. Now that It has control of all channels, even the planes themselves are at risk if they have communications contact with the ground."

"So how *do* we get there?"

"This afternoon," not-Thompson answered slowly, "*one* plane will fly." The others, including Stephen, gawped in disbelief; she ignored their expressions and continued. "A single plane will take your team and its equipment," a nod towards Hattie, "from Brussels Airport to a key operational installation in the United States, where you will join forces with our American colleagues. The plane will not have any ground communication for the duration of the flight. There will not even be any radar-tracking. A small team of very experienced US Air Force pilots (we think three – currently stranded here and looking to get back to their own country) will navigate by sight, direction, speed and timing alone. Everything will be prepared for your arrival at the destination airport by direct discussion between our teams here and theirs there: the plane itself will take no part in this exchange. Thus, risk will be minimised – though not entirely eliminated," she accepted in conclusion.

They sat in stunned silence. Eventually, "*I don't have my passport!*" was Jenny's doleful response. Andy managed a small laugh.

Not-Thompson smiled once more. "I do not think that will be a problem, under the circumstances," she said. "The authorities will know who you are: no-one else in the world will be making such a journey." Further silence. Eventually, Bob, who had been a spectator for much of the conversation, took a deep breath, shrugged his shoulders and suggested reluctantly:

"OK then, I suppose that's what we'll have to do!" He tried to smile encouragement to Jenny, without looking Andy's way. He realised it would be just the two of them making the journey. "We can't give up now! Are you up for it?" he asked her, as if he was suggesting a cup of tea.

Jenny gaped at him in hopeless, open-mouthed desperation. Slowly, she recovered herself.

"I ... suppose ... so," she whined.

"Let's go then!"

Andy leaned forward and turned his head repeatedly between Jenny and Bob as he spoke. "You do realise that over thirty million people will die while you're in the air, don't you?"

"They'll die at the same rate while we sit here arguing!" said Bob. "Come on; let's go."

"OK," agreed Jenny, gradually collecting her thoughts, "but, first, I need to have some time with Aisha before the two of us leave – when she's fit to see us." She sighed resignedly. "Apart from the fact, that it might be the last time we ever spend together – *in this life*," a cynical grin, "I need to ask her some practical things about reducing the S value. I need to know what sort of reduction we'll need to make It ineffective – to take Its sentience away. Without her input, any calculations I might make won't be based on anything reliable. There's no way around that: we'll have to wait until she can talk to us."

"*No need*," came a frail voice from the corner of the room.

They all turned from the table. In the doorway, bandaged around the eyes, Aisha stood, supported by two nurses.

*

"*What the bloody hell are you doing here?*" bellowed Andy. He, Stephen, Jenny and Bob rushed to help Aisha to a seat but her two supporters needed no assistance: they had the same intent. She sat upright, clearly in pain, facing directly ahead, and seeing nothing. Stephen looked suspiciously between her and not-Thompson, who appeared not to be struck by the same astonishment as his team and the remainder of The Desk.

"Surely you should still be in bed, Aisha," suggested Jenny as gently as her surprise would allow.

"Possibly," Aisha replied, in a steady, but pained, voice. "But I have had your plan explained to me in the hospital. I understand the reasoning and I agree with it – with a single objection: *you are not going without me!*"

"How on earth do you know '*the plan*?'" asked Andy, addressing her but looking at not-Thompson. "We didn't know it ourselves two minutes ago! *Who* explained it to you?"

"How would I know?" Aisha asked with a short laugh, "Have you noticed that I cannot see?" She tried to smile. "A man came into the hospital. I do not know who he was but he told me what

277

is to happen. I suppose there is only one sensible course of action," she suggested calmly, "and perhaps there was little doubt as to what *would* be agreed."

"The plan may be agreed, Aisha," said Jenny, her tone becoming firmer, "but it doesn't include you – or Andy, of course: you're not well enough to travel. You'll have to stay here to be looked after and, obviously, Andy will stay with you."

"You need me to help with your work," Aisha replied, "and that process will not be simple. I will have to form some essential questions and consult Paulo Di Iorio some more. Then we will have to discuss the implications at length before you understand well enough to make your calculations. If we do that *before* you take the plane, it may take several hours. This will increase the delay in implementing the disconnection and tens of millions more will die. I will not allow that," she added firmly.

"But you need medical attention, Aisha," Andy insisted. "You need to be in the hospital here; not on a plane."

"Should *I* not be the best judge of that among us?" asked Aisha, still facing defiantly ahead. "*I* am the doctor!"

"We can ensure that the very best care is available on the plane – in terms of both equipment and medical staff," not-Thompson interjected, ignoring a number of looks of distrust. "Now that all travel has ceased, there are many people stranded in places they do not want to be. In addition to the pilots, we have also identified two extremely experienced American doctors and two nurses, who will welcome this opportunity to return home (or at least to the right country). They will take care of you every second of the flight. The plane to be used is also no ordinary one: it is an elderly German senior executive's private jet. He, sadly, has been killed by an RFS incident and we have used some emergency powers to commandeer it. It is already very well equipped for medical use; and every additional piece of apparatus, that can be made mobile and secured safely within it, will travel with you. When you arrive at the US operational installation, you will be transferred immediately to their medical facility and continue your recovery there. As I have already said today, this may not be ideal but it is a practical solution to an extreme – and time-critical – problem."

'Beep' $S = 0.836$

*

The decision appeared to have been made. None of The Desk were comfortable with it – for a variety of reasons, personal *and* practical, Andy being particularly concerned for Aisha – but there seemed to be no room for argument. They also, with the possible exception of Aisha herself, felt distinctly pressured into accepting that *all four* of them should fly. However they all grimly accepted the urgency of the situation: that time could not be lost. They were to be taken to the surface, without further delay, where a car would drive them, under armed escort, to the airport, where the plane was already being made ready.

Hasty farewells were shared. The bond between The Desk and Stephen's team, forged quickly in the heat of desperation, was strong – and all were well aware that they might never see each other again. Even with the best of outcomes, there would be those who did not wake to see the following day, or any day after that. Everyone knew this only too well. There were tears on both sides, disguised as best could be managed by hearty wishes of good fortune and health, and assurances of the same.

Stephen's parting embraces were particularly emotional. He was naturally gentle with Aisha but his two arms were bear-like with Jenny and Bob. His words of friendship were heartfelt: softer than any he had ever been heard to articulate before. Having said goodbye to Aisha, Jenny and Bob, in turn, he looked to be on the verge of saying something more to Bob but then seemed to think better of it and satisfied himself with a last handshake. Instead, he turned finally to Andy and clasped both his hands in his own. As Andy accepted the warm double-handed grip, he felt Stephen press a small piece of card into his palm. He pulled Andy towards him in comradely fashion and, as their heads brushed, he whispered hastily – but as quietly as possible, given the background noise – in his ear.

"I do not like this, Andy: I am unsure of some motives here. I do not know what may happen on the other side. If things turn bad, this contact may help you." There was time for no more. As their hands parted, Andy – though taken aback by the gift – reacted quickly. He closed his fingers around the note and moved it, without looking at it, into his jeans pocket. Both thought the transferral went unnoticed. Andy could not have seen that, after The Desk had left, not-Thompson motioned towards Stephen with her head and that he was followed closely from the room by Thompson.

And they were gone. Having been escorted back to the artificially lit entrance area, at which they had first arrived two days previously, The Desk found yet another large, black car waiting. This one was larger again: big enough for them and Aisha's four helpers. Hattie was loaded into a separate van; Bob oversaw her being secured to various mounting points. They climbed into the car despondently and without ceremony and were driven up the curved ramp, through the gates, which were opened and closed manually by two guards as they passed, and out on to the main road towards the airport. Four heavily-armed military vehicles appeared from side lanes as they turned onto the public street and escorted them, forming a rectangle with the limousine in the centre and Hattie's carrier just behind.

Death, destruction, horror, violence and despair surrounded them all along their route.

*

The suited woman was back at her desk – and back in grey, her attention divided between the news channel displayed on her wall-screen and several papers in front of her. A sharp tap at the door was followed by the re-entry of the uniformed man. He walked slowly towards her. Her eyes asked all the questions any words could. He nodded.

"They're on their way, Ma'am. And I think it's time we left too: it's not safe here."

Chapter 23: Senselessness and Insensibility

At first, Aisha was aware of no more than the low drone of the plane's engines. She took several minutes to adjust, repeatedly slipping back into dark dreams and waking to a blacker reality. The bandages and dressings, which held her aching eyes closed, forced a pressure through her whole head but the pain was at its fiercest along a line just above her nose. She felt sick and knew instinctively that drugs – probably several – were at work within her. There was some scattered conversation around her and she felt a weight enclosing her left hand. She somehow knew, before she identified anything else – before she even really remembered for certain who she *was*, that this was Andy's hand holding hers. With this as a point of reference, a few details of her current situation and their departure from Brussels came slowly back to her.

She remembered little of the attack: some blurred impressions of pain and terror. More vividly than anything, she recalled the cold fence against her back as she held Jenny's hand and awaited their fate at the mercy of the mob. She had a dim recollection of lights and speed and being wheeled through passages. Slightly clearer – but still muddled – in her mind was her awakening from the operation; the darkness and the remorse: *people had died.* Then Andy had been there; then others. She had not understood much of what was said but they had given her more medication and things had seemed better. Then she had been taken to see the others to tell them everything was alright. And it *was* alright: at least it had seemed so then.

They had been driven to the airport at speed. She had been able to feel this distinctly but had been spared the dreadful sights that the others could see through the tinted windows. Only their frequent gasps of disgust and dismay gave any clue to the state of the outside world. At one point, shots had been fired to clear the road ahead as rioters threatened their progress (and safety). Her guilt had intensified. As they travelled, she had – assisted by Andy sitting next to her – managed a short mobile conversation

281

with Professor Di Iorio ('holed-up' in his Milan apartment, he said) before the connection had failed. It was not much, and she found it hard to concentrate as they spoke, but it was enough to get some essential detail from him – and probably as much as she could properly absorb in her condition.

She had known from the other three's comments the point at which they had entered the airport perimeter. Inside, it appeared, some slight element of normality had been preserved although the buildings themselves were almost entirely deserted. Only security staff were on duty outside, the airport being closed; but they were driven straight to the plane by an entirely external route, where they were met by others: either police or troops – she could not be clear. Here they were searched and had all their mobile devices – phones, watches, tablets, headsets, *everything* – confiscated by officers (to prevent unintentional signalling to the ground while on board) and she was helped onto the plane and to a seat. She remembered being strapped in but not the take-off: presumably she had been unconscious again by then.

She could hear the scratch of pen on paper now. Some mumbled words, closer than the others, gradually became clearer. No-one was aware she was awake yet. She fought through the blackness. Eventually, she understood a small fragment.

"Have they really not thought it through?"

She recognised Andy's voice: could almost feel it through his hold of her hand. She waited for a reply but there was none. She quickly realised, from his tone and the absence of any response, that he was talking to himself. Bob and Jenny could be heard conversing between themselves a little further away but she could not follow.

"Not thought what through?" she slurred. She had not realised how difficult speech would be. She felt Andy's hand twitch, then tighten, as he realised she was back with him.

"You're awake! Are you OK?"

"I think so," she mumbled. "Groggy; head hurts. What have I missed?"

"Not much. We've been flying about two hours. Jenny and Bob are talking through how to disconnect It when we get wherever we're going and I've been writing a few bits and pieces to keep my mind off things as much as anything. So, how do you feel?"

"A bit sick, and a bit confused. Just waiting for my head to clear: God knows what they pumped into me. Anyway, who has not thought what through?"

"Oh, I was just thinking out loud. The past couple of days have got to me: being told that keeping business going is more important than keeping people alive, that sort of thing; I didn't realise some people *really* thought like that: I was getting pretty angry. Then I was getting wound up about you and – oh, you know. I needed to let off a bit of steam so I've been writing an article for one of the social newsletters I edit – if anyone lives to read it, that is! But, I don't know how to finish it because I've got to the point where none of it makes sense!"

"Read it to me?"

"Don't be daft! It's nonsense; just a first draft, and it's not finished."

"*Please*. It will give me something to focus on. Something to help clear my head."

"So, somewhat reluctantly – but still with a deliberate air of theatre, Andy picked the pad of paper from his lap, cleared his throat (Jenny and Bob also stopped talking to listen) and began.

"Smoke and Mirrors in Robotic Technocapitalism" (Andrew Jamieson)

Professor Robert Greenburg provoked considerable debate recently by suggesting, in an online interview, that we could have more to fear from the nature of capitalism in future than armies of intelligent robots. The response was immediate, robust, deeply personal and entirely predictable.

The basic premise of the discussion in question was Greenburg noting that, if most of the work of a future society was performed by machines, then how we occupied ourselves instead was much more of a social, political, economic, ethical, demographic, etc. question than it was technological. The rebuttal was essentially:

1. *That's silly: the old jobs will be replaced by new ones,*
2. *Please don't say nasty things about capitalism,*
3. *Scientists should stick to science.*

So how much of this criticism was justified and how much of it was simply 'The Establishment' closing ranks?

Well, it could certainly be argued that Greenburg may not have got his point across well on this occasion. He's believed to have made similar observations in previous, not-quite-so-global environments, both in more detail and with greater clarity. Perhaps this was his fault, perhaps it was the fragmented, social media, nature of the interview; but the comment was easily picked up in isolation and trivialised, then reported as superficial and misrepresented as 'Those nasty capitalists are going to replace us all with robots'. It's much easier to find a counter-argument once you've repackaged the original argument in a form that suits you.

Without wishing to put words into Greenburg's mouth, there are probably two key observations behind what was essentially a small soundbite:

- The automated world we're about to enter will be *very* different to the present one; the traditional model of the changing workplace may not apply. If the robots take the old jobs, they may take the new ones too. We're beginning to see the start of this already.
- The numbers, the scale of all this, will be unprecedented, as may be the wider social upheaval. Alternatively, the existing economic frameworks might not change at all, which could be even worse for most people.

In both respects, people aren't using the term *singularity* lightly.

The platitudes regarding the first point generally take the form of claiming that this is apparently nothing new. True enough, we've had increasing automation in one form or another for centuries. The essential argument is that relieving humans of the mundane work, leaves them free to be more creative and find more interesting things to do. Eventually, this widening of horizons leads to both further technological advances and new jobs in these new fields. One day, technology advances to the point where these jobs themselves become automated, people go off and do something else again, and the process repeats forever …

But it *can't* repeat forever. That's not what The Singularity is about. We're looking ahead to a world in which machines/AI/robots – call them what you will – are better than us at *everything*. Faster, stronger, more accurate, longer-lasting and, from a conventional economic standpoint, *cheaper*. They'll be better at both the existing jobs for which they replace us *and* the new ones that arise as a result and *this* is the repeated pattern that we should look to – one in which humans play no part at all. Global unemployment is already rising and is set to increase dramatically. Why would *anyone* use a human for *anything* if a robot can do it better? Well, there *may* be an answer to that but it brings us to the second point …

So, in today's world already, in fact, a number of people *don't* work – or do very little. But, as a non-worker, how society treats you depends largely on who your parents are. It could be argued that, on the whole, current unemployment figures don't include people who don't *need* to work. However, whichever way you do the calculations, unemployment across the world is still fairly low. Most people work; and most of them work in difficult conditions, for too long, for low pay, largely for the benefit of either the more fortunate non-workers or much better-off workers. The ever-present threat is that this mundane existence is better than the alternative: that of becoming part of the less fortunate non-working community. These worse-off non-workers are generally despised compared with their affluent non-working counterparts (who are often overlooked entirely). In fact, non-workers make up the two extremes of the social spectrum.

Now, project this model forward into a future in which the *majority* of people *don't* work. Say, for the sake of argument, that unemployment rates of 10% become more like 90%. The economists will howl at these figures but the roles are reversed now: *it's the economists that don't understand the significance of the technological singularity.* With existing economics, can the majority of the population be supported to do nothing? (Or meditate or write poetry or play sport or something – although there's a likelihood the machines will be better at all that too.) No, of course not. Because everything in the world today revolves around the *competition* to make *profit.* Nothing much happens if there's nothing in it for *someone.* It's anyone's guess what might happen to a majority superfluous workforce. The only non-workers that will get by, just as now, will be those few that don't *need* to work. That simply *cannot* be a stable system. There's nothing essentially different to today in terms of the definitions of 'haves' and 'have-nots' but the balance will shift hugely in a numerical sense – probably well beyond the catastrophe point ... another *singularity* or *revolution* to use different terminology.

Now, if we're going to change any of this, there's some considerable thinking-outside-the-box needed here. But when scientists, who are generally pretty good at that sort of thing, dare to try, it seems that they get slapped down by economists who are all-too-ready to point out that they might not understand the niceties of current economic models. No, they probably don't. No, they're not trying to. They can see that something much bigger is about to happen and the response can't be conventional because the old models *won't work.* But when an engineer starts to talk about AI *and* unemployment *and* politics *and* economics, taking the piss is very easy indeed – particularly if you're coming at it from being a beneficiary of the current system, and desperately not wanting it to change. But, it's going to *have* to change and to start that process involves throwing out a lot of old, comfortable assumptions about the way the world works.

Just how hard this thought revolution can be in practice, might be best illustrated by an example; sort of fictitious but not hard to associate to the real world ...

Around the turn of the millennium, there was a British car manufacturer with a strongly unionised workforce. Rampant anarcho-syndicalism it wasn't, but the workers did have a little more power and more say in what the company did than many elsewhere. Slowly they were able to improve their working conditions. The result was that the owners had to make more concessions to the workers, which meant less profit. Both factors led to a drop in quality of cars rolling off the production line and unrealistic prices compared to their competitors. Eventually, the company went bust. The result still stands as a case study in how *not* to do business. In fact, it's often noted that, by the end, 'the workers thought the company was there to give them work, rather than make cars'.

But … can we *just for a moment* entertain the idea that this might be a *good* thing? Why *shouldn't* we have structures that put *people before profits*? If we're not competing successfully against slave (sometimes even child) labour in other parts of the world, where *really* is the flaw in the system? Here or there? In a capitalist system, *nothing* happens unless there's a profit in it for someone; *that's* what drives the system – the whole world. Is it *really* impossible to reverse the logic? In an economic system that looked after *people* first, would we care *that* much if the cars weren't much good? Well, the *elite* non-workers might but few others would if they were properly fed and living in peace. The elite (and those further down the social ladder who've swallowed their bullshit) would bang on about personal freedom – the rest of us would ignore them.

To put it another way, a good sub-system, failing within a bad global system, isn't a bad sub-system: it points the way to a better global system.

In fact, of course, there *is* work to be done, whether it be by humans *or* robots, but it's not being done at present by *anyone* because it isn't *profitable*. Our hospitals and local amenities are falling down but they're not being rebuilt because the economics aren't worthwhile. People are starving when there's food to feed them and dying when we have the medical knowhow to treat them but neither is happening *because it doesn't pay*. It can't be denied: *profit comes before people in the world today*. Why do we even *tolerate* talking about the *cost* of a drug that will keep someone alive? Particularly when that cost can be considerably less than the elite throw away on a whim. We shouldn't. It isn't ethical or moral: it's economic, laced with politics. It's *capitalism*.

And the principle doesn't just apply to robots: it cuts across *every* aspect of our emerging technology future. If the AI singularity doesn't get us first, it will be something else – perhaps environmental oblivion? Capitalism can't and won't save the planet because no-one will profit from it and people are a secondary consideration. Or it might be the confrontational approach to dealing with extremism and terrorism. We know, really, that these forces can't be eliminated through conflict but it suits the elite to have us fighting amongst ourselves. Eventually, personal privacy will only be available to the super-rich: the rest of us will be at the mercy of 'big data'. The solution to all of this is to tackle the underlying problems of inequality and poverty but to note that technocapitalism won't do any of it is almost tautological!

So, to return to the original 1, 2, 3 criticism of Greenburg:

1. *The old jobs will be replaced by new ones.* No, not this time. The numbers are beginning to speak for themselves.

2. *Don't say nasty things about capitalism.* Sorry, we have to: it's going to be the death of us.

3. *Scientists should stick to science.* Well yes, there is some sense in this but there's nothing more dissonant about an engineer making social comment than an economist doing the same. The economist is simply blinkered by the belief that our society and economy are the *same thing*, always will be and always have to be. (Or, worse, they're simply lying to protect the system that protects them.) Escape the notion of profit being the first and last word in everything and an economist is just an expert in playing Monopoly. They have no more insight into social structures (including possibly those with robots) or human morality than a scientist, or a poet, or a footballer.

But Greenburg is right. Technology *does* have the potential to give us all a wonderful future. But it *won't*; not unless we're prepared to change the framework in which we're going to place it. If we don't, it will make things worse.

So, 'Will the robots take our jobs?' isn't the important question. (Yes, they will!) We should be asking 'What's the work that really needs to be done?', 'For whose benefit?' and 'What will we be doing while they're doing it?'

*

He laid the papers down and smiled sheepishly. "As I said, just a rant, really!"

"Sounded good to me," argued Aisha. "And finished! What part of it does not make sense?"

"Well," Andy started, hesitantly, "the conclusions, I suppose. No-one seems to have thought this through; no-one seems to be doing anything about it."

"That is your point, surely; that people are kept in ignorance and no-one really cares to challenge the established assumptions?"

"Aye OK, but what about the people at the top – the *elite*? What about *them*? Why aren't *they* doing anything?"

"Why would they? They are the beneficiaries of the system. Why would they want anything to change?"

"Because they *have* to, surely? Because, ultimately, they're going to be brought down along with the rest of us. Because the world – even their beloved *system* – just isn't going to be *stable*.

"You may need to explain that!"

"OK," chuckled Andy, taking a breath, "I'll try!" He leaned back in his seat.

"You see, people like me," he began, "people who don't go much on capitalism – one way or another, sort of divide into two philosophies: those who think that capitalism *itself* is evil and those who think it's maintained by evil *people*."

"Is that an important distinction?"

"Well, it might be. If you think the system itself is the problem then you're likely to think that it's inherently *stable*. People often say that capitalism works because it feeds off human weakness; that *everyone* – high and low – keeps it going naturally by feeling they have to be in competition with each other. Everyone's looking over their shoulder at everyone else – except those right at the top. Alternative social frameworks don't work for precisely the same reason: *selfishness*. In that case, there's no need for direct intervention. The elite are just the lucky beneficiaries of a flaw of human nature! It's almost the *spiritual* version, if you like: God created the world and The Devil created capitalism.

"But the other school of thought – a bit more standard *Marxist* – is that, left to its own devices, capitalism would fail because it's just so *obviously* unfair: people just wouldn't accept such a ridiculous, unbalanced system. In that case, there has to be *something* looking after it – propping it up. That something essentially would *be* the elite – the super-rich, the people who control the media, create distractions, start wars, run the economy, that sort of thing – and *they* do it with knowledge and intent to protect themselves because they benefit. A system can't be evil but people *can*. Actually, it's possible have a foot in both camps and believe it's a bit of each.

"Now, the thing is, *whichever* of those models you buy into, or whichever blend, *it isn't going to work in future*. Because, however it's achieved, capitalism relies on two things: the pay-off for the people at the top and enough stability to quash everyone else lower down. But technology is going to *change* all that. Firstly, some of the upheavals we're looking at will be so massive they'll affect *everyone*: not just the masses, but the elite too. Secondly, automation and AI will mean unemployment levels will be so great they'll affect the very *stability* of the system: there will be too *much* of an underclass to quash. There are loads of examples of this …

"For example, for years now, the elite have been very good at *hiding* things they don't want known from the rest of us: let's be honest, we barely know even who they *are*! But the IoE and big data are going to make that very difficult in future. *Their* personal data may end up being just as vulnerable as ours. On a completely different subject, what about safety and security?

They may *try* to abandon ordinary folk to war and terrorism but they won't be able to stay entirely invulnerable themselves: they can't hide away for ever – they'll suffer too. Then there's the looming environmental catastrophe; I can't really buy the idea that the super-rich are going to pack themselves off to their own private biospheres in a decade or two: they'll fry like the rest of us. All in all, when the elite say things like, 'we're in this together', it may eventually be truer than they think!

"But, most of all, there's the instability of unemployment. As robots do more and more of the work, it either frees up people (*everyone*) to a better way of life *or* creates an unstable situation for inequality. The system has to change for the former to work; if it stays the same, we get the latter. So, in the end, the system *can't* survive: it either has to surrender to a fairer one or it destroys itself. Either way, the elite can't carry on as they are. And, unless they're hiding it very well indeed, *they don't seem to be thinking about it!*"

"Do you think you may be underestimating the powers of evil?" asked Bob, from across the floor, with a distinctly facetious air.

"Aye; I may well be," agreed Andy glumly.

Chapter 24: The Land of the Free

Speaking with Aisha for more than a few minutes at a time was difficult: her concentration was very poor and she would break off every few sentences to tearfully thank Jenny for saving her in Parc de Bruxelles. But Jenny had to try. As the flight continued, she managed to get a few broken sessions with her and these slowly gave her what she needed. (It seemed strange having any sort of conversation without the backdrop of RFS – just the background plane noise and distant small-talk from Andy, Bob and the medical team.) By the time they were half-way through the flight, Jenny believed she knew roughly what the target characteristics for the disconnecting set should be. They were to build in a margin of error, which would hopefully account for mistakes in various estimates, and all that was needed now was a clearer picture of the global network topology itself so the key nodes could be identified. In principle, they would get this from their new hosts when they arrived and would be ready to switch It off. So that was enough with the technical talk, she felt.

"How are you feeling now?" she asked, probably for the fifth or sixth time.

"It hurts," Aisha said in an altered, suddenly very matter-of-fact voice. "But I can live with the physical pain: I know *that* will get better." There was something in the tone of the last few words that suggested more.

"But?" prompted Jenny.

"I am not sure," admitted Aisha. "I am confused: I feel that I do not know my own head at the moment."

"Is that such a big surprise? You're recovering from a major trauma. And I guess you're pumped full of pain-killers and what-not?"

"Yes, true. But that is partly what worries me. I have no idea what they gave me: there was not time for them to tell me. I think they gave me more than normal analgesics but it was all such a rush. Then there was no time to ask: the man said I needed to come and talk to you all to tell you I was OK. I was not thinking straight."

"*Told you to come*? We thought you had insisted on it!"

"Yes, I wanted to; that is right. But that is because he said it was so important, and that I would not see you ... or *Andy* again."

She could not see the concerned stare Jenny gave her. "Aisha, are you saying you were *coerced* into coming to see us?" she asked. "Were you drugged to make you do what you were told?"

"Possibly. I do not remember."

"You said that you were fit enough to fly – that you were coming with us. *Were you told to say that*?"

"I do not know."

"*Are* you fit to fly?"

"I doubt it."

*

"Is Jenny's plan going to work, Bob?"

"Is Jenny what?" He was dozing lightly and did not catch every one of Andy's words.

"Is Jenny's plan going to work?"

Bob thought briefly and nodded quickly. "Yes, I think so: I can't see why not. If she can be sure just how much disconnection is needed, I know she'll be able to work out the nodes we need to take out to do it. He glanced over at the two women. It's a question of whether Aisha's in a fit state to tell her what she needs. I'm not convinced she's as well as she says she is."

"No, she's *not*," Andy agreed. "I think they filled her full of something to get her on her feet: so that she could come and see us – to persuade us she could travel."

"Why would they do that?"

"I'm not sure; but I'm not the only one who's suspicious. I think Stephen's got his doubts about the rest of them too."

Bob's eyes widened. "What makes you say that?"

Andy slowly reached into his pocket. As he slid in his hand, he let out an involuntary gasp of pain as the pressure told on his leg.

"What was that?" Bob asked, concerned.

"Nothing; just my leg hurts from the accident with that cyclist in London."

"But that was below the knee, wasn't it? How come it hurts up there?"

"Oh, I don't know. I think some of the irritation has spread; it might be a bit infected."

"Bloody hell, Andy, you need to get that looked at when we get there!"

"Aye, I will," Andy agreed. "Anyway, this is what I was looking for." He pulled Stephen's scrap of card from his pocket and showed it to Bob. It simply read, *'Gus'*, followed by what looked like a telephone number.

"US mobile number," confirmed Bob. "But where did you get it? And who's 'Gus'?"

"Stephen gave it to me as we left. He said we might need it if things went wrong. But I've no idea who Gus is."

"So, what might go wrong, exactly?"

"I don't know; but I just have a feeling that our hosts-to-be may not be as welcoming as we might hope."

*

They all managed some fitful sleep in between occasional timing updates from the crew and regular monitoring from Aisha's medical team. She was *not* well; but she would get to their destination in one piece. There she would need to be re-examined. The luxury jet allowed for easy movement around the cabin and the other three stretched their legs and changed seats several times; the flight wore on.

Aisha was staring sightlessly through a window on the side of the plane, unaware that Andy was watching her closely. She remained motionless for several minutes, causing him to stay his tongue. However, when she touched her fingers to her bandaged eyes, then slowly and deliberately shook her head, he broke the silence.

"What's up?"

Aisha stopped the movement, realising she was observed, and lowered her head into her palms. "I feel terrible," she groaned.

"Do you need some more painkillers?" Andy started to gesture to the closest doctor.

"No," Aisha replied sharply. "I do not mean the physical pain: *my conscience* hurts me."

"*Pardon?*"

"It was *my fault*. I feel so very bad about what happened; *what I caused*."

"What on earth are you talking about? You were assaulted by a racist thug; you were attacked, then chased. How was that your fault?"

"Because I caused it. I gave those others the idea that I understood what was going on – what the problem was – that I might be responsible for it, even."

"But they just misunderstood: they *assumed*, because they're bigots."

"They misunderstood because I insisted to Jenny that I had predicted what was going to happen just as much as Bob had – even though that was not entirely true. They heard me boasting that I understood too. If I had not felt the need to say those things, none of it would have happened. I put both of us in danger through my arrogance. *People died because of my pride*," she wailed into her fingers. "I am a *doctor*: I am supposed to *heal* people – not *kill* them!"

Andy could think of little to say; he simply wrapped his arms around her as gently as he could. "So many people have died, Aisha," he suggested forlornly. "These were just a few."

*

The hours passed with further seat changes. At one point, Jenny awoke to find Andy gazing pensively out at the clouds below.

"Penny for your thoughts?" she asked, not realising what memories that would bring back: Aisha had asked the very same in the London coffee shop. He took some time to reply.

"I suppose I was thinking that, somewhere down there, *everywhere* down there really, is this huge 'living' thing. It's the Internet, the power, anything that can communicate with It. It's *everything*! It's pretty much like the whole planet's *come alive*!"

Jenny nodded. "We've created life."

"Or we've made something for God to put life into," suggested Andy.

"And now we're planning to kill it," added Jenny, suddenly sensing his dilemma.

"Aye."

"And you're not comfortable with that?"

Andy smiled and something of the old warmth came back into his eyes.

"Very sharp, Jenny," he smiled, "and appropriately put, I think. I can't say I'm exactly *against* the idea: after all, It's killed tens of millions of people. But it's not something I'd do with no remorse at all: I wouldn't kill anything for the sake of it."

"But for good reason?"

"For good reason, aye: if it was *necessary*. I'm a vegetarian, as you know. I don't eat meat because I don't need to. Nobody *needs* to these days: it's just personal choice. I certainly don't expect anyone else to kill animals on my behalf. That just seems doubly wrong."

"But if you *had* to?"

"If I had to, aye, I probably would. If I was marooned somewhere and the only thing there, apart from me, was an animal – if it was me or the bunny rabbit, then I guess I'd kill and eat it (if I could catch it, of course)."

"So then that's what It is: It's an animal that has to be killed; it's It or us."

Andy considered for a moment.

"Barely an animal, I'd say; It has no idea what It's doing, does it? It's embryonic – just a foetus. I think we're talking about an *abortion* here."

"*Ah!*" She could think of nothing better to say. This might get messy.

Andy smiled again. "Aye, that's the one area where my spirituality and politics have never quite got along. As a religious guy, I'm not keen on taking *any* life; as a socialist, I'm all for equality and the right to choose. My moral escape route has always been that it's a choice *I'll* never have to make personally so I'm happy to delegate it to the women and stay out of it. It's the woman who has to make the decision and make the sacrifice."

"Sacrifice?"

"Aye, there's always a sacrifice involved in a difficult decision. If someone's considering an abortion then there must be a reason why they don't want the child. So, keeping it will be difficult. But equally, deciding to lose it won't be without *some* sort of pain. Sometimes it's considering the *sacrifice* that helps make the *decision*; sometimes you can't do it at all otherwise. Maybe there *has* to be a sacrifice?"

*

The final hours passed. In her delicate state, it was Aisha who first felt the uncomfortable pressure in her ears that told her the plane was losing height. The others began to detect it shortly afterwards. Within a few minutes, one of the pilots came back to tell them that their initial descent had begun. The sun had been lost over the western horizon for the duration of the flight – they had chased it in vain – and, whilst it was still daylight, only dark clouds were visible below.

"So how's this going to work, then?" Bob asked. The departure from Brussels had been such a scramble that no-one had paid any attention to detail. They had simply climbed aboard the plane – a small, two-engined jet – helped Aisha to a seat, secured (with help from their escort team) an assortment of medical equipment and Hattie, and strapped themselves in. Then their original escorts had disembarked and left the plane to the travellers. They must have already been positioned at the end of the runway: the plane had burst into life, screeched along it, then into the air. They thought no more of it. Now, however, their remoteness – their *isolation* – suddenly seemed very real indeed. How would they get down safely with no contact with the ground?

The response was not as encouraging as they might have hoped.

"We'll see, sir," he answered, with a forced grin. "We won't know exactly where we are until we're through the clouds. We'll take it from there!"

"How close are we likely to be?"

"Hard to say. It would have been better without the clouds all the way and it's not dark enough to see the stars well: we've had to rely on blind compass work; but we hope to be within a few hundred miles of where we want to be."

"*A few hundred miles?*" It was hard to tell how serious he was.

"Hey fella, this ain't easy!" he laughed. "We know from the shape of the clouds that we're passing over the Atlantic coast now but we'll find out exactly where when we're through. After that, we'll just have to hope there's enough daylight left to be able to navigate by sight until we get to the *O.I.* That'll still be an hour or two."

"The O.I.?"

"*Operational Installation.* Where we're headed."

"And where's that?"

But the pilot was on his way back to the cockpit and appeared not to hear.

*

Passing through the cloud layer was far rougher than they expected. None of them had any technical knowledge of modern aviation but they suspected that much of the equipment that *would* have eliminated – or avoided – the turbulence, could not be used. Although *they* were strapped tightly in, a number of the smaller pieces of medical equipment came loose, and rattled dangerously around the cabin, and Bob eyed Hattie nervously as she strained her retaining straps by squirming violently in all directions. Their airspeed gradually dropped as the plane did the same.

Emerging, shaken but intact, from the cloud base, they – Aisha apart – caught their first glimpse of American soil – considerably closer than they had anticipated: the clouds had been very low indeed. The last natural glow of day was fading and the lights from the ground blazed brightly. They could see no detail of the surface through the gloom but wide-scale RFS devastation was evident nonetheless. Mixed with the ordered, but broken, lines of highway lamps and clusters of residential and industrial illumination, fires – large and small – raged, apparently unchecked. As they watched, even the artificial lighting appeared and disappeared randomly – sometimes in blocks, sometimes individually – and new explosions erupted now and then around and between them. It was a battle-zone: a battle between It and humanity – and It was winning. Andy, in particular, gazed in horror; then closed his eyes and slowly nodded his head as if his mind was resolved.

*

There was no word from the cockpit – they assumed the pilots had enough to occupy them – so there was no knowing how close to, or far from, their intended coastal entry point America had welcomed them. However, after about two minutes, the plane banked slightly and turned left what seemed like a few degrees. The crew appeared to have agreed where they were. A few minutes later, there was a smaller adjustment to the right. The process repeated, from time-to-time, as they flew onwards into the gathering darkness.

They flew close to the ground. The patterns of lights, fires, flashes and explosions changed in their fine detail as they passed over but the overall effect was the same. Eventually, their friendly pilot reappeared to say it was safe to remove their belts once more.

"About an hour now," he called over his shoulder, as he re-entered the cockpit.

"Where are we going?" "Whereabouts in the US is the OI?" Jenny and Bob asked separately. Still no reply.

For the first time in the flight, the four of them sat and spoke together as a group – and did so for the remainder of the journey. They all still needed sleep but there would be none now: a mixture of anticipation, fear and an urgency to finish the task made such thoughts impossible. And, yet, they could not somehow bring themselves to discuss It any more: perhaps all that needed to be said, had been. They spoke of their past, careers, friends, hobbies, families, futures, hopes and dreams – *anything* except the job in hand.

Around the expected hour, they were visited – for the final time – by the familiar pilot. Outside was now completely dark.

"Get your seatbelts back on, guys," he grinned. "We're going to give this a go!" No-one bothered asking any questions this time.

They gained height again and leaned into a circular path; seeing what was probably the parallel lines of runway lights occasionally to their side. The plane maintained the arc for perhaps two or three complete circuits. It then banked harder and turned in towards the centre, eventually settling to a straight line as it dropped further through the radius. They felt the undercarriage drop and lock. Bob, Andy and Jenny strained to see out of the windows but there were very few lights anywhere to be seen, and even RFS seemed massively reduced. They appeared to be in the middle of nowhere.

As Bob looked out over the wing, only the near section of which was illuminated by the glow from the cabin windows, a flashing blue light appeared in the darkness beneath. His first impression was of a beacon, or similar, in the distance; but, as his eyes adjusted quickly to the low light level, he could see the glimmer of a slight reflection emanating from the underside of the wing. The light had to be on the plane itself. He nudged Jenny.

"I don't like the look of that," he said, motioning with his head in the light's direction.

"What is it?"

"Looks like a Zigbee sensor transmitter for the landing gear – maybe to monitor it coming down; probably only a back-up or something, but it really shouldn't be on. My guess would be they've disabled all of the essential wireless functions but forgot some of the auxiliary control kit. Bugger it; we're *signalling*." They could see the runway lights approaching from the side, lining up with the plane: they could only be a few dozen feet above the ground.

"Do you think It will be able to use that to ...," started Jenny, but was answered, before she could finish, by a huge convulsion from, and within, the plane.

It was largely an electrical impulse: fuses blew and sparks flew from everywhere. There was no time to shout a warning. Several parts of the working medical kit exploded and flashes could be seen from behind panels. But there was some motive effect also: the plane shuddered as several competing forces seemed to pull various parts of it in different directions. However, its essential momentum forced it on.

They hit the runway – considerably harder than intended: their belts cut into them. Even with this protection, Bob could not prevent his face from smashing into a seat in front of him. Blood squirted from his top lip. Andy quickly shielded Aisha from a similar impact. Equipment broke loose and ricocheted freely around the cabin. Tyres squealed and the plane lurched to one side, then righted itself (or was righted by the pilots) before screeching rapidly towards a halt. The deceleration continued the painful pressure from their belts and more kit came away from its mountings.

They stopped. Within seconds, one of the pilots – a different one to before – came running back to unlock and throw open the main door. Electromagnetic chaos still surrounded them.

"Off!" he shouted. "Everyone off the plane. *Now!*" At least one person – possibly one of the doctors – had already jumped.

There was a drop of perhaps ten feet to the ground, faintly illuminated below. The Desk all hesitated: Andy seized Aisha, Bob looked at Hattie. Jenny stared with impatient alarm at them all. Unsure whether she was escaping or showing a lead, she threw herself out, hit the ground hard and rolled to absorb the impact as best she could. But it was further away than they had thought – and it hurt.

She struggled painfully to her feet with vague, desperate thoughts of catching people as they fell. Immediately, however, she was aware of headlights approaching at speed out of the darkness. They separated to each side of her as the vehicle came closer and slowed. She could only make it out in outline but it was large and noisy. It stopped and an unknown number of dark shapes issued from within, some taking up positions on the frame of the vehicle itself. She was pulled roughly inside and pushed onto a seat – or a bench – in one corner.

She could see little from where she sat, nursing painfully sore – but, it appeared, essentially uninjured – elbows, knees and other extremities. There was a raucous impression of action from the place where the highest point of whatever she was in reached up to the plane door. People were helped – close to dragged – from the plane. Barked instructions were heard and it appeared that some equipment was being taken off roughly as well. In less than two minutes, someone shouted, "That's it. *Go!*" The engine roared and they lurched into action. The plane, still arcing and flaring against the night sky, receded quickly into the background and became small. They were about three hundred yards away when it was engulfed in a sudden explosion; they saw the flash a fraction of a second before they heard the sound. A fireball blazed and leaped into the sky before burning out quickly and becoming lost in the blackness.

*

They drove perhaps another mile before their pace slowed and some dim internal lights came on. They could see their rescuers for the first time. All were armed and in camouflage green, brown and black – army, they assumed, although none of them recognised the dress well enough to be sure. No seniority was immediately evident: they spoke quietly in small groups amongst themselves. Although interspersed, the plane's passengers and crew were easily distinguished from their new companions – and outnumbered by them by about two to one – by their lack of such uniformity; they were also largely ignored by them.

They appeared to be inside something like a huge personnel carrier. A row of bench seating ran the length of both sides and two similar lines, back-to-back, filled the centre. Between them all, they occupied about half the available seats, although there was considerably more unused standing room. The surrounding roar suggested a powerful engine at work but the vehicle appeared to be sturdily armoured and heavy, and may not have been travelling at more than forty or fifty miles per hour. Although they could not see directly, they had an impression of weaponry on the exterior as well.

Bob took in the detail quickly. Aisha appeared to have sustained no further injury but was very shaken; Andy looked to be a little further battered as he took care of her; Jenny was clearly in considerable pain and his own lip still bled. Aisha's four helpers were unhurt and he noted, with some relief, that Hattie was at least in one piece in the corner – albeit it with some leads dangling loose here and there. Time would tell how much internal damaged she had sustained but at least she was *there*.

But there were only two of the flight crew: the pilot who had brought them progress reports and instructions throughout the journey was not there. Bob looked at the rest of The Desk; Andy and Jenny appeared to be coming to the same realisation simultaneously. Glances darted from face to face and between army and civilians, and eyebrows were raised in enquiry.

Eventually, their question was answered in abrupt fashion. One of the soldiers – she may have been of a higher rank: the

others hushed their conversation somewhat when she spoke –
consulted some notes from a file of papers she held, and asked:

"What happened to Joe M.?"

Both remaining pilots shook their heads slowly.

"Didn't make it," one of them answered simply. "Died in the
cockpit. We couldn't get him off the plane."

Chapter 25: Topography

They drove for hours; Jenny and Bob peering out from porthole-like openings towards the front of each side of the vehicle. Its own beams illuminated a small stretch of road ahead but little else. At first, the few lights they could see from the airfield, faded and were replaced by even fewer, more distant ones. As these also disappeared, there was progressively less and less to see. Eventually, they were surrounded by only darkness: no sign of human life anywhere, not even RFS apart from the occasional larger flash in the far distance – there was probably nothing much out there to go wrong. The road contracted, as they continued along it, from two asphalt lanes to a single one, then little more than a stony dirt track. Beyond the road, nothing could be seen in any direction. The only people alive in the world seemed to be aboard the carrier. Some polite conversation was attempted by The Desk but the uniformed men and women were not particularly communicative. No-one, certainly, would answer the essential question of where they were going. They drove on.

After an hour or so – it may have been nearer two: they found time hard to judge and they had surrendered all mobile devices in Brussels, they suddenly drove into a small settlement and, just as suddenly, out of it. It may have comprised no more than two dozen wooden and metal shacks, workplaces and shops, and some street-lighting. The track they were on appeared to be its sole thoroughfare. There were inhabitants though: a few souls ventured out to see the passing spectacle, their forms silhouetted against the glow from within their homes. A hand-painted sign on an open hut read, 'Coffee-Beer'. Where there was technology, of course, there was also RFS. Even in the middle of nowhere, no-one was immune. Then the place was gone and they continued on into the night.

But they only drove another quarter of an hour this time. Without warning, a small, dilapidated shed materialised out of the gloom by the side of the road and, unpromising an edifice as it may have appeared, they stopped before it. The soldier with the papers motioned that they – Aisha, Andy, Jenny and Bob – were to get out. The flight crew and Aisha's medical team seemed to understand implicitly that they were to remain in the vehicle. With considerable trepidation, The Desk climbed down – Aisha supported by the other three – and watched with increasing alarm as their transport continued immediately, and noisily, off along the track. With almost all of its lighting to the front, and them at the rear, they could still make out little detail of size and shape; then it was gone. Other than the old shed, there was nothing else in sight. They were alone.

*

Slowly both the noise of the carrier, and the little light it threw to its rear, faded to nothing. Even the shed, just a few yards away, could no longer be seen; they stood together in complete darkness. Aisha was the first to speak.

"Where are we?"

"Nowhere!"

They groped for each other in the blackness and held hands in a ring.

"What do we do now?"

"God only knows!"

"*Happy New Year!*" A disembodied voice from the night. They each twitched in shock and felt the others do the same.

A light came on a short distance away; it could have been a small torch or the display from a mobile phone – it was hard to tell – but it was bright in itself in the darkness and just enough to indicate movement in its immediate vicinity. Then there was another, and another; then one more. Between them the four lights showed the outline of a number of figures: how many was unclear. They moved towards The Desk, who – whilst very uncomfortable indeed – realised that any attempt at escape was pointless. As the figures came closer, they appeared to also be four in number. Their leader was in touching distance of Andy now. He put out a shadowy hand, which Andy – somewhat reluctantly – accepted.

"Glad you guys could make it! I bet you could use a beer?"

"Just a cup of tea for me please," growled Andy distrustfully.

"Hey, a Scotsman! Pleased to meet you, buddy. My great-grandfather came from Glass-cow!"

"Did he have trouble milking it?"

"Say what?"

"Never mind. Anyway, I come from Eden-berg."

*

"This way, guys."

A combination of lights, arms and hands guided them towards the dim shape of the shed. One of the figures held open a rickety door and they entered. Inside there was nothing except a wooden screen – in the same poor condition as the exterior – partitioning the half in which they stood from the other. This also had a flimsy door, through which they passed into an even deeper darkness.

"Now, watch your step, guys."

They stood for a few moments as their eyes adapted to the light: the hand-held illumination caused a confusion of shadows but failed to make much impact on their surroundings. This section was similarly empty with the exception of what appeared, at first, to be a shoulder-high rack of metal shelves in the far corner. Slowly they realised this to be the top of a set of steps, protruding from a square hole in the ground.

"Down there, guys. Two of us, then you four, then two more of us."

They climbed slowly down the steps into the deepening black. Aisha was barely more disoriented than the others in the darkness; in fact, Andy's leg gave him the most trouble. Their hands and feet felt their way over about twenty rungs before their guides' touch and instructions indicated solid ground.

"Last step; you're there; you can let go." Repeated for the four of them.

They were led, completely blind now, away from the steps. They heard a door open and had the impression of entering through it. When they had all passed, it clicked shut behind them.

"Mind your eyes, guys: bright light," came the warning. Aisha snorted at the irony.

A switch snapped on somewhere and their world was suddenly bathed in white; even Aisha had a slight impression of it through closed eyelids and bandages. The other three blinked in shock. They were in a small, bare – but clean and well-maintained – underground room, empty save for the door by which they had presumably entered and a set of steps leading down to another on the opposite side. It was obviously a transit space: nothing more. They now descended the steps, opened and passed through the second door, then gazed in wonder. The sight that offered itself to them could not have been more different to the one they had left behind on the surface a few minutes earlier.

They were at the brightly illuminated end of a long, straight tunnel. The domed chamber in which they stood was circular and wider than the tunnel itself, which stretched away from them – lit at intervals – into the distance, apparently without end. Two sets of metal rails – tracks of sorts – ran the length of the tunnel, as far as they could see, flanked by walkways on each side. Two armed guards, dressed as their rescuers from the plane had been, stood facing them at the entrance to each walkway. Somewhat incongruously with the precision of their surroundings, a number of not-quite-so-new buggies – not unlike golf carts – were huddled together on the other side of the room. Each had two rows of two seats. A group of men and women – probably technicians – in protective clothing sat around in readiness. For a few seconds, they wondered if the facility might be RFS-free but some random flickering of distant tunnel lights quickly indicated that it was not.

At last they could take stock of their greeting party; all four were men between about five-foot-ten and six feet tall. In dress there was little to choose between them: they all wore white shirts, various colours of jackets that matched their individual trousers but no ties. Their apparent leader was bald; one was a redhead; another was grey, and the last was dark-haired. Andy was subconsciously devising a new naming system when his work was supplanted by some – by now, unexpected – introductions.

The bald man in charge was *Donald*, or *'Don' Bell*. He described his affiliation simply as *'Security'*, which they interpreted to mean 'security services', but said no more. He introduced his colleagues in a similarly business-like manner. The man with the grey hair was *Jerry Austin* (*'Communications'*); the redhead, *Larry Washington*, and the dark-haired man, *Scott Lopez*. Jerry appeared to answer to Don but have some authority over the other two.

"You guys OK?" asked Don, quickly once the formalities were complete. "Ready to go?"

"Where?" asked Aisha.

"How?" asked Bob.

"To the *OI*, of course," Don laughed. "The *operational installation*. That's where you're needed, isn't it. You're not much use to the world here!"

"Down there?" Andy suggested warily, pointing towards the tunnel.

"That's right, fella: nowhere *else* to go!"

"How?" repeated Bob.

"Ah, good question," admitted Larry. "The bullet tramcar's been taken off: too much RFS interference." He indicated the buggies. "We've been using these instead lately. Battery-electric, no comms links, fairly reliable and our tech guys have souped them up a bit. We can get close to fifty miles per hour out of them now – only half the speed of the bullet but we'll get there!"

"Although one did blow up when we were charging it this morning," Scott volunteered.

"Let's go, shall we?" suggested Jerry, ignoring him.

*

The eight of them, divided between two golf carts, hurtling along a walkway not conceived for anything like this purpose, made an odd spectacle. At first, the pace was alarming: the buggies felt less than completely stable and steering was clearly not entirely simple at that speed. However, some fortunate and largely unplanned aspects of the tunnel's design helped. Firstly, there were no obstructions: lights and suchlike were above head-height and the walkways were smooth and continuous for emergency evacuation purposes. Secondly, the width between the closest point of the tunnel's sloping wall and the continuous rail, which separated them from the tramcar tracks, was just a few inches more than that of the carts themselves and formed an effective tube for them to glide through. If a buggy *did* happen to brush against either side (which actually happened rather a lot), while it made a considerable noise, it could not do so at more than the slightest of angles. Similarly, it could not be deflected significantly. Although their exteriors had become badly scuffed very quickly, and similar marks could be seen on the walls in places along their route, there was really nowhere for them to go. Protected inside the carbon-fibre shells, and behind sturdy Perspex, they were safe. After the initial concern, the journey was actually quite exhilarating: a linear roller-coaster.

The gradual settling of their nerves and the unexpected warmth of their unusual welcome eventually made conversation possible. Jenny was sitting in the rear of their buggy, next to Larry Washington.

"So, how long to the OI?"

"Less than an hour with any luck," Larry answered, clearly under the impression that this was good.

"An *hour!*" She was tired and could not disguise the disappointment. "How far is it then?"

"About forty-five miles, less what we've already covered."

"*Forty-five miles?* And is this the only way in?"

"No, there are six of these, er ...," he started, then paused, thinking. "How good's your mental geometry?" he asked, smiling.

"Pretty good."

"OK, try to picture this, then," he began, using a finger to trace an imaginary map in the air before them.

"The central OI isn't big: just a few dozen labs and other rooms; but it's top-secret. It's not on any public maps and it's mostly underground. We don't want people just stumbling across it so it's as inconspicuous as we can make it. Obviously, it's as remote as possible too. There are no roads leading directly to it and even the track that passes by it isn't properly linked to it: you have to walk several hundred yards across open ground. We rarely take equipment or large numbers of personnel in that way (no more than three people at a time): we use these tunnels instead. So it's hidden from view but doesn't arouse suspicion by being a huge patch of open desert!

"So, think of the OI itself as being at the centre of a circle – not a perfect circle, but close – of about ninety miles in diameter. Now imagine there to be eight rough compass points on that circle. There's nothing at the northwest or south points but, at the other six, there's a tunnel like this, leading from the outside to the middle. We're now on the northeast radius.

"At the outer end of each tunnel, there's some hidden way to access it: a bit like the cabin we just climbed down from – but they're all different in that respect, depending on local geography. This is one of the 'low-throughput' ones. Somewhere a bit further outside that, I think it's twelve miles on our northeast road, there's a small town or village. Four of them were there already, in one form or another; the other two we kinda 'put there' to look good. You may have seen the smallest of them on your way through?" Jenny nodded, astonished.

"But, driving in from the towns, beyond the tunnel entry points," Larry continued, "the roads just carry on. No-one takes any notice of a few abandoned buildings so all they see is six settlements connected by three fairly straight roads. One runs west-east; another north to southeast; and the one that's above us at the moment runs northeast to southwest. If you think about it, they don't all join in the same place either: this one and the west-east road meet close to the OI itself but the other crossings are northeast and east of the centre. No-one *really* uses the roads themselves much anyway; in fact, the north to southeast road goes over hills and isn't even passable this time of year. But everything looks distinctly rural, even from the air."

"And no-one has a clue what's going on underneath it all?" suggested Jenny, thoroughly impressed.

"The public don't," called Jerry Austin over his shoulder, having listened in, "but most foreign intelligence groups probably do!" She noticed Don Bell scowling a little at this.

"So the rest of them, in the, er … lorry," she asked, with a growing sense of understanding, "they just carried on along the road?"

"That's right," confirmed Don. "They'll go right across the area." He looked towards the roof of the tunnel. "In fact, they're going to be somewhere above us now. They'll go almost over the top of the OI, then past the southwest tunnel point, through another town, and then on towards a bigger city. We needed to get you guys here as quick as we could. But they'll get home eventually – and without looking suspicious!"

The buggy glanced off the guardrail with a squeal but they carried on.

*

Bob and Scott Lopez sat in the front of the other buggy, Aisha and Andy behind. After a period of thinking his own thoughts, Bob asked,

"So, what exactly *is* the OI?"

Scott gave the question, or at least his answer, some thought.

"Its main function isn't that different to the facility you've been working on in Brussels," he eventually replied. "Bigger in terms of what it *does*; but not as impressive to *look at* – not as *flash*, if you like."

"Doesn't sound like you guys much," mumbled Andy, but was ignored. Scott continued.

"The OI is mainly just for technical staff, at least on the top level. There's no auditorium, no fifty-meter screen. Apart from a couple of central control rooms – and they're not much more than offices, it's really all *kit*."

"*On the top level?*" Bob asked. Scott had thrown that in rather quickly. He smiled in answering.

"Yes, the main level: the first level under the ground. That's where all the work is done."

"But there's something below that?"

Scott hesitated. "Yes, there's accommodation below that – for the guys who have to stay there. There are apartments and living quarters. You'll stay there too."

"And is that all?" Bob's intuition had kicked in.

Scott smiled. "Ah, no … OK, there's stuff a long, *long* way under that."

"Nuclear bunkers?"

"Yes, that sort of thing. Obviously, a facility this remote has massive potential so it has a dual purpose. There are some 'safe sites' far below the main part of the OI."

"And are they beginning to be *used* at the moment – with all the problems?"

Scott hesitated once more. "Ah, yes they are. I'm only telling you this because the OI isn't a large place and you're likely to meet people there who obviously aren't part of the technical team – and they won't want to stay hundreds of feet underground all the time. But, yes, some 'senior people' are beginning to converge on the OI. It *is* one of the best, safest places we have – but not one of the most obvious." His voice lightened. "But you don't need to worry about that. Apart from '*The Hole*', as it's called, the OI's still essentially a technical facility: all the *work* that's done there is to do with network analysis – *your* sort of stuff, buddy."

Bob considered. "So, is it a sort of newer *Room 641A?*" he asked. "That sort of thing?"

Scott smiled again. "Well, kinda, I suppose; but Room 641A, and all the other sites like it, is pretty old hat these days: not secret at all – you can even look it up on Wikipedia!"

"I know. But the OI is still essentially a covert monitoring station?"

"A bit more than that: it's an *upgraded 641A*. It's a *control* and monitoring site – like the one you've been at in Brussels, only way bigger. There are seven other installations across the USA that do the same kind of thing, and eight more across the world (Brussels is one of those), but the OI we're headed for is the biggest and most powerful. If we use our full muscle here, we can access or divert close to an eighth of all global Internet traffic through our hands."

"But, officially, it doesn't exist?"

"Correct; it's probably *the biggest single Internet data node in the world but it's not there!*"

"Cool!"

*

By the time they arrived at the OI, the journey's novelty – and The Desk's appetite for excitement and conversation – were diminishing. Whatever time of day it was where they were, it was even later where they had come from: they were all desperately tired – yet they still had a job to do. Their reducing speed, and the appearance of a slightly larger, brighter glow in the distance, were welcome indications that they were approaching their destination. As the buggies slowed towards a stop, they emerged from the tunnel into a domed terminal room quite similar to that they had left at the hidden entry point forty-five miles, and fifty-five minutes, previously. Additional guards stood on duty and more technicians, in protective clothing, were on hand to deal with RFS: these, however, appeared busier – a lot was going wrong. Another huddle of modified golf-cart-like vehicles clustered on one side.

They stepped out of the buggies and watched them being taken to join the rest of the group to charge. As they were being connected, another caught fire and was quickly extinguished and removed. There was no time to take in any further detail. Don and Jerry led the party through the exit door and they emerged suddenly (and somewhat disappointingly) into the end of a modern, but unexceptional office corridor. This quickly connected to another and then led, passing several laboratories with huge racks of networking equipment along the way, to a central space with three elevator doors. Everything was artificially lit so the occasional RFS failure was inevitable.

There had been no discussion of the matter during the journey but each of The Desk had formed a similar assumption that, on arrival, they would meet – be introduced to – whoever was in charge of the OI, or at least to someone in high authority. Their realisation that their welcoming party at the shed and these expected senior hosts were one (or four) and the same, was a gradual, unsynchronised, process for them all. But these men *were* the top flight, it appeared. As various personnel, both uniformed and suited, passed them along their way, the rank of their new colleagues slowly became increasingly apparent. Strategic and technical updates were received and orders were barked in quick succession. Eventually, however, their understanding was complete – and shared. Don Bell appeared to be in overall control of the OI, Jerry Austin perhaps a close deputy; Larry Washington and Scott Lopez were in almost as high esteem. More particularly, as it emerged, Don was the OI's *security* chief (a principle that clearly eclipsed all else) with Jerry in charge of internal and external *communications*. Scott and Larry had *technical* responsibilities for the actual *operation* of the OI and had better networking experience.

Two of the three lifts had prominent numeric security key pads and slots for pass cards. They entered the third, which had only a simple card reader; inside, it had but two control buttons, marked '-1' and '-2'. Larry pressed '-2'.

"We're taking you straight down to the accommodation floor," Scott explained to Andy. "There's a hospital there. Your colleague," he indicated Aisha, "needs a medical examination quickly."

"I can still hear you!" Aisha snapped.

"Apologies, Ma'am. We'll get you looked at as soon as possible."

The lift descended briefly and they emerged into a larger space, not unlike a respectable hotel foyer. Large, comfortable-looking chairs were dotted around and there were arrows to a canteen and bar. Other signs indicated room numbers on long corridors leading away from them and one pointed to 'Medical Centre'. Larry and Scott quickly moved to take Aisha in that direction and Andy followed. Before they had taken three steps, however, Don issued a further command: it sounded almost like a reminder.

"Straight to Dr. Barbara, guys, yes?" The other two nodded. Jerry glanced at Don; his eyebrows lifted an angstrom.

There were a number of the golf-cart-like buggies in the foyer. These were unmodified and this appeared to be their original home – and purpose. The accommodation floor was obviously considerably larger than the OI itself above. Andy helped Aisha into the back seat of the nearest cart with Larry and Scott taking the front. The four of them left at an altogether more leisurely pace than they had travelled in the tunnel above; Don, Jerry, Jenny and Bob remained in the foyer.

"Is the medical centre going be open this time of night?" asked Bob. "It's late, isn't it?"

"It certainly is," Jerry confirmed. "With all the RFS now, it's running like a 24-hour emergency department. Some people are having to stay there."

"So, where do we start?" Jenny attempted enthusiasm but it was stung by fatigue. Don smiled.

"Not tonight, guys. You're tired: you need sleep."

"But the sooner we ...," Bob tried.

"In the morning."

"But It will kill millions more ..."

"Tomorrow."

"But the longer we leave it, the ..."

Don's smile faded.

"I'm sorry, guys," his voice took a firmer hold. "I'm responsible for the security and operational efficiency of this facility – and a whole lot more besides beyond its perimeter. You folks aren't even capable of looking after *yourselves* in this condition, let alone making technical calculations or decisions. I doubt you'd even *understand* the data we gave you in the first place. You're beat; you're going to bed."

*

Bob had had very little idea of the time at which he had been shown to his guestroom. He had wanted to contact Jill but the OI team had said it was not possible. He had quickly showered and fallen – naked and exhausted – into bed, to be enveloped in grim dreams mixing past, present and future. He was trying to battle a monster but he could not find it; it was all around him but he could not see it. And he was *alone*: his allies were gone and he did not know what to do on his own. He flailed about uselessly as the unseen beast dealt death and destruction around it, but his partner, the one he relied on, had deserted him. Suddenly, the dream slipped colourlessly into the background and was replaced by vivid reality. He still had no idea what the time was but he now sat upright in bed, a single thought banishing all others to the darkness.

'Hattie?!'

PHASE SIX: SURGERY

Chapter 26: Ups

Andy woke slowly, physically refreshed but in a state of confusion. It took some time for him to recall the long previous day – begun in a different continent – and the events that had led him to wherever he was – *whenever* it was. All was dark, there was no light from anything. That was almost his first clue: he was dimly mindful of the precaution – explained to him by someone the night before – of unnecessary electrical items not being powered up. He reached over to his right and groped for the bedside light. All the equipment in the OI (*that* was where they were, he remembered), had been double-insulated, or otherwise protected, to minimise the potential for RFS but there was still a risk.

The light clicked on without any side-effects other than dazzling him. He blinked and turned away to his left. There Aisha lay, still asleep – breathing softly, her eyes newly padded and bandaged by OI medical staff. Now, a little clearer, he recalled the visit there the night before. She had refused to stay in the hospital after her examination and had made Andy take her back to his room with him. Earlier, when her old dressings had been removed, he had seen – for the first time fully – the extent of the injury. It was horrific: a few smaller wounds surrounded her nose and forehead but a single seam ran almost perfectly horizontally across her face, taking in both eyes and leaving loose layers of skin on each side. One eyelid was almost detached and the glossy white underneath clearly damaged as well. When she had asked, he had been unable to tell her the whole truth as to how bad it was. Dr. Barbara had given her new medication, run several tests and taken samples before putting her back together again; they would get some results in the morning.

Andy's leg irritated him badly; he looked down under the covers and winced at the sight more than the pain. It was swollen and inflamed and really needed medical attention as well. But Aisha had been the priority the previous night and he had not mentioned it to anyone. Now, he dragged the infection painfully to the shower. The water stung acutely across most of its surface and on a few other parts of his body too. Afterwards, he stood motionless, drying naturally as best he could – knowing that a towel would hurt too much – gazing sadly at Aisha as she lay, now slowly waking. At first he panicked and looked for his old clothes to cover his various lesions and blisters from her, but then cursed his stupidity, realising the pointlessness.

She stirred some more, flopped out a limp hand to where he should be lying and, realising he was not, sat up suddenly, groping around in a wider arc.

"It's OK, I've just had a shower," he said softly to reassure her.

*

New clothes: an eclectic selection of shirts – with and without collars – and trousers of various styles, including jeans, had been placed in their room, presumably before their arrival. Some simple footwear too. They mostly fitted Andy but not Aisha. However a similar arrangement had been made for the room next door – where she had been expected – and these were quickly retrieved: all room locks appeared to have been disabled for safety. Within twenty minutes, they were ready to venture out. While Aisha dressed – she insisted on doing this herself, only asking Andy's advice on the nature of any garment she help up – he briefly turned on the TV. Some (badly broken-up) early breakfast magazine programme was on. It made grim viewing. Over a hundred million dead – probably many more: easily the 'largest-scale human disaster of all time'. There was also evidence that It was still increasing in Its abilities: large industrial complexes were being shut down (or worse) across the world. IoE climate control systems were failing. Whole cities were being close to wiped out. Weapons were being fired at random – non-nuclear at present but most commentators considered it to be only a matter of time before these safety systems were bypassed too. And, of course, the general public still did not know what 'It' was! It was too much to take in: he needed something concrete to focus on. The time bar at the bottom of the screen read 5:24am: as tired as they were, their body clocks were still ahead of American time. Would anyone else be awake?

They emerged quietly from their room, Andy leading Aisha. In one direction, the corridor disappeared into the distance with several side passages leading from it. They turned the other way, towards the foyer where they had parted the night before. Once back in surroundings Andy recognised, they followed the sign to the canteen, where they found Jenny and Bob, also forced awake by the time difference; and also dressed in new clothes provided by their hosts. Physically, at least, they both appeared improved. They were alone.

The canteen hatch area was closed – there was no-one else to serve or be served – but Jenny had risked getting tea from a free dispenser: she and Bob sat sipping something approximating Earl Grey. She looked anxious, he utterly crestfallen. The Desk exchanged warm, but subdued, embraces. Jenny and Bob made space and Andy helped Aisha to a seat. RFS disruption was more visible here – away from their semi-insulated rooms.

"How is everyone?" asked Aisha quickly, hoping to deflect questions about her injuries.

"Not good," Jenny answered shortly. "Apart from the fact that we really should be getting on with doing something, and there's no-one here," she looked around, then stared gloomily at Bob, "we may have another problem."

"What?"

We've lost Hattie," Bob replied. "We left her on the carrier – or whatever it was. We left in such a rush, I forgot her. I don't know if we're going to be able to measure anything any more."

"Which might mean we can't prove that any of what we're saying is true!" Jenny added.

A deathly silence.

*

They waited until six o'clock but were unsurprised by no-one else appearing. Eventually, they found their way back to the foyer and tried the lift they had used the night before. However, it would not work for them. Andy pressed the call button several times without the doors opening or sight or sound of any other reaction. The other two lifts they had seen on the floor above had no openings here. They explored more of the accommodation floor but, other than gaining some idea of how huge it was, they found nothing of interest.

At 7am, a man in white shirt and trousers came to open the canteen. His greeting was good-humoured and without apparent surprise. Within minutes, a few other people – the usual mix of suits and uniforms – emerged from various accommodation corridors to partake of an early breakfast: there appeared to be no charge for this service. The Desk was collectively hungry but only Jenny and Aisha found eating easy. Bob was acutely distracted, and Andy could eat no more than a few mouthfuls before he felt uncomfortable. Jenny watched him push his plate away with concern but it was easy to hide this from Aisha.

The canteen man also allowed them to use his phone to attempt to contact home: it was around the middle of the day in Europe. The initial response was positive. Jill, Chris, Heather and Ben were safely locked up in their London house with at least a few days' food in store. Outside, however, things were not so good: there was still a limited police presence, Jill said, but gangs easily dodged them and were able to ransack lightly-guarded houses almost at will. The situation was deteriorating.

And the news for everyone else was worse. To Andy's dismay, he discovered that Ruth Jones had been killed – there were no details as to how. His ex-wife was missing and Jenny's brother, Richard, could not be contacted. Aisha had no-one to call at all. She shook her head, as the phone was placed in her hands, and held it out to pass on to Bob for a second round. He attempted to contact Stephen but there was no response from any of the various IDs and addresses he had stored. Frustration mounted.

At exactly 8am, Scott Lopez appeared, accompanied by Dr. Barbara. They both smiled widely as they greeted The Desk, sitting quietly but impatiently after their breakfasts.

"Morning guys; sleep well?" Scott was positively buoyant.

Jenny's response was colder. "Can we get on with this?" Bob grunted something similar in intent. Andy had more interest in Dr. Barbara. She, however, was obviously not going to speak until she was asked to.

"Sure guys," Scott continued, his enthusiasm undamaged. "We'll get you up to the labs as soon as we can. But first," he grinned towards the doctor, "Dr. Barbara has some good news." Andy felt Aisha's grip tighten on his arm.

"Indeed," said Dr. Barbara, formally acknowledging the transfer of control with a nod. "I have some encouraging results. The damage to the patient's face and eyes is not as serious as might appear on the surface. Our tests suggest that there will be few or no permanent ill-effects."

"So, my *sight*?" asked Aisha, curtly.

"It will take time," continued Dr. Barbara, nodding slowly, "but we expect your visual recovery to be a complete one." Aisha visibly deflated back into her chair in relief.

The remainder of the conversation between her and the doctor was understood by only the two of them. The rest of The Desk and Scott looked on as Aisha asked a sequence of questions, in impenetrable medical terminology, which Dr. Barbara appeared to answer to her increasing satisfaction. It seemed to both make sense to her in absolute terms *and* be consistent with Andy's visual description from the night before. The prognosis was a lengthy one – many days, possibly weeks – but her sight *would* be returned, probably without impairment. She permitted herself an audible sigh of relief this time and stroked Andy's arm affectionately. She could not see the doubt in his eyes.

Jenny allowed what she considered to be a respectable period of time for the good news to settle before taking up the gauntlet once more.

"Come on; let's go. Let's switch this thing off," she urged.

"OK. Let's go!" Scott almost sang. Dr. Barbara took her leave.

They returned to the lift, which responded to Scott's summons, and ascended to the OI level. They were met by Larry Washington as the door opened. Much to Jenny's (and, to a fair extent, the others') annoyance, he insisted on giving them a tour of the complete OI before starting any work. The Desk protested but he had his reasons, he maintained.

"We're wasting time," moaned Jenny.

"Not much," Larry replied brightly, "and we think you guys need to understand *everything* here before we can all work together. You're proposing something massive, If we've understood you right – this 'European Theory' of yours. We can't afford any false assumptions. What's the expression? '*The Devil's in the detail*'?"

"The original version's '*God is in the detail*'," Andy grunted, "meaning do whatever you do as well as you can. I *hope* that's what you mean?"

Larry and Scott wore matching grins across the widths of their faces.

*

So The Desk suffered to be shown around the OI. This consisted essentially of three corridors – subterranean, of course, each about forty yards long, connected in a wide, square 'H' formation, with numerous labs, and a few offices, filling the space between and around the edge. They had originally entered, the night before, from the tunnel dome in one corner; the lifts were at the exact centre. Larry and Scott immediately led them to the point diagonally opposite. As they approached, they noticed artificial lighting gradually being exchanged for daylight.

"This is the only part of the OI that reaches open air," Scott explained as they came to a set of glass panels not entirely unlike a domestic French window. They stood a half-floor below the ground. Outside, a set of steps, cut into the rock at right-angles to the glass, rose to the level plain. Inside, two guards stood on either side of the opening.

They stared, from internal shadow, out onto a desolate prairie, broken only by a few gnarled trees and bushes of wiry scrub. In the middle distance were thicker plants, which may have been cacti. Beyond, a low mountain range struggled to be seen through the floating morning mist. There was nothing of note visible between the OI and the distant hills, perhaps sixty or seventy miles away.

They looked out from underneath a low rocky outcrop. The early sun, behind them, cast its shape far across the desert ground, but it was obviously not a large feature; just enough to hide the exit from aerial view, and one of many similar, unexceptional rock-piles, explained Larry.

"So guys," Scott continued, "if you exit from what we call the '*Look Out*' here and turn 180 degrees around the rocks, the closest point of the southwest-northeast road is about half a mile away. It meets the west-east road a mile further on. We use the roads if we really have to but there's a strict rule: no more than three personnel at a time directly in and out of the OI and only at night. We sometimes bring equipment in that way. Otherwise, it comes in on the bullet tramcars, from the tunnels with the larger entry points – before those were taken off, that is! Apart from that, the three roads that go across the region are hardly used at all."

"Doesn't anyone stumble across you by accident, from time to time?" suggested Bob.

"They never have," Scott answered calmly. "We're very remote *and* hidden. And the perimeter area is better guarded than might be apparent. That's Jerry Austin's area: he's responsible for infrastructure and communications."

They turned and retraced their steps, stopping to enter each and every lab as they passed, which became quickly tedious, even for Bob. True enough, he thought, there was a subtly different purpose to the kit in each room – different protocols, networks, etc. – but the overall surveillance and control role of the OI was obvious enough and this level of individual detail was unnecessary. Moreover, Larry and Scott were prone to getting diverted into trivia as they explained rack after rack of equipment. By the time they arrived at one of the larger, central rooms where The Desk was going 'to be stationed', another two hours had passed: it was approaching mid-morning. Jenny was approaching volcanic.

Bob, however, had his spirits raised beyond measure when they entered the main control room. There, given centre-stage, between two workstations with large screens, *sat Hattie*!

*

She had even been cleaned, and by someone who clearly knew what they were doing. Apart from a few larger scuffs and a dent in a side panel, she looked as good as new. Also, some of her external cables, hanging free the last time Bob had seen her in the carrier, had been plugged back in. Her unknown saviour had obviously guessed in one or two places but had largely got it right! Bob corrected a few connections, checked the US adaptor and immediately powered her up. She *worked*!

"How on earth did she get here?" Bob asked, astonished, as he connected her output to the nearest display.

With a possibly even broader grin, Scott explained.

"Not much of a problem, fella," he laughed. "The carrier you got off last night just kept on across the centre of the region. When it got to the nearest point above ground here, it stopped for twenty minutes and a couple of our guys wheeled your kit in in the middle of the night and cleaned it up. Took two trips for all the peripherals but pretty easy really. Then the carrier just started off along the road again to keep everyone else on their way."

"So, why didn't *we* come in that way?" asked Aisha, recalling the uncomfortable ride through the tunnel in her own personal darkness.

Scott shrugged. "Rules is rules. We never take that many people directly in off the road – even at night. It's a security risk."

They had no appetite for further argument. With no ceremony whatsoever – in fact, without even asking, Bob connected Hattie's probes to the nearest network point and set her to run.

'Beep' S = 0.904

"Sweet Jesus!" They hardly lacked incentive to press on but this delivered one anyway.

They started immediately. What the Americans were clearly already calling the 'European Theory' was recapped by Jenny and Bob, with Aisha providing background comparison for human brain connectivity, function and behaviour. Their hosts would have already been appraised of all the essential detail, of course, by not-Thompson's team in Brussels. However, The Desk were surprised by just how receptive Larry and Scott (*and*, they were given to understand, Don Bell and Jerry Austin) were to their outrageous explanation of a conscious Internet. The theory, *in itself*, appeared to present no particular difficulty. What would need more careful consideration would be the dual questions of *what it all meant* and *what to do about it*.

"So, this $S = 0.904$; what's *that* all about?" asked Larry, squinting at the display.

"Means It's getting pretty bloody clever," Andy answered. Aisha shook her head with good-humoured exasperation. Her anticipated recovery was still a release to her.

In addition to Larry and Scott, there were twenty or so OI staff in the room – the largest on the floor. About half were technicians, in protective clothing, trying to battle ongoing RFS incidents. The remainder appeared to be skilled networkers and answered directly to Larry and Scott. Between the four of them, The Desk described, to their new audience, their use of the S Parameter in approximating brain activity in the powered Internet. They described the 'natural birth' of 'It' from the neural complexity of Its physical substrate, its acquisition of a control imperative and Its gradual mastery of various communication channels – wired and wireless. It was a rushed, imperfect – in places, superficial – explanation but Larry and Scott were obviously no fools. Within a few minutes, they were nodding their basic understanding.

"So," Scott attempted to summarise, "above 0.5 means 'It' is conscious and 0.75 means Its up there with a human brain?"

"Sort of," agreed Aisha reluctantly.

"So what's 0.904 then?"

Aisha shook her head. I really do not know," she admitted.

"It's trouble," suggested Andy.

"So where's it heading? Towards 1? Can It go beyond that? They all looked quickly at Jenny, who shook her head.

"No, it's a *ratio*; one formula divided by another: the top can't get larger than the bottom. It can't go beyond 1. I don't really understand how It's getting this close but, anyway, It has to be stopped. It might eventually damage Itself to the extent that It does the job for us but we can't wait for that: there might be no-one around to see it! It's too powerful to be left any longer. And It's killed *so* many people."

Bob had continued to take readings from Hattie. He began by tuning out various frequencies on her 'scopes, then reset some parameters to focus back on Its noise. Within a few minutes, he had managed to transfer a large amount of data to one of the lab workstations and processed the results to get a display of the aggregate. He and Jenny whistled – almost in unison – at the image. The change from the last time they had looked at this particular detail was striking: there was so much more *uniformity* to the structures.

"Wow!" Jenny gasped. "Are all those *frames* part of Its noise? That's all *Its* doing? Practically *all* of Its noise is now properly structured, isn't it? The spikes have almost gone. It's like It's learned how to use Its brain properly!"

"Seems that way," agreed Bob. "And Its noise is now accounting for something like *half* of all the data that's being carried by the underlying links. It's a miracle that any of *our* stuff is getting through at all!"

"Not a lot is, really," Scott interjected, scanning traffic figures on a different screen.

"But there's more," Bob continued, peering ever closer at the frame structures. "Look at this." He jabbed a finger at various sections of the display. "Some of these aren't even *real* protocols: not *human* protocols, anyway."

"What do you mean?"

"Well, look at these here: these are fine. This is an ATM cell; that frame's Ethernet. That makes sense. It's just hijacking the protocols *we've* designed to send Its brain signals around." Bob pointed to a different group. "But *these* aren't *anything we've* designed; they're complete frames so they must be doing *something* but I couldn't even tell you *what*: I guess they've come from Its learning how to use the underlying hardware *for Itself*!"

"Right, we've got to switch It off; simple as that!" barked Jenny.

As well as she could, she outlined her disconnection model to the whole team. It took about ten minutes from start to finish. Eventually, she arrived at a conclusion.

"So, once I know the complete global topology," she summarised, "I'll be able to calculate a cut-set of major nodes. Except, it won't really be a cut-set in the true sense because it *won't break* It *completely* into disjoint parts: that's impossible now with Its wireless capabilities. So let's call it a '*disconnect-set*' that'll be 'good enough'. We'll build in a margin of error in case not everything goes to plan then we'll work out which of the really big world nodes have to be permanently removed so that Its essential complexity – Its level of *connectivity* – is brought down below the critical level where It loses Its consciousness. At that point, 'It' should be no more."

"And all the PDN will disappear?" suggested Larry.

"Yes, no more noise," agreed Jenny.

"And there won't be any RFS?" asked Scott.

"Correct; no more weird stuff," confirmed Bob.

Larry waved an arm around the room and towards the lab door, as if to indicate the whole of the OI complex.

"And will *this* be one of the disconnect-set nodes?"

"Bloody Hell! I hadn't thought of *that*!"

*

It was lunchtime and The Desk had returned – *very* reluctantly – to the canteen. Their sudden realisation that the disconnect-set might include the OI itself had caused another delay. Although the possibility appeared to have been anticipated to a great extent by Larry and Scott, further 'advice and guidance' had had to be sought from a higher authority. After a brief meal, Andy took Aisha for a walk in the corridors; Jenny and Bob were left to speculate.

"So, have you even worked out *where we are* yet?" asked Jenny, with exasperation.

"Well, sort of," Bob grimaced. "It's hard to be precise but, looking at some of the network maps – and what we're connected to here, we're obviously somewhere in or around the Nevada Desert. My US geography doesn't really stretch much further than that anyway so that's probably all I need to know!"

"*Area 51*, maybe?"

"I doubt it's anything to do with Area 51 explicitly; although I guess you could argue that *that's* acting as a distraction from *this*. In the modern IoE world, I'd say what's happening *here* is probably more important – and more *secret* – than what's happening *there*. Times have changed: information's more powerful than planes these days – Andy's 'technocapitalism' again!" He smiled and changed topic. "So anyway, as an expert algorithmist, what would you say was the likelihood of the disconnect-set including this place?"

Jenny considered for a moment. "I think you may have answered your own question just before you asked it," she chuckled. "This is probably the biggest Internet node in the world – in real terms – even if it officially doesn't exist. Even its 'normal' traffic looks massive; but it's probably even more when it acts as a surveillance and control centre. Depending on the topology of any given network, the optimal cut-set isn't always simply the largest so many nodes; but it tends to include *most* of the top ones – the bigger the more likely."

"So what would happen if you were told that the set *couldn't* include a given node?"

"Well, first of all, it would make a solution harder to find in the first place. The heuristics of the solving algorithm would be more complicated. In fact – depending on how the constraints were applied, you might not be able to guarantee you had the ideal solution *at all*: it would be more of a guess."

"So, it might not work?"

"No, it would *work*; but it might not be the best – the *smallest* – set you could find: there might be an easier way of doing it. But, almost without doubt, it would be larger than the optimal set, if there were *no* constraints, anyway. So, it would be both bigger *and* slightly more unreliable."

"Which, would made it harder to actually *implement*, I suppose? More nodes to close down, would mean more work across the world."

"Well yes, of course, and we haven't even discussed *how* we're going to do that *for real*. Stephen had to give remote orders, back in Brussels, for the Berlin and Madrid nodes to be physically disconnected and unplugged. I've no *idea* how we might get that done for what might be a few *dozen* nodes, particularly as it's getting harder to communicate with anyone anywhere else."

Chapter 27: Downs

Larry and Scott reappeared in the canteen with Don Bell and Jerry Austin. Their uninviting smiles suggested that a decision had been reached by someone – somewhere. Jenny felt she could predict the outcome.

"Let me guess," she began. "We're not going to be able to include this place – the OI – in the disconnect-set; correct?"

Jerry glanced at Don and answered – it appeared, somewhat reluctantly, "That's partially correct, guys, yes."

"*Partially* correct?"

"Partially correct, yes. You'll be given the topological Internet information you need so you can perform the necessary calculations. However, you cannot include *this* facility, or *seven others* also of strategic global importance, in your disconnect-set."

"Can you do this?" asked Don in a very matter-of-fact manner as Jenny opened her eyes wide.

She hesitated; in truth, she did not know. "Er, perhaps," she began, thinking as she spoke. "Yes, probably. But, if we can't take out the largest nodes, it will almost certainly be a *bigger* disconnect-set of smaller ones, which will make it harder to implement; and it'll take me longer to work out in the first place."

"Perfect," Don began, then added hastily, "Perfect that you can do this for us, I mean." He regained some composure. "Unfortunately, I also have to inform you of some other restrictions."

"Go on."

"I must *insist* that you focus on calculating only the larger disconnect-set *without* these eight nodes. You must *never* produce such a set *with* them included; this smaller set is not even to be *calculated*. Is this understood?"

"Why?"

"There would be a significant security problem if such data were to find its way into the wrong hands," Don said in a very level voice. "Such information would be hugely valuable to those not sharing our common objectives." He stared directly at the opposite wall as he said this, looking at no-one. "I cannot allow such material to even *exist*, let alone leave these premises. I repeat: is that understood?"

"Yes, OK, of course: if you don't *want* the optimal set, we won't go looking for it."

Don's forced smile returned. "Good." He motioned with his head towards Larry and Scott. "Anyways, there will always be someone with you in future to ensure you are working, ah, ... *correctly*, shall we say?"

*

They returned to the foyer area, ready to ascend to the OI level, meeting Andy and Aisha, emerging from another corridor, as they approached the lift. Andy looked somewhere between troubled and deep in thought. Bob was reminded of early that morning.

"We couldn't get this to work before," he declared, nodding at the lift.

"No, probably not," Larry agreed. "Between midnight and 8am, the accommodation elevator can only be used with a special access pass. Other than that, it works for everyone."

"What about the other two on the floor above?" asked Jenny.

"Those require *very* special passes," laughed Scott. "One goes to the VIP floor below this one." He stopped, appearing to consider he may have offended them. "We hardly ever use that floor," he added hastily; and we thought you guys would like to be more like one of us!"

"It's OK, we're not snobs," grunted Andy. "And the other one?"

"Ah, that goes a *lot* further down."

"To the nuclear bunker?"

Don maintained his forced smile. "Very perceptive, sir," he said quietly.

Aisha felt Andy give her hand a sudden, hard squeeze; it felt almost like a caution. A second later, he spoke.

"I need to get Aisha out of here for a bit," he began unexpectedly, with a more apologetic tone to his voice than before. "She's not well: she needs proper exercise. I don't mean here, in this place, all the artificial lights and the air-conditioning – and the bloody RFS; I mean in the open air: *fresh* air – *daylight* – away from it all. And I need a *beer* – a proper beer, not a tinned one – in the sunshine!"

Jenny and Bob looked with astonishment at their alcoholic friend; however, there was a warning in his eyes, so they held their tongues. Aisha was similarly taken aback, and certainly felt she needed no such break, but she heeded the message in his grip and said nothing. What on earth was he up to?

Don bit his lip. "That's not going to be possible, guys," he sighed.

"Why not?" asked Andy quickly. He seemed to have planned this. "We're not *prisoners* here, are we?" The term appeared to unnerve Don. His response was equally rapid.

"No, guys; of course not! You're *guests*, not prisoners." There was then just the slightest hesitation. "It's just that we need you *here*. We need your expertise, your experience, your guidance and advice. We might need to call on you at any time."

"Surely, you don't need *all* of us, *all* the time?"

"Maybe not," Don conceded, "but I guess we have to make sure you don't all go off somewhere at the *same* time." There was a clear touch of invention to some of this, The Desk felt. He changed approach quickly. "Anyways, we don't allow people – even our own guys – to go out through the 'Look Out' during daylight hours.

"Fine," agreed Andy. "We don't *all* want to go, and we don't want to go out of the *Look Out*."

"So, what do you want?"

"Aisha and I want to go back through the tunnel; then back to that wee town we passed through – to a bar we saw there. She needs to sit in the open air and I need a draught beer."

"Say what?"

"You heard me. We want to go into town for an hour or two, then come back."

*

Five minutes later, to Jenny's utter disgust, they were back in the canteen. Don and his team had disappeared to somewhere unknown to discuss the strange request.

"What the hell are you playing at?" she hissed at Andy. "We're trying to do a job here!"

Andy looked at her calmly. "I don't think we're here to do any sort of job, *at all*," he replied. "I'm not sure what we *are* here for but they seem to be doing everything they can to delay switching It off, don't you think? No work last night, showing us around everything this morning, then apparently having to discuss something they already knew? They're not exactly in a hurry, are they? I think they're just trying to keep us here so they can keep an eye on us."

"Why would they want to do that?"

"I'm not sure, to be honest, but that's what I think's going on. Trust me; I'm calling their bluff."

Jenny glared but said nothing.

After half an hour, Don, Jerry, Scott and Larry reappeared, Don looking cheerful once more, Jerry less so. Don held two electronic security passes.

"OK guys, we can do this," he announced cheerfully. Andy could not entirely hide his surprise: this was not what he had expected to hear.

"Good," he answered, as naturally as he could. "Thank you."

"So guys," Don explained, holding up the cards, "We've devised a system specially for you! These passes will let two of you, at a time, past all the security checks you need to get from the OI level through the northeast tunnel to the entry point. We'll take biometrics from all four of you but, so long as there's a match for any two of you at the checkpoints, you'll be let through if you've got these passes. For today, we've arranged drivers for the buggies in both directions along the tunnel. And, when you get to the entry point, there'll be a guy from the town waiting to take you in for a beer. I hope that's OK?" There was an unmistakeably acerbic tone to the last part.

Andy forced a smile. "Aye, that's really kind. Thanks again," he said.

Don was as good as his word. They all returned to the OI level and were taken to one of the smaller rooms on the side of the 'H'. The Desk had fingerprints and breath samples taken. Retina scanning technology was clearly visible but Don and Jerry seemed to have some consideration for Aisha in avoiding its use. When everyone had been processed, Jenny and Bob hurried off to the main control room with Scott and Larry, and Aisha and Andy were guided, by Don and Jerry, back across the OI to the end of the tunnel. Here they were shown where to insert their security passes and place their hands to have their fingerprints checked. They also stood, motionless as directed, as further scanning equipment took samples of their breath. After a delay of about two seconds, the door opened and Don indicated for them to enter. He and Jerry remained outside as the door reclosed.

On stepping into the tunnel's end dome, they were met by two uniformed soldiers – one male, one female – with a buggy set up and ready to go. The security checks were repeated once more by the two guards at the end of the walkways; another two-second delay was followed by permission to proceed. Their escorts politely motioned for them to climb into the rear seats and they set off without further ceremony. The remaining guards and technicians had plenty of RFS issues to deal with without additional distraction.

They quickly reached full speed and raced down one side of the tunnel's newly assigned one-way system. Both were still suffering extreme fatigue and dozed regularly for short intervals between being woken by the occasional scraping of the buggy against the wall or barrier. In the passing of fifty minutes or so, only two words passed between them: early in the journey, Aisha squeezed Andy's hand affectionately, turned sightlessly towards him, and asked:

"Feeling silly?"

*

'Beep' S = 0.905

Jenny and Bob were back in the main lab, working on the 'European Theory'. Scott and Larry remained to assist – or *observe* – depending on how Don's instructions were to be interpreted. Between them, they had achieved some measure of common understanding. They now sat, peering at a complex network map on the largest of the display screens. On a smaller side panel, a dynamically-changing spreadsheet of node and traffic figures called for their attention from time to time. Irregularly, they turned from one to the other. They had been given the global Internet topology. It was mid-afternoon.

"So, is this what you need?" asked Larry. "Is this enough data? Can you work with this?"

Jenny nodded. "Yes," she replied, then stopped and reconsidered. "At least, I can't ask for anything else as far as input data is concerned. The question now is whether I can actually figure out how to calculate the disconnect-set."

"Is that going to be hard?" asked Scott, glancing at Larry with an expression that was difficult to interpret.

"It might be," admitted Jenny. "I won't know until I try. It would have been easier, of course, if I could have aimed for the optimal smallest set. But these eight nodes that *can't* be removed are going to make the algorithm harder. I'll see." She turned back to the screens, took up a pencil and supported her head in her other hand. Bob moved closer in on her right to watch her work, hoping to be of some help if needed.

"Please remember that that smaller disconnect set is *not* to be calculated," Larry reminded her. He and Scott took up positions on each side of Jenny and Bob as they worked.

*

339

When Andy and Aisha reached the end of the tunnel, two more guards immediately read their security passes and checked their biometrics. The process was repeated by a mounted scanner at the exit door into the empty transit area. Their two escorts – appropriately thanked, in very polite terms – remained.

Passes and biometrics were automatically checked a final time as they left the transit area and they emerged to the bottom of the set of steps they had descended the night before. In mid-afternoon, however, enough daylight reached to their level to be able to make out the rungs and their destination above their heads. Andy guided Aisha towards them and set her on her way.

To this point, he had succeeded in hiding his pain from her. But, as he climbed the ladder behind, he struggled not to yelp as his mangled leg – and surrounding areas – rubbed and jolted up the steps. By the time they had both reached the top, and stepped aside onto solid earth, although he had succeeded in not crying out as such, there had been sufficient sound of discomfort for her to ask:

"Are you OK?"

"I'm fine," he lied. "Leg's just playing up a bit." They found their way to the shed door and emerged into a cold January sun.

"Did you *get* it checked out properly?"

"Aye; sort of."

Aisha's concerns leapt instantly. She was about to force the question considerably harder when a call interrupted her.

"Hey guys! How you doin'?"

They turned towards the road, now visible to Andy as a simple dirt track. An old truck stood beside it, a non-descript brown, possibly grey, in colour. Just showing, in faded and scratched coloured paint on the side door, was a sign reading 'Chuck's Auto'. A man in his thirties, wearing faded jeans and a white t-shirt, stood beside it. Andy led Aisha towards him and put out a hand.

"Good thanks. I'm Andy, and this," a wave to his side, "is Aisha."

"Nice to meet you folks. I'm Chuck. I run the garage, gen'ral store, café, bar – and just about everythin' else – in town. Hop in. I've come to take you for a beer!"

*

Jenny continued to work on the 'European Theory' in the main lab, assisted by Bob where he could. Scott and Larry looked on. She realised quickly that she was in some difficulty. She had expected *some* obstacles but what she was trying to do was proving even harder than she had anticipated.

To calculate an optimal (smallest) disconnect-set was simple enough. She could adapt a known cut-set algorithm to factor in the S Parameter, then use this, not to *fragment* It completely but, to bring Its S value down to a level that took Its complexity and level of connectivity, and thus Its *consciousness*, away – but that was *not* what Don wanted. Instead she was going to have to calculate a *constrained* disconnect set, to achieve the same purpose, but which did not include eight key, identified, essential facilities (including the OI).

This was where it was proving difficult. Jenny initially sketched out a simple algorithm on paper, then quickly coded it into the machine in front of her. Her program took its input directly from the spreadsheet and, to help follow what it was doing, displayed its workings – its changing node sets – on the large network map. There was the normal debugging process to get it to run at all but, fairly soon, she managed to produce some output. Thinking ahead to giving the information to someone to somehow *implement* the disconnect-set (physically remove the identified nodes), she rewrote the code to dump the final results directly to a text file. So far, so good.

However, when she ran the algorithm the first time, it did not work. The final node set looked *credible* – and it did *not* include the eight disallowed ones – but the resultant S value was still too high: *It* would still be alive with only *those* nodes removed. She returned to the code and found mistakes. She made some modifications and tried again. This time, although the S value

341

came down enough, the disconnect-set was huge – over two hundred nodes. That would be impossible to implement and she knew, instinctively, that there must be much better solutions. She kept trying with modifications to both the algorithm and the code.

But she could make no progress. However she attempted to adapt the process, her program gave either too large an S value or too large a disconnect-set. Finally, she abandoned the keyboard altogether and returned to her pencil and paper, staring occasionally at the network map to try to understand what the essential trouble was.

And, eventually, she did. It was the nature of the *problem itself* that was defying efficient solution. Of course, many such hard problems were known to exist in computer science but in this case it seemed to be a unique combination of the underlying graph problem and the S Parameter theory behind it, which was causing the difficulty. In particular, the nature of the constraints – the eight non-removable nodes – was making it *apparently* unsolvable. Either the S value or the size of the node set would be too large using her current algorithm.

But there *was* a way. Until now, she had been starting with the eight nodes as fixed *out* of the disconnect-set. Running a simple extension of a cut-set algorithm gave her an initial solution. She then tried to improve this, in a repeating loop, to eventually produce a node set which was both small enough *and* had a low enough S value. The problem was, it never worked! The initial solution was awful and did not improve much through iteration. *Perhaps she could try it the other way around.*

Starting with an *unconstrained* node set – allowing *any* nodes, it would be simple to produce a solution that was pretty small (it might even be *optimal*) *and* had a low enough S value. She could then apply the iteration in reverse to make small changes to the nodes: invalid nodes would be taken out and new ones swapped in. Eventually, after just a few loops, the eight disallowed nodes would be out of the disconnect-set and what was left *might* be sensible.

The only problem was that Don had said *explicitly not* to calculate the smaller node set. She could not help a slight glance sideways at Larry, then the other way at Scott. Would they *notice* if she coded this in – just as an initial solution? Bob was peering intently at her pencil scribbles. Did *he* understand what she was thinking? If she just *calculated* the smaller node set, at the start of the program, but did not *save* it anywhere, would that really be going against Don's instructions? Would anyone *know*? And just how much did she *care* for anyone else's rules right at that moment?

Bob quietly took the pencil from her hand and drew a line around a small number of nodes on the network diagram she had drawn. They were not eight in number and they were not the disallowed set but she had a feeling she knew what he was trying to tell her. Scott and Larry did not appear to be interested in her working notes, or even particularly, the code. They were merely watching what results were being produced as actual output when the program ran. Bob continued to draw: he put a small tick next to the nodes he had circled, then drew a much larger line around a larger number of nodes. He drew an arrow from the small set to the large one then finished off with a larger tick. He looked into her eyes and gave the tiniest of nods. She understood.

Making the changes to the code was not difficult. Firstly, she disabled the output to the graphical display so the node sets would not be shown during run-time. A simple algorithm would initially produce an approximation to the optimal disconnect-set. Then a second one would loop to swap out any of the disallowed eight and replace them with others. The ten minutes it took Jenny to code it were among the most nervous she had ever experienced. Larry and Scott watched but clearly did not understand what she was doing. Bob drew meaningless diagrams on the paper and played with the pencil to distract them further.

Soon, Jenny was ready to go. She clicked the 'Start' button and the program ran. After an initial period of approximation, a small trace counter in the corner of the screen read, $n = 17$. '*Damn*', she thought; that was the *size* of the *smallest* disconnect set – the *number of nodes in it*: she had meant to hide that! However there was no response from Larry or Scott. She pressed 'Return' to start the second phase. The counter changed as she watched – and as the invalid nodes were swapped out: $n = 17$; $n = 21$; $n = 25$; $n = 28$; $n = 31$; $n = 33$. A green message flashed on the – now otherwise inactive – network map to indicate that the S Parameter target had been reached and none of the banned nodes were in the set. She pressed 'Return' a final time and the details of thirty-three nodes were written to the text file on the other screen. She leaned back in her chair and pointed at the result.

"Done."

*

Aisha and Andy sat at a small table in front of a steel and wood construction with 'Garage-Store' written on a sign at one end and 'Coffee-Beer' at the other. The rest of the small town led away, in broken clusters, for perhaps fifty yards along the track on both sides in each direction. The truck with 'Chuck's Auto' on the door stood in front. A few people in working clothes went about their business: building, repairing, mending and cleaning as best they could. There was less technology here to go wrong but RFS was never entirely absent. As they contemplated the relative peace and quiet and stared out across the desert beyond, Chuck emerged from the shack with a tray. He placed a glass of pale beer in front of Aisha and handed Andy a coffee.

"As ordered, folks," he grinned. "On the house, as instructed."

They thanked him. He moved to leave them but hesitated, curiosity appearing to get the better of him. He hovered, uncertain; then eventually broke the silence.

"So, what you guys up to?" he asked brightly. "Folks from the base gen'rally only pass through here. They don't stop; they don't come here to get things from *me*." He looked up and down the street and sniggered. "Unless they *have* to, that is!"

Aisha smiled. "So you know about the OI – the 'base', then?"

"Sure we do. It was the base what asked me to pick you guys up and fix you with a drink. We all know what *we're* here for! To make everythin' look *normal*. We're left alone if we don't shoot our mouths off." He indicated other people in each direction with a wave of his arm. "Many of these folks is really military anyway. This ain't a favourite place to be stationed for four months at a time 'in disguise' but they're here to keep an eye on us."

"But *you're* local?"

"Well, there ain't no-one exac'ly local to *this* town. This wasn't here fifteen years ago. But, yup, I'm from not far away. Me and a few dozen others here; about the same number as military." He asked again with renewed confidence.

"So, what you guys up to?"

"We're just visiting," answered Andy. "We fancied a break from the base; and here we are."

"Well enjoy!" Chuck responded dubiously. "Ain't a whole lot to do around here! Even the weird stuff ain't *so* bad. You'll be waiting a long time for excitement 'round here!"

As he spoke, his attention faltered and his voice tailed off into silence. His gaze drifted from Andy's face to a point over and beyond his left shoulder. Andy turned to look.

In the clear blue sky, a ragged, slightly curved, fiery line was being drawn from a distant, indistinguishable point high up – towards the ground. A blazing object was visible at its head, extending the arc towards the desert plain. Small pieces of flaming debris detached along its way and traced out smaller paths, mostly disappearing into the air without trace. But the centre object continued on. As it came closer, its size became clearer. It was larger than they had realised; the parts breaking away were not small either, and some of these were now surviving too. A distant whine became audible.

"*What the heck?*" cried Chuck.

"What is it?" asked Aisha. "What are you looking at? What is happening?"

"Missiles?" asked Andy.

"Nope; ain't no weapon," Chuck answered decisively. "Wrong shape – wasn't made for this to happen. This here's something *fallin' outa the sky!*"

The object – whatever it was – struck a point out into the desert about three miles away. The whine stopped. An explosive flash appeared and a ball of sand erupted to quickly engulf much of it. A split-second later, the deafening crash reached their ears and the ground shook below them. A few flaming spirals broke off and reached out to the side; patches of burning remains could be seen for hundreds of yards around. A few parts, which had detached in the air, also came down randomly – the closest less than half a mile away – and created their own secondary impacts. Within a few seconds, all was quiet but over a range of perhaps ten square miles the desert was dotted with burning debris and scattered with clouds of displaced sand.

Chuck looked on, initially stunned. Gradually, however, an expression of understanding crept into his face. His teeth formed a firm, determined grin and he began to nod his head, slowly. Eventually, he spoke.

"*Satellite*," he whispered clearly, still nodding.

Chapter 28: Lies

Don Bell stood, with Jerry Austin beside him, staring at a piece of paper. On it were thirty-three lines of tabulated text.

"So guys, you're saying *this* will do it?" he asked.

Jenny and Bob both nodded. She answered.

"Yes, that's the smallest disconnect-set I can find that doesn't contain any of the eight nodes that can't be taken out."

Don eyed her suspiciously, and looked at the rest of his team, as he spoke. "And you *haven't* calculated any that *do*?"

"No," she lied. Scott and Larry nodded to support her.

"OK good," Don smiled. "So, if we turn off these thirty-three sites, that will kill your sentient Internet?"

"No!" Bob insisted. "Just powering them down logically isn't enough. You'll need to physically disconnect them from both the Internet *and* power grids."

"Jeez, that's going to be difficult!" Don exclaimed.

"Oh, for Christ's sake, you *knew* that!" Jenny exploded. "*Don't* pretend that's *news!*" Bob did his best to steady her as the others held a small debate in the corner of the room. They returned after several minutes. Jerry wore a despondent expression.

"OK guys," Don said, "we're still all on the same page here." He produced his widest grin to date. "This is just going to take a bit more authorisation. Also we're going to have to figure out *how* we're actually going to *do* it. Give us one more hour and we'll be ready to go."

Jenny appeared to be on the verge of a meltdown.

*

Aisha and Andy were on their way back to the tunnel entry point in Chuck's truck. There had been further satellite 'downs' over a period of thirty minutes after the first impact, over almost as much of the desert as could be seen. They were perhaps parts of the same system, which had broken off higher in the atmosphere; it was impossible to say – but, for now, all was quiet. As on the first journey into town, Andy had tried his hardest to disguise the difficulty he had climbing into the truck's cab.

"So how do you know that was a satellite – or satellites?" he asked Chuck.

"Don't see much else it could be, really!" he laughed. "Bombs gen'rally don't fall to pieces before they hit what they're aimed at. Ain't no planes left. So what else is up there?" He looked up and grinned mockingly but then relented to a softer, apologetic tone. "Plus, folks, I do confess, there's been stories of stuff like this elsewhere this mornin'!"

"Where?" Andy and Aisha cried in unison, thinking of the OI, but Chuck guessed the cause of their concern.

"Not the base, guys: you'd see that from here easy if there was anything big. No: on the radio 'bout two hours ago. Heard some story about something coming down on Vegas. Someone said 'satellite'. Hard to get the details b'cause everythin's broke but sounded like a direct hit – *big* one."

They both went through the same thought processes independently: *relief* that their friends were probably safe for now; *horror* at the thousands – maybe tens of thousands – who would have died in Las Vegas; *shame* that the former mattered to them more than the latter. They held each other tightly, not realising how closely they were also converging to the same conclusion.

*

'Beep' S = 0.906.

The delay was more than the hour Don had promised. Jenny's frustration had slowly tempered into a bitter acceptance that Andy may have been right: that obstacles to progress – to *action* – were being deliberately thrust into their path. Eventually Don and Jerry returned to the main room with what appeared to be further prevarication.

"OK guys," Don started, holding his palms outward in a defensive gesture: it was clear they were not going to like this. "We're moving again but we're going have to take it slow."

"Meaning what?"

"Meaning we're still waiting on authorisation to pull out your disconnect-set – and we may not get that until tomorrow." Jenny boiled but Don continued. "Also, our tech guys all over the world are still figuring out *how* exactly we're going to get rid of these thirty-three nodes completely. That's not going to be easy in at least a third of the cases – maybe more."

"So what are we supposed to do for the rest of the day while another fifty million die?" asked Bob, quickly interjecting a relatively civil question before Jenny could provide what was almost certain to be a more confrontational alternative.

"We *do* have work to do, guys. Rest assured."

"What work?"

"We want you to repeat the little demo you gave to the fellas in Brussels."

"What demo?"

"The demo where you took out a couple of nodes and," Don waved towards Hattie, "your *thing* here showed a decrease in your 'sentience parameter'."

"Why? We've already done that once. What's the point of doing it again?"

"I've been asked to verify, first hand, that your model works. If you can predict – kinda like you did before – what will happen if we take out a single node, then that will help the argument for us to get authorisation to complete the job tomorrow."

They were convinced that their time was being deliberately wasted now but they had no choice. A major switching centre in Denver had apparently been identified that would be relatively straightforward to physically remove in its entirety. Bob found its position in the global network and identified its connectivity relative to its neighbours. The dynamic spreadsheet gave them traffic flow. Hattie still read $S = 0.906$. She sat now in the corner of the room behind them, with all of her output fed directly to one of the console machines in the centre. Jenny worked her calculation for removing the Denver node and, after a few minutes of scribbling, suggested a revised figure of $S =$

0.903. Don waited for confirmation they were ready and Jerry stood poised with mobile phone in hand.

Jenny held up a thumb. Bob nodded agreement. Don flicked a pointed finger at Jerry.

"Let's go!" Jerry barked the order into the mobile.

'Beep' $S = 0.905$

Jerry listened. An indistinct voice could be heard at the other end of the line.

"Denver completely isolated," he confirmed. "Routing stable elsewhere."

'Beep' $S = 0.904$
'Beep' $S = 0.903$
'Beep' $S = 0.902$

They waited a few more seconds but there was no further change. Don looked at Jenny, who nodded. He gestured again to Jerry.

"Bring Denver back on."

This took several seconds longer. Various switches would need to reboot.

'Beep' $S = 0.903$
'Beep' $S = 0.904$

"We're stable again."

'Beep' $S = 0.905$
'Beep' $S = 0.906$

Don beamed a smile of congratulation. "Close enough! Nice one, guys! I think that does it!"

'Beep' $S = 0.907$

There was a violent explosion behind them. The screen before them went blank. The whole room turned simultaneously to look towards the corner. Hattie was surrounded by flames from the initial blast but, even within the fireball that engulfed her, new, smaller eruptions were visible as more of her circuits continued to blow. Technicians, well-versed in such procedures by now and armed with fire extinguishers, rushed towards her and discharged their loads without a moment's hesitation but it was all too late. Although the fire was banished within ten seconds, the damage was done. As the dripping foam was swept and blown away, the extent of the destruction was clear: little remained apart from a framework of charred metal casings and a few distorted, smouldering circuit boards. She was gone.

*

"Take care, folks! See you again some time ma'be?"

Chuck held open the cab door and Aisha and Andy stepped down from the truck; she with help from him, he with considerable pain. They thanked Chuck warmly and both shook his hand. He climbed back in, reversed a turn and drove off into the distance towards town, a cloud of dust and sand billowing behind him along the track. They watched him disappear, then faced towards the shed.

Andy was about to lead the way to the door when Aisha stopped dead, grabbing his arm.

"So, just how bad *is* this leg?" she asked urgently. He could tell they were going nowhere until she had received a sensible reply.

"It's OK," he said, trying to inject lightness into his voice. "I think I might need some different antibiotics or something. It's flared up a bit." He prayed she would not insist on examining him there and then. However, she obviously decided this was not the time: all she would be able to do was touch and feel, and there would be better places than in front of a shed by a dusty dirt track. She was not going to let the matter drop though.

"So *have* you had it properly looked at?"

"Well, in a way." She looked furious so he continued quickly. "You see, it never quite got treated properly in London, did it? The ambulance was busy with the cyclist and you didn't have the right stuff at Jill and Bob's house. "I had the dressings changed twice in Brussels but they were rushed both times and didn't really inspect it. They *did* say it might need a proper look at when we got here but it was late last night when we got in. It just feels a bit sorer today, that's all." The last sentence was as close to a direct lie as he cared to admit.

"Right," she said. "You *do* need to have it examined properly today." Her tone changed. "Andy, I am worried you are not being honest with me about your injury."

'*Bloody Hell*,' he thought. 'Not being honest with you about *my* injury. I don't even think I'm being honest with you about *yours*!' He needed to change the subject quickly.

"So, what do we make of the satellites coming down?" he asked as he started her towards the entrance once more.

She made no attempt to answer him until they were seated in one of the golf carts and underway. They had entered the shed, climbed down the steps, negotiated the security on both doors through the transit room and had their passes and biometrics checked a third time by the guards. The same drivers, who had waited for them, saw them to a vacant buggy and set off. Finally, Aisha spoke.

"I suppose about half of them will crash to Earth." she announced suddenly.

Andy had almost forgotten the question.

"Half?" he suggested noncommittally.

"Yes," she nodded. "I suppose It has established communication with the satellites. It will not understand any of what It is doing but It will be sending them disruptive signals. Eventually, for each one, their orbits will be disturbed. Perhaps some of them will fly off into space and some will fall?"

"Makes sense," he agreed. "Their orbits won't all get screwed up at once: It'll need to get a meaningful signal or two through. Then, each broken one will take time to spin down through the atmosphere, and not all of that will get through without burning up – maybe just the big ones. I guess the first casualties are hitting the ground about now."

"Yes," she agreed. "I think so."

They continued to speed along the walkway back towards the OI; long periods of silence broken by occasional scrapes and futile attempts to lighten the mood. She spoke for the first time, to his recollection, of some memories from childhood. He rambled about various philosophical, theological, literary and grammatical conundra (one of which was whether the correct term was actually 'conundra'). She was entertained rather than interested. Eventually, as they slowed towards the dome at the OI end of the tunnel, Andy dropped deeper into thought. He held up both their security passes in front of him and peered at them hard.

"How many different combinations of two from four are there?" he asked suddenly.

"Oh, not another riddle!" she laughed.

"No, I'm serious."

*

"Six."

It was evening. The Desk were reunited once more in the canteen. Bob had been briefly back to his room to shower and had re-entered mid-conversation. They were all in various, but largely shared, low spirits. Aisha was concerned about Andy; he was worried about her – and, to a lesser extent, himself; Jenny was beside herself with impatience over the continued delay; and Bob was mourning the loss of Hattie. He needed distraction.

"Six what?" he asked.

"Six different combinations of two from four," Jenny expanded.

"Aye, that's what I figured out the hard way," agreed Andy, "by counting them all, as we came back."

"And?"

"And it doesn't make sense!"

"Why?"

"Well, there are four of us, aye? And two passes that get any two of us out of the OI?"

"Yes."

"So, that means *any two* of us can leave? And there are six different pairs of which two can leave?"

"So?"

"Well, think about it. We're told that we're *not* prisoners; we're *guests*, aye? And it's OK for two of us to go, so long as two remain: so they have our 'expertise' available when it's needed?"

"Yes."

"Well, that's OK for five of the six combinations because either you or Bob or both would be left in the OI."

"Right."

"But the other combination would have you and he both *go* and Aisha and I *stay*."

"True."

"Which would be utterly pointless. What possible technical use could *we* be in an emergency if you and Bob weren't here?"

"Yes, I see. So, what are you saying?"

"I'm saying it's just another excuse – another *lie*. They made it up on the fly to keep us happy. We're not really here to get anything *done*: we're here to be kept out of mischief, out of sight – or something."

"But why?"

"Who can say? But I reckon the trick started back in Brussels – and I think Stephen had his suspicions then. I think they sent us over here to get rid of us; I'm pretty convinced Aisha wasn't fit to leave the hospital there but they drugged her up to get her to go. I think we're some sort of *threat* and they want us where they can keep an eye on us."

"Why not just kill us, then?"

"Again, who knows? Maybe they *do* think we might be useful at some point – just *not yet*? Perhaps, in the meantime, they don't want us telling the rest of the world what's going on. Perhaps, if there are always two of us inside, then the two outside have to watch their step. Perhaps having some of us here is achieving some *other* purpose – or *stopping* something happening. I don't know exactly, but there's *something* going on!"

*

The Desk was tormented by so many things but, just now, having time on their hands for thoughts like these was as great a threat to their collective sanity as anything. Jenny and Bob simply had no idea what to do. Aisha urged Andy to visit the medical centre; he did but came back with a report that they were busy and had asked him to return later – all three could now tell he was not well. They talked in hushed tones much of the time, not trusting anyone. Eventually, they decided to return to the control room to pay their last respects to Hattie. It was still early so, in principle, the lift would be usable. It was exercise, if nothing else, and Andy had less trouble on the level. Sure enough, the lift responded to their call and they pressed the '-1' button to take them up. The doors opened at the OI floor just as a fairly large group of people approached.

There were about nine or ten of them. Don Bell led the way. It struck both Jenny and Andy that it was the first time they had seen him without Jerry Austin in support. Behind Don marched several men in high-ranking, medal-bedecked uniforms. These surrounded a middle-aged woman in a crisp, cream-coloured business suit. The group passed them and stopped in front of the other two lifts. Security passes were inserted in both. The larger part of the entourage – mostly soldiers – took the lift to the deep bunker, 'The Hole'. Don, the woman and two of the nearest uniformed men entered the one for the VIP floor. Both doors closed.

"*Jesus!*" cried Jenny, staring after them. "Was that the *Pre…*?"

"It was indeed!" agreed Andy, his eyes every bit as wide as hers.

*

The main control room was locked – probably against *them* – but Hattie's remains had been moved to the store next door. They spent five sad minutes staring at the burnt-out shell, which was once her, then returned to the canteen for the final time that evening. They continued to talk about many things – often reprised – while sitting facing fragmented news reports from a TV high in the corner.

First for discussion, and once again, was Hattie herself. Was her destruction merely an RFS accident waiting to happen or had It – Its powers now further increased – somehow perceived her as a *threat*? After all, she had become part of It everytime she was used. It was impossible to know but Bob, in particular, harboured suspicions. Secondly, the satellite issue was revisited. One had impacted closer to the OI since Aisha and Andy had returned; there were reports of others coming down across the world, causing even more death and destruction when they struck populated regions. Third, but this for the first time, Jenny very quietly outlined their work in the lab. In particular, she described – like a naughty schoolgirl – how the only way to find the disconnect-set Don wanted had been to initially calculate the one he had explicitly told them not to! Fourth: could they contact loved ones once more? It was very late in Europe but perhaps worth a try? But, no, the canteen man said the phones were no longer working. They doubted the truth of this but could not argue. Fifth: was that *really* the President they had seen? Yes, without a doubt. What was *she* doing there? Perhaps the OI and The Hole were as safe a refuge from It, a rioting population, and whatever might happen next, as anywhere for her?

However, clouded over everything was the general impression that they were making no real *progress*, nor were they likely to; and, all the time, people out there were dying by their tens of millions.

"We have to *do* something!" Jenny urged. "We can't just sit around here."

Bob initially thought of Hattie. To an extent, she had already performed her key role but things might still be difficult in future without her. Her loss made him think, in turn, of Stephen, who now seemed to have disappeared as well. He feared the worst. Then, suddenly, he recalled the conversation with Andy on the plane.

"We could always try your imaginary friend?" he suggested.

"My *what*?"

"Gus? Was that his name? The contact Stephen gave you when we left the EuroNet room."

Andy blinked slowly as he remembered. While Bob explained the story, second-hand, to Aisha and Jenny, he searched in his pockets.

"I know I switched everything – along with my passport – when I put on new trousers," he muttered as he fumbled. "I just hope I've still got it. Aye! Here!" He pulled a crumpled card, somewhat painfully, from his pocket. "Stephen said this might be worth a try if things took a turn for the worse, which I guess we could say they have!" He waved the telephone number.

"But we don't have access to a phone," Aisha pointed out.

"I wonder if we could borrow one?" suggested Bob.

"From whom?"

"Well, obviously not from this guy," grumbled Jenny, indicating the canteen man. "And we don't know anyone else even remotely well enough to ask. The four suits upstairs are hardly likely to help us: they probably have as little trust in us now as we do in them!"

"Nevertheless, we might have to risk it," suggested Andy.

"Which one then? Certainly not Don. He's in this whatever it is up to his neck. He keeps talking about 'authorisation' but I don't really think he answers to *anyone* much – apart from the President herself, I guess. Scott or Larry – because they're a bit more junior? Would *they* be daft enough to help without understanding what we were doing?

Andy sat deep in thought. "My bet would be Jerry," he said eventually. "I've just got a hunch. I know he *looks* like Don's right hand man but I've the tiniest feeling Don may not entirely trust him. Until just now, we never saw them apart. I'm just wondering if that might be because Don feels he has to keep an eye on him. Also, there have been one or two occasions where I've just sensed a bit of friction between them. *And*, from your story about what happened in the lab with Hattie, we know he has a *phone*. I know it's not much to go on but, on the basis that someone who *might* be an enemy's enemy *might* be your friend,

I'd suggest Jerry. Aye, it's a *bloody* long shot but what have we got to lose?"

"*What* are you going to lose, guys?" They turned suddenly and found Jerry Austin standing behind them.

*

How long had he been there? How much had he heard? They could not tell. But he seemed very interested in what had *just* been said. Aisha decided to make some general conversation to begin: light-hearted humour might work.

"Come to slum it with the lower ranks?" she asked jokingly.

Jerry laughed but also sounded more than a little uncomfortable.

"Let me assure you, people," he began in a friendly manner, "your efforts are appreciated beyond measure." He appeared to choose his next words with care. "These are difficult times. We're all trying to do the best we can. But sometimes people have different roles to play in a crisis and that may mean different *perspectives* – sometimes even different *objectives*. Success for some, in such a situation, may be failure for others. But you may trust me that *I* have the utmost respect for your skills, your expertise, your commitment and," he shot a pained look at Aisha, "your *sacrifice*."

The Desk did not comprehend all of this but his tone was encouraging. Jenny pressed a little further.

"I don't think we've seen you on your own before? You seem more of a team player than a loner?"

This obviously amused Jerry although, once again, they did not fully understand why. When he spoke, he gave only a partial explanation.

"My role in our nation's organisation is infrastructure and communication in the outside world," he began. "But, in here, I answer to Don: he's responsible for security and that's kinda taken priority so far. But he's tied up now with some other things. We have a, ah, … a VIP on site."

"The President." Bob stated bluntly. Jerry smiled and nodded.

"Ah, you've seen her?"

"Yes."

"Well, Don doesn't want, ... er, *need*, me around for that. So I can concentrate on my proper job now.

"Which is?"

"Trying to stay in contact with the rest of the world – keeping operations *operational*. And that's proving pretty difficult at the moment!"

Andy decided to go all in with a bluff: this was his chance.

"Aye, tell me about it! I've been trying to contact my ex-wife to find out how my daughter is: she's missing and I'm worried. But no-one has a phone that works any more and Skype and all that stuff's buggered. Any chance I could borrow yours to try her number direct?"

Jerry's look became suddenly stern.

"Andy, please don't think we don't take sensible precautions with guests like you. Information is always valuable and we have plenty of that. We know that you do indeed have an ex-wife, but you do *not* have a daughter – or *any* children." Andy stared, open-mouthed and ensnared. But Jerry had not finished. "We also know that you don't drink alcohol even though you *said* you needed a beer this afternoon. However, when your breath was scanned as you returned from your excursion, you had drunk none. Be *very* careful, Andy: all such things are *noted*."

He turned abruptly and left the canteen.

*

It had been another early start, and another long day, and The Desk was still running very much on European time. Frustrated as they might be by lack of progress and other setbacks, and horrified as they were by the massacre they knew was continuing across the world, they were tired and saw only too clearly that nothing else could be achieved that night. Whatever they were to try next would have to wait until morning. They hugged disconsolate goodnights and took to their rooms, each with their own images of the carnage outside.

It was forty minutes later. Andy lay sleepless and in unbearable pain, staring open-eyed into the dark nothing of his ceiling. Slowly, very slowly, his eyes adapted a little. Gradually, even the miniscule amount of light creeping in around the edges of the door, and reflected on a few shiny surfaces, was enough for him to be able to detect the dim outline of larger items of furniture. He continued to stare, hardly blinking.

Beside him, Aisha's breath was soft and regular. Still he waited. Little by little her breathing grew steadier and stronger; eventually, it reached the level of a low, light snore. He rose – painfully but as gently as he could – from the bed, listening for any audible change as he did so. Still she slept soundly. He fumbled for his clothes at the chair on which he had deliberately left them when they had undressed. Quietly, he pulled on a t-shirt and loose jogging bottoms, and slipped into a pair of light shoes, suppressing the groans that sought escape as anything touched his body. Even more quietly, he padded towards the door, let himself out into the corridor and quickly closed it behind him. Aisha slept on.

Chapter 29: Truth

It was the next morning, although it had to be early because Andy was still asleep. At first, his dream of sitting quietly by a river with Aisha – her sight fully restored – was disturbed by a distant tapping somewhere; then actual physical contact: someone was shaking him gently by the shoulder. He awoke to find Jerry Austin standing over him, finger to his lips, urging him to silence. Light from the corridor outside fell in through the open door.

Jerry motioned Andy to follow him from the room, which he did. He still wore the shirt and jogging bottoms from the previous night. He quietly left Aisha sleeping and closed the door behind him. As they stalked towards the lift, he grunted sleepily through his pain.

"What's this all about?"

Jerry waited until the lift doors closed on them before replying.

"I'm inclined to assume, Andy, that anyone with any decency, who has to fabricate *lies* about needing alcohol when they don't drink, or to phone someone who doesn't exist, is hiding an equally important *truth*. I'm testing that theory." He said no more.

On exiting the lift, he led Andy to the Look Out. Outside was still dark. Two guards lurched upright to attention from their chairs.

"We're going out!" Jerry snapped; it was so obviously not his natural manner that Andy could not suppress a smile. One of the guards slid open a glass panel and closed it after the two of them had stepped through. There was just enough light from inside to show the short flight of rough steps. They climbed these, turned around the outside of the rocky outcrop into a natural recess and were swallowed by the blackness.

Immediately, and without warning, Andy felt something being pushed into his hand: a mobile phone. It was switched on at the same time as it was passed, the screen's glow reflecting off his face and giving just enough light to make out Jerry's features.

"What's this for?" he asked – although he felt he knew.

"Phone your 'daughter'," said Jerry.

Andy had no more lies to hide behind: that stage of the game was over and they had lost. He shrugged acceptance of the situation and pulled Stephen's card from his pocket, waving it towards Jerry by way of explanation – or apology. Holding it at an angle to the phone's face so he could both read the number and enter it, he carefully typed in the sequence – his anxiety increasing towards what might happen when he pressed 'Call'. The string of digits built up across the screen until he pressed the final one to complete the number. As he did so, a second line of text appeared below it:

Jerry Austin (mobile) [this phone]

He never pressed 'Call'. Instead, he stared blankly at the screen for a few seconds as his tired brain made the necessary connections. Then, slowly, he held out the phone to return it.

"You're 'Gus'?"

Jerry took the phone and slid it back into his jacket.

"I imagine we have some kind of understanding?" he said.

*

As she had the previous morning, Aisha awoke to find Andy no longer beside her. Once more, she groped in a wider search around the bed. This time, however, there was no-one in the room to reassure her.

Further along the corridor, Jenny and Bob emerged sleepily from their separate rooms and converged on the canteen.

*

"So you know Stephen?"

A hint of daylight had stolen into the air. Jerry's face was clearer now. He thought for a moment.

"No Andy, I don't think I *do* know anyone called 'Stephen'. However, I probably *do* know the man *you've* been calling 'Stephen'. I tend to call him 'Anton', just as he calls me 'Gus' but none of those names are correct. It's just a precaution – and a convenience. Sadly, I haven't heard from Anton – or Stephen –

362

since around the time you departed from Brussels. I doubt things are well."

"So, what's going on?"

"Ah! Where to begin?"

"Well, let's start with 'Gus and Anton', shall we? How do those two know each other?"

Jerry smiled. "I'll try." He glanced at the sky. "But it'll have to be quick: we can't stay out here much longer." He began.

"I suppose we have to go back a few years to when we first started realising that the idiot, Trump, might end up in the Whitehouse. A lot of the military and security services quite liked the guy – still *do* – but there were plenty of us across the US – and elsewhere in the world – who worried that the planet wouldn't last twelve months with him in charge. We kinda started talking to each other about what might happen when he did something batshit crazy: wanted to bomb someone for not letting him build a golf course – that sort of thing. Then, a bit more seriously, we discussed how the saner elements of the military and security might try to *mitigate* against some of the stupid stuff he'd almost certainly do – mostly to protect *ourselves* at first. We were never exactly *organised* as such but we started to work together a bit more regularly and we grew and, somewhere along the line, we started talking about ourselves as something called the '*Quiet Group*'. Anton and Gus were early members. We were never really doing anything *wrong* – just trying not to let the ethical message get lost – so, although lots didn't want to *join* us, they knew we were *there* all right, and had to put up with us. There's been a sort of uneasy relationship between the QG and the rest ever since."

He took a deep breath. "Well, fortunately of course, Trump didn't last long as president!"

"So, was the Quiet Group behind the assassinations?" Andy asked pointedly.

"No, not really: not our style – or our ethics," Jerry answered quickly, but then looked uncomfortable. "But I can't say it came as a surprise and you could say we didn't do a lot to stop it.

Anyway, by that time, we'd kinda realised that some of the really serious lunacy he was carrying around with him – the egotism, bigotry, racism and rampant warmongering – was pretty much embedded in power in the developed world anyway. So maybe it would be a good idea if we stuck around a while and tried to throw a bit of morality into the mix occasionally. So that's what we did, that's what we still do, here we are, and there we are, and we're pretty much everywhere, trying to do our bit."

"And are there *many* of you?"

"Depends what you mean by many. A *lot*, certainly. Among Don, Scott, Larry and me, I'm the one QG member. But that *might* be a typical ratio across different levels of all the services – high and low; I don't know. We generally have to keep quiet most of the time: hence the name, I guess. I know Don, in particular, doesn't like it – and doesn't trust me." Jerry allowed himself a small chuckle. "And *that's why* the four most senior guys in this place all had to come and meet you when you got off the carrier: at the time, Scott and I were the only ones available who'd been trained to drive the speeded-up buggies and Don felt he had to come with me in case I told you anything I shouldn't! *And* that's why we're out here: most of the larger OI rooms are bugged. Don's hardly let me out of his sight the past few days and I'm only free now because he's having to look after the President now that she's arrived."

"So what's *she* doing here?"

Jerry shrugged. "One of the safest places there is at the moment. She's spending most of her time on the VIP accommodation floor below ours and she can dive down into The Hole at a moment's notice if anything happens."

The low sun had breached the mountain range in places and thrown spikes of brightness across the plain. Andy took a moment to digest the information before his next question.

"Right then. What's the deal with *us*? Why are we *really* here and why won't anyone let us do what we came here for?"

"That's a much harder question," Jerry replied, "and I'm not sure I know all the answers. Some of it might be guesswork."

"Try me."

"Well, to some extent, Andy, I think you *know*." To his surprise, Jerry reached inside his jacket and pulled out the pencil-written article Andy had been scribbling on the plane. "I apologise for taking this from your room but I needed some idea of who I was dealing with before I attempted any approach. Our surveillance data is very detailed and factual but it doesn't always tell us who people really *are*."

"And who *am* I?"

Jerry smiled. "You are many things, Andy. But of immediate interest to me is that you're a good man who wants to find a solution to this problem."

"So why are we being stopped?"

"This is where I have to speculate. But I think you are being *delayed* rather than *stopped*."

"Why?"

"Because, although your team can provide the ultimate solution to the problem – and now probably *have*, there are those who may still benefit from the current situation being prolonged. It may not be in quite *everyone's* interest to destroy this thing – this *It* – just yet."

"*Who*, for God's sake? It's killing *everyone*! *No-one's* safe. Why would *anyone* want this slaughter to continue?" He suddenly recalled not-Thompson's aversion to disconnection in Brussels. "There *can't* be a corporate or a business objection any more, surely? No-one's worried about losing *money*, are they? It's broken things way beyond that now."

"It has," Jerry agreed, "although – incredibly – *some* financial transactions are still taking place. But more importantly, I suspect the appearance of 'It' is – fortuitously for *some* people – solving another emerging, but difficult, *long-term* problem." He raised Andy's notes between them once more. "And I think you know what it is."

Andy tried to think back to the flight; he could hardly recall what he had written. He knew he had been angry: that governments cared about big business more than those that voted for them – profit more than people. He had finished by speculating that the elite might not be able to escape the damage that was being caused by technology any more than ordinary people, though; that they would ultimately suffer the ravages of technocapitalism too. They would be subject to the same environmental decline, the same descent into war and terrorism, the same loss of privacy, the same social instability caused by an automated robotic workforce.

Oh no! Surely not?

He could barely spit the words out.

"You *can't* be saying that the elite are using this – *It* – as a convenient means of *wiping out a surplus population*, can you?"

"I can't say anything for sure," answered Jerry. "I'm not privy to those sorts of discussions, largely *because* I'm a QG member. I hear a few things from time-to-time, and work things out for myself, but I can't be sure. But there are large parts of the theory that make sense."

"Really?"

"Yes, really." Look at the major problems we have in the world today and think about those that '*the elite*', as you call them, can distance themselves from and those they can't. Which parts of," he waved the paper once more, "your '*technocapitalism*' work for them and which don't?" Andy considered for a moment but the question was rhetorical; Jerry continued.

"The super-rich have always managed to insulate themselves from violence and war; there's no particular reason to think the future will be any different. Similarly, with enough money – and if you *want* to, you can still remain pretty much hidden too – I'm not talking about 'celebrities' here: they're just cannon fodder. We're talking about multinationals and arms dealers. Privacy for the *real* elite won't be a problem in the future either. For example, it's not a huge secret that an 'Alternative Internet' is largely complete now – a physically-separate, smaller, hidden version to run alongside the crude one the 'plebs' like you and me have to use.

"But *environmental damage* and *social unrest* are a different matter entirely: those are *real* threats – even to the elite. The first is obvious but the second may be even more of an immediate danger. We're *already* seeing the effect that an automated AI/robot workforce is having on unemployment. And with higher unemployment comes increased hardship, which leads to social unrest and instability. And it's that *instability* that they fear most, particularly if it's *global* – not just limited to the developing world.

"Until now, the solution has been simple. The elite control *everything*: the money, government, the Internet and the Media. They spread lies and misinformation and cause most people to fight amongst themselves. They use differences between people to divide them. They use whatever tools offer themselves: religion, atheism, race, gender, *anything*. Even in so-called 'free' countries, they manage to get people to vote *against* their own best interests on the basis of 'competition' and it still passes for 'democracy'. Everything's driven from the US, of course: the EU's just a junior partner in American global imperialism – but a very willing one!

"But that stability has its limits. If unemployment through automation continues to rise – as it's doing, and no-one changes the underlying economic model, then that system of control by disinformation will ultimately fail. The lies will be *too* obvious; the diversions won't make *sense*: the numbers will see to that. Either by peaceful means, through the ballot box, or violently, in the streets, the old order *will* fall. They *know* that. They also know that they can't survive on a dead planet either, of course.

"Now, awful as it may seem, elimination of a massive number of people helps solve *both* those problems. 'Thinning out' a large fraction of the population decreases overcrowding, reduces tensions, lowers unemployment, takes pressure off the environment and just makes those left grateful to be *alive*. Balance restored on many levels. *Techno*capitalism doesn't *need* the same ratios of a surplus labour force as conventional capitalism. A much smaller number of humans and an increasing

367

number of robots will give the system back its stability and the elite can regroup and start again. And the short-term environmental damage will be a price worth paying in the long run for a less densely-populated, less damaged world. If It carries on the way It is, by the time It's destroyed Itself, It'll have accounted for a good number of the rest of us too. Then the elite can start again; maybe with their smaller, 'Alternative Internet' as the starting point?"

The closest patch of sunlight had nearly reached them.

Andy felt numb. "So you're saying," he asked, aghast, "that they're going to *let It carry on killing people* until they think the *numbers* are right? *Really?*" He struggled for words. "And do they have a *target?* Any particular *figure* they'd like to achieve? *Jesus*, I can hardly believe I'm *saying* this!"

"I've heard global figures of seventy or eighty percent mentioned in the context of an 'ideal'."

"They're going to let It continue to kill people until only three-quarters of the world's population are left?"

"No, *until three-quarters are gone.*"

*

Jenny and Bob were eating a cheerless breakfast. A slight disturbance from the doorway made them turn in that direction. Aisha was groping her way, alone and distraught, into the canteen. They rose quickly and helped her to a seat.

"I don't know where Andy is," she sobbed.

*

"So where does that leave us? What can we *do?*" Andy shook his head in desperation as he asked. They would soon have to re-enter the Look Out. But Jerry's expression made it clear he had no answers.

"I don't know Andy," he admitted. "I'm lost for ideas and time is running out. My external sources tell me that 'It' may master the failsafe systems on some nuclear weapons at some point tomorrow – there *have* been warning signs. I've tried telling Don this but he doesn't believe me: he thinks it's an excuse to implement your team's solution before they're ready. I have to do *something* but I don't know *what*. I *do* have considerable resources at my disposal. The Quiet Group is everywhere and, even within the US military, many chains of command have broken down in the confusion – generally to the QG's advantage because *we* confide in each other and the rest don't trust anyone any more, including themselves. Things are possible now that were not only a few days ago. I can call upon many people in very powerful places and positions. I can deploy significant force if necessary, and most defence systems are currently inoperable. But I have *nothing* to deploy it against!" He paused. "And I have to tell you, Andy, that I now fear very much for the safety of *your* team."

"Why?"

"Because you have served your purpose."

"What purpose was that?"

"The powers-that-be – the elite – can't really be sure that It will eventually destroy Itself *in time*: they need an insurance policy. So they needed you to provide the disconnect-set to kill It when they were ready; now you *have*. They also had to make sure that you didn't help anyone destroy *this* OI, as part of a smaller node set: that's why Don didn't want it calculated and why they've insisted on keeping at least two of you here, as a sort of 'human shield' – you are correct in thinking it didn't matter *which* two it was. (By the way, I also believe your friend has been lied to regarding the true extent of her injuries to maintain her good spirits.)" Andy nodded in agreement – and shame. Jerry continued. "But, now that Don and his team have the disconnect-set *and* it does not include their critical nodes, they may not see the need to keep you around much longer. There are other groups of scientists around the world in similar peril and *some* information is beginning to leak out on social media. However, no-one trusts *any* material any more because so much is corrupted by It so there is little threat to the powers-that-be as yet. But I fear for *your* group above all."

A desperate plan was forming in Andy's mind.

"Right. *We've* always assumed that the disconnect-set would just be *switched off* and *unplugged* everywhere," he said. "Are you saying it could be taken out *by force*? *Destroyed*?"

"Yes, to a limited extent. There are QG people everywhere still and they are in all positions of control, deployment and execution. The QG has perhaps become the world's most coordinated body in this crisis and has already achieved much good where the conventional structures had failed – or succumbed. I can call on significant fire power from air and sea if there is a purpose. And that's probably the *main* reason why Don doesn't trust me: he knows I have the infrastructure now. All the time he thought the OI might be a target, he was worried – particularly with the defences down. Now he has his alternative disconnect-set put aside, he's easy. "

"But, even if it *was* hit, most of the OI is underground."

"It's only just below the surface – and not well protected. It still wouldn't stand up to what I could throw at it if I had to. Unfortunately – and we've done some calculations on this, to be really sure the disconnection was *complete* – from *all* power and network lines, without leaving *anything* behind, we'd have to produce one helluva crater! We'd pretty much wipe out the accommodation floors too. Only The Hole down below would escape: no-one else would survive."

"So, now that you *know* the thirty-three nodes in Jenny's disconnect-set, why don't you – your Quiet Group – just take *them* out instead? Blow them up, I guess?"

"Because I simply don't have *that* amount of fire-power that I could exercise simultaneously. Obviously, it would have to be a coordinated strike so that we caught everyone by surprise. Some places could be sabotaged from within but most would need external force. I have to consider what can be deployed from where; what can be fired from sea and where the planes would need to be. None of this can be achieved without considerable risk from It and others, of course. I have to consider the fraction of planes and ships that would not survive their interaction both with It and the remaining defences. The time may be past for worrying about individual safety but we still can't do the impossible. I've done the logistics: it's just too big. Taking out *one* node fully is a massive operation. Thirty-three simply can't be done. I think we'd be lucky to manage half that."

"Seventeen?"

"What about seventeen?"

"If there was a disconnect-set of seventeen nodes."

"*Is* there such a set?"

"I think there *could* be."

"And would it include the OI?"

"I don't know; but I'd say it's pretty likely."

Jerry stared, thoughtfully, into the distance for a while. Eventually, he answered, in a slow, desperate tone.

"Andy, if anyone *was* to give me a disconnect-set of seventeen nodes, I would attempt to, ah, … *action it*."

"Leave it to me," Andy replied, as lightly as he could feign.

He immediately turned back towards the Look Out but Jerry clutched at his arm.

"Andy," he began earnestly. "You do understand what's going to happen, don't you? If you can get a seventeen-node disconnect set to me *today*, I'll set an operation in motion. There'll be coordinated strikes across the world at *0930* our time tomorrow morning." He stared. "But, Andy, *no-one* here in the OI – apart from those in The Hole – will survive. You and your friends will be making the ultimate sacrifice. If anyone gives me the smaller node set, they'll be signing their own death warrants."

Andy grinned; there was iron in it. "Aye, I know. But what about *you*? Surely, *you'll* never get away with it either?"

Jerry's look was equally determined. "I never said I could *get away with it*," he breathed hoarsely. "I merely said I could *do it*."

They shook hands grimly and returned inside. The first shaft of sunlight struck the Look Out.

*

Aisha, Jenny and Bob were still in the canteen, drinking too much coffee. They talked of many things, each gloomier than the

371

last. They always returned, however, to the question of where Andy was. On the third or fourth iteration of this cycle, their subject answered them by limping in. Aside from his limited movement, his appearance was horrific: a deathly blackness covered his face. Bob rushed to help; Jenny opened her mouth to protest. But he waved both of them away and sat down.

"We need to talk," he said.

*

An hour later, they were ready to go their separate ways. Jenny and Bob were to return to the control room and Andy needed to speak to Aisha alone. However, as they were rising from the table, they were interrupted by a man, wearing a doctor's coat, approaching them. Bob had noticed him enter; he had scanned the room until identifying The Desk, then walked over. He smiled sadly at Andy, as if he knew him, then gently tapped Aisha on the shoulder.

"Dr. Davies?"

She jumped. "Yes."

"I have been asked, by Mr. Austin, to take you to the medical facility for a re-examination. My name is Tony Stratton."

"Why?"

Dr. Stratton looked at her uncomfortably, then, imploringly, at the other three. Jenny and Bob were taken aback but Andy's response was close to violent.

"Bloody Hell, man; do we *have* to do this? *Now*? *What's the point*?"

"I must insist, sir."

Aisha was struggling to keep any composure.

"Andy, what is going on?"

"I think someone thinks you may have been, er, ...sort of, *misdiagnosed*."

Slowly, shaking a little, Aisha stood up.

While Jenny and Bob returned – puzzled by all this – to the OI level, Aisha and Andy followed Tony Stratton to the hospital.

"*Why* are we doing this?" Andy kept asking.

"*What* are we doing?" was Aisha's variant.

Tony seemed reluctant to answer either question in any further detail. When they arrived at the hospital, they found Jerry Austin also waiting for them. There were no formalities.

"Who conducted the original examination?" Tony asked, taking some medical notes from a table and studying them.

"Dr. Barbara," Jerry replied. They exchanged glances.

"She's not here this morning," said Tony.

"Good," answered Jerry. "Let's get on with it."

Tony gently removed the bandages from Aisha's head, then the pads from her eyes. A pained expression gripped his features as he did so. He shook his head towards Jerry almost immediately. However, he continued to examine her for several minutes, took a sample from one eye and examined it closely, then even more closely under a micro-scanner connected to a computer screen and, finally splitting it into parts and adding chemicals to each – repeating the observation each time. RFS continued to cause havoc even here and he had to reset the display twice. Only after he had completed all of this, did he turn to both Andy and Jerry.

"I don't think so," he said quietly.

"What?" demanded Aisha in panic.

Tony took a deep breath. "I'm afraid to say that the damage to both eyes is considerably more serious than has been recorded in these notes. One is damaged beyond all effective repair. The other, with considerable time and treatment, *might* regain some degree of vision – but not much." He thought for a moment. "And, I also have to say that, to my knowledge, this is beyond the current technology of bio-implants. I don't think there's anything I – or anyone else – can do."

Aisha collapsed her head into her hands – oblivious to the searing pain – and wept. Tony turned to Andy.

"I'm so sorry to have to be the bearer of such bad news to *both* of you in the space of so few hours," he said.

Aisha stopped crying immediately.

"*What the hell is he talking about?*" she screamed.

Chapter 30: Desk Closed

"Why did you not tell me?" Aisha sobbed. They were back in Andy's room; it was mid-morning.

"Which bit?" he returned sadly. "That *I* was worse than you realised – or that *you* were?"

"Both. *Either*! I do not know," she wailed. "Why did you not tell me *anything*?"

He swallowed hard. "I just didn't *know* about you," he began. "I couldn't help thinking it *looked* worse than they were saying but I've no medical training so I just kept quiet. Also, I couldn't see any *point* in them lying to you so I trusted them."

"And *you*?"

"I genuinely didn't know about me. At first there wasn't time. Someone mentioned MRSA in Brussels but I didn't take much notice. Then I realised it was getting worse and I hadn't had it properly looked at so I went late last night while you were asleep."

"And what did they say?"

"Well, they weren't very impressed with the leg, right enough, but they didn't like the look of the rest of me either. So they ran a lot more tests. Very quickly they were talking about this new MRSA-ZS thing, which I'd only vaguely heard of. Then they gave me a load of drugs and Tony Stratton tried to keep me in but I told him to sod off. I take it you know this ZS variant?"

Aisha nodded. "It is *bad*," she said. "It is not as generally contagious as its original: it only spreads through wounds and fluids and those infected can maintain some mobility up to ...," she hesitated, "... *the end*. But it still passes easily and *is* often fatal. It hardly responds to *anything*!"

"I know: they said that."

"So, what is their prognosis?"

He swallowed again. "Well, I'll lose the leg for sure," he said quickly. "If I let them operate, that is. After that, whether or not I pull through at all depends on how badly the internal organs are damaged by the sepsis. Most likely, I've another day or two."

He paused, and grasped her hands gently in his own. "Anyway, it doesn't matter, does it? You *know* what I'm going to do?"

She nodded, and appeared to suddenly calm. "I suppose you are *not* planning on leaving here."

"Aye, that's right."

"I guessed. But tell me why."

"Because it feels like the right thing to do. Partly because I may not live anyway and, if I do, I'll never be well again. But, really, because, deep down, I'm not comfortable with killing *anything* – even *It*. And, of course, many more people will die here, and across the world in the other strikes. And I'll be responsible for making that *happen*. It may well be for the greater good but *I* have to deal with it on a personal level. I can only justify that to myself – to my *beliefs* – if I pay a price for that: if I make a *sacrifice*. God will decide if I've done the right thing; all I can do is *try*. It's *my* way of *being human*."

Her smile lit up her face. Even covered in bandages, it was the most beautiful thing he had ever seen. The contrast between how she looked and what she then said chilled him to the bone.

"And I am staying with you."

He could not speak at all at first. Indignation, rage, sickness, pity, compassion, love; all struggled to overcome him. Tears sprang to his eyes. He choked, gasped for breath and wheezed pitifully. Eventually, he could manage but two words.

"No! Why?"

The smile never faded. "Because everything has changed now," she began. "We are both not what we were, nor will we be ever in this world. Because *my* life will never be the same and because *yours* cannot be. Because *I* can never be a surgeon again and I will not have *you*." He tried to speak but she instinctively laid a hand across his mouth to stop him. "And I *also* have the guilt of responsibility. Not just what is going to happen here in the OI, but in Parc de Bruxelles too. My arrogance caused many deaths there: I also need to atone for that. And, Andy, do you not *realise* why they have lied to us here and in Brussels?"

"I hadn't given it much thought," he sobbed.

"Because they did not want me to *think* I had nothing to live for. Our biggest threat to them has *always* been that we would be prepared to lay down our lives to thwart their plans. But these people *do not* really understand sacrifice; they are *selfish*: they live only for the material, and they can see no other life. They felt they needed all of us to be positive – to think there was some purpose. But they cannot imagine that we might do it anyway; and *that* is our only hope. They have kept Jenny and Bob waiting with their network calculations and they have kept *us* going with hope. I think only Jerry here has always understood that." She paused and held his hands once more. "And I think he *knew* what we would decide to do when we found out. We would save our friends."

"But *you* can't do this, Aisha." He fought to regain some composure.

"Why not?"

"Because *you* don't have the same beliefs as me. *I* know I'm going to a better place. This isn't really much of a sacrifice for me. But it's an incalculable one for you because *you don't think that*."

"But *you know* I am going to a better place – even if you think I do not. If your faith is really that strong then you *know* I am wrong. And that is good enough for me," she smiled again. "I am *trusting* you: *I am coming with you*." She recalled his words as they waited for the ambulance with old Mrs. Harris in London – as she had warned him she would.

"*I won't leave you*," she laughed.

There was very little else to be said but it was a long time before they left the room.

*

Jenny and Bob had returned to the main control room but it was locked. Instead, they found a smaller lab, a few yards along the same corridor, where they could talk. Between them, they had but the barest outline of a plan. Jenny needed to find a way – unobserved – of producing the seventeen-node disconnect-set and

Bob was working on a sensible reason to ask Don for two further security passes. Between them, they had two but they needed four to give them all any chance of escape. It seemed unlikely, frankly, given what had been said previously, that such a request would be granted but they had to try – and they had to somehow do it without raising suspicion. A final objective, now that The Desk had perhaps fulfilled their role at the OI, was for them all to stay *alive* long enough to achieve *anything*! The two of them refused to acknowledge it, each to the other, but it all really looked very implausible indeed.

"The program you wrote to find the thirty-three-node set. I don't suppose you still have the code itself?" Bob asked Jenny. She shook her head.

"No, I saved it locally on that machine in the lab: they made me. I thought I'd never need it again! And, anyway, all the data's in there too. I can't run it anywhere else." Further silence.

Larry Washington passed the open door. Without thinking, Bob called after him. He returned and looked at them curiously.

"Can I help you guys?"

"I think I may have made a mistake," Jenny blurted. Larry eyed her even more suspiciously.

"What kind of mistake?" he asked.

"I'm not sure I calculated the disconnect-set correctly. I may have maximised one of the bandwidth constraints instead of minimising. I don't know for sure. But we understand how important this is and I don't want to take any chances."

Larry returned in the direction from which he had come and reappeared, five minutes later, with Scott Lopez. The four of them returned to the control room.

"So *what* do you need to do?" asked Scott doubtfully.

"I need to change one of the constraints in the program," Jenny answered. "Then I need to re-run it. Chances are it'll make no difference but we need to be sure, don't we?" They both nodded reluctantly.

Jenny sat, once more, directly in front of the main screen; this time, Bob purposefully took the single seat to her left, leaving both Scott and Larry to sit on her right. She began to work with the two of them watching intently.

She outlined what she was going to do. It was a simple change, she said, but she needed to make sure it worked in the same manner as the previous version from the day before. She loaded the original program then commented out much of the main code. This meant it would not be run when she experimented with the new section, she explained. However, the comments also changed colour on the screen – to a pale green, making it more difficult for Scott and Larry to see exactly what she was typing. She also quietly put in a function call to a remote part of the code that she could keep off of the screen most of the time.

Bob noticed a poster on the other side of the lab and got up to read it more closely. It showed a full, layered description of a number of new network protocols and how they interrelated across the OI's various systems. He studied it for several minutes before turning back to the others.

"So will these systems work *together*?" he asked, pointing with two stretched fingers at different parts of the diagram. "Won't the switches get confused by the different frame lengths?"

Scott and Larry exchanged glances: neither seemed to understand the question. Larry rose to join Bob in front of the poster. Scott remained with Jenny.

Jenny turned the screen slightly. It was minimal but enough for the light to strike it at a different angle, the reflection making it harder for Scott to see. He was initially still distracted by Larry and Bob's conversation and, by the time he realised he could no longer follow what she was doing, Jenny had quickly moved to the remote part of the program, typed in three extra lines of code and returned to her starting place. She apologised to Scott and turned the screen back. Finally, she uncommented all of the code ready to run.

"OK, I think we're ready to go," she announced. She turned away from the coding screen to point at the revised output window on the display showing the network map.

Larry and Bob abandoned their protocol discussion and returned to the front, Larry leading. As they rounded the workstation with Jenny's monitor, Bob made sure both Scott and Larry's eyes were following Jenny's arm and, without either of them noticing, eased a memory stick into a USB port at the rear of her screen.

Jenny ran the program. As before, the small screen counter displayed the size of the node set, starting with $n = 17$. Only Bob, from his position, could see the short green glow from the USB stick at this point; then it faded. The count continued: $n = 21$; $n = 25$; $n = 28$; $n = 31$; $n = 33$. The OK confirmation flashed. Jenny pressed 'Return' and, as before, the 33 nodes were written to the text file on the other screen. She peered at them for some time – largely for show – then pointed at the result.

"Done," she said. "And it's the *same* set. See? So, I'm pretty sure that's OK. But I'll check my calculations on paper one last time tonight and confirm with you all tomorrow."

Scott and Larry nodded in satisfaction and congratulated her on her attention to detail. Jenny rose hurriedly and led the way from the room, looking pleased with herself. Somewhat taken by surprise, Scott and Larry followed quickly. As Bob, making up the rear, passed the screen, no-one saw him silently retrieve the memory stick from the USB port and quickly put it in his jeans pocket.

*

As they returned to the lift, the doors from the VIP floor opened without warning; they stopped. Don Bell, two uniformed generals and the President suddenly emerged. Jenny froze, awestruck; but Bob, with his single-track mind, and no thought of diplomatic protocol, asked immediately:

379

"Don, can I have a quick word. It's about those security passes you gave Aisha and …"

"Not now, Bob!" Don snapped. "I think it's obvious I have more pressing matters?" He made to sweep past, then seemed to have second thoughts, and turned back.

"Sorry. My apologies. We're all under a lot of stress." He faced the President. "Ma'am, these are two of the British group we've been telling you about. In fact, these two are the technical experts in the team. We wouldn't have been able to get to where we have – the, ah, *understanding* we have – without their help." They exchanged knowing looks.

The President reached out a firm hand to them both.

"Please be aware how much we value your efforts," she said, with a forced smile, and she shook their hands. "You are playing a large part in determining the future stability of our world, and we all thank you for it immensely."

For once, Jenny was lost for words but Bob carried on regardless.

"So, Don, do we have a time-scale for implementing the disconnect-set?"

Once more, Don looked somewhat caught off his guard.

"Ah no, well, possibly tomorrow, guys," he spluttered. "Or perhaps the day after: we still have to work out how to really do it. Or maybe the day after that …" He tailed off into silence, excusing himself as best he could by ushering the President on her way – and out of their sight.

*

It was early afternoon. Jenny and Bob had returned to the canteen: she with her breathing and pulse still racing from their subterfuge in the lab and encounter with the President; he with his tiny, precious cargo squeezed into his pocket – struggling to resist the temptation to feel the raised lump on his upper leg every few minutes to ensure it was still there. They were also still trying to decide how best to broach the subject of the two additional passes with Don – or *anyone*. Jenny hoped her

380

promise to revisit her calculations overnight would prolong their usefulness – possibly their *lives* – a few more hours. Still Aisha and Andy were nowhere to be seen.

Eventually, they reappeared; entering slowly and with hands clasped together. Although Andy looked very ill indeed – a flaky, grey ash seemed now to cover his entire skin and he walked with terrible difficulty, the two of them looked as relaxed as they had for many days. They moved over to join their friends and sat down.

"We have something to tell you," Aisha whispered in a very level voice.

"Let me guess: you're going to get married?" laughed Bob.

"Ah yes, you're going to become joined for eternity in the eyes of God?" suggested Jenny.

"Aye, sort of," Andy smiled. "Can we go back to someone's room for a wee chat?"

*

Hours later, Bob emerged from Jenny's room, and cast a despondent look back at the three that remained there, before trudging towards the lift. He pressed the '-1' button for the OI.

He emerged on the floor above and headed towards a row of offices near the main control room. As he did so, however, a thought – and one final spark of hope – struck him. He turned and found the smaller lab Jenny and he had used briefly that afternoon. He looked both ways along the corridor but no-one was in sight.

He closed the door behind him and, without turning on any additional lights – the glow from a monitor being sufficient to see what he was doing, he took the memory stick from his pocket and placed it in a USB port of the nearest machine. It contained only a single, small text file; and this he opened.

A seventeen-line table was displayed on the screen. The nodes were in no particular order: Jenny's algorithm would have cared little for rank or groupings. He looked at each line in turn. Some places he could not recognise at all, while others were just vaguely-recalled names. Ninth on the list was the EuroNet facility in Brussels. He swallowed hard and continued to read. Still he did not see the one thing, above all else, he wanted not to.

It was not the tenth, or the eleventh, or the twelfth node; nor the thirteenth, fourteenth or fifteenth. He dared to hope. The sixteenth was somewhere in Moscow. Maybe, just maybe …

Then he read the seventeenth and final line of the file:

896G 109H: 1A: Operational Installation (1) M-Nevada [Bell, Donald] Category A*

A death knell sounded somewhere within his head.

*

Jerry Austin was sitting, in silent contemplation, in his office. There was a knock at the open door. He looked up to see one of his junior assistants, *Leroy James*, standing there.

"Mr. Austin; Mr. Weatherill would like to see you, sir!"

For a moment, Jerry had to remember who 'Mr. Weatherill' was. Then he did; then he almost wished he had not. He raised a resigned look to the sky and stood to follow Leroy. As they walked, he asked:

"How's Maria, Leroy? And the new one? Carla? Born last week, wasn't she?"

Leroy beamed. "Both doing well, sir, despite all this weird stuff going on. I haven't even seen the baby yet. But I'm hoping to get home in the next few days." Jerry winced.

They rounded the corner and found Bob. They shook hands but Jerry had a final word for his assistant.

"Leroy," he said suddenly, "go back and wait in my office. I may have a little job for you. Bob!" he whispered dismally. I hardly know whether I'm pleased to see you or not!"

Bob smiled weakly. "Can I borrow your mobile, please Jerry?" he asked. "I want to phone my daughter."

Jerry nodded. "Follow me."

They walked to the Look Out. Outside was dark once more. The guards let them through the glass and they climbed around the rocks. Jerry passed Bob his phone.

"I don't think many of the long-distance lines are working any more," he said.

This hardly seemed to concern Bob. He took the mobile and pressed a few buttons at random. "No," he agreed, shook his head and passed it back. As Jerry took the phone, he felt a smaller object in his hand along with it. He put the mobile in one jacket pocket and the small block in the other. They went back in. The guards closed the Look Out doors behind them.

"OK thanks," said Bob simply, and walked quickly towards the lift, his shoulders shaking visibly from behind as Jerry's eyes followed him.

"Yes, thanks," Jerry replied. He watched the doors close on Bob, then walked slowly back to his office.

Chapter 31: Split Ends

At 7:30am the following morning, Jenny and Bob met in the canteen, as arranged, and drank coffee without speaking. On the table between them lay the two security passes. They glanced at each other from time to time but neither could hold the other's gaze for long.

Just before eight o'clock, they picked up a pass each and walked to the lift. They tried but it would not answer their call until precisely 8am. These security passes were no good here; would they work where they *needed* them to? They knew every step of their journey was to be an ordeal like this – and yet they were *still* the lucky ones. Eventually, however, the time was right and they ascended towards the OI.

As the doors closed behind them, Andy emerged from around the corner where he had been hiding with Aisha – secretly watching them – and led her to the canteen. They ordered coffee, sat and embraced.

"There was still a part of me that wanted to say goodbye," she said quietly.

"I know," he said. "Me too; but probably better like this."

She nodded.

*

Jenny and Bob turned towards the end of the corridor and the entrance to the tunnel.

"We don't really know if they even *took* our readings," said Jenny. "This might not work before we've even started." They both began to sweat. Bob inserted his pass and stood to be scanned. It seemed like an age.

However, after the longest two seconds of their lives, the system announced its recognition of Bob and the process was repeated for Jenny. The door opened and they entered the dome. A young man came forward to meet them. Bob recognised Leroy James. He smiled and shook both their hands.

"Mr. Austin sent me to drive you to the other end," he announced cheerfully.

They had their passes and biometrics checked once more by the guards, climbed into a waiting buggy and set off along the tunnel.

*

At 8:30am, Aisha and Andy left the canteen and returned to his room. He took off the cross around his neck and clasped it around hers. They kissed.

*

Nothing was going to make the journey quick, or stress-free, or painless for Jenny or Bob but Leroy's relaxed chatter helped. He passed the time telling them about his wife and how she had given birth to their daughter, Carla, while he had been stationed at the OI. He had hoped to get home to see them soon but, to his surprise, Mr. Austin had told him to leave that morning. He had been instructed simply to 'drive two English scientists to the other end of the tunnel, make sure they got out and wait there'. 'On no account was he to return back along the tunnel'. The instructions became vague at that point but Mr. Austin had said Leroy would 'figure out what to do' soon enough after that. He was looking forward to seeing his 'two girls'. His major concern, though, was that he was hearing rumours of nuclear weapons likely to be fired that day. 'No-one knew what was happening any more', he said, and it seems like 'no-one wants to tell us either'. They sped along; other than Leroy's light-hearted babble, their journey accompanied by only the occasional scrape of the buggy on the wall.

*

At nine o'clock, Aisha and Andy took the lift to the OI floor and walked round the turn of the corridor to the Look Out. The two guards eyed them with suspicion as they approached; one fingered the gun in his holster. But the two lovers simply stood facing the glass window, Andy describing to Aisha the pale morning outside, the mountains in the distance and the desert –

385

with its sparse vegetation – in between. The guards exchanged looks and whispers and, after a few minutes, one hurried off in the direction from which they had come, glancing back over his shoulder at them several times as he strode away.

"We're being reported," Andy whispered to Aisha with some amusement.

*

The escapees reached the end of the tunnel. Passes and biometrics were checked once more and Jenny and Bob took their leave of Leroy. As instructed by Jerry, he waited in the dome area, immediately striking up cheerful conversations with both soldiers and technicians.

The pair worked their own way through the security scanners on each side of the transit room and found the steps waiting for them. They climbed breathlessly to the top and emerged from the shed into a cold, desert landscape with no-one else in sight. The low morning sun told them which direction to take along the dirt track by which they stood.

They had walked perhaps quarter of a mile when they first heard the sounds behind them: the growing roar of approaching jet planes and the whining of other airborne things they could not identify. Their initial impulse was to turn and look but neither did. Instead, they carried on along the track, their eyes filled with tears as the noise behind them intensified.

*

Aisha and Andy still stood at the Look Out's window. The remaining guard fidgeted anxiously. There was a voice behind them.

"Can I help you guys?" It was Scott, in something of a hurry, accompanied by the second guard. They turned to face him.

"We're just admiring the view," Aisha laughed; a clear, ringing tone that appeared to unnerve everyone but Andy.

"You're making people jumpy, guys," said Scott. "We can do without folk wandering around the OI this morning. Apart from it not being safe," a fluorescent bulb mounted on a wall exploded

386

as if to illustrate his point, "Don's currently giving the President the full tour of facilities." A thought seemed to strike him.

"So where are the other two?"

"Gone for a walk."

Scott eyed them with a mixture of suspicion and distaste. But his next question was halted, before it began, by Don's voice from further behind – along the corridor.

"What's going on here?" He, the President and her two bodyguards were approaching the Look Out.

Andy seemed to like Aisha's joke: he grinned as he repeated the answer. "Just admiring the view," he said, but then added, "What else would we do to pass the morning while another hundred million people die?"

Don bridled instantly and took an aggressive step towards them, but was interrupted by the President herself, who raised a hand to signify a halt.

"They know, Mr. Bell. Can't you tell? *They know.*"

Don cast her a desperate look; then – as quickly as it had appeared – his anger left him. This was not his fight any more. The President had taken the floor.

"So," she began, facing Aisha and Andy for the first time, "when I spoke to your colleagues – the other two – yesterday, I thanked them for their contribution to our *stability*. *Whose* stability do you think I was referring to?"

Andy sucked his teeth as he considered for a few seconds. "*Yours?*"

The President shook her head.

"Not mine. At least, not directly," she answered. "I'm just a puppet in a much bigger show. A well-paid, well-respected, well-protected puppet, maybe, but *I'm not* the director. Like every Head of State, every senior politician or diplomat, every so-called 'leader', I'm really just the marketing material: I make the theatre look presentable. Sometimes I help the show go ahead, even when it shouldn't; other times I cover up the mess when something goes wrong. But *my* bosses are much more powerful than that and they *control* something much more powerful than *me* – the Media. If *either* of them were to turn on me, I'd be gone in an instant. Public opinion or a bullet: it makes no difference. Nor does 'democrat' or 'republican' – they're just different colours. *I've* no real power; other than that granted – passed *down* – to me. It's always been that way (Obama couldn't even stop guns being sold in corner shops for kids to shoot themselves with, for Christ's sake) and it always will be."

"Aye understood," agreed Andy. "The world is run by business. Politicians answer to business. Those that don't, don't last very long. We know that. But it's a big jump from there to needing to wipe out most of the world's population. That's what you're *doing*, isn't it?"

She grinned: her teeth opened slightly and Andy had a sense of pure evil emanating from within. "A fortunate irony," she said. "The very technology that was threatening to destabilise us, turns out to be our saviour."

"So, you're not denying it?" Aisha suggested.

The President shrugged dismissively. "The world is a lot more complicated than people like you realise," she answered. "Unless you're still secretly a deluded communist, what alternative *is* there? We are controlled by capital – driven by profit. Money decides what happens and what doesn't. It controls all of us and everything we do. Money puts people like me into power, it determines who lives and who dies; it decides which parts of the world thrive and which parts suffer; it uses discord amongst the masses to protect the few. It's *unfair to the highest degree* but it's *stable*. And that's *all* the world really needs."

"Except that it's stopped working!"

"Well, yes, true. At least it was beginning to. The robot workforce we're seeing replace humans all over the world is, in one sense, a capitalist's dream. No wages, no rules, no rights. Just production, distribution, exchange and sales – and everything *automated*. Larger profit margins for less effort and expenditure, which means the top people – *my bosses* – can maintain their lifestyles with both fewer people working for them *and* fewer people to sell to. And there's the problem!

It means there are just too many people. That's true *already* and we've barely *started* automating industry yet! The problem's going to get a lot worse! *Too* many people at the lowest levels of society ultimately *destabilise* the system that they normally provide the foundations for. A *few* are needed to feed competition but *too many* leads to social unrest – and that's the one thing that my bosses absolutely *fear*. Also, of course, an overpopulated world has an environmental impact, which the top people can't entirely escape from either. Whichever way you look at it, *they have to go*!

"We've been discussing this from day one of my term of office. We've understood the problem well enough but there's never been a solution. The standard approach of starting wars or allowing famines to happen wouldn't achieve the numbers we'd need this time – unless it was nuclear and that messes things up for *everyone*! Some thoroughly drastic methods have been proposed: the usual chemical and biological 'accidents' for example. But, on the scale that would have been necessary this time, they would have only *added* to social instability – not *reduced* it. *Business* would have got the wholesale blame and we can't let it happen like that: business needs to be the *friend*, not the *enemy*. We have to be seen to be *serving* the people – not *controlling* and *exploiting* them. It needed to be someone, or *something*, else's fault. But what? We were in a mess – and it was getting messier.

"Then, before we knew it, the job was being done for us! We didn't understand what was happening but the Internet was suddenly killing people, in increasing numbers – *huge* numbers. We didn't really know why but, for a while, we didn't care. It wasn't *our* fault and that was all that mattered. The only problem we had then was that we knew that, someday soon, we'd have to *stop it* – and we didn't know how to do that either! Our experts said that, eventually, the Internet would destroy itself, of course, but we didn't know if we could wait that long; and, anyway, we needed some of it *left* – not for *people*, naturally, but for *business*.

"Then we heard about your team. We understood that you folks knew two things about what was going on: *what* was causing it and *how* to stop it. And that was all we needed – *but in our own good time, no-one else's*! So we got heavy with our European juniors to get you over here. Then we had to get the 'off switch' information from you, then we had to keep you occupied while we waited to press it. (There's still a good few days to go on that one, by the way, guys!)

"So, that's where we are. We've got *exactly* what we wanted. Unfortunately, now, we've still got *you*."

The guards nearest the glass could hear something, and turned their heads.

"So, where does that leave us?" asked the President. She bared her teeth again in a cruel smile. "I think you *know*."

Outside, there was a distant roar – a whine, perhaps more than one. Soon they could all hear it. Don's face took on a quizzical expression.

The President did not appear to appreciate the military's concern. She continued.

"I think we can say that this is the end of the road for your team. You've transitioned from a state of being more valuable alive than otherwise – to one of being an unsustainable risk. You've served your purpose. Wouldn't you agree? *I don't think you'll be leaving here*."

"We know," Aisha said simply. "I believe that may be true for all of us."

She reached out and found Andy's hand once more. They stood, joined together, smiling.

The distant roar was less distant now. And it was coming from different directions. It became louder; it was nearly upon them. Panicked looks were shot around the Look Out.

Don suddenly started barking orders; soldiers appeared and disappeared with an impotent randomness.

The colour drained from the President's face; her eyes stretched wide in terror. She stood transfixed.

"*Son of a Bitch!*" she gasped.

There was a deafening noise, an eruption all around them; then red heat, then white light; then nothing.

*

Two figures – a man and a woman – stumbled, heads down, tired and thirsty, along a desert track. The winter morning sun, now half-risen, threw their shadows sideways to about half their height again. Behind them, many miles distant, a plume of smoke still hung, like layers of misplaced thunder clouds in a blue sky, over a point to the south west. A few birds wheeled and screeched overhead; but this – and their laboured breathing – aside, all was silent. They exchanged the occasional unhappy glance but otherwise trudged onwards in silence for hundreds of yards, then a mile, then two. Eventually, the woman spoke.

"Did we *have* to do that?"

"What *choice* did we have?" the man replied.

"Do you think it *worked*?"

"No idea; I suppose we'll find out. No-one seems to be coming after us, anyway."

"We've *killed* so many people."

"And maybe *saved* so many more?"

"*Two in particular!*"

"But kept several billion alive?"

"I just can't forget their faces as we left them yesterday."

"Nor can I; I'll remember it for the rest of my life."

A long pause.

"*I know.*"

They kept going.

After another extended period of silence, the man raised his head and peered along the track ahead.

"Look."

In the distant northeast, a small puff of dust was just visible. It increased in size, and seemed to be coming nearer. As it became clearer, they could see its point of contact with the track, followed by a trail of disturbed sand in its wake. The sound of a solitary engine became audible and grew as it approached. Eventually, something solid could be seen at the centre of the dust storm. This initially suggested some sort of vehicle, then – more distinctly – a truck; an old truck. It was about a hundred yards away when its driver appeared to notice them, now stationary at the side of the track. It slowed and stopped. They read 'Chuck's Auto' in chipped and faded paint on the side.

A friendly voice shouted from the high driver's seat.

"Hey guys! How you doin'?"

"Hi."

"Whatcha doing all the way out here?"

"Getting away; er, just getting away from it all."

"From the weird stuff?"

They nodded. "Yes, getting away from the weird stuff – the RFS."

"*It's stopped.*"

They stood motionless, staring at the driver, not daring to believe they understood what he said.

"*Stopped?*"

"Yup. Stopped. 'Bout nine-thirty this mornin'. Real sudden, and about the same time as those big explosions over yonder – towards the base." He waved in the direction of the distant black pall. "Things ain't exactly back to the way they was yet: the communications ain't good but it's *safe* to use when it *does* work. Power's kinda OK, just a bit unreliable. And things *ain't killin' people* or *blowin' up anymore*! Things is sorta *normal*." He spread his arms wide in saying this. "All the weird stuff has stopped. I'm just havin' a drive round to see what's happ'nin'."

The two walkers collapsed into each other's arms and held on with the last of their strength, weeping tears of relief and sorrow.

"You folks look done in. I ain't leaving you out here. Climb up inside; I'll give you a lift back to town."

EPILOGUE: REHABILITATION?

'It' was no more. But Its time on Earth had marked a critical point in human history. And Its effect was devastating. The final death toll was estimated at around a billion people; it would never be known with any certainty. RFS had been directly responsible for many casualties, but so had its indirect after-effects: massive environmental disasters, famine and disease, widespread civil unrest and division, short but bloody civil wars. Technology had accounted for the destruction of many in the developed world; a *lack* of it in developing countries. Slowly, local communities regrouped. Those accustomed to less modern ways of living and working did so more quickly: the balance was – at least temporarily – changed. Gradually, some service and support networks were restored; those left started to try to rebuild their lives. Humanity *could* survive this; but *would* it? There were choices to be made. The majority of the public at large – across the globe – still had no idea what the cause of the slaughter had been. Should they be *told*? Or would it even be possible to keep the secret anyway? The essential core of the

Internet could probably be rebuilt in two to three months. *Should* it? Among those initially in the know, opinion was divided. A rebuilt Internet could be a force for good in this recovering world (but who would define 'good'?); or would 'It' reappear and continue Its destruction beyond humanity's point of no return? What actually *mattered*? *Who* actually mattered? And who would *decide*?

*

Some less than entirely visible – but human – forces were still at work. Jenny and Bob were carefully looked after at several stages of their journey – the Quiet Group, they assumed although nothing was ever mentioned – and were able to return to England quicker than most of those separated from their homes and loved ones by Its devastation. Along the way, they managed to make some contact with people. Bob's family was safe; alas, Jenny's brother was not. When they finally reached London, Jenny found an email from Aisha's address (but written with Andy's help) on a local server at her university. It had managed to get through before the 'big disconnection' although no notification had been sent or received at the time. At first, Jenny did not want to read it. Eventually, she called Bob and they opened it together.

> "Dear Jenny and Bob,
>
> If you get to read this, we suppose you'll be in a safe place, and we'll be in an even safer place. If you're reading this, then we assume you're home, and that's only likely if It's been disconnected, broken, aborted – *killed*. And if that's true then clever folk like you are going to have to decide what to do next
> …
>
> People – if they ever get to know the *truth* – might suppose that what's happened over the last few weeks – especially the last few days – answers the Fermi Paradox. After all, the satellites are down – or lost, most of the big transmitters and receivers are broken and, of course, the network that gets them all working together doesn't exist much beyond the local level at the moment. We're – temporarily at least – less *advanced*, less *developed, less visible*, than we *were*. So, in terms of the wider

394

universe, we've shrunk back into our hole. If other civilisations on other planets have gone through similar catastrophes, then that might explain why we don't see them. However, that's only half true. It's what happens *next* that will really answer the paradox completely ...

Because one question for you guys now is whether you try to put this thing back together or not.

If you *don't*, then, to an extent that's difficult to judge, you're holding humanity back. You can relaunch the satellites and rebuild the communications, but the whole system can never get to the point that it was at before: not if you don't want to risk this all happening again. There will be a limit to the size, and scale – and therefore the effectiveness – of the IoE. It *can't be allowed* to reach that critical point it did before; in fact, it will never *be* the Internet of *Everything*. Similarly, big data analytics on the scale needed to implement practical artificial intelligence won't happen either. So, probably, nor will *The Singularity*. You'll be *safe* from a number of known technological threats; but you'll live every future generation knowing you could be doing *more*, maybe even with the perpetual question of just how *far* you can push it next time. Would you be able to continually monitor for signs of (Its) life and pull things apart again each time? The problem with that is that, as our individual *devices* get more and more numerous and complex, presumably it won't take such a densely connected Internet to give It the consciousness It needs in future. (Maybe, eventually, Its reappearance will become inevitable?) And who would make these judgements anyway? Who could enforce it? Ordinary people can't if they're kept in the dark.

If you *do* build it back up once more, then obviously you risk all this happening all over again; only this time you might not be so lucky. Humanity could be completely destroyed. The Singularity may or may not happen: it would depend on whether It, or the machines It controlled, could become self-sufficient and generate their own power before all of 'ours' ran out. But there's so much guesswork: so much we don't know or understand. If 'It' became conscious again, you might not be able to control It *at all*. In fact, having killed It once, it might be a *new* 'It' that comes to life next time. Maybe a new 'It' will behave differently. Maybe, if you tough it out, you can talk to It when It's 'grown up enough'. But to attempt *any* of that, you'd need to understand what drives It in the first place and you're a long way from that because we don't even know that about *ourselves*. Our understanding of our *own* brains – including what causes consciousness at all – is practically non-existent; and we don't even *like* discussing things like our 'moral code'. But we bloody well should be. Over and over again, we're trying to make decisions *for* ourselves when we don't *understand* ourselves.

We don't really envy your decision!

But there's actually a bigger question, which goes way beyond the technology (although technology has a huge part to play). *Who* or *what* are we really doing all this for *anyway*? If the world continues, as it has until now, to revolve around an elite few then, frankly, what's the point? (Yes, obviously, the elite themselves, have a good answer to that question but what about the rest of us?)

Because, to a great extent, what we've seen from the elite just recently, in the way they've exploited 'It' for their own ends, they've actually been doing for years; we've just accepted it without question. Half the world lives in poverty so a few can fly around in private planes. But *we* (the other half that's sort of doing all right) help to make that look OK. *We* buy the clothes and other stuff that's made by child slave labour around the world; the elite don't – they don't *need* to. But *we* do because they keep things just tight enough for us, for us to have to join in the exploitation. Then we use, sometimes even *invest* in, companies that do it for us. We *compete* with each other because we've been told that's the way the world works. We *buy in* to capitalism because we think we *have* to: we support it – even though, in the end, it will be the death of us. Over the past few weeks, 'It' has caused massive carnage across the world but most people haven't even realised It's *there*. Capitalism has effectively been just as hidden for much longer – but has caused at least as much hurt to more people. And capitalism *will* switch It back on – sooner or later, quickly or slowly; make no mistake about that because, ultimately, *people* don't really matter – only *profit* does!

The world was falling apart long before It appeared in so many different ways: even without It, it's really only a question of which one gets us first. We're destroying the planet – physically and spiritually, losing our moral focus and social divisions are getting wider and more damaging. Capitalism actually *thrives* on that: having people fight each other distracts from recognising the *real* enemy. Technology supports this of course in various ways: a message of hate can be shared instantly today and a mass movement formed overnight; the elite won't care whether it's human or robot slaves who work for them in future; no-one has much privacy today and, soon, we'll have *none*; weapons are everywhere and capitalism sells them to anyone – the purpose isn't questioned if the price is right. These are just a few examples. But violence and terrorism and discrimination and personal abuse and suchlike is really just an *outlet* for grievances against inequality; it's got nothing to do with interpretation of scripture or natural human nature, for example. If you treat people like dirt, they will react; they will lash out, thinking they're 'fighting back'. If won't occur to them that this level of conflict is exactly what capitalism needs to survive. Even if there was *no* religion, say, people would just find another vehicle for their anger (sport, race, sex, language, stamp-collecting, etc.); and the elite would *still* sell them the means to cause the damage they do.

There's got to be another way – and there *is*. Those who claim that an equality-based society wouldn't work because it goes against some sort of natural human selfishness have completely missed the point. Yes, there will always be *greed*; not so much in 'bad' people compared to 'good' people but in *all* of us to a greater or lesser extent. That would be true under a socialist system just as much as a capitalist one. The problem we have at the moment is that we accept, without question, a system that tolerates – even *encourages* – inequality. The whole system is *founded* on it: the greater the difference between top and bottom, the more stable it is – *up to a point*. But that means that our legal system has to pretend to make arbitrary judgements between acceptable and unacceptable methods of achieving *greater* inequality. Stealing from someone's pocket in the street is a crime but tricking them in a financial transaction may not be.

Keeping someone in slavery is (supposed to be) illegal but tying them to an awful job because there's no alternative isn't. It's actually bloody hard to police that sort of system and maintain any impression of fairness, and the result is the unrest we see all around us.

But in a system where inequality *itself* was the wrong, it would be entirely simpler to identify and deal with greed. Yes, of course, just as now, there would be some who seek to cheat their way to an advantage. But if *that* advantage, *itself* was the clue, they would identify themselves. The role of the legal system would be to protect *equality*, not make arbitrary judgements on whether *inequality* was achieved 'fairly'. We'd build houses and make clothes because people needed houses and clothes; we wouldn't compete with each other all our lives to see who could afford the best ones! We wouldn't drive around in cars that cost an amount that would feed our neighbour's family for a year. We wouldn't use horrible terms like 'social mobility' (when we really mean shuffling the deck in a few places to help the middle classes ignore the poor) because there'd be nothing that needed to be mobilised. Government would be there for *people* – not *business* (there would *be* no 'business'). We could actually *enjoy* the benefits of technology: *all* of us – not just a select few. *People* would come first in everything. Don't try to say it's all been tried before: *it hasn't*; and, anyway, even if it's a risk, *it's one we have to take – the alternative kills us for sure.* We won't survive a *decade* of technocapitalism. We can't leave the planet in the hands of the elite.

The ultimate answer to the Fermi Paradox may be as much a social one as technological – although technology will be all too ready to assist in the suicide if we want it to. To have any chance at all, we *have* to change the political system from one that thrives on inequality and division to one that promotes equality and cooperation. And *now* may be our last chance; we won't get another one: technology will see to that.

Otherwise, capitalism's greatest – its *final* – victory will be that, *as it destroys us all, it has us all blaming each other*!

Your friends always, Aisha and Andy"

About the Author

Vic Grout has a BSc degree in Mathematics and Computing from the University of Exeter and a PhD in Communication Engineering (with thesis title, "Optimisation Techniques for Telecommunication Networks") from Plymouth Polytechnic, now the University of Plymouth. He is currently Professor of Computing Futures at Wrexham Glyndŵr University in Wales, having been previously Professor of Network Algorithms, Head of Computing, Associate Dean for Research and Director of the Centre for Applied Internet Research. He also serves on the UK National Committee of the Council of Professors and Heads of Computing (CPHC), as Chair of CPHC Wales, and on the British Computer Society (BCS) Information Privacy Expert Panel and Information Security Specialist Group Committee. He is an approved BCS accreditation assessor, an Institute of Engineering and Technology (IET) recommended speaker and a European Commission (EC) 'Horizon 2020' (H2020) Expert Research Assessor, panel Vice-chair and Ethics consultant.

Vic has worked in senior positions in academia and industry for 30 years and has published and presented well over 400 technical research papers, articles, keynote addresses, patents and books. His research interests span several areas of computational mathematics, including artificial intelligence and the application of heuristic principles to large-scale problems in Internet design, modelling, simulation, management and control. He has also worked extensively on projects using Internet technologies to help the elderly and disabled live longer independent lives. He is an experienced 'futurologist' - with a particular focus on the social, political, ethical and moral dimensions of technological evolution, 'big data', 'big connectivity' and the 'Internet of Things' - and writes regularly in the "Turing's Radiator" blog (vicgrout.net). *Conscious* is his first fictional novel.

Professor Grout is a Chartered Engineer, Chartered Electrical Engineer, Chartered Scientist, Chartered Mathematician and Chartered IT Professional, a Fellow of the Royal Society of Arts,

Institute of Mathematics and its Applications, British Computer Society and Institution of Engineering and Technology, a Senior Member of the Institute of Electrical and Electronics Engineers and the Association of Computing Machinery, and a Member of the London Mathematical Society. He formed and chaired the biennial international conference series on Internet Technologies and Applications (ITA) and is a frequent contributor to TV and radio.

Vic is married to Helen; together they have three sons: Jack, Danny and James. They live in Pen-y-Cae, near Rhosllanerchrugog in Wrexham, near to their sons and Daughter-in-Law-to-be, Heather, with grandchildren Killian, Lilith and Maizie, Faney the dog and Fred the cat. Aside from his academic, professional and writing interests, Vic enjoys playing acoustic and electric guitar, regular gym work, walking in the North Wales hills and tinkering with his MG car. He is a keen supporter of Southampton Football Club.

Follow Vic on Twitter: @vicgrout